Finalist for the Flaherty-Dunnan First Novel Prize
The 2014 Honor Book for Fiction for the Black Caucus of the ALA
One of the 5 Breakout Brooklyn Book People of 2013, *The L Magazine*

"Powerful ... full of impossible hope ... Jackson's prose has a spoken-word cadence, the language flying off the page with percussive energy."
—**Roxane Gay,** *The New York Times Book Review*

"There is nothing pretty about selling drugs or doing crack, yet Hurston Wright Award winner Jackson makes it literarily beautiful in this debut novel."
—*Library Journal* **(starred review)**

"Jackson's voice is defined by a striking juxtaposition of street smarts and book smarts ... Reading such writerly turns of phrase, it's hard to believe Jackson wasn't composing poetry in the cradle." —*Portland Monthly* **magazine**

"Jackson's novel is beautifully written and sad and hopeful in a way that aches."
—*The Portland Mercury*

"[A] searingly forthright and honest confrontation with the mean streets of urban decay." —*Kirkus Reviews*

"Jackson's dedication to the shadows and unhappiness of his characters shines through." —*Publishers Weekly*

"Jackson's poetic prose is a joy to read." —*Booklist*

"*The Residue Years* is an inspired testimony to the death of the American Dream. Or perhaps it is a rebuttal to the idea that there ever was one."
—**Bookreporter.com**

"Authenticity and a rhythmic prose propel Jackson's debut novel."
—*Time Out New York*

"Beautiful sentences that mix urban slang with pitch-perfect lyricism, resulting in a new way of expressing American English." —*The Paris Review*

"This novel is written with a breathtaking, exhilarating assurance and wit. Terrific." *es*

"In this raw heartwreck of a novel, every bit of personal wisdom is hard-won. The author is entirely persuasive, such that Grace and her sons, given vivid voice, are one of the fictional families I have cared about most."

—**Amy Hempel, author of** *The Collected Stories*

"It's so tough to write beautifully about ugly things but Mitchell S. Jackson makes it look easy. *The Residue Years* is the story of a man and woman trying their best to overcome the enormous hurdles life has put in front of them. This is a memorable, powerful novel and Mitchell S. Jackson is a genuine talent."

—**Victor LaValle, author of** *The Devil in Silver*

"I was touched by characters whose lives were often as real for me as my memories of growing up. The language invented to tell their stories engages, challenges, clarifies the American language, claiming it, enlarging it—"

—**John Edgar Wideman, author of** *Philadelphia Fire*
and *Brothers and Keepers*

"The language in this book is as gut-wrenching as it is stunning, at once an elegy and an anthem. Fiercely honest and intense, this is a beauty of a book."

—**Maaza Mengiste, author of** *Beneath the Lion's Gaze*

"Inhabit Jackson's song, a ballad about family, struggle—and struggle for and with family—while finally seeing the face of systemic racism, gentrification, failed hoop dreams, and a misguided drug war that makes criminals of victims. See the face and feel the breaking heart. And also be lifted up because this fantastic achievement speaks ultimately of love."

—**Robb Todd, author of** *Steal Me for Your Stories*

"Mitchell Jackson writes brilliant sentences, so full of the energy and beauty and tragedy of life." —**Michael Kimball, author of** *Big Ray*

"I know these characters well. I know the language they speak: voices redolent of struggle and the South displaced to our country's far northwestern corner. A wrenchingly beautiful debut."

—**Jesmyn Ward, author of** *Salvage the Bones* **and** *Men We Reaped*

THE RESIDUE YEARS

A Novel

Mitchell S. Jackson

BLOOMSBURY

NEW YORK · LONDON · OXFORD · NEW DELHI · SYDNEY

Bloomsbury USA
An imprint of Bloomsbury Publishing Plc

1385 Broadway   50 Bedford Square
New York   London
NY 10018   WC1B 3DP
USA   UK

www.bloomsbury.com

First published 2013
This paperback edition published 2014

ISBN: HB: 978-1-62040-028-9
       PB: 978-1-62040-029-6
       ePub: 978-1-63286-220-4

Library of Congress Cataloging-in-Publication Data

Jackson, Mitchell S.
The Residue Years : A Novel / Mitchell S. Jackson. —First U.S. edition.
pages cm
ISBN 978-1-62040-028-9 (alk. paper)
1. Drug addicts—Rehabilitation—Fiction. 2. Mothers and sons—
Fiction. 3. Drug dealers—Fiction. 4. Street life—
Fiction. I. Title.
PS3610.A35434R47 2013
813'.6—dc23
2013016977

6 8 10 9 7

Typeset by Westchester Book Group
Printed and bound in the U.S.A. by Berryville Graphics Inc., Berryville, Virginia

To find out more about our authors and books visit www.bloomsbury.com. Here you
will find extracts, author interviews, details of forthcoming events, and the option to
sign up for our newsletters.

Bloomsbury books may be purchased for business or promotional use.
For information on bulk purchases please contact Macmillan Corporate and
Premium Sales Department at specialmarkets@macmillan.com.

In memory of Jamal

For Rhonda
For Justice and Jaden

Every decision you've made has brought you to this moment.
—Lillie Dora Jackson (Mom)

All stories are true.
—John Edgar Wideman

PROLOGUE

We know what *really* happens this visit is this.
—Champ

IT'S YEARS BEYOND the worst of it, and it's your time, Mom, a time of head starts and new starts and starting and going and not stopping—of re-dos and fixes, of gazing at full moons and quarter-moons and seeing what before were phantasms for-reals. If this streak keeps up (it will; why not?), you've got the rest of your life, hell yeah it's a life, minus fatmouthing no-accounts. You hope—no, we hope (you and your eldest) that this year, next year, and the years after are an age of heartbeats, steady breath, and a healing for your harms. Smart money says you and I are in for seasons and seasons of pewter sunups and cold-ass sunsets and rain. In this state, who can get away from the rain? Shit, you used to think maybe it was the rain. This will be a time of cruising rainy days by your old bus stops, unsoaked, semi-warm, and daydreaming. To be true, Mom, we'll likely see days upon days of yearning. But hey, this might also be the time, after a long-long trial of bootsie-ass suitors, of your white gown and bouquet; it might be, but Mom, let's keep it funky, if ain't been in forty-plus years, there's a helluva chance it won't. You know I would take care of it all if I could but at present—enough said, so meantime, you're on your own for new gear: for age-sanctioned tops and blouses; jeans and dresses; khakis and slacks, work suits; until they cut me loose, it's on you to foot new heels and flats and sandals—yep, sandals, but closed sandals, please, for those sacrilegious toes! Plus, Mom, set aside enough to keep spruced, to make this year, next year, and all the ones to come, months of pedicures and manicures, of consistent appointments for weaves, of waxes and peels and scrubs and tweezing, but no foundation. It ain't never, no matter what fly-by-night wannabe beauty expert claims it, the year for caked-on makeup. It's also never, and I mean never-ever times count as high as you like, a moment for punkish men, no Old Joes, none of those grown-ass juveniles I wished far-far away from us when I was young; on the other hand, it's the time for your young bastards—KJ, Canaan, and, despite my predicament, me too. Some say this is the time of love. The suckers always do. You give it and you get it, that's what the suckers say. The born-agains preach we might be upon the Second Coming. We might be, but since we ain't been for eons, best not hold our breath. What else? What else? This has been seasons of long letters, of kites that arrive with their seals broken, handwritten kites with words scratched out or under-lined, kites approved and delivered, just a few kites declined.

This has been weeks and weeks of steady visits, of seizing every chance to taunt the superintendent's bunk rules, a miraculous year of Grace and Champ, of mother and son reaching out.

My ex answers your call like shit is sweet, says, Good to hear from you, so fake you want to reach through the receiver. Next thing, she drops the phone minus nary a pardon and leaves you on an indefinite hold soundtracked by the blare of some rap video cranked beyond good sense. Meanwhile, you carry the noisy cordless into another room, crack the blinds, and watch a pair of baseheads, both thin as antennas, push a half-wrecked sedan down the street. The baseheads, they've got the sedan's doors flung open, and seethe at each other across a scrappy ragtop roof. Farther, they jog their hooptie to a slow cruise, jump in on the run, and sputter off. It's still plenty of lightweight action on the set. The old lady dressed in a who-gives-a-what-about-the-heat getup (down coat, snow boots, thick wool scarf) tugging a shopping cart full of thrashed cans. Down a ways, boys riding wheelies for distance on dirt bikes with mismatched rims.

Finally, our Princess, my baby girl, your grandbaby, picks up. She announces she's doing well, offers up a story about school, and follows her report with a plea for ice cream—beseeching to which you concede. You assure our Princess you'll be there soon, that she should get ready, and hang up hoping her mother, my spiteful ex, will for once keep her word.

Next thing, you search your bedroom closet for an outfit, pick Capri pants and a halter top, and iron them both on a burnt towel laid across your bed. You get the clothes nice and pressed, then model the getup in the same mirror where you keep posted a picture of your boys, my brothers, of which the baby is now a teenage bastard. You try on the clothes, only to decide the granny-still-got-it fit ain't comfortable, not respectable for a day with our Princess, not even close, so you option look after look before settling on a cotton shirt and khakis, which is the best move, since the more skin you show, the more these recalcitrant good-for-nothings make you a show.

Dressed, you collect from under your mattress the fist-sized stash you've been saving for months and peel off a stack of bills. You dump the cash in your bag, grab your keys, and hike outside to where your raggedy Honda is parked too far from the curb for you to have owned a license for as long as you have. There's a trick to starting the Honda, which you've learned after getting stranded beaucoup times: pumping the gas a few times but not so many it floods the engine.

Outside my ex's crib, the Honda coughs and wheezes and goes mute as you pull the key. You hop out and shuffle into a yard strewn with a pink and purple Big Wheel, hula hoops, and a candy-cane jump rope, stroll up a set of unbanistered steps, and rap a door knocker the size of a prison guard's key ring. You'd have to be blind to miss how they've let the place go, to miss the paint peeling eczema-like from the walls, windows dirtied to damn near dark as limo tint. How you doing? my ex says, with that supercilious smile that used to be a wellspring. She steps aside to let you in and vanishes, leaving you inside a living room packed with shit I bought: leather couches, big-screen, black lacquer coffee and end tables. It don't take long to spot her punk-ass new boyfriend standing shirtless over the stove, a clown with one of those inverted builds: legs like arms and arms like legs, not to mention the sucker's tatted as if he's gangster, when it's a good bet he's weak as one-ply. But hey, who isn't, or hasn't been, at least, some kind of soft, so maybe I should cut him some slack.

Negatory!

Our Princess is all done up in a long dress, frilly socks, and matching pigtail ribbons, and flares her dress jumping the last few steps to a spot near you. You kiss her forehead and fix (relieved you and me both she didn't inherit your sacrilegious toes) her wrong-footed sandals. She asks again for ice cream and you say sure, swelled up with the fact that, unlike the past, our Princess and all else can double-trust—no, overtrust—your word. Holding her at arm's length, you ask who bought her gold bracelet and matching gold chain. She says his name, and when you repeat it, the punk dips out of sight as if your voice reminds him of his sensitive side, of all the ways he can't measure.

Ain't shit sensitive no more about my scandalous-ass ex. She don't bother to see you off (should've seen it coming, what she'd become, but I was sprung); what she does is yell what time she'll be back and instructs her tissue-tough boyfriend to escort you and our Princess to the door, a feckless half-ass gesture since you're halfway to the car by the time the sucker peeks his tattooed neck outside, and by the time he reels in his paranormal-shaped dome you're working the famous trick to starting the Honda.

You drive with the windows down, hot air whistling, and gospel tunes playing on the tweaked six-by-nines you bought off a neighbor for a jug over what they were worth. You've lost some savvy these years, which is a fair trade, you might say. At a red light, two boys strut by, speed-licking ice cream melting fast in the heat. Logo'd headbands noose the boys' throats; their slouchy striped tube socks are hiked to the calf of their thin bowed legs, and they've got the swarthy skin of youngins who've balled outside all summer. In the crosswalk, the shorter one drops his cone and morphs into a cherub statue till a pileup of cars honk him manic and out of the street. The mother in you eases away checking your rearview, shaking your head.

★ ★ ★

Boom! The Honda backfires in the parking lot of the ice-cream parlor and freezes everyone in earshot, embarrasses you into scanning for witnesses before escorting our Princess past a waist-high pile of bikes to the counter, where workers are crumpling under the weekend's midafternoon crush. The only grown-up in the whole joint is an old man searching for a table with a wrist-thick newspaper tucked to his side.

Our Princess, just tall enough to see into the display, tugs at your Capris with premature strength and whispers her order. Sure, baby, you say. Whatever you want.

Double-scooped sundaes in hand, you find a seat near the old man, stuff napkins in the neck of our Princess's dress, and she half eats/half wipes her face with strawberry-topped vanilla ice cream while you wade through kiddie talk to the nexus of what's what, a part of which is whether or not my ex's punk-ass boyfriend has shacked up full-time. Our Princess spoons a mouthful and confirms the punk goes to sleep every night with her mom.

Hell, yeah, it's a mistake, but who ain't done it? Ask a question that—when posed to a child who hasn't yet learned the value of a white lie—leaves you wide the fuck open. Do you like him? you say, and brace. Our Princess licks sprinkles off her fist (the full extent of her musing) and confirms she likes the punk *a lot.* Well, don't forget your daddy loves you, loves you more than anything, you say, with a voice more limp than you'd like.

After ice cream, the Honda backfires again at the mall, *boom,* and coughs an ozone that panics a couple strolling the lot arm in arm. Soon as you and the Princess make it inside, in so many words, she lets you know that, yeah, you might got plans, but she's got plans too, and her plans include a visit to the toy store and a new summer outfit. Okay, Princess, you say, anything you want, as long as there's time left after we've bought your daddy's gift.

Our Princess names the wrong name.

No—your real daddy! you say.

The stores on the first level are picked over to the utmost, to the point where what's left is not worth mentioning. Worry builds while you browse, a feeling spiked by checking your watch and seeing, beyond the ticking hands, a shotgunned trip that ends with what might be your first time late for last-visit. Our Princess can sense it too. She hurries up the escalator and waits at the top. The two of you flit hand in hand to the next stop, a shoe store where the salesman, one of those cooler-than-thou types, is leaned over a counter. It don't take much to see he's one of those junior clowns who fronts like he's clocking big dough, when it's a good bet his hourly ain't but a buck, if that, over minimum wage; he's a young poser, but to be true, Mom, aren't we all, or at least I am a bit of one most days. (How else to make it?) Young Cooler-Than-Thou offers help and you ask for whatever won't cost you an arm and a leg. He suggests a style, shows you a pair of low-tops in my size, gives you the rundown of color. He segues into the shoe's genesis: a script that's dismissible, but you let him finish anyhow, figuring he's no less than somebody's baby boy trying to flaunt what he knows while he hides how much he don't.

New kicks in hand, you tug our Princess to the gift shop, chiding her the whole way to hurry. Just inside she dashes for a stuffed animal display, grabs a big brown teddy off the floor, and strokes it against her cheek. Next scene she's struggling behind you with a bear twice her size. The new duo stake out a space in the aisle while you browse cards, feeling your heart catch speed. You make a choice right before your hope for making one fades, and, with our Princess trailing, shuffle up to the register, where a cashier with white hair and capricious hands calls her a pretty young lady and smiles gamma-esque.

Today my real daddy birthday.

That's wonderful, the woman says, and how old are you?

Without a word our Princess uses two hands to make three fingers.

Wow! Such a big girl, the woman says, then to you: You have a beautiful daughter.

Agreed, her mistake ain't surprising. In the past, just a glimpse of you could stop a strong heart: a man's, a woman's, no matter, but at present, that effect's been oh so vitiated; though who knows, maybe your powers are on the comeback. The lady says good-bye, and our Princess waves like a beauty queen.

In the visitors' lot cardiac miles later, our Princess unbuckles herself, twists around for a better view of the building. She mentions how big her daddy's house is, a comment you don't hear for being distracted, for searching your bag too long for the card and a pen, for waiting for what might feel like all a nigger's good time spent in the hole for words, a single word, to show its face.

My eldest,

Happy birthday! Happy birthday! Happy birthday!

Let me tell you, I had a lot of trouble finding a card that said the right things. Till it dawned on me, there aren't any right things to say. Only to do. So from now on, no more sorry or I

promise or I swear. But what I will say is keep watching . . .
Mad crazy Love,
Mom

You fix your hair and glance at our Princess, whose face is pinched at the blank space where her visor mirror should be, a frown that strikes a gong in your chest, not to mention, if the car's clock is right, you're late for last-visit. But check it, you ain't the only one running on the late show, so is the big-boned Indian chick one of these smooth-talking rogues brags he hooked playing Collect Call Lotto. The Indian chick shows up every week wearing filthy jeans and laceless Keds with a sumo baby wedged on her hip, looking just the right type of desperate to accept a hella-pricey call from an unknown prisoner and open her heart to unortho-dox love. Soon as you step foot inside, our Princess asks about the bars and you explain, the best way you can, if there is such a way, that the bars make sure nobody leaves without permission.

Daddy on time out?

We could say that, you say.

The buzzer sounds and you and the Princess stomp, huff, hike to the end of a line. Up ahead there's a cluster of anxious convicts waiting by the visiting room entry, all of them penitentiary-fresh in clothes stiff with smuggled starch and their cleanest canteen-bought tennies. We have to ask that man to get him, you say, and point towards reception. And when it's our turn, you let him see our gift.

Dude working reception is a redneck, probably from one of those towns farther south where they chop logs, breed behemoths, and keep tacit population caps on anyone resembling us. The cracker has a buzz cut, square chin, hard green eyes, and lips lean as a basehead's word. Lucky for us, our Princess is oblivious as she rushes up and holds the gift high.

This for my real daddy.

The redneck ignores our Princess, scans your license against the list, announces with a smirk that he can't find your name.

Please, you say. Sir, can you please double-check.

Look, miss, there's nothing wrong with my eyes, he says.

But it must be some mix-up, you say.

He darts his green stones over the list and drags a thick stump thumb down the columns. He seems sad to find your name, but perks up at the sight of our Princess holding the gift. Contraband, he says, snatching the box out of her hands and tossing it aside, and though you shouldn't give him the joy, stand and stand your face collapsed and shoulders heaving till he shouts, next, next, looking into a part of you that ain't for him to see.

One of our few black COs is working the visiting room. Dude was cool months back, but got passed over for a promotion and, ever since, has made it extra tough on everybody that ain't white. Dude's extra-heavy-handed search is misdemeanor assault everywhere in the first world. To top it off, he stalks you all the way to your seat, the last of seats near light. With care you help our Princess climb onto the seat.

HOLD THE FUCK UP! That ain't what happens. Enough with this fantasyland shit. Our Princess with you on today's visit, who the fuck am I fooling?

We know what *really* happens is this: We urge at each other through the window and who I don't see—our Princess—gives me the feeling of a weight-lifting wonder knocking me breathless. You sit down and stand up, sit down and stand up, sit down and stand up, your smile disassembling. I called her all last night, called her all this morning, and nothing, you say. She never once picked up.

Am I surprised? Try not. This place ain't built for dreams. Out back sits a rusted pig-iron weight pile and a dim-lit rec room stuffed with slanted pool tables and mended chairs. The radios, the TV's: Everything electronic here is from another era. It's no wonder the PA translates speech to garble. This building is as old as everything—B.C. See wire punching holes in weak Sheetrock, hear water gagging through old pipes, and, my word, the air most days is thick enough to choke you dead. Late nights, guards with keys to unlock every bolt ever produced patrol our dorms, funky boxes crammed with the noise of grown men snoring and the slosh of no few of us undersexed heedless convicts touching ourselves.

Mom, here's the truth of the truth of the truth: There ain't an expectation these walls can't change, not a one, though truthbetold a nigger should be steeled against this grief, should, since I'm seasons and seasons into my set, have spent days and days and days gazing through cyclone fence, spent months of wake-ups and lights-out and chow time and count time and (a time or two) hole-time. Everywhere inside this place is flaking fish-colored paint, which is proof the white boys in charge would give not a shit if we died from breathing lead. And believe me, sometimes it's as if I *could* die here, fall comatose on a mattress so thin, it takes prayer for a wink of sleep. Weeks and weeks go by with no more than the Wednesday transport to get me through, the tiny comfort of seeing dudes more inconsolable than me slug off a bus dressed in a dingy one-piece and the orange plastic slippers that chafe your feet to bleeding.

It's no wonder why years later this year could mean more yearning—at least for me.

But hey, Mom, there's a chance you'll find love—the suckers might be right. And hey, let's take heart, you're sober, off-paper, working—swelled with what gets you, me, a human through.

Look around. See the room bathed in borrowed light, couples whispering across tables, intractable-ass kids darting between the seats, hear the vending machines ejecting snacks and coins, the kitchen crew knocking pots behind the rolltop gate, an officer or two snickering under his breath.

This is what we have, Mom, what we made, and we must make do.

So we reach out, the two of us, you and your eldest young bastard, and hold one another for a time that flouts the limit of allowed contact.

De Paul Drug Treatment Center

DIVERSION CONTRACT

Name:_____ Case No:_____

I here by agree to enter the diversion program. By doing so I understand I must adhere to its obligations and responsibilities as mandated by the judge, program manager, field supervisor, and other approved treatment providers.

CLIENT RESPONSIBILITIES

1. I must tell the truth
2. I must attend all court sessions as ordered
3. I must follow the treatment plan mandated by program personnel
4. I must not violate the law. (If I engage in any criminal act, I may be prosecuted for the charges pending against me)
5. I must obtain gainful employment within 90 days of release into phase two
6. I must tell my field supervisor within 48 hours of a change of address or telephone number or change of employment
7. I must get permission from my field supervisor before I leave the state of Oregon
8. I must submit urine samples upon request
9. I must complete at least 40 hours of community service or pay $500
10. The program is at least 12 months and I will pay a monthly fee of $50.00. I must have a zero balance in order to move on to complete the program.
11. If restitution is owed, I must pay the amount in full as ordered by the court.
12. I must follow the directives given to me and remain drug free. If I fail to do so, the judge may impose one or more of the following therapeutic or punitive responses:

A. Additional community service   B. A period of incarceration in Mult. County jail
C. Extra individual counseling sessions   D. Extra AA / NA meetings
E. 48 hour intensive relapse intervention program.   F. Program termination

CLIENT RIGHTS AND BENEFITS:

1. During the time that I am in enrolled in the program the prosecution of the criminal charge(s) against me will be stayed.
2. If I successfully complete the program, the criminal charges against me will be dismissed and I can never be convicted for those charges:
3. I can quit the program at any time, but if I so choose, I will be prosecuted on my pending charges
4. If I quit the program or I am terminated, anything I have said concerning my drug use while in the program cannot be used against me in court.
5. If I am terminated from the program my conduct while in the program may be considered by the judge at sentencing

Client signature   Date

WHITE / CLIENT   YELLOW /CASE WORKER   PINK / PROGRAM

Had them planned, changed them, and
changed the changed ones.
—Grace

THE DAYS. OUR DAYS.

DePaul Center rehab days: Breakfast at 6A, group counseling
at 8A, one-on-ones at 10A. We take lunch at noon, and we can
eat or not with what seems most mornings as no matter to them.
Afterwards it's another required group: either NA or AA, though
neither of which are any anonymous. At 2P or 3P depending, it's
our last afternoon group, then lo and behold a bit of free time
after that—what amounts to a few of us in the TV room and/or
our room and/or wandering halls and/or sitting outside enjoying
a smoke. Two or three hours to do as we please, save their long
list of rules, before we're back once again on their clock. Dinner-
time's at 5P, and a girl—when am I not one?—should get something in her stomach if she hopes to survive. The after-dinner
meeting is optional, though if we're lucky or blessed or what-
haveyou, it's forsaken for a visit, which, by the way, they arrange
by letters: A–J on Mondays and Wednesdays and K–Z on Tuesdays
and Thursdays.

But this or that week, Sunday to Sunday, sunup to all hours,
what you'll find here are experts—or else a bunch of them that
make the claim. As in my sweet neighbor, who just reached the

halfway, who can name almost any sixties slow tune. As in the former debutante always stitching or crocheting. As in the handsome guy from the top floor who swears he can name most any car trouble just by listening. It seems forever I've been an expert at reading people, and, like everyone else here, the *here* being a place we call by another name, I've also been an expert at other things, the worst of which is lying—to others, to myself.

In this city, it rains, rains so much you best get to liking the rain, so much I've come to love fixing my face to the sound of the rain, love to draw my brows and paint my lips and glue my lashes and, day by day, dot a mole on my cheek—my beauty mark. Most of these females act like just cause we're here, how we look don't count, but I got news for them, program or no, inpatient or out, looking good is a full-time occupation. And it ain't no days off!

No time off if you're smart from reading people either, which is a skill, a talent white folks have stamped with fancy names: rapid cognition or off stage thought or automatic processing, though I call it what my grandmother—God bless her soul— Mama Liza did, which is your first mind, and like Mama Liza would say, we all got a first mind; it's just some of us are too fool to follow ours.

I flow past chattering TVs and trilling alarm clocks, past rooms swelled with whispers or troubled breath, flow past posters of quotes, past a boldface placard of the center's rules, skip right on down to Girlfriend's room. Girlfriend's got her door swung wide while she fusses over a closet of what must be hand-me-downs from a shaky stool. Really and truly, she's always straightening this or that or sweeping or running a rag along dusty sills or hand-mopping her floors or tucking her bunk with corners made for hospitals, or an army base.

By the way, your first mind comes to you in seconds—or less. If you're listening, it tells you how much you'll like a person, if you can trust them, it tells you where to rank them; with your first mind you figure how old, how smart, whether they keep a bank balance or specialize in bounced checks.

Girlfriend, who holds her weight—who don't?—in the wrong places, quakes off the stool. Hurray, she says. Hurray. This time next week. This time next week and you're on your way.

What she means is I've almost reached the end of this stint, which, so help me, is my everlasting last.

She scans a letter from the pile that sits beside a framed five-by-seven of her boys, letters sliced along the edges and crayoned, which, if my mind serves me right, was what got me and her to speaking. Before that you couldn't get her to open her mouth, couldn't nobody ply a single word from her till the day we happened upon each other in the hall, she hurrying with her mail and me lugging an armload of books to my room. That day we exchanged hellos and, for reasons neither of us could name, we chatted through both morning groups, through free time, blathered right through lunch. Next thing we knew we were taking all of our meals together, sitting through Sunday services, and swapping stories well past the time everyone else was asleep. Come to find out we were both raised Baptist, lost our mothers as young girls, and have the habit, excuse me, *had* the habit, of choosing work-allergic roguish men.

Try to split us apart now and you can't, but who knows beyond my stay what will become of our bond?

Who knows but how could we, how could any one of us, when this life is not that life? When we've spent this long dissembling. How could we, though those that know us best or maybe don't know the risk coax our truest truths into view: that we have problems accepting love, that we don't know how to let go, that we're not so good in judging who or what should be kept, that on our worst days, it's tough to find reasons?

We stroll to the kitchen, my heels clicking and her flats whisking along. If you've seen one cafeteria, you've pretty much seen them all: a windowless room with soft white walls and gray tile and workers—stone-faced new residents themselves—who at mealtimes serve just enough to keep us alive and no more, which must be why a good few residents look the victim of third world hunger. We are victims of the morning's longest line, heirs of cooled oats, shriveled links, and shallow juice in cups the size they use for urinalysis.

We find seats and right off she asks me if I heard about the girl who got out last week and relapsed so fast she was back by morning group the next day—sad, sad, yes, but not outside our fates. We come and go. We come and go: the timid ones, the stubborn ones, the worried. Girlfriend sips at what's left in her cup, which, as I said, wasn't much to start.

Your boys. You must be about to bust, she says.

Explode. Yes, I say.

Now's the time for those plans, she says.

That's the thing, I say. I've had them, changed them, and changed the ones I changed.

We watch the latecomers drag in—their eyes full of blood and hair tight-napped at the neck or spun around their head—and catch the last scrapes from the pots and pans. She and I don't say much else. We are not the last to leave but close, and she walks me to my room. There's a note under my door that says for me to report to the nurse.

Should've known they'd hit you with that last UA, she says. I'll leave you to it.

What they won't say here is how we can never know, when we get this close to leaving, if someone would rather see us stay. What they won't say is what they'll do to keep you if they choose: botch exit papers, switch UA results, quiz you to tears on a false report from the staff. They keep secret the ploys they use to stretch your days into months, tricks that will send us to places we escaped to serve suspended time, to serve new time, reason why when you reach the end it's nerves, nerves, nerves.

The UA line stretches far down the hall and I shuffle to the end of it behind a girl from my floor with gobs of white glue caked between the tracks of her weave. You can hear someone curse inside the restroom—what might be a scheme gone bad which wouldn't surprise me. I once saw a so-called slickster's balloon of prepackaged urine fall from his armpit, burst, and soak a fussy nurse's brand new white shoes. Down the line the counselor gapes at us from her office—the wall of champions looming behind her—while the nurse moseys out bearing gifts: twist-cap prelabeled sample cups, and here and there packets of pills.

Which of us experts believes themself a bootleg chemist? Who's ready to bet against the odds, will hedge against the time it takes to pee clean; against whether they test our urine, or our hair, or our blood.

The counselor slinks out, a wrist noisy from a sleeve of gold bracelets rubbed half-silver. She works her way along the wall frisking us each with just her gaze, waiting for an eye to rove, for a nerve to spark in someone's balled fist or leg. She reaches me and takes my hand in her hand till my heart slows. Come see me, she says. You be sure to come see me soon.

My turn comes and I hover over the toilet and catch a weak stream in the cup and twist the cap tight. I stand in the dank for a time, braced against the sink, listening to the voices float in through the door. When I come out, I see a new resident, too young for this life, carrying her intake issue—blankets, sheets, a flat pillow—with arms so thin you could rub them for fire. Below bangs hacked to a slant across her face she gives me meek eye-to-eye and slugs up a flight of stairs. She could be me years back my first time in a place like this, though let's hope she arrives at the truth sooner than I:

It's no use trying to fool ourselves.

Sometimes fooling ourselves is the only strength that counts.

But time has taught me my options (who knows about the
next man's?), *my* options, are full of fast-twitch muscles.
—Champ

HERE COMES A WOMAN, no coat, with her wet hair mat-
ted. Closer, she looks about Mom's age and, like Mom, makes
you wonder if she's lived a hard-knock life or not. My mother
will be out soon, and I can predict the promises she'll make, a
script after years I can recite verbatim, speeches she may believe,
but maybe doesn't. But that matters not. Whatever plans Mom
has this time, grand or small, starry-eyed or dull, my plans will
be under her plans holding them up.

OneverythingIlove. We. Won't. Lose.

The woman from a few seconds ago, she's hocus pocus in my
rearview—poof. Vanishes, and when I swivel to see where to,
there's an unmarked patrol car idling at the crosswalk. Your boy
keeps cool at first (clean records create reckless confidence), but
when they start towards me, I push the sack in my boxer briefs,
hop out my ride, and shuffle towards the nearest house, a place
that favors our old house on Sixth—home. Two sets of stairs to
reach the front door, and I climb each one slow. As if I'm cursed
with early arthritis, a janky hip, a trick knee. Truth be told, I'm
giving the kind officers time to get busy with another call, to find
more pressing work elsewhere, anywhere but here, but wouldn't

you know it, there must be nothing pumping in Northeast, nada,
and since it ain't, I'm the object of the officers' affection, their
one and only true love, and right about now they're sending
their amore through a searchlight, stabbing it all inside my ride,
which, Ibullshityounot, bucks my eyes the size of silver dollars,
and buries my breath down deep where it's hard to find.

And peoples, trust me, you'd be breathless too, or worse, if you
knew what I know about the Feds' famous math: 100 to 1—a.k.a.
the Bias Effect, à la Len Bias, the former college star who over-
dosed himself into old glory's cocaine demigod.

What I see: a porch junked with trash bags big as boulders,
old bike parts, rusted tools, busted cardboard boxes, a mound of
soggy clothes. What I feel: my heart stall, a vein in my neck grab.
When my heart gets to pumping again, I pound at the door.
No—my bad. There I go being a hype man for myself. On the
forreals, it's a feathery-ass knock, but I'm ready to strike a convo
with whoever answers.

Hello, sir, I don't mean—

Excuse me, miss, I know it's late, but—

Hey, lil man, let me holler at—

But see here's the problem: Through the thin curtain covering the window the whole house is black. Ain't enough light in
there to make a shadow. In a nimbus I harvest my cell and make
a Broadway show of dialing my homeboy Half Man. No lie, it
sounds as if someone installed an amp in my earpiece. Wouldn't
be surprised if the whole block heard it ringing over and over,
heard me calling my homeboy to no avail, which shouldn't be
no big old surprise since dude could make a career of being
absentee: Gayle "Half Man" Kent: the CEO of Mr.-Never-There-
When-Need-Be, Inc.

A car splashes past, bass turning its trunk into a booty music live show. Soon after I lay a second round of heavy-ass knocks on the door, pounding that sets (sans self-hype this time) my knuckles afire and ratchets my pulse to the sound of a siren. And peoples, let's call that siren freedom's theme song cause that's what it is, trust and believe, cause the ones who disbelieve are either doing time or indicted.

Police pan the light across the yard, the house, then relentless again on me, and meanwhile, I'm glancing this way and that, and feeling the sack crawl down my crotch towards the loose elastic of my boxer briefs. Any second they'll order me off the porch with my hands held high. Another second and they'll trap my wrists too tight behind my back. And right between these fates sits the crossroads.

Run or stay?

Toss or keep?

Felony or misdemeanor?

Life has options! This is what they preached to us in my old youth program, what I tell my bellicose brothers whenever they'll listen, which ain't if ever often enough.

Options. Options. Calling Kim, my sweet thing, is on the list. My girl don't sleep sound at all, so she says, unless we're lying side by side which means she's likely up, but since she's also a first-rate worrier, it probably ain't worth the trouble. The trouble of lying. Of inventing an excuse for why I'm breaking my embargo on hitting licks this late, a rule I let her impose in the first place. Not to be no sucker, never that, but Kim is special, so special. Yeah, most, if they could, would choose the chick of their dreams, but if you ask me, fantasy girls are never seen in full. My girl's the girl you'd pick if you were wide awake with time to think, and though, between you and me, I may here and there indulge in a shot of ancillary pussy, I ain't in earnest down with risking our good thing.

Life has options, my old program preached, but on the other hand, here's the incontrovertible truth about those options: Act too slow and they put on track shoes and sprint right the fuck off.

The patrol car shifts into park. The doors swing open. A pair of officers hop out and plod my way. I swing around just in time to see them (those flashlight-bearers of love) stop at the base of the first set of steps. Them looking up at me and me squinting into the inscrutable. You live here? the one without the flashlight asks. He's heads taller than his partner (picture a giant on his tiptoes in heaven), with a voice that sounds beefed up on performance drugs. No sir, I say, hoping the *sir* sounds sincere, honorific. I'm looking for my friend. Haven't seen him in a while.

The officers turn towards each other, black silhouettes set in effulgence. And on my life, it should be a crime how long they stay silent.

They busted this place the other day, one says.

Busted! You sure? I say, and start towards them.

So let's get this straight. You haven't been here in all this time and you stop by at almost midnight to say hello? the taller one says.

The three of us stand on the sidewalk, face-to-face; face-to-chest. They're older and maybe slower, but they've got those radios no mere man can outrun, and even if by chance I could, I'd still have the problem of this slithering sack in my crotch. Check it, if it's true that life has options, it's also true those choices are full of fast-twitch muscles.

How about you show us some ID, says the shorter officer, though calling him short is gratuitous to the utmost. Homeboy's all of five feet nothing—no lie, we're talking centimeters off a certified dwarf. With hands no good for shooting pool or poker, I give the dwarf my license and watch him (in a hundred frames per second slowmo) march to his car and sit with the door swung open, one foot inside, one foot hovering. He runs my license on speaker, and just like that, my legs are no better than a beat-up ride with bald tires and alignment shot to shit.

The taller officer asks my name once more, and before I can answer, his partner shouts it out.

Wait, aren't you the one that used to play ball? he says, and shakes a finger. Aren't you the kid that wore those colored socks in the tournament that year? The homunculus appears, looking smug and slapping my license, neither of which are good signs.

Here comes the chorus of freedom's theme song. Here it comes and here's why. One of my homeboys (dude probably never so much as jaywalked) spent almost a week in the county thanks to a handful of faulty warrants in his name by way of false reports to officers by his full-time, lifetime, thug-life cousins. Now, I should be straight, but that's the thing about this business: You think you know, but you can never know for sure whether you're in the system.

The legal-sized dwarf returns my license and turns his eyes into hot flares. Tonight's your night, he says.

This boy here could shoot that ball, the taller officer says. I seen him score thirty-something points one game, must've been five or six three-pointers. He turns to me. Youngster, you supposed to be in college somewhere scorching the nets.

Oh, you were at that game? I say, and offer my best impersonated smile. It was seven threes that game, sir, I say, still hoping the *sir* sounds sincere and honorific. I tell him how I'm in college, about how close I am to earning my degree.

You balling? he says.

No, sir, I say. Just the books for me.

He fixes his face into a frown you could almost call authentic. You got the right idea, he says. For sure. You could be out here running amuck like the rest of them. You keep on.

When they pull off, the part of my brain that makes good decisions says, Leave now! Leave now! Leave now!

But what do I do?

What they should tell you in those youth programs is that reckless confidence breeds bad decisions, that avoiding a felony can swell almost anyone with a superfool's sense of safety.

Back in my ride with window cracked, it's Northeast in concert: tires whirring over slick streets, water rushing down a sewer, a dog barking in somebody's backyard. It's Northeast on stage: a stray cat rummaging through a curbside recycling bin, a small black thing darting into the lot across the street. This is the same lot where years ago, I'm talking back when we were living in the house on Sixth (our home then and now though we don't own it), me and my homeboy Half Man and a couple of my patnas from King Elementary would play stickball or football or kickball against dudes from another neighborhood. On days when everyone showed we had enough for six-on-six, but attrition is a motherfucker. It'd be slim pickings for our reunion squad: Half Man, my boy with the lazy eye, and maybe my wannabe pimp patna, but only if we could coax him away from the beefy white broad he brags to anyone who'll listen is paying what she weighs.

Bam! From nowhere a basehead appears at my window. Say, boss, I'm doing bad out here, he says. Let me get a little bump to set me straight.

Dude's a veteran smoker. Used to see him my second go-round

at curb-serving. Good sense says I shouldn't speak one word, but I speak two: Beat it.

Aw, boss, don't do me like that, he says. I'm not askin for no handout. He waves his arms, fans a noxious funk of mildew, smoke, and highgrade piss and backs into a snatch of light. In that snatch you can see he has a nappy beard that runs all the way down his throat and yellow eyes, my alcoholic uncle Pat's yellow eyes. Right after we'd left for the first time the house on Sixth, back when my moms kept the family level, balanced like the weight you use to zero a digi scale, my always-soused uncle Pat would pop up unannounced plying at her with sob-ass drag: Grace, I just need a place to lay my head a few nights, he'd say, and parlay that few nights into a week, into a month, into a year of living rent-free, drinking the last of the 2%, and spending whole days beached in front of our TV.

I ask dude if he's police cause back in my crucible days an old head told me asking the question would protect me against police entrapment. Dude scratches his head and bores into me with spangled I-get-zooted marbles. C'mon, boss. I'm fucked up out here, he says, as if the shit isn't explicit. I raise the window and shoot him a glare that's the same as thorough ass-whooping.

This veteran basehead, nappy beard, my drunk uncle Pat's yellow eyes, he drags to the other side of the street. He stops, plucks a small bit off the ground, and, with the rain slapping his skull something vicious, holds it to the sky and cocks his head. He leaves his arm up until it tremors. Then he drops his arm and shakes his head and tosses his find aside. He turns his back to me, slugs off, and in the distance, a shadow swallows him whole.

It won't be an issue at all.

—Grace

THE COUNSELOR—she wears her hair short as a man's and handmade clothes—glances from a desk messy with papers and pens and a multicolored coffee mug. Hey there, she says. Just finishing. When I sit, my feet won't keep still, so I fold my hands in my lap and dig my heels in the floor and don't let the clock tick off but a few seconds before I get around to what's most important: Where? She picks up my file and runs her finger along the top sheet, her bookish frames free-falling down the slope of her nose. She tells me my housing assignment, the Piedmonts, and you couldn't pick a place with more addicts and dealers, a place with more to tempt. Oh my, I say. Is there any place else?

I'm afraid not, she says, and tweaks her frames. She goes on about denied grants and budget cuts and program closures—excuses she must think consoling, but aren't in the least—and takes out a triplicate-copy contract and asks me to read it.

She tells me that my caseworker will have the details, but that the gist is I give them nine months to a year clean as an outpatient, and they set me free and clear, clean slate. She flashes teeth coffee-stained to light ocher. Here's my best advice, she says. Affirm, affirm, affirm, and do it every day. Find a new group of friends if the old ones are users. Choose new places to hang out if the old places are triggers. You should also do yourself a huge huge favor and take up a hobby, she says. Reading, drawing, cooking, sewing. She leans over her desk and points at the sheet and explains the penalties for breaking rules. She claims she's confident I won't. She waits for a response that isn't forthcoming. Let me be the first to congratulate you, she says. Don't mistake today for anything but progress. For the next nine months you're pretty much free to do as you please save breach the contract or break a law. Just nine more months and we cut you loose.

They tell us in times like these to affirm.

I am a child of God.
I place my life in the care of God.
I believe in a power greater than me.
Before I say I can't, I will say I try.

Grace, Grace, she says. Are you here? Do you anticipate trouble? No, I say. No issues, I say. None.

She tears apart the copies and hands me the bottom sheet and bullies me into a hug. Nerves are natural, she says, and steps back. But you have the tools to make it. You have the tools and you have us. So if ever you need, you stop by, she says. It's open-door and I mean it. She hands me a voucher for food and toiletries. We are a resource, she says. We are your partner. She takes out a camera and poses me against the wall and snaps a portrait. She tells me when I finish outpatient, she'll post it on her wall of champions.

In my room, I fold and smooth shirts, pants, blouses, my one skirt, audit socks for matches, check stockings for runs, couple bras to panties, and pack it all in my nylon suitcase and duffel. I swipe ledges for dust, sweep and resweep the floor, inspect the desk drawer; I count empty hangers left in the closet, take apart my bunk, and turn my sheets and blanket into squares. I lie across my bunk and, for the umpteenth time, read old letters, greeting cards, my old intake papers, the last few months of progress memos.

I throw on my jacket and slide a picture into my front pocket, the only one I can find of all my boys, together. It was taken at Canaan's first birthday, ten years ago now, the year KJ started first grade, Champ finished junior high, the year Big Ken and I split for the last time. This was also the year my word, in ways that measured most, began weighing less than it should, a time before my case and the sentence that sent me down state and my boys, my precious loves, for a time with their father.

I loll in the hallways, peek into my friend's rooms, coax them into long-winded good-byes.

You wait so long to leave and when it's your turn you wait as long as you can to leave.

I am not alone.
I am capable of change.
I am the change I want to see.

At last, I end up under a covered bus stop with my duffel slung and my suitcase squatting by my side and my cherished birthday picture tucked in the pocket over my heart. There's only one other person down here with me, a rugged-faced man wearing a stained work shirt and thick-soled boots. The man pats his pockets with an unlit filterless cigarette teethed between his lips. He asks for a light and I offer my Bic and he cups his hands against a gusty wind. He gets it lit and takes a drag that must be Zen, and though it wasn't on my mind, I tamp out my slim menthol and light up myself. The bus arrives before long and I crush my cig under my foot and lug my duffel and suitcase on board and haul them to the back, where a boy—he got to be somewhere between the ages of my youngest two—with spiked green hair is slumped in a seat with a battered skateboard laid across his lap. It's fall, but the boy's wearing a T-shirt that, without even look-ing, you can see right through it, cutoff shorts, and dingy tenny shoes with no laces. He thumps his board and jerks his neck to what must be a song in his head, oblivious until we reach North-east, where he signals his stop, leaps into the street, and skates off against traffic.

Stops later, a bad wind blows a familiar face on board—Michael. Well, well, well, I'll be gotdamned, he says, swagger-ing my way. Ms. Corporate America in the flesh. Fuck a month, ain't seen you in a year of Sundays.

Hello, Michael, I say. Please call me Grace. Those jobs were years ago.

Once in corporate America, always a corporate American, Michael says. You know how it is, most times it ain't where you at, but where you been and with who. Michael smiles, unveiling missing teeth and a wrong-colored tongue. He rubs an unshaven cheek and stabs his cake cutter deeper into his kinky afro. The man smells as if he should bathe in hot bleach.

Say, where you been hiding? he says.

Hiding, I say. Haven't been hiding nowhere. More like lay-ing low.

Sheeit, ain't nothing wrong with that, he says. Come to think of it, somebody tell me, I forget who, that you was in diversion.

Judge sent my black ass there when I caught my first possession. But after living a coupla months with all them rules and regulations, I told em, fuck it, send me to the penitentiary. He picks something out of his teeth and flicks it on to the floor. He plops in the seat next to mine.

Now, they cuisine, he says. From what I recall, they cuisine wasn't all that bad. Indeed it lacked a certain je ne sais quoi, but every blue moon you'd close your eyes and that shit was damn near fine dining. Michael chuckles and scratches his head and checks the bed of black gunk under his jagged nails. You finish all them phases, or they still got you leashed on that paper? he says.

I give him my back and watch the blocks scroll—the apartments, the duplexes, the record store, Check Mart, a black-suited Muslim hocking papers outside the beauty supply.

Oh, oh, I got it, Michael says. Cool, didn't mean no harm. You know me. Might get it fucked up every now and then, but a brother mostly means well.

There's a spotted run of days between this man and me. So many times of us stumbling into a plasma center at the end of a week run, and blowing, with no qualms whatsoever, the few dollars they paid, plus whatever change we had in our pockets, of us striking out with smirks, buying from the nearest dealer, and racing to get loaded: in an alley or abandoned building or, in a bind sometimes, the unisex bathroom of a resturant in Old Town.

Michael looks at me and I look at him and we trade blame, pit against each other our past, strength, will, pride, faith.

By the way you looking, I say, about now, an in-patient program would do you good.

Cool, cool, I see you up there on your stallion, Michael says. But check it: make sure you hold them reins real, real tight.

He don't hazard my way again. He opens his window, and fake busies himself with emptying his pockets of junk. He gets off on Skidmore and waves good-bye at half-mast.

Stops later, when I get off, it seems as if I've stepped into a movie on pause the whole last year. I tug my things past a totaled car and yards of ankle-length grass, past a bent street pole and a pair of tagged stop signs, tug it up to the front gate of the Piedmonts, a weathered apartment complex enclosed by a tall wrought-iron fence. I buzz and smoke the next-to-last cig in my pack while I wait. The lady that shows clasps my hand in hers with strength. She leads me to a building in the back that houses an office furnished with an oak desk, lawn chairs, and a rack of color-coded keys. She hands me a sheet and tells me to read it with care. It's our rules, she says. Rules beyond your program contract. She tells me the complex is a drug-free zone, that any tenant caught on the premises with drugs or paraphernalia will be reported to the police and put out.

She leads me to my unit, offers a canned script of assurances, and skirts off the moment I turn the bolt. I drop my bags and kick my heels off by the front door. Someone has slapped fresh paint on the walls, shampooed streaks in the carpet, nice touches, but a front room won't tell you whether you can stand a place. To know that, you best get to checking the bathroom. How wide this bathroom is, if you stretch out your arms you can palm both walls, and how high, if I hadn't kicked off my heels, I could almost touch the fan. The tile is mismatched and curls where it should lie down. The tub and toilet are scrubbed to off white. When I turn the faucet, it spits rusted water that takes a moment to stream clear.

You've been here before, I tell myself. Weaker and with less to lose.

I take a long breath in.

Let a big breath out.

Take a long breath in.

Exhale—enormous.

Air sucks through the fan. Cold tile bites through a hole in my stockings. I take out the picture of my boys and wedge it in a corner of the mirror and hit the light switch. The bulb flickers to a soft glow and I finger the photo's curled edges—see my three boys, my precious loves, in all the light there is.

> . . . but it's tough when most years, most days,
> she looks so vintage.
> —Champ

BACK WHEN WE WERE STRAIGHT. When we were living with my great-grands in the house on Sixth, home, back when Mom's checks kept me and KJ laced in new shirts and laden with toys, back when she kept a corporate job that paid a bonus, back then Mom came home at the same time day in, day out. I'd sit at my window and watch her pull up (we kept a new ride back then), and would book to the top of the steps and damn near implode waiting for her to sway through the door dressed to impress the world in wool-blend pants and silk blouse or a skirt suit with a broach pinned to her lapel, plus jewels you could hock for a new self on her fingers and wrists. The routine. Mom would say my name the way only she could, the way only she can, and flash a smile that never seemed even infinitesimally fake. Then she'd call me down, doff the tenny shoes she wore to and from work but never anywhere else, bright white shoes she kept stitched with sparkling double-knotted laces yanked so tight it's a wonder her feet never fell off from lack of blood. My mother would grip me in one of her spine-bending-breath-stopping hugs, set me free, and, while I was working to catch my wind, would shuffle off towards the kitchen where my great-grandparents,

Mama Liza and Bubba, were waiting to hear of her day. My M.O. was I'd lag, wait till Mom was well out of sight, snatch up her tennies, untie her tight-ass knots, loosen the laces so she could slip them on the next morning no hassles. Set them side by side, and vanish before anyone in the house witnessed. It was the most I could do for her back then and may be the most I have done for her since.

Mom is outside the gates glancing.

She's smoking a nasty-ass cigarette and wearing clothes that might be secondhand. This is the first time she's seen my ride, which is probably why, right off, she don't move, not until I tap the horn and pull up close.

She climbs in and the first thing out her mouth is, Whose car is this?

How about hello? I say, but already Mom's shimmying in her seat, running her hands along the dash, opening vents, and saying, Wow, wow, the whole time.

No, Champ, serious, whose car is this? she says.

Mom, I say. C'mon.

Mom what? she says. This cost, what? What did this cost?

Nothing, Nothing, I say. No worries.

She twists to give me the side of her face and lets her window down. Okay, I'll let it be, she says. But for now.

I ask why she didn't call me the day she got out. Tell her I would've picked her up.

Some things you should do on your own, she says. Some days it's best to be by yourself. Mom touches the door handle, and smiles at me, the way she might've half my life ago. Look at you, she says. Look at you. She can't decide on where to eat, so

I drive us to the diner where my high school coach would take our hoop team during state tournament time, a spot with a waffle breakfast that could bring a nigger to tears of joy. The hostess seats us in a booth near a window and gives us menus and ice waters. Our waiter appears, asks if we need time to decide. Mom does, so I busy watching cars wheel Broadway while she over-thinks her choice. She closes the menu and our waiter reappears pad in hand.

So, how's it going? she says.

Cool, I say.

Just cool? she says

Just cool, I say.

And Kim, she says. How is she?

Cool, too, I say.

You haven't had a conversation with me in umpteen months and all you can say is cool? she says.

Just being honest, I say. Ain't gone put nothing on it. Ain't gone to take nothing off it.

Boy, you silly, she says. What's the good news?

That's a lot of pressure, I say. What if it ain't none?

Mom lifts her head. Her eyes, they're oceans. I've seen them roil with storms, but now they're clear, becalmed.

Boy, life's pressure, she says. You best prepare.

How about I'm free and alive? I say. There's the report.

Mom holds her water glass as if it's a chalice and sips. There's a whole lotta difference between being alive and livin, she says. There's a whole lot of folks walkin dead on they feet. She pauses and clamps her eyes. And I should know, she says. Believe me if anyone should know that, it's me.

I slide out the booth and slink to the register and take my time buying a paper. I glance over the front page and lollygag more before I make my way back. Mom ain't interested in reading a section, says she'll pass on the bad news. What she does is scrounge her purse (that joint's big enough to bury an elf) for her compact, fogs a tiny mirror, wipes it with her sleeve, gives herself a once and twice-over, and drags a finger across brows she's forged since my wee bit days.

The Metro headline is news of another judge handing out another Measure Eleven charge (you've got to love those mandatory minimums!) to someone I know, this time to this Blood dude who warmed the bench on my Biddy Ball team. Every other week, I see a name I know, an old friend, ex-teammate, a face I recognize from summer camp, in the Sports or Metro, more in the Metro than Sports, which, when you think about it, proves a point: there's a gang of dudes (you might could count me in) out here who love to be seen, felt, heard, most of whom (you got to count me out) though, will accept the shine how it comes.

Mom smoothes her ponytail, bats lashes hard to tell ain't hers. You try and give her the gift of seeing her new, but it's tough when most years, most days, Mom's so vintage. She asks me about school and I mention this class I'm taking that begins with the prof posting a quote for guided free-write. Last week's quote was by Oscar Wilde: A man's face is his autobiography. A woman's face is her work of fiction. Mom puzzles those brows. And just what's that supposed to mean? she says.

We linger after our meal, and when we leave, Mom says she wants to stay out, so I drive to Irving Park and park on Fremont, two wheels on the curb and two wheels in the street. Since we don't do publicity (no public hand-holding, public hugging, public kissing), me and Mom walk uphill with a little space between us to the masticated bench that overlooks the covered court where down below the Mexicans play eight-on-eight full-court with a tricolored ball. Mom swirls her heel in a mound of damp leaves. A team erupts over a three-point make.

So what you been doing since you got out? I say.

She zips her jacket, worries the buckle on her bag.

Not enough, she says.

Well, why not? I say. What's the plan?

She shakes out another smoke, turns to watch a car maneuver the islands on Seventh Ave. The plan's to keep planning, she says, and lights up.

Right, I say. But you got something a little more defined?

Yes, she says. She takes out a folded sheet, her diversion contract. It lists rehab mandates, how long she has to get a job, how much she owes for her fines and fees. Don't get no more defined than that, she says. So right now my plan is their plan.

Okay, so now we know what's what, I say.

We? she says.

Yes, we, I say.

Enough about that, she says. You know what, I was thinking about finding me a new church, she says. One where worshipping is more important than who put what in a plate.

Again? I say.

Is that a problem? she says.

The problem is them church saints persecuting almost all of mankind. Like I saw one of your old friends on the corner the other day. And you know what she was doing?

No, but I bet you'll tell me, Mom says.

Spiking a slapdash cross and singing "Happy Birthday" to Jesus.

MITCHELL S. JACKSON

That's a bit much, Mom says. But there's nothing wrong with committing to God.

Nothing wrong with commitment is right, I say. But what about what's beyond that? Mom smirks and shakes her head.

Oh, so it's that time, huh. Time to rededicate your life to your Lord and Savior? I get to my feet and, imaginary mic in hand, pace in front of the bench. Umm-hmmm. I spoke to the Lord today, amen, and he said put a lil extra in the offering plate. I said, I spoke to the Lord today, amen, and he said God blesses those that give. Cause the church, amen, needs money for new paint. Cause Reverend Bootleg, amen, amen, needs money for a new car.

Boy, you best quit mocking the Lord, she says. For lightning snap out the sky and strike you down. Mom crosses her legs, knocks a wet leaf from the hem of her frayed jeans. She takes off a shoe (Mom's toes are a sight) and shakes out something worrying her foot. How's your brothers? she says. When's the last time you seen them?

Now, them jokers need Jesus for real, I say. But not to worry, we got em.

Who's the we this time? she says.

Big Ken, I say. And me. Mom, trust, the boys are all good till you're good. Let's worry about getting you off this paper. With them, it's no rush.

With them it's all the rush, she says, and groans. You won't understand until you do.

Hey, I'm with you. On the home team. Us versus them, I say, and throw up my hands.

Mom's smile, silver caps, missing molar and all, could burn off high clouds. Something else, she says. What you think about me going back to school? Or picking up a trade? I'm so tired of them tossing me pennies. Mom scrounges for her compact, digs out a tube, and swipes her lips. Hey, I say. Whatever it is, whatever you need, I got you.

More Mexicans show—a squad, and we watch the game till a fight breaks out over a foul, our cue to leave.

We stand. I ask her if she ever thinks about the old house.

Which house? she says.

The house, I say. Home.

Mom swirls her shoe in a tiny treasure of leaves.

But Champ we don't own it. It's not ours, she says. She turns to me her eyes oh so oceanic. Son, don't get attached to what they can take away. And what can't they take away?

We link hands (to hell with old rules).

But what if we did? I say, and squeeze.

You do it all once, do it all twice . . .

       —Grace

THE DEPARTMENT OF COMMUNITY JUSTICE.
Never mind the temperature, there's always a draft in places like this, and never enough places to sit. A riot of folks pushed up against walls papered over with posters and announcements. Folks thumb pamphlets and screen papers—applications, affidavits, recc letters, pay stubs—and dash after restless kids, everyone resisting as much as they can the urge to look too much into each other. There's a man posed by the restroom, holding a tiny cup, his feet dancing as if he couldn't piss clean if you paid him gold bricks, and he's who I trek past to a front desk helmed by a girl who don't hide one bit being bothered. Wordless, she points to the sign-in and drops her head over what must be in no small way worth more of her precious, precious time.

Thank you very much, I say, wishing I could crush her with the glint of my teeth.

They call names. I find a speck of open space and listen for mine.

It's tough to find comfort here, takes but so long to know no one with sense would choose this for themselves.

A woman calls my name—once, twice; she waits for me to rouse and sidestep bodies to where she stands. Grace Thomas.

You are Grace, aren't you? Come, she says, and hustles down the hall. She tells me her name, that she's new to the county, that I've been reassigned to her load last-minute. She stops at an office that could be the office of any of them—too many papers and too little light—and takes a seat in a padded chair, and thrusts a thin manila file across the desk. This about sums it and isn't much, she says. Can you catch me up to speed on the rest?

Where to start? I say.

Well, that, she says, you should know.

She straightens her desk. You can't help but notice she's got her nails clipped and polished clear, wears a wedding ring sized for show. She opens my file, leafs through the top pages, leaves the folder splayed.

Okay, Ms. Thomas, I've got a billion appointments, so let's make this brief. UAs, we do them by color and yours is blue. You call in the morning. You call weekdays and weekends, and when it's your color you come in. No excuse. Be warned as well, she says, and please don't mistake this as an empty threat, that noncompliance carries consequence. Furthermore, you can count on house calls, she says, count on a number of unannounced visits. Now, employment, she says. Per the job search contract you've got sixty days to show a pay stub or we mandate job-readiness classes. Meanwhile, we'll need to see job logs, one entry per lead, she says. And let's not forget your substance abuse programming. For now it's NA twice a week and a bi-monthly woman's group, both of which require the group leader's signature to count. Well, Ms. Thomas, that's about it, she says. I believe that about does it for now. We shall see one another soon.

★ ★ ★

Daybreak the next day the hunt. You rise and search the cupboards and icebox, hoping to find food heavy enough to last the
day, to spare yourself from spending the pennies you have left.
You stuff yourself to a paunch and carry a day-old paper to the
front room and plop on your scraggy couch and search the want
ads for jobs that list a starting pay of no less than triple the state
minimum wage: an office manager and a payroll clerk and an
executive assistant . . . You check job after job and stuff the sec-
tions in a bag and head into the bathroom and spend more time
than anyone should penciling your brows and painting your lips
and stroking your weaved locks. You prep in your cracked bathroom mirror and whisk to your room and dress in old pants and
a blouse with stained pits and your favorite heels, the half-size-
small heels you bought at full price because the salesman convinced you they were the last pair to be found. You dress and rub
your neck and wrist with smell-good and high-step outside,
prance beneath a beautiful blue sky—a day for movies or post-
cards or love songs—to a corner stop, where you wait for the first
bus of buses you need to reach the first culled hope: an executive
assistant job at a sportswear business, its office in a red brick
building with a lobby that lets in the sun. You greet the front
desk girl cherry, but she eyes you pore by pore and slaps a clipboard of papers on the counter and warns against leaving questions, any one question, blank. You print answers in your best
hand and give it back to the girl. You work to keep your feet and
hands still while you sit, until a man—he's got a shaved top lip
and blonde strands clipped high around the ears—shuffles out
and calls your name and leads you into an office decked with ab-
stract art and a plastic fern. Your smile sags when, all too soon, he
prods you over your spotty work life. You answer in truth and,

all too soon, he pops out of his seat and offers a mock thank-you-for-time and rushes you right back into the lobby, a room more narrow and dim than it was breaths ago, and under the receptionist's harsh gaze it dawns on you—these people and their papers, all their papers—to fill out a JOB SEARCH REPORTING LOG: *what is the name and address of the company and what is the title of the position and to whom did you speak and what is the name and phone number of a contact and what was the outcome of the visit?* You scratch the answers and double-check the scribbles and gather your things and stride out and amble blocks and catch a bus and then the light rail and then another bus to apply as a secretary at a real estate firm, a business that isn't holding same day interviews, so you leave wondering when and if. You head from there to a warehouse in Southwest, which, as of a day ago, needed a shipping clerk, but just your luck, highway traffic is at a halt, froze so you crawl a few feet in an hour, which means the hours to apply at the next place have come and gone, so what to do but get off at the next stop and cross the street and wait in mist that will soon be rain. You perk when a super-long accordion guzzler arrives, a bus empty save a minor cast of strange sorts: a man who shouts *I'm a Vietnam Veteran and homeless, which should be a crime, but here I am,* another man with a melon-colored moon-shaped bruise stamped under his eye, a woman with a canal dug in the center of her flaky scalp. You ride the double-bus and then the light rail and then a second grumbling engine to your stop in Northeast. You stop in Big Charles's store on the way home and buy an *Oregonian* and a *Nickel Ads* and stuff them in your bag and, feet aching, dodge puddles. You drag inside—the heels you had to have have shrank to ancient Chinese bindings—and doff your soggy clothes and, too lazy to cook, fix boiled wieners and

Ramen, which shouldn't be a decent meal anyplace. You're intent on marking the papers before bed, but by the time you eat and let your stomach settle and watch a second or two of what's flashing across the TV, your eyelids may as well be bricks. Heavy, so you slog into the bedroom and swathe in old sheets and spend half a night chasing sleep or rather a whole night thrashing in and out of sleep till outside your window birds chirp and your alarm clock trills. You wake at daybreak the next day and call the UA line—today's not your turn—fry almost a whole bag of spuds and a pile of scrambled eggs and bacon that could cause a weak heart to stop. You cook food for a family, though it's only you, and mark the day's classifieds and shower till the water runs cool and so slow, so slow, fix your face and your hair and put on your clothes, and, with a man's steely can't-stop-won't-stop untouchable tick in your chest, you stomp out the door in flats—lesson learned—with your oriental heels stuffed in your bag and your head cocked to a gorgeous cloud-specked blue sky. You do it all once, do it all twice, and it's another week of more of the same: trips to deep in Northeast and Northwest and Southwest and Southeast and Gresham and Clackamas and Troutdale . . . routes that take on the feeling of sojourns across seas; then one ash-gray morning you call the UA hotline and today's your turn, so you skip breakfast and dress in a rush and leave, find yourself flitting under a sky made of gauzy white cloth. You reach the office in no time and scratch your name on a list and wait to be called, and, wow, wow, they call you faster than you thought they would. You bop out of the office before noon dead sure you sampled clean with yet another checked-to-death classified stuffed in your bag, listings for a home healthcare aid and a customer service rep and an inside sales rep and an account specialist and a personal assistant and an administrative assistant and a day-care attendant and a telemarketer and a mail clerk and a nurse's aide and a nail tech trainee—prospects with an hourly pay falling closer and closer to the state's minimum. You search and search and spark the rare times they invite you into a conference room or office for an on-the-spot interview, though you don't know why, since they never fail to grill you over your work gaps and conviction and quote the same trite script: *we'll be in touch and thank you very much for your time and the position has been filled and it looks as if you're under-qualified and it looks as if you're over-qualified* and what happens this week is what happened last week and soon the can't-stop-won't-stop tick in your chest blights to should-you-quit-when-will-you-quit, and those evenings especially, you trudge home wary the phone will sit mute a day, a week, a month, a life, that the world is scheming against poor unemployed you; those days you feel trapped on the wrong side of faith until it dawns on you that it could be worse, much, much worse, and that comfort stirs you out of bed the next daybreak. You drone through rote prep and drag out the door—the sky is a sea of heather gray—and catch this and that bus to this and that place to fill out app after app after app and this time who knows; who knows this time what they will say on your nth hunt.

"Mom, don't fret, it's no big deal . . ."
—Champ

BEAUTY LIFE. A passel of females (grandmas, teenyboppers, twenty-somethings) seated in fluorescent chairs pushed against the walls, women mute and cross-legged and lost in beauty mags or prattling across a center table fixed with a gaudy vase of fresh tulips. A few stylists back in the back, dressed in all-black smocks. One of them painting white slop on a client's near-to-bald scalp, another sifting through a mess of combs and scissors and curlers, another whacking a grandmother's gray locks into an atavistic bob. Mom finds the last empty seat and leaves me to hold up a wall. She flips through a style book, shows me a few choices, asks me what I think. Don't none of them move me, so I tell her to choose whichever she likes most. So much for input, she says. Whose idea was this? Whose? she says, and slaps the book closed. We don't say nothing more till a stylist sways over, wearing plastic gloves glazed in auburn goop. She asks Mom if she's picked a style. Not yet, but I want something new, Mom says, and turns to me to affirm. Something fresh. The stylist tells Mom no problem and escorts her to a station and I skip back outside feeling eyes on my back. That car is parked close. I get in and let the seat back till I'm almost lying down, and watch the shop's clientele: a female saunters out patting a spume of loose curls, another one slicking severe blond streaks; I watch a girl hop out the passenger side of an old school sedan (seen the driver around town; he's one of those recalcitrant brass-knuckleheads who loves to provoke beef) booming with unbalanced treble—business that's semi-interesting at best short-term, but in the long run is a vapid-ass hobby, so can you blame me for dozing? Who knows how long later, Mom stirs me with a knock at my window. She's sporting a new short cut, her hair bone-straight and sheened.

Wow! I say.

You like? she says.

I love, I say.

Me too, she says. Can we tip?

It's hella cliché to claim all the nail shops are owned by Asians, but it's true almost all the nail shops in the city are owned by Asians. A woman with an apron stitched with the shop's name asks what service Mom would like and I tell her manicures and pedicures for us both. Mom says, *Both*? and I say, Yeah, *both*. They seat us in padded chairs beside each other and run foot tubs of water and I don't know about Mom's, but my tub's a Fahrenheit to scald. Too hot, the tech says. Too hot! I say. Mom chuckles, slaps my leg, tells me to take it like a man. You told me you was a grown man, she says.

A moment after, when the nail tech slips off Mom's heels, it's plain to see adding this trip to our itinerary was sagacious as shit. The verdict is out, though, on whether Mom will feel so too.

Let me mention, the smell in this piece, oh boy, this is your brain, this is your brain about to burst. Must be why in some shops the workers wear those white face masks. But I endure, breathe slow and shallow, work my yogaesque peace till she gets to the part where she rubs my soles, the part that, between me, you, and the walls, makes me squeamish as shit and takes all my man-strength to suppress a punk's titter.

I see we're still sensitive, Mom says.

Hey, I say. Hey.

They do our feet and, right where we sit, they balance manicure bowls half-filled with marbles on the arms of our chairs. This close, I see my tech's got a jagged half-moon chipped from a front tooth stained the shade of dry mud. She looks the youngest and thinnest of the workers and ain't said word one since almost boiling off my fucking foot.

Not so for Mom, who, minus their little language chasm, has been gabbing with her tech like they've been friends since birth. That's Moms for you. Never seen a conversation she couldn't fuel.

They sit Grace the Gabfabulous under hand and foot heat lamps, and I bide time watching another nailtech apply inch-long claws on the fingers of a chick a nigger wouldn't want no problems with in a dark alley. Can't understand why a chick, any chick, would think them joints are in anyway attractive, though it's probably best that I don't. A worker ask Mom if she'd like a wax, peel, or massage but Mom declines.

We (me and Mom) stride out so close our sleeves touch.

Feeling good, I say.

Mom makes a fist, touches her rose-red nail job. Feeling more of myself, she says. To be continued.

Downtown: the Justice Center, the blue-capped tower, the State Building, the trillion-windowed federal courthouse, the county courthouse, the courthouse square, the city building with *Portlandia* looming over the entrance. We end up in North-

west on a street lined by furniture stores, vintage stores, boutiques, ATMs.

Before we start, let's agree on what we're after, I say. On what
you want and what it is you need.

Is this a shopping spree? she says.

Just like TV, I say.

But this isn't TV, she says. Son, I love to see you do well,
trust me I do, but you've been spending and spending and I
don't know how you can, she says. Where it all comes from.
I don't know and I know you won't tell me. I don't even know
if I want you to tell me. No, I know I don't want you to tell me.
I won't be able to stand it whatever it is.

Mom, don't trip, it's no big deal, I say. Let's not make a big
deal out of nothing.

At the first spot a woman wearing a kiloton of costume jewels
rushes out of a back room to guard the register as if it's the Fountain of Youth or Fort Knox or both. She snaps open the till and
busies with some insignificance only she and God can see without
saying shit (not hello, not be right with you, nor how may I
help you) to Mom nor I. We're on the fool side of patience and
still she don't budge a quarter-step away from her post. Just when
I've had enough, I tow Mom outside.

No such civil rights moment at the next store. This saleslady is
on us so quick she stumbles. Welcome, welcome, she says, with a
glee that's damn near satiric. Mom makes her way to a rack, sifts
through the hangers, and spotlights a long-sleeved blouse. This
is cute, she says. Then get it, I say. I find a seat beside a silver plate
of cheese and crackers and half-pints of water while Mom and
the saleslady browse the racks, the tables of folded sweaters, the
trunks. Mom floats back every so often to showcase her picks

(skirts, more blouses, slacks, a single-button suit) and fuss over a price.

If you want it, get it, is the script.

Are you sure? she says.

Mom, get what you want. Let's not worry over nickels and dimes.

To be true, today's tab is liable to put a dent in my re-up funds, but somebody tell me, among all my so-called concerns, what should be above my mother's joy?

Mom builds a nice-sized pile on the counter while the saleslady grins like a first-rate sycophant. We leave with arm-loads of new threads folded in bags and a discount card good for an eon.

This is too much, she says. Just too, too much.

Says who? I say.

I'm serious, she says.

So am I, I say.

There's a clot of cars on I-5. I take the Fremont Bridge and get off near the hospital. Just past the bakery I ask Mom if she's ready to call it a day. She isn't. Then it's movie time, I say, bend the next corner, and cruise to the theater by the mall. Mom insists we haul her new threads inside. If we're keeping them, we may as well keep them, she says. No sense in letting someone steal them.

The box office line is no line at all, a minute wait if that, but since it's no such luck on showtimes, we settle for a flick (the only one we can agree on) that by my kick-around watch (no jewels around Moms) is an antagonistic wait-time from previews. We buy the tickets and a bundle of snacks and head inside a theater with the lights still up. Mom drops her bags in the seat beside her and dives last-supper-style into the tub of popcorn I was loath to oversalt.

This is how you know we're hella-early. The screen is dead and gray and the only human in the theater besides us is a slender (true, I got nerve calling dude slim) attendant sweeping a row a few rows up. Minus dude, this scene would've been prime for us (the us being me and my boys), who weekends would run CIA-like subterfuge on movie workers. We'd hop a back fence, dash through a low-trafficked exit, and trade the rest of our day for the gem of free flicks.

Ah, those sweet, sweet salad days.

The sound comes up. Then a marathon of ads and trailers. Then the movie starts with a boy making a bedtime wish to bring his dead father back to life. Mom coos and I give her the look. What? she says, and gives me the look back. The flick is straight hammy, but at least keeps me awake (minus an odd nod here and there) till the end, which for a nigger who can fall comatose at any time, in all places, is a feat. When we leave it's gloaming and the lot's lit by high halogens. There's a trickle of couples strolling towards the entrance. The light rail clatters past. A pack of fatmouthing youngsters stomp towards the mall. Farther, my ride gleams. Mom climbs in and I load her bags into the backseat. Now, I say. How do you feel? Mom blows a lift in her new bangs and smiles a smile that's less her heart. Honest, how I feel is the old me didn't measure, she says. That I'm someone new I don't know, she says. But someone, though, I might like to meet.

Sooner or later we all face two options.
—Grace

IT'S COME TO THIS. Me in my new interview clothes in
another part of town, a two-bus-transfer part of town. But early
too. I head straight for the bathroom and work the routine: I
press my lips together and slick my hair and fasten my coat buttons and brush lint from my sleeves and send my smile through
warm-up.

When I come out, I drag in line behind a man wearing construction boots splattered with paint and snug jeans. The man orders off a sheet for his whole crew and stands aside picking paint
flecks off his tattooed forearms. He's the show until it's my turn.
The girl working the counter is as slight as I was at that age. She
fixes the fishnet halo under her visor and asks to take my order.
Not placing an order, I say. But may I see the manager, please. I'm
here for an interview.

She disappears.

She comes back, asks me to step aside, and simpers at the
next customer. Not too long after, a woman built to survive
rambles out with a clipboard in her hand. She says her name is
Pam. And you must be . . .

Grace, I say, and give her a once-over. What my first mind

54

says about Pam: She's been through the fire and got a soft spot for folks that seen the flame.

We sit in a booth near a window muddied with specials. She has a hairy mole on her cheek that's tough to ignore. She slaps my app on a clipboard and checks it with a red pen. I can't watch. I can't *not* watch. I left the felony question blank, and when she gets down by where it's at on the page and crisscrosses a red *X*. I turn to the window that looks onto the playground, see two boys tumble out of the mouth of a winding purple slide while a small girl stands by applauding.

There's a huge difference between lowering your standards and adjusting your expectations. One day you're driving your boys to a restaurant and ordering whatever they want off the menu and stuffing dollars in the donation box, and the next you're interviewing for a job with, if you hadn't of called your eldest, bus fare home and not much else. Sooner or later we all face two choices: either we can adjust our expectations or have them adjusted for us.

Pam wrinkles her brows. Hmm, no food service experience, she says. Do you at least have your food handler's permit?

No, no food service on the résumé, I say. But I got three boys with big appetites, and I've kept them fed.

To tell the truth, the experience isn't crucial, Pam says, but you couldn't work without your permit.

Permit? Oh, I can get one, I say. I'll go and get one as fast as you can.

Great, great. But first let's talk about these work history gaps, she says. She points to one of her red *X*'s. I look away, see through the window behind her happy kids riding a carousel.

Work history, I say. Well, I was getting state checks for a few years. Then had some personal problems after that.

Problems? she says.

Yes, I say. But I'd rather not discuss, unless it's necessary.

Who ain't had them? she says, and flips the sheet. The way I see it, you here now, and that's what matters. You could be back in that welfare line just as easy.

I nod and feel a flash of buoyance.

Oh, I see here you graduated from Jeff, Pam says.

Yes, I say. I'm a Dem.

Did you know Ronnie Reid? she asks.

Ronnie Reid with those colored eyes? I say.

Yes, him, she says.

Who didn't know Ronnie Reid? I say

He's my cousin, Pam says.

Wow, I say. Haven't seen him in years.

You aren't the only one, she says. They got him down there in Salem, gave him ten, but he's close to home now.

Pam lays the pen on top of the clipboard and pushes it across the table. Looks like you left this blank, she says.

And there it is again: *Have you ever been convicted of a felony?*—a blinking neon billboard.

The choice is yours: Choose wise.
We either are or we aren't.
Where we go, there we are.

Oh, I say, and force a smirk and grab the pen—a weight.

Don't let them tell you otherwise; there's a big, big difference between lowering and adjusting. Sooner or later there aren't but two choices for all of us. Will they check if I lie? How long will it take for them to find out the truth?

The first few times you tell the truth and hope for goodwill, but afterwards you take your chance on lie.

Must've overlooked it, I say, and check the wrong box.

She rubs a finger. The light catches on one of her gold rings.

She would have hired me anyway, would have. If I'd explained how I'd been broke, out days, and scheming on a hit, if I'd told her how some guys I knew, but didn't really know, but had been out with, told me about a hustle, if I'd told her how they'd promised that returning the TV they'd heisted would go down without a hitch. No probs, baby girl, is what they said. No problemo. On the other hand, they couldn't do it, cause they were men and they were in bad shape and no one in their right mind was going to let them return anything, return nothing at all, looking the way they looked. So all I had to do, they explained, was take it back to the store and say I didn't want it. Take it back and, they promised, we could split the money three ways even. And puff till our heads burst. Smoke till our lungs collapsed. But of course they were wrong, and I was caught and charged and convicted. Pam would have probably still given me the job if I'd come clean about that first conviction and the fraud—collecting state checks in two states—that finally earned me a trip downstate. If I'd explained what I told the judge about the troubles of raising three boys who outgrew clothes by the month, boys who deserved new tenny shoes and the latest games, who were worthy of much more than I could afford on the funky few hundred Oregon was giving me, which is why I kept the Oregon address when I moved across the river to Washington, kept the address and the state checks, not because I wanted to, but because I had to, and even though the judge just shook his head and gave me a year and a day, Pam would've understood why I'd agreed to the TV scheme, why I'd kept the checks, and even why I'd just checked the wrong box.

The kids rush in with a breeze whipping behind them. The girl working the counter dumps dirty trays. Elsewhere, the soda machine churns ice, meat sizzles, a knife knocks against a cutting board.

"That's a good question."
—Champ

DREAM WITHIN REACH, that's our motto (and by *our* I
mean me and Mom) though over the years, once a year, we allow
ourselves leeway. Most years that leeway's named the Street of
Dreams. What is it? It's this showcase they hold every year for
homes built for fools who could own the average life times over.
They build these show cribs in the burbs (surprised?), blanket the
city with ads, and for a month or so, lure an interminable stream
of hella wishing gawkers. We got caught in the crush our first
couple visits, but you learn what you learn or else and ever since,
me and Mom, my bad—Mom and I, have took to sneaking a tour
after the tour is officially closed.

Mom's hunched outside her job, outside her normal perk,
her uniform drooped over her shoulders and off her waist, her
bag gripped by the handle, the long strap looped to concrete.
She climbs in and wilts with her head leaned back.

Looking kinda beat there, Grace, I say. You sure you still want
to go?

I do if you do, she says. Do you?

Don't you know it, I say. Today's the day for my ladies. First
you. Kim later.

We strap in and hit the road. This year they built it up in the

West Hills, way up past where Burnside becomes Barnes Road, up where you make a few turns and *boom!* it's a whole new universe, a cosmology of its own. The tour's been done (yes, we're still on that) for weeks, but the sign is still up: WELCOME TO THE STREET OF DREAMS. You can see the first house, stories upon stories high, looming behind what must be the gates of heaven, see a sand-colored Mediterranean joint with a fountain out front, a landscape crew tending what's damn near a forest in front of another. Most years Mom and me would be oohing and aahing by now, but we won't and I know it and I pull over feet past the sign.

Nah, this ain't it? I say.

What isn't? she says.

Let's make it a new start, I say. A new tour. And my vote's for Northeast.

There? she says. But what's to see?

Everything! I say.

Mom's dull eyes brighten. She sits up. We strike a deal and the deal is, she has to show me spots from her day.

We float back to Northeast and get off on Kerby. We ain't about to hop out and hoof it, but if we did, no hype, on this side we could reach any place worth being in minutes on foot. I ask Mom where to first.

Well, since we're close, she says, let's start with the school.

Mom's old high school is my old high school. She tells me in her day everyone she knew wanted to go there. That the ones her age, whose older brother or cousin or sister took them to visit the campus, would come back bragging of cool kids who were swaggered outside the gym, or by the bricked front entry, or near the bleachers by the track. Mom says when she went there (like when I did), the school was known for what happened in its back halls, for throwing the livest school dances, for basketball and football and track teams that were always among the best, for being the school every year that entered a black princess in the Rose Festival courts.

Let's see, she says. Where should we go?

I'm thinking we should roll by where ya'll used to kick it, I say. Where ya'll went when it was time to shake a leg.

Mom titters, tells me she never snuck in the clubs before her time, not because she didn't want to, but because she never had a fake ID nor looked old enough to not need one. But my friends though, she says, now they were a whole other story. She says they'd steal or borrow ID, hit a hot spot all dolled up, tell her to hold tight, and leave her iced in a car for hours while they partied. That's exactly why when I turned twenty-one, I was everywhere, Mom says. All the trendy spots in Northeast and North, the one or two in Southeast, even the ones in the boonies: Earthquake Ethel's, Turquoise Room, The Cattle Yard. I'd waited too long, she says. No one was going to stop me from having my time.

We cruise down Williams and stop outside the building that used to be a bar and lounge. Mom says this was where you went after a day at the beauty shop, where you'd go when you wanted to flash a new dress or jewels. She tells me the owner wore a uniform: a sailor cap, double-breasted big-buttoned blue sport coat, and wing tips polished to mirrors. He'd tip his cap and flash a smile, Mom says, that made you feel like you were the star.

We cruise by what was The Social Club and Mom tells me to stop. Now this right here was it, she says, and goes on about how The Social Club was also the afterhours, the place where old men knocked dice to wee hours in a smoky back room, where they served the stiffest drinks you could find, where you could order a burger big as a dinner plate stuffed with sausage, eggs, and whatever else they had in the kitchen. They never had music or a dance floor, Mom says. But my oh my it always boomed with grown folks having the time of their natural born lives.

The Social Club's on the same block as the building that used to be Rose City Auto Repair. Mom says the owner (a freckled Creole named Mr. Black who wore clean coveralls with his name patched on his chest) must've fixed every knock and ping in Northeast. She says old man Black could keep your Chrysler or Buick or Ford running well past when your mileage turned over. Says he was loved for giving free car washes to customers and always quoting a fair price. And if he knew your people, Mom says, he might let you work out payments.

We ride by what used to be Burger Barn. Gosh, you sure did love them burgers, Mom says. Just couldn't get enough of them burgers but everybody else was stuck on the chicken baskets. Them and the desserts. Mom says half the folks she knew would've pawned an arm for even a teaspoon of their banana pudding or peach cobbler, for the thinnest slice of their sweet potato pie. She tells me twins (who pimped on the side and would let their prostitutes rest in back booths between shifts) ran the restaurant day to day, but that the hoes were only there on weeknights since the after-church crowd ruled the weekends.

Figures, I say. You know how the Christians love their after-church grub.

Those were the days, Mom says. Those were the times. She tells me we should ride by the mall, that if it's about her day then we have to. We wheel down MLK to Weidler where I pull into the underground parking, see mall security patrolling in a jeep, an old couple strolling for an entrance, wild kids rollerblading between parked cars. Remember those Saturdays after I got paid that we'd come and make a day of it? Mom says. That was everything. I'd shop all my favorite stores for clothes and shoes, then swing by the discount shop to check the ninety-nine cent specials. Mom admits that, while we thought it a treat, the times she sent us to the ice rink were times she didn't feel like being bothered. But least ya'll got some junk out the deal, she says, and reminds me how we never left the mall without a trip to the Candy Shack and a blessing of our pick of cotton candy or an XL box of caramel corn or an XL box of caramel and cheese corn mixed or a just-the-right-ripe caramel apple.

We take Seventh Ave up from the mall—past Broadway, Siskiyou, Knott, Monroe. Mom points at Irving Park and I circle an island and pull near the day care center across the street. Nothing doing on the courts but dudes playing a scrap-game of one-on-one. Talk about summers, she says. Me and my girls couldn't wait for the sun. Couldn't wait to put on high cut shorts, stroll up here, and make an afternoon of parading around the fields and courts, while the guys huffed and sweat through games. We'd traipse till our legs hurt then make our way to the street, where there was never a shortage of highsighting guys sitting on their hood or trunk with their eight-track blaring a Motown hit.

We (Mom and me) have been how long out? Neither one of us have checked to see. She asks what I have planned for Kim.

Oaks Park, I say. Gone hit the rink.

Oooh, skate night, she says. Now that should be fun.

It should, I say. You wanna roll?

With these knees? No, you two enjoy. Enjoy yourselves just

you two. You need that sometime. Mom turns to me and flashes a seismic smile. Soooo, what about you? How about you show me a spot or two?

What comes to mind first is MLK: the used car lots, the liquor store, the barbershops, the beauty supply, the car washes, Albina Bank, the precinct, the Job Corps office, the gas stations that sold that cut-rate low-octane ethanol shit that gave my ride the coughs.

Can't let you off that easy, Mom says. Lets see them. Let's go.

The first spot of mine we hit is the hand carwash on MLK. This is where, soon as there was a inkling of heat, the hustlers would gather with their old-schools: chameleon-painted Mustangs, Monte Carlo Super Sports, '64 Impalas tricked with dual exhausts, El Caminos customed with trunks of big-ass woofers. You'd see the carwash packed with flossy rides, with dudes cooling against a fender or craned by the ear of a blushing young broad. What I don't tell Mom is how I'd sputter by in my hooptie (a Buick Regal with a faulty alternator) and dream of being among the go-getters, of being posted beside a late-model four-door on pristine five-stars swathed in low-profile meat—how I longed to seize a place in the life.

I cruise a couple blocks up to Quickies, the brick convenient store where, after a long day of park balling, me and my hoop patnas would slog to (T-shirts drenched and feet on hell in high tops) intent on copping a sports drink or juice, and if we had the loot, a hot link or jo-jos or a flaky bean burrito. We'd hit the store and either tramp back to the park for the close-to-sunset runs or trek back home to wash our sweaty nut sacks. Then around the time I hit my growth spurt, about the time the old heads started letting me ball on the main court, niggers caught in that red and blue strife were turning Quickies' lot into the

Wild Wild West. Got to the point where you'd bop out carrying your half guzzled drink and sack of JoJos and get caught in ballistic funk. Quickies is where one of my homeboys from grade school got shot in the chest and lived, where the brother of a JV teammate got shot in the neck and died.

Where do we end up?

Where could we end up but the corner of Sixth and Mason.

I park across from the house and for a time the both of us sit quiet and gaze. The light is dying behind the clouds. Whatever was left of the season's heat has been sucked out the air. We get out and walk to the fence. They've got the lawn cut and the porch painted, a new screen door. What I think of about then is this, I say, and sweep my arm.

Mom nods. She nods and smirks. Tell me what you remember most, she says.

When Mama Liza would keep us hostage for hours of prayer and devotion. Stealthing into Bubba's fruit stash for a kiwi, plum, or mango. Oh yeah, and remember the year you bought me that rolltop desk and encyclopedia set? I say. The one I talked my boys into playing school all summer?

Yes, I do. Yes, I do, she says.

Mom, have you ever thought? I say. Sometimes I think, I say, how we spend all this time looking further and further, when what we need was behind us all along?

Yes, Champ, she says. It would be nice, it would, if we were all at some point sprinkled with light.

Mom asks how often I come by the old house.

That's a good question, I say. Not that often and often, I say. Or whenever I feel the need.

★   ★   ★

Skate night. We (my girl and me) swank in late with our arms looped. Ain't been in here in a hot minute, but ain't much changed. Walls wood-paneled, raggedy carpet, a glass case filled with old skates and trophies, lockers with the paint rubbed to patterns. And it's dim in here too, disco dim with a light machine playing colored swirls across the rink. We find a seat in the lobby and I help Kim pull off her boots and carry them to the counter, do that and ask the counter girl for new skates for my girl if they have them cause I should. You shouldn't have, Kim says, and slips on the new wheels. She gets to her feet and scissors her stilts apart this way, then that. Then who walks in but this funnstyle super-skate dude who's been a mainstay at the rink since my old summer program was coming here on field trips. He lopes in dressed in a field jacket and fatigue pants and carrying a metal box. He finds a seat close by and lifts a pair of calf-tall skates (black leather joints with zebra laces and neon rubber wheels) and small can out the box, drips oil on his axles, and gives each wheel a spin. He swanks on his custom skates, ties the zebra ropes in intricate-ass bows, locks his combat gear away, and rushes onto the floor.

That man means business, she says.

Can't mean no more business than that, I say.

We laugh, and there isn't anything in our laughs but truth.

Tonight the rink's crackin; I'm talking a fusillade of couples, of cliques, one or two drowsing in solo-dolo, a few dudes I balled against in grade school, a trio of chicks in flourescent leggings—one of whom I smashed too recent for me to be blithe about it. The chick gives me the eye, gives Kim the eye, and she's modest about the shit like none, a sign hard to ignore but I hope my girl ain't peeped it.

You know her? Kim says.

Yes and no, I say.

And that means? she says.

In passing, I say. Why, cause she's mugging us? That ain't nothing but hate.

Hate on who for what? Kim says.

Cause look at you, I say. Look at us.

Alright, Champ, she says. Whatever you say.

I slip on my skates and lock away our stuff. The next song muddles over the speakers. Slow-mo skaters lap the rink. Kim stands and pirouettes and faces me. What a great idea, Babe, she says. Why can't we do stuff like this all the time? She puts out her hand and says, Come, let's show them how to do it.

I tell her to give me a sec, but only so I can watch her make the rink alone. What's better than watching your girl swoon through a crowd under strobes. Oneiric is right, damn near everywhere we go, my girl's *the* girl, that dark skin, eyes always one color and then another, legs you could climb to heights. I love, love it. Love being out with her. No lie, when we're out my nuts swell up from seeing (as long as that shit don't approach disrespect) mortal niggers awed.

The DJ calls couple skate and plays a slow jam. Here comes Kim gliding off the floor, her hair floating behind her. Babe, come, she says, reaching out. Get up, will you.

Now? I say.

Yes! she says, and tugs me off the bench and onto the floor. We catch each other hand in tender hand and lock a tandem stride for laps. The DJ mixes one slow song into the next. The chick I hit rides by snickering with her bright-clothed crew. Superskate flies by in a backwards scrawl and nudges me into a stumble. My girl grips me tight, keeps me steady.

Look at us, she says.

Right, I say. Look.

That I've been searching for the same things ever since.

　　　　　　　　　　　　—Grace

IT'S LIKE LIGHTNING, like love, like the cure. And if you haven't felt it you can't judge—or at least shouldn't. If you haven't felt it, how could you ever really know what us addicts, us experts, are up against in this life of programs and counselors and sponsors, what we face because of or in spite of our earned expertise? Ask, and if any one of us is telling the truth we'll admit that our kind of lying is like a religion.

This is why they say no one does this alone. Why they say once an addict equals always one. Why they say your program membership should be lifelong. Why they mandate ninety meetings your first ninety days. It's tough to guess how many are here except to say that it's more maybe than expected and never enough as it should be. Up front a new group leader—he's a shaggy redhead with freckled arms—sits on a table and sips a steaming mug. He raises a hand and waits until the gabbing stops, until the members scrape their chairs into place; he waits and clears his throat and sets aside his drink and stands.

Hello, I'm an addict and my name is Randy, he says. Welcome to the Learning to Live chapter of Narcotics Anonymous. I'd like to open this meeting with a moment of silence for the addict who still suffers. This settles us. Randy hops off the table and pads near a portable chalkboard.

Is there anyone attending their first meeting? he says. If so, welcome. You are the most important people here. All we ask is that everyone present follow one law: Never attend a meeting with drugs or paraphernalia on your person. If you're carrying, please take it outside and leave it and we'll welcome you back. This protects our meeting place and the NA fellowship as a whole. Randy moves near the first row of seats. He's short and soft, a mix that usually gives grown men a complex, but somehow commanding. You have to make five years or more to lead a group, which means for us—or at least those of us who've been in this place, those who've tried and failed, who've quit and joined—Randy is an apostle. If you've used today, please seek out a fellow member at the break or after the meeting, he says. It costs nothing to belong. You are a member when you say you are.

As is my habit, I scan the shoes of the members in my row—it ain't a clean pair among them—then off to my sides. My neighbor's arm is sprent with needle pricks, his thumbnail discolored. No way to justify this life, my life, but slamming a needle is a whole other harm. Randy leads us in the *we* version of the Serenity Prayer: *God grant us the serenity to accept the things we cannot change, the courage to change the things we can, and the wisdom to know the difference.*

We finish and members volunteer—everyone's always so eager to submit—to read from the basic text.

Who is an addict?

What is the program?

Why are we here?

How does it work?

The twelve traditions.

The meetings begin the same. So goes a theory of resurrection.

An addict, any addict, can stop using, lose the desire to use, and learn a new way of life, they say.

They say and they say and it sounds so easy, as if living clean is no more than hitting the right switch, as if it takes something less than heroics to face history dead-on, to accept the life we've earned. The meetings are meant to be havens, but not everyone comes for safety. I wasn't but few blocks away last meeting when this guy approached me—breath smelling like the worst breath—claiming he had what I need. I'd seen him in the meeting, reciting the steps, even stuffing money in the seventh principle basket, seen him running his glazed eyes up and down the rows. No, I think I got what *you* need, I said, and offered him a handful of mints.

We make fearless and searching inventories.

Hello, I'm an addict and my name is Mark. My drug of choice is meth. I used to deal it, then, *bam*, my first hit. Couldn't breathe without the shit after that. Every day spent chasing the next score. The next hit and nothing else. Up for a friggin week straight sometimes, getting high, no food, a sip of water when I remembered. A real addict too. Would piss myself if the dope wasn't finished and a trip to the bathroom meant missing a hit. It wasn't long before people I'd known all my life turned their heads when they saw me coming, seen someone resembling the old me, with the way, on a good run, I'd shrink down to a percent of myself, skin with a few sharp sticks inside. Got so bad I couldn't friggin stand to walk past a mirror. The dope dropped me so low that I broke in my mom's place and stole her wedding ring. Worthless man, no other way to put it. Scum who didn't deserve to live.

We make fearless and searching inventories and tell the fearful to keep coming back. Keep coming back and it works. We can stand up and testify when we so choose. But what would I tell them? That the first time I took my eldest. That Dawn, my best friend, promised I'd feel better and forget. That I've been waiting for that to happen ever since. Though when we tell our story, a bit of our trouble becomes another's, there will be no fearless and searching inventory for me. Not today. My business is my business until it isn't.

Randy announces Cleaniversaries, and awardees stroll up to accept their tags. It makes me think of the time I earned a tag, years ago, my first stint in NA. Was proud of it too, but not proud enough to show it. Too afraid of what people might think, or, worse, what they might say. The awardees palm their foil-scripted color tags and stroll back to their seats while the rest of us boom our hands together. Honest, it makes me jealous seeing them. Makes me anxious for my time to come. And when it arrives this time, who cares who sees? When it comes this time, let them all see.

We pass around the seventh-principle basket. We search for something to give, singles mostly, a few fives and tens, an odd twenty. I scrounge for dollars, the best I can do. We read up to the twelfth tradition, the first one I learned by heart: *Anonymity is the spiritual foundation of all our traditions, ever reminding us to place principles before personalities.*

★　★　★

The other night I watched a show on drugs. It talked about this study where they rigged rats to a machine that shot them with cocaine every time they pressed a bar. The man on the show explained that the rats pressed the bar at the expense of food, sex, sleep, pressed even when it meant they'd suffer electric shock, kept right on pressing for hits until they fell out dead.

"But what if this is?"

—Champ

AIN'T A SPOT TO SQUEEZE in nowhere in sight, which shouldn't really be no big old surprise, since most days, meaning a day like today, finding a place to park near campus is like defying physics or catching a lightning bolt or slapping bullets out of midair. Been so bad, twice I wrote a letter (didn't send either one of them, though) to our crater-face school president beseeching him to increase the meter count or better yet build a new garage so fools don't have to wander miles upon miles trying to find a spot for their ride. By the time I find a spot, by my kick around watch, I've missed almost half of Professor Haskins's Advanced Speech class. With no change for the meter and no time to get none, I leave the car parked on a prayer, meter blinking expired, leave it paralleled, throw on my backpack, and zip down Broadway, hustling around the tennis courts to the canopied park blocks and the pebble-paved pathway where last winter I slipped on a patch of ice and busted my ass.

And here's the cold part about being late to Haskins's class: The room is too small to sneak in unnoticed, not a chance of it, so I burst into a dead sprint. Okay, okay (there goes the hype again), something close to a dead sprint is more like it, what with leaves on the ground and the ache of bruising my ass-cheeks months back still fresh on my mind. My legs kicking and my arms pumping so fast they blur the words of the dude with the Santa Claus beard proselytizing from an overturned bucket. Legs kicking and arms pumping past nerds plowing through notes, past pretty young things lap-balancing encyclopedia-thick texts, past jocks strolling with knotted tenny shoes looped over their shoulders, past huddles of exchange students, all the while the smell of roasted lamb, roasted chicken, and seasoned ground beef taunting my empty gut. But ain't no time for snacking. *Pow!* I duck into one building, blast through another and another with that juiced-up Olympian speed, me zagging through clogs of striving Einsteins till I reach Haskins's room, stoop to catch my breath, fix my laces, and pull my shirt from where it's stuck to my skin from sweat.

A head or two twist around when I walk in. Haskins pauses long enough for me to find a seat. Mr. Thomas, he says, his voice deep and scratchy. (Imagine an old blues singer: a B.B. this or Muddy that.) Nice of you to join us. I was worried you'd miss your turn, he says. How long before you're ready? The thick of Haskins's specs, you'd believe him if he claimed he could see outer space. He twirls a stick of chalk. He settles in a desk in the front and crosses his legs.

It won't take long, I say. I fleece my pockets for a tissue, pat my face, search my bag for my speech, and ramble up to the lectern. I clear my throat, look out at the room, a class as full as it's been all quarter, at Haskins sitting in the front row, a critique sheet on his desk. Good morning, I say. My name is Shawn Thomas and my speech is called "The Bias Effect."

★ ★ ★

Here's the forty-four-billion-dollar question:

What's the link between the NBA lottery and America's War on Drugs?

The answer: Leonard Kevin Bias.

The über-ballyhooed Len Bias, that is.

[Pause. Eyes.]

This year marks the tenth anniversary of the night the Boston Celtics selected the former Maryland Terrapin with the number two pick in the NBA draft. The six-foot-eight small forward with the liquid jumper and bionic legs was everybody's pick for the next coming, a talent to rival Michael Jordan, some said maybe better than Jordan, a player who could fuel the league for years to come. Well, Bias didn't transform the B-ball universe alive, but his death from a cocaine overdose forty-eight hours after that draft sure has metamorphosed America.

[Pause. Eyes.]

Soon after Bias's death, House Speaker Tip O'Neill (rest in peace), let's call him Commissioner Tip O'Neill, inflamed by the death of a player who'd become a neutron star in what was known as the DMV, and whom Tip, not ironically the representative of Boston, believed had died of a crack overdose because he was black, convinced his Democrats they needed a swift and stern response.

If you think Commissioner Tip's game plan was all about Bias and pursuit of the greatest public good, think again. It was an election year and the donkeys were dead set on socking it to the GOP, who'd won two years prior in no small part by convincing voters their rivals were "too soft on crime."

All right, so even if the Dems' motives weren't wholly pure, at least they had the sense to seek counsel. There was no way an experienced group of lawmakers could fathom drafting a bill without research, facts, testimonies, expert opinions.

Wrong! Wrong! Wrong!

[Eyes.]

The response of Commissioner Tip and his collective of vote-seeking senators was about as soft as the bad-boy Detroit Pistons. That answer was called the Anti-Drug Abuse Act of 1986. The bill, which volleyed for a spate between the House and the Senate, was ratified that October; it passed sans a single secondary expert opinion, with all of zero hearings, without conversation the first with a single person from the Bureau of Prisons, minus insight from even one judge, sitting or retired or dead and brought back to life.

[Eyes.]

It was a tough, big, attention-grabbing bill, infamous for a draconian-like feature that had been outlawed since the 1970s: a mandatory minimum, more specifically the hundred-to-one ratio.

[Pause. Pause. Eyes.]

What that ratio means is this: it takes a hundred times the amount of soft cocaine to trigger the same penalty for crack cocaine.

Tip and his boys set the triggers for first-time offenders at five and fifty grams. Five grams of what old-school dealers called "ready rock" earns a five-year federal bid. Fifty grams earns a ten-year set. By contrast, you'd need five hundred and five thousand grams of soft cocaine for that much time behind bars.

[Pause. Eyes.]

Let's put that in further perspective? The average role player wandering the streets with five grams, what amounts to a few rocks, in his pocket would receive the same sentence as a team starter toting a half kilo.

It means the sixth-mantype dealer arrested with fifty grams on his person, what amounts to the size of a jumbo meatball, is subject to the same sentence as an all-league dealer caught with five kilos!

Now that we all know the numbers, can we agree they don't add up? That the math adds up in the worst way.

[Pause.]

Now here's another billion-dollar question. Which ethnic group is most sentenced to the unsportsmanlike bids?

Answer: The lion's share don't look nothing like Commissioner Tip and his team of rah-rah politicians.

[Pause. Eyes.]

Before you accuse me of playing the race card, check out a few more stats

Nationwide, blacks make up eighty-two percent of the cocaine defendants, while whites and Hispanics make up two-thirds of cocaine *users*!

Nationwide, blacks receive eighty-eight-point-three percent of the mandatory crack sentences!

In Bias's home state, the stats aren't any better.

There, blacks make up sixty-eight percent of all people arrested for drugs.

There, blacks now land drug-related prison terms at eighteen times the rate of whites!

I could go on. Believe me, I could.

[Pause. Pause. Eyes.]

It's safe to say—no, it's *true* and *right* to say—Commissioner Tip and his Dream Team of legislators not only dropped the ball on drug laws, they exacerbated it to the crisis of a forty-four-billion-dollar (take *that* salary cap!) annual blunder. Commissioner Tip has passed on, so the new question, the question for all the bank, is this: Which politician will have the guts to amend what has become the biggest mistake of twentieth-century American law?

*   *   *

Even a super-senior such as myself don't know what to make of this silence.

Haskins stands and tucks the hem of his African-colored ethnic print shirt, the light turning his natural into a gibbous black globe. Polished wing tips, pregnant wallet stuffed in the front pocket of slacks cinched at the waist into the specs of a corset. This is what the activist-turned-professor look looks like live in vivid color. He saunters up, and I make my way to the back to a seat. He makes a comment that I don't hear from eyeing the Filipina chick across the room.

Would anyone like to offer feedback? Haskins says. Or ask a question. I sit up, roll my neck, press my toes to stretch my calves. The pugnacious earthy chick with the tangled hair, who stay shooting me a cryptic eye, shoots up a hand. You make it seem like some big conspiracy, she says. She pulls her knees to her chest, leaves her demolished boots hanging off the lip of her seat. As if America has some goal to put blacks in prison. Like, that's just so ridic, she says, and waves her hands past her eyes. Like beyond ridic.

I kind of agree, a dude from across the circle says. He don't raise his hand cause, shit (his T-shirt is two sizes too small and jeans are shrink to snug!), if he did he might bust a seam. Hey, I'm not prejudiced or anything, he says, but it sounds like

excuse-making to me. Do you really think Congress has it out for
blacks? C'mon, bud, he says. People commit crimes and criminals
go to jail. It's simple. Everything's not about race.

If this was another year, my freshman or sophomore or junior
year, those quarters my brain's alchemy was tweaked by a legion
of black studies courses (you'd be surprised how riled the right
reading list can make you), if this was then, those days I spent
stalking campus with a militant's scowl, I'd say something to set
dude's snug-ass jeans aflame. But this ain't then; it's now, my last
year, and the real is, no matter what I say, white folks won't ever
hate themselves like us.

You're right, not everything's about race, I say. But what if
this is?

No one else says another word.

Quiet or no quiet, how I feel about most of them most days,
especially the rare ones when I'm carrying a package with my
books and papers, how I feel those days especially, is these suckers
would be ecstatic if they saw me arrested. Oh, the dreams I've
had, the nightmares of officers raiding my class, clapping me in
cuffs, and parading me to a car parked conspicuous as shit in the
Park Blocks, horrors of these squares blabbing to some local reporter how they always thought me up to no good, the vision of
my suckerfied classroom nemeses running his weak script for all
the world: People commit crimes, criminals go to jail. Simple!

Haskins yanks his hella-cinched slacks well above his hip
bones. He calls on the next speaker and the next—one speech
on recycling, another on organ donors, both of which real talk
might've been better than mine. Haskins asks at the end of class
if I'm keeping my appointment, and I know I should say no, but
why, this moment, do I feel as though I can't. He packs a vintage

shoulder bag and we leave while the next class files in. His office is in another building, and I drag a step behind him the whole way there. Haskins offers me a seat on a green tweed couch, re-tacks the WHO WILL SURVIVE AMERICA poster that's come loose at one end, shelves a stack of books from his desk.

Your speech, he says. It was strong. You could tell by their response.

But I don't think they got it, he says.

Sometimes it's not what they think, but *if* they think, he says.

Haskins leans back in his seat, clasps his hands behind his head. So what're your postgrad plans? Grad school, I hope.

Grad school, I say. No plans for that.

Well that's disappointing, he says. Is this a certainty? You'd do great in political science.

You mean politics? I say.

Yes, politics, he says.

Oh no, I say. Politics aren't for us.

Wrong, he says. He takes off his specs, rubs the bridge of his nose. Politics are especially for us. Give it some thought before you dismiss it.

Haskins swivels to face his crowded bookcase, plucks a dusty hardcover off a shelf, shoves it at me. These are some of the great-est speeches of the century, he says. Go ahead and take a look. I think you'll like it.

I'll give it a read, sir, I say. But I'm pretty set.

Give some thought, he says. The program is two years. Trust me, time will pass no matter. You might as well do something with it.

Careful not to open my bag too wide (the stench would be

tough to explain), I stuff the book inside and quick-fast zip it shut.

When I leave, there's a cluster of students wearing shirts and ties with buttons pinned to their chests campaigning for the school election. I push past a flyer-bearing future politician (me one of them?) onto Broadway, stopping by the phone booth (it beats a cell for business 24/7) under the sky bridge to call back a lick. My guy says he's on his way down. He wants a few zips which won't buy no mansions, but ain't nothing to scoff at neither.

Every campus has them, self-aggrandizing weed men. Around here it's the anarchistic muralized white boys who hock the nickel bags, twenty sacks, and eighths of green to the school's ubiquitous weed hypes. Got to admit they make me jealous too, cause though the money's less, unless they get greedy or hella-reckless, they can semi-stealth their business sine die, no troubles.

But there ain't no charitable apathy nor no promo for this illicit shit. Anyone vending what I vend best keep it to themselves. Which I do. You won't catch me selling to anyone affiliated on any level with this fine, fine institution. But just because I don't serve the student body, staff, or faculty don't mean the campus is off-limits for business. Believe you me, there is no safer place for this than here. The Bias Effect. Tough to count the days my backpack's freighted with more than books, with what's a sure trigger for a federal charge. Shit, if the Feds emptied my bag today, if they found what's sealed off in clear plastic, I'd be knee-deep in middle age when I paroled.

Farther up, I find an empty bench between buildings and wait for my lick. I crack the book from Haskins, but can't focus for shit with this sack in my bag, with the automatic doors opening, with the pitter-patter of people walking past, the *schwock* of a tennis match, with the boom of the bearded man still ranting from his overturned bucket.

You mind? A guy asks me for a spot on the bench and I make space. He's carrying a leather briefcase and wears a beta-male blue suit. He asks if I'm a student and I nod, push my face in the pages, but eye him from my peripheral. He covers his face and sighs. He takes his hands off his face and rakes his hair. He picks up his briefcase and lays it across his lap and thumps what could be Morse code for backup. I get up, grab my pungent, freighted backpack, and scuttle the fuck off.

Am I, paranoid? *Hell* yeah! But check it, the moment right after you stop being noid is the moment you should make sure your people ain't blocked collect calls from jail.

          . . . they'll see for themselves.
                  —Grace

ONE OR THE OTHER, cause it can't be both. The football
or the basketball. Either will put a dent in my so-called savings.
The itty-bitty money I'm socking away for when these people
let me off their papers—and they will. I choose the Spalding and
buy a pack of needles and a hand pump, at prices that leave me
with too little to mention, so I won't mention it. There's a boy
that's more or less between my firstborn and my middle boy
dipped over a station and listening to headphones loud as bull-
horns. The boy's holding a CD with a cover that shows a guy
wearing a suit and scarf and fedora with his head tipped low. The
boy closes his eyes and snaps his neck back and forth. The next
song that plays samples an old soul favorite of mine, and I listen
until as a mother I can't anymore. I tap the boy and he snatches
off his speakers. I ask him to suggest an album that's a bit less
explicit. He bops down to another shelf and picks a colorful CD
off the rack. This one, he says.
    I buy the CD and the Spalding and straggle out the automatic
doors with my purchase double-bagged and my previous few
dollars fewer. As soon as I get outside, the cold snakes inside me.
I'll have to wait until the paycheck after next for a coat that puts
up more fight. Payday is Friday, next Friday, but it's also the

week my court fines are due. Traffic plods along. A hard wind whips up my leg.

This is how it is until the bus comes. The driver is a young woman. I find a seat, but move for a guy who cracks his window in this cold. It's a long ride to my transfer. I wait under a covered stop for my next bus. There's a pay phone inside the stop that keeps ejecting coins. The bus rumbles up I-5 and across the bridge and off on the city center and into the bus depot. The depot's surrounded by pawnshops, old brick buildings, slant parking spots, parking meters made of copper. The last bus carries me across the city. Vancouver, Washington, VW, is lush and unlittered and no one needs to be anywhere fast. I get off and slog what passes for a busy street carrying bags—a heft. Kenny lives in a subdivision, rows of new homes painted tan or blue or gray, homes with double-car garages and neat piles of leaves in the yard—this is the other side of living check-to-check.

If he'd told me about this place—his tongue has never been a conduit for the truth—I would've called him a bald-faced lie.

The address he gave me has a big picture window with its curtains drawn apart, fluffy upholstered couches, a glass table, an oil painting of a bowl of fruit.

I am loved.
I am strong.
I am patient.

No one answers. Not the first time I buzz. Not the second. It's a long time before I hear a voice and the light clop of feet, longer before someone comes to the door. It's Helen. Are my boys here? I say.

She smirks and slaps a hand on her hip and huffs a lift in her bangs. I sit my bags beside me and cross my arms. I see we still rude as ever, I say.

Did Kenneth know you were coming? she says. She looks past me, and it's no telling what she sees.

Kenneth, I say. Who's Kenneth?

Wait, she says, and slams the door shut.

But I won't let her do it; won't let her wreck my day. I take out my cigarettes and count what's left in the pack.

Kenny comes to the door dressed in a starched white shirt and creased khakis as if he just might be other than who and what he is. Well, well, well, he says. Look who finally dropped in.

Needed time, I say. Don't start.

Don't we all, he says. How'd you get here?

A spaceship, I say. A hot air balloon.

Still got jokes, huh, I see. But check this out, all jokes aside, call ahead next time, he says. Helen ain't too fond of surprise guests.

You got my boys a few days and now all of a sudden you calling shots, I say. Trying to tell me when and where?

They're our boys, he says. Canaan and Kenneth Jr. And how all this time add up to a few days? C'mon, now, Grace. We're too old for new math.

You wouldn't put it past this man to have been feeding my boys a bad script about me, but my boys are bright; they'll see for themselves.

My youngest comes up, calling Kenny. He spots me and yells and almost falls over himself trying to make it outside. He pulls me tight, shoots something out of me, shoots something into me. I missed you, I missed you, I say, and stand back to have a look at him. His father, if that's what he is, struts off. My baby leads me inside and asks if I want to see the rest of the house, and I don't have the heart to say no. He shows me a crystal chandelier in the front room, a kitchen fixed with granite counters and oak cabinets, bedrooms posterized with basketball gods. He tugs me into the basement where my middle boy is sitting in the semidark, eyes locked on the giant screen, thumbs drumming a game controller.

Ta-da! I say.

He looks at me, a glimpse, says, Hey mom, and goes right back to his game.

Wait a sec, that's it? I say. That's all you got for your mama after all this time, after I hiked across the world for you?

He pauses his game and slogs over and presses his head to my chest for a thump, that's it.

You would think it was this middle boy and not my baby that marks time but it isn't. It's Canaan I was pregnant with the night I caught Kenny, the night he called one time too many and said he wouldn't be home. It was my youngest kicking in my belly the late night I broke a phone, threw on clothes, and blew red lights all the way to her apartment. By then I'd steamed outside her place many a night, had busted car windows, knifed tires, had keyed curses onto the hood of her car, but of all the times that was the first time I'd ever had the gall to knock on her door. She answered in a robe that was a match of one he'd bought for me, and it must've been a reflex how fast she tried to shut me outside. So quick, but I jammed the door, pushed through, and stalked her into the bedroom where I caught Kenny—he seemed the gift of my life to that point—lying butt naked in bunched sheets. He didn't say a word, didn't stir when I turned and fled.

That night, I drove home and butchered his suits and dumped them in a tub of bleach. The truth is, though, it was as if I'd done nothing—nothing at all to heal.

He and she bicker above us and it's a boon for me.

The boys open their gifts and precious hours go on.

They are priceless, my sons; they're all I need, or else they're not enough and I hope to never know.

> But that's how it is for us.
> —Champ

THERE'S A BUCKET UP AHEAD spitting a big-ass plume of dirty white clouds. Cars ahead, cars behind, car across. Shit, you could start a squad (hoop, football, soccer (though we don't play no soccer in these parts)) with the fools waiting for the shop clerk to flip the sign, and let us in, and scrawl our names on a list nobody but nobody but her can touch. Niggers ready to Olympic-joust for first in the chair. When the clippers are cold, sharp, precise, before a showing late can mean a whole afternoon on ice. Believe me when I tell you, fresh cuts are serious business, especially at The Cut Above, which is damn near an institution. Soon as the sign flips we (the *we* being me, KJ, and Canaan) surge across the street with the rest. The barbers in prep mode, zipping their smocks, oiling their clippers, tooling their stations. The clerk puts us down on the list and sends my bros searching for seats.

The shop meanwhile fills.

See you got your nappy-headed brothers with you, one barber says, the resident shop funnyman.

Damn, homie, I say. Hatetrocity at the crack of dawn? Let us live.

You know me, he says.

Yep, I say. Your hate runneth over.

89

My bad, he says, twisting the top off a bottled juice. But I wouldn't have to say it if you brought them in here more often. Your bros be lookin like Nigerians by the head by the time you think they need a cut.

Gimme me six feet, I say, and ask Famous, the shop's manager, to get a handle on his workers. Famous, by the way, is this type of guy: a being-caught-without-a-fresh-fade-is-a-crime type of guy. A man after my grooming heart.

Mr. Funnyman asks about his first client and the clerk says it's baby bro.

C'mon, young Kunta. Hope you don't break no teeth on my clippers.

The clerk unmutes the TV in the lounge and teases the shop with a commercial of kids singing. The rest of the lounge, a couple dudes haranguing who's the best high school hooper in the state. Near them this tight-jawed quasi-mute, a dude they say got a bad habit of taking stuff that ain't his. A handful of unmentionables. And it's one of them (thought I was the only one who caught it) that glimpses a white girl jogging past the shop. Look at that shit, he says. Got pork Prefontaine-ing in the hood now.

Big deal, someone says.

Damn right, big deal, someone says. It'll be marathons next. Million dog march after that.

Why ya'll mad? someone says. Make it easier to knock the pork.

Pork, what's pork?

White meat, fool.

Who wants that?

All the smart niggers, that's who. Trust the porkologist. You ain't lived till you had a taste.

Man, you silly.

Sheeit. Knocking a white broad is a black man's civil right. Even Malcolm approved.

Malcolm approved, my ass.

Real talk, boss. Check the history books.

The clerk stomps into the lounge. She's the girth of an NFL lineman (a few pounds off, no more). She don't need to do more than wrench her lips for fools to quiet right the fuck down.

It don't matter why they're here, they're here, Famous says. You see them coffee shops and boutiques and bookstores down the block. Who you think they built them for?

Famous got his nickname cause someone said he lived life like a movie. Most people would say that's extra, but I say, a life with no stories, what's the point?

KJ's ambivalent about his cut. Looks to me, with his shoulders hiked. My bro is always demurring, always deferring. But since it's 0.00 percent of reclaiming a vacated seat, it won't be no assurance from intimate distance today. Give him a low one-lengther, I say from my perch. Dude's averse to cuts, I say.

Averse? the barber says. Averse! There you go with those SAT words. Man, don't you know the shop got rules against that smart boy vocab?

Funnyman's got jokes, but maybe it ain't no knee-slap. How else to explain dude on the other side who used to go to grade school with me, who used to get teased something terrible about his droopy eye, who spent recesses befuddled by chapter books, needed extra time on tests, and slogged the halls past the last bell with low ambition pinned to his chest like a Cub Scout badge? How else to explain, how now, like most of us other frauds, he plays like he's too tough for TV, a muthafuckin man of steel. But hold up before you knock it. That's how it is for us. How they made it. How it must be if we are at all to be. Cause how it is where you're from, who knows, but around here, you're either a soldier or a sanguine sucker.

Check it, though, deep down in the place sealed off from the world, what I know is, no civilian should have to be that tough.

Someone mentions white broads again. Calls up a snicker.

I was just talkin to my grandmama about it, Famous says. She said it used to be nothing but white folks living here. Said we used to be out there by where Delta Park is. Then, after the flood, we moved on this side and white folks moved out. So really they're just reclaiming the neighborhood. Don't y'all watch the news? Didn't ya'll see the big story on gentrification?

Gentrifi-what? Famous. Not you too with SATs. We thought you was from the streets.

You fools can joke if you like, Famous says. But when ya'll livin on the outskirts cause you can't afford rent, see who's haha'ing then.

Shit, send me to the burbs. That's loose pork central.

You fools keep on, Famous says. And when they got Northeast under sovereign lock, watch how fast us niggers are extraterrestrials.

The bell sounds. A latecomer arrives. He gapes at the crush and walks right back out. Funnyman makes a show of snatching the cape off my brother.

The bell sounds. The hot-food-plate man strolls in and posts by the clerk's desk. Good morning, my brothers, he says, and tips his brim. He reels off a menu: hash browns, grits, eggs, tuna melts, pancakes, French toast. Plates are five dollars, he says. But if you're hungry and ain't got it, get me back next go-round.

Damn, brotherman. You ain't got no swine?

Now, now, now, my brother, he says. I do not encourage the black man's consumption of the hog.

Brotherman scratches orders in a black pad and marches out to his truck. He whisks in with plates covered in foil and sweaty bottled juice. We appreciate the business, my brother, he says after every sale.

The clerk calls my turn for the chair. She stands up and stretches, and trust me, it's a universe away from even a half-sexy sight. She calls my name for next in my barber's chair, and I call KJ over to cover my seat.

What's shaking with you, bro? says my barber.

Shit, I say.

Shit is right, he says, and swings me around. Look at that!

By *that* he means the girl in the threshold holding a little boy's hand, the one dressed in spindly stilettos, a low-cut shirt, and jeans tight as a blood pressure cuff.

The off-duty stripper fit's extra for my tastes, I say. But she might could get it on the late night.

True, true, he says.

He starts to prep. To say my barber works at his own speed would be a huge huge downplay. The homie's slow as shit, but he's also hella-skilled, which is mandate number one for me. Number two is, nothing I ever tell him gets retold.

Bro, I ain't tryin to be in your business, he says, but I was ear-hustling and overheard some fools with your name in they mouth. And it wasn't positive.

Forreal? I say.

Yeah, he says, somethin about you and a chick.

You catch a name? I say.

Nope, he says. Sure didn't.

My barber used to live around the block from me when we lived in the house on Sixth. Back then he was cutting in his basement, shearing sharp-ass flattops in janky light. But I had to find a new barber for a sec when he moved. His people being one of the first in the neighborhood to sell off, to give up their place to white folks. This is why I mention to him my plan to buy the house.

You serious? he says.

Dead serious, I say.

Well, if that's what you gone do, bro, he says, you best put the hurry-up on it. You seen the signs? These house prices is so high it's disrespect.

The house on Sixth, home, ain't even up for sale, but I leave that bit of info out. How I'd hustle enough money to buy it if it was—tis a question, a damn good question.

The bell sounds again. The bell is always sounding on Saturdays.

My barber swivels me towards the wall of fold-up chairs where Canaan and KJ share a seat and sit quiet and watchful, and oh what a difference a decent fade makes; we look as if we could be some kin.

Ding! There goes the bell. A white man strolls in—I'm talking the average white man, the everyman's white man, as in there couldn't be a whiter white man in all of America, as in the man has his Oxford shirt elbow-rolled, his collar flipped, and pennies in his penny loafers.

The clerk calls down to a barber, the only barber in the shop who takes appointments, and he motions at the white man. You should hear how fast the shop is overcome.

Well I'll be goddamned! Look at this!

He's my client

And what's your client's name?

My name is Jeff, Jeff says.

Jeff, okay, Jeff. If it's not too much of us to ask, where do you live—close?

Yes. Moved a few blocks away a few weeks ago.

We see, we see. So how you likin it?

It's a wonderful neighborhood!

WONDERFUL NEIGHBORHOOD! Ya'll here this?

Jeff moseys down to his barber. The barber snaps on the cape, wets Jeff's stark-blond strands, combs them over his eyes, plucks a pair of scissors from his supplies. He swivels Jeff to face us.

And this is how you spell mistake.

Jeff, if it's not too much of us to ask, do you mind telling us if you're buying or renting?

Buying, he says. Isn't owning a home the American dream?

That's what they say, Jeff. So, Jeff, the shop would like to know, did you have much trouble finding a bank to finance that dream?

What are you implying? he says.

Famous, tell him. Let him know.

Hey, buddy, I'm not the bad guy here, Jeff says.

My barber snaps off my cape and I step out the chair and brush my sleeves. I look over at my bros both caught in shades of juvenile angst.

He's right, I say to the shop. Right about it being a dream.

Oh boy, look who comes to his defense.

No defense. Just truth, I say.

Jeff's barber twists him away from the crowd.

Got eyes on my back while I bop over and ask the shop clerk how much I owe and give my bros dollars for tip. These shop hawks caught for the moment in a rapture, but then a big mouth self-appointed hoopologist chirps about last night's ticker and just that fast the shop is back to its chattering self. The doorbell sounds and in swanks a wicked ex Crip who's grand among us for beating a racketeering beef. He and I nod at each other—a silent salute, before we (the we being me and my bros) push outside. Outside, I look far this way and far that way.

Would you believe me if I told you there ain't a single pale-skinned-home-owning-dog-walking distance runner in sight?

That's it, just a month?
—Grace

OF ALL MY BOYS, Champ was the most collickly. When he was a baby, he'd pitch fits, crying and flailing his fists to where you couldn't do nothing to calm him. We were living with my grandmother Mama Liza then, and sometimes, to keep him from wailing the whole house awake, I'd strap him in the backseat and drive. After a few blocks with the radio low and the engine humming, instead of crying he'd be cooing and rubbing his booties together. It never took more than one side of a cassette and a smooth road to lull him to sleep. But after a while the rides were as much for me as they were for him. Whether he was crying or not, I'd steal out and venture to Laurelhurst or Lake Oswego or Gresham or Milwaukie or the spot on Marine Drive where I would sit and watch the planes take off. Most nights I was back before the last newscast, but some nights I wandered until the TV snowed off-air.

Champ shows late morning playing a slow song from the sixties.

Your music, I say. You act like you as old as me with this music.

Well, you about as old as me by tastes, he says. So don't that make us even?

We wheel out to a lot on Division and park a few blocks away because my eldest has a theory about never letting a salesman see you pull up.

There's a circle of salesmen near an office huffing cigs. One of them stamps out his smoke and hustles over. Welcome to Treasure Auto, he says. He pats the breast of a ragged wool coat and takes out a card and thumps it and offers it to Champ. He says his name, a name you forget, and asks if my eldest and I are siblings.

So who's leaving here in a new car? he says.

He flashes a mended smile, shakes a finger scorched from days, months, years of smoking to nubs, and this is why, while he and Champ tour, I drag feet back.

Soon as you see what you want, you let me know, he says, his breath making wreaths in the cold. And I'll make sure you leave here with it.

You could loll a day care of upset babies to sleep with how long it takes him to show us a car that's worth our time. This one's gray and boxy with a lightning-shaped crack in the windshield. Champ gets in and starts it up. The engine sounds like an engine should—I've heard enough sick ones to know—and the inside's nice too, as if the old owners kept it covered in plastic. Champ revs the gas and tests the heat and checks the glove and flips the visors and twists on the wipers—high speed, low speed, intermittent, and it all checks out, plus the price falls within what Champ said we had to spend. But it's a Dodge, and I can't get past the thought of me wheeling by every person I've known in life, in a car meant for someone twice my age. The salesman asks if we wanna take it for a spin.

No, thank you, I say.

Not a good fit, eh? he says. Not to worry, we've got a car that's right for you or I'm in the wrong business. We let him lead us farther and farther into a used car abyss: a Rabbit with a dented bumper, an Escort with stained cloth seats, a Pontiac built before power steering. Name your price, he says, and taps a hood. No reasonable offer will be refused. Unreasonable offers may be considered.

Champ stops him midway through another pitch. Thanks, he says. But we're going to check a few more spots. He grabs me by the arm. He's never had a tough time making choices, or not as tough a time as me.

Hey, don't leave, he says. Wait a sec. Wait a sec. We have more.

But my eldest has already made up his mind.

If not for me calling and calling Champ after shifts for a ride, we might not be here. It was a few shifts ago when he offered. He'd come to pick me up from a double and I was outside enjoying a smoke.

You ain't gone stop till there's a hole in your throat? he said.

Do we really have to start? I said.

Yes, he says. We do. So I've been thinking, and here's the deal. You quit that nasty habit and I'll buy you a ride.

You're just talkin? I said.

When am I just talking? he said.

Give me a month, he said.

That's it, just a month? I said.

Yes, he said. Have you made it a month before?

Guess not, I said.

I know not, he said.

They say the first one's the toughest, he said. That it takes at least a month to form habit.

Then what? I said.

Then you'll have a new car and a new chance at best health. So let's start soon, he said. No, let's start right now, he said, and stuck out his hand.

I fished out an old pack, the pack I'd just bought, the loosies I kept in the side pocket.

We stand alone in a lot for so long it feels flagrant. Champ trots off, checks sticker prices, peeks in windows, while I pop a stick of smoker's gum and slow-chew, waiting for my craving—how will I make it a month?—to die down. There's a stoplight a block off and bouts of traffic stop and go without anyone coming to help. When we turn to leave a man dashes out too late after us.

No such trouble at the next lot, where the salesman blurs to our side, tells us he has the perfect car, coerces us over to an electric-blue Honda. He raises the hood, shows us a small clean engine, and recites facts about pistons and horsepower and miles per gallon. He gets in and fires it up and the engine sounds like an engine. He asks if we'd like to take it for a test drive, and there isn't a hint of desperate in his voice.

We roll off the lot with the windows down and the music high. We're out in Southeast, but what I wouldn't give to be in the old neighborhood, sailing early mornings past crowds at the bus stop. What I wouldn't give to be seen zooming away from an NA meeting or pulling warm and dry up to my job.

The wheel shudders, and I let off the gas and check the mirror to see if Champ felt it too. You take care of this and it'll run for one-fifty, two hundred thousand miles easy, the sales guy says. I take 205 north for a ways. I get off and get on the southbound side and head for the lot. We end up in the office, a mangy mobile home that smells of mildew. Our sales guy hunts the manager, and the manager—my first mind says he's lived for years off faux-pride—sits a slab of papers on the table. Looks like today is your day, he says. Let's talk numbers.

My credit score, these days, is slapstick. Who'd believe me about the brand-new rides I drove off lots—the Spitfire, the Mustang, the Taurus, the Datsun? Who'd believe the times they gave me low-interest loans, no-interest loans, incentives up the yang? Champ asks if I'm sure I want it. He flips through the top few sheets and slides them back to the manager and asks me to wait in the lounge. I hear him tell the manager he's paying in cash.

When you've got a new car and a full tank and nowhere to be, you ride. You ride the freeway, ride local streets; you roam, hoping for witnesses, with your windows cracked and the heat blasting; you whip by the same bus stops where most days you can't stand more than a few heartbeats without someone you know tooting their horn. Time on my hands, so I wheel by Alberta market and the mall, ride past the parks; I cruise Ainsworth, Dekum, Lombard, dying to be seen. But there isn't anyone out today but strangers, and I refuse to share this feeling with strangers. This is why it's time to find Pat. My brother Pat is in one of a few places always: either at one of his kids' mother's house or the tavern. I stop at the house where his boys stay, and tap the horn. Someone cracks the curtains and fast shuts them closed. I toot another time and Pat's youngest boy shuffles onto the porch in pajamas. He stops at the top of the steps and squints to see who's in the car.

Where your mama at? I say.

Who that, Aunt Grace? he says.

Yeah, your auntie, I say.

He disappears in the house and returns with his mother clomping behind him.

Hey, girl, how you been? I say. My brother there?

Girl, this the first week of the month which means that brother of yours is MIA. Liable he's somewhere guzzling up his half of the rent.

Well, when you see him, can you tell him I came by? I say.

As I said, Pat's at one of a few places always. One of his favorites is the tavern. The one tavern in all of the civilized world that sells 40-ounces by the bottle. By car it's a hop-skip from his woman's place. To be true, too near for his whereabouts to be in question, but that's my brother. I haven't stopped in—why would I?—since forever, though forever ago this place was about what it is now. There's a man racking pool balls, another one playing a pinball machine, old men collected around a table slapping cards. Pat's among the cardplayers doing what he does best—running his mouth. His back is to me. He jumps when I touch him.

Say, sis, don't be creepin up on me like that, he says. You almost got fired on.

Boy, you ain't about to fire on nobody, I say. What you doing besides boozing away the rent?

Oh, I see you been by my lady's, he says, and swigs his 40. Well, I'll have you know this here ain't the rent. That gone yesterday. This here's the light bill.

Sometimes I think my brother's the happiest man alive—drunk, sober, or any state in between. Once, when he was staying with me—he's stayed with me off and on for years—I asked him his secret. He said he'd show me. Said to stand still and don't look ahead nor behind. Now feel, he said. Feel the right now. That's all we have, he said. You wanna know what it is, that's it.

Pat's wearing a checkered shirt and jeans and combat boots and needs a haircut in the worst way. Waste not, want not, he says, and downs the last of his beer, and pushes away from the table.

What's the word, sis? he says. I know you ain't swung through to shit talk with me and the fellas.

Right, I say. Come.

Pat staggers out behind me and waits swaying while I open the car and climb in.

Who ride's this? he says.

Who you see in it? I say.

That right, he says. Thought you said they had you down there slaving for them nickels and dimes, he says.

They do. Champ bought it, I say.

Oh, he says. Well, I'll be good and gotdamned. Nephew gifting cars now, eh? He must be into some mighty sweet shit.

What you trying to say? I say. Why can't you let me have this?

Sis, have it, he says. Have it all you want. But you and I both know anything seem sweet as this got that bitter marching right behind it.

Pat, please, I say.

Say no more, say no more, he says. He climbs in and straightens his seat and fingers the upholstery and fiddles the disc player's controls.

Look like you and old neph picked a winner, he says. What this, bout an '86, '87? What the miles on it?

What miles matter? I say, and start the car—it starts easy; it should all be this easy—and lower the windows and crank my system. My music stomps into the street.

But maybe it's just here. In my city. Not yours.

—Champ

PEOPLES, YOU LISTENING?

Bet.

This is how it go.

If you're cold enough they name you.

Clutch or Jack Knife or K-Dub or 3-D or Dead Eye or D-Reid or Big Third or Smooth or DaBell—score twenty or thirty a season, and *bam*, you're Stu or Pickle or Free or Fish or Big Blass or King Cole or Doc—they've christened you T-hop or B-hop or Pooh or Fluff or the Honey Bee or Houseguest or B-Moore or J. D. or Bookie. Handle your biz lugis luge and everywhere they'll say your name, call out T-Cage, T. T., Gumby, Banger, A-Train, Nickle, Action, P-Strick, JoJo, L. V., T-Jones, Blazer.

We're talking MVPs and state champs and first-team All-Everythings, dudes who any day you wanted it would kill your weak ass at the park.

In my city, hoop's the hegemony.

In the Rose City, the P, what the deal is, if they name you, you're anointed. And in the P that's what we cherish, what we love if nothing else: Year after year after year we harangue who's greatest of the ones who dropped 40s and 50s *pre* a three-pointer, which phenoms scored 60! 70! 80! Guys named J-Bird or

Zelly-Roo or T. B. or D-Stoud or Slash or T-Bone or T-Ross or T-Hamp or Juice or Ice or Silk—middle school man-childs who played not a lick beyond the eighth, or the luckier-than-thous who hangtimed off to college handcuffed by the city's collective hope. The General and 2-Ounce and Stretch and Big City and Slider and Truck and Duke and the one we named the GOAT: legends, a few of them, all-leaguers in every league they played.

My word, a nickname is a christening, meaning you got a shot, meaning they think you can go, which is one chance more than most of us, so no wonder the chosen are all there is to speak of. No wonder when, for most, hoop's about our only shot to be better and bigger than the rest, to secure a life that counts.

But on the flip side, fall short and then what?

Best-case, you join a city league and/or wake early on the few weekends reprieved from rain to hit Wilshire or Irving or Laurel-hurst for full-court four-on-fours; you catch a rare weekend park run and on Monday semi-limp, half-swank onto your dronerific of a nine-to-five, fatmouthing to anyone with ears about who beat who by how much. You carry that same chatter to the shop or the grocery store or just outside the entrance of whatever club is crackin that month, carry it to the sidelines of an open gym or to a perch in the crowded bleachers of games between—the likely highlight of a nigger's week, month, winter—your old high school and an archrival.

Not a failed life for most, but fordamnsure not no dreamland neither.

Worse-case, you're addle-brained and haggard and wandering a main street with a decrepit semi-flat hoop rock tucked at your side or shooting air jumpers at a rim nobody but nobody but you can see. Worser, you're left plotting on a way to prolong the cheers: you're peddling hard or soft, or gangbangin or dumping seeds in every used-to-be-sorta-bad who saw **your name** bolded on the front page of Prep Sports—BKA slipping raw dog in community pussy. Fall short, and what the fuck can you do? Catch a sex-abused-low-esteemed-runaway teen girl on a humbug and risk your heretofore faulty luck: first as the dude who strong-arms the paltry tips of an amateur stripper, then as a local pimp sending runaways, strippers, the de-esteemed on escort calls, then graduating to a road show, hitting Cali, Vegas, NY, and all ho-strolls in between.

Let them quit screaming your name, and worse-case you just might rob a bank (who gets away with that?), just might hatch a (hand to God this happened) a flawed murder-for-insurance plot.

But maybe it's just here. In my city. Not yours.

Canaan dickers for snack funds, leaps the bleachers, disappears out the gym. Next dead ball, the ref shoos youngsters too close to the baseline, too close by the sideline, most of them wearing team sweat suits and sandals with white socks peeking from their open toes—neophytes who I can't help but think right about now ain't lived near long enough to even earn a single real foe. A crowd of some fortunate-ass young bucks plus a few teenybopper chicks dressed for spring or summer, which I suppose ain't all that bad since, though it's cold and damp outside, inside this heat is cranked to Africa.

And before I forget (me hypermnesic? Yeah right) about enemies, let me say this: Fuck a sycophant. The way I see it, you ain't lived till somebody don't like you. Shit, a few somebodies.

Grown folks loitering by the door chomping on pencil hot dogs or oversalted chips, slurping pull-tab pops, all of them held captive by the sign: NO JUICE OR FOOD IN THE GYM NO EXCEPTIONS! The old man who runs this sweatbox roosting by the entrance, guarding against anybody who so much as looks as if they'd break a rule. Side note: I used to think this same old head was one of those ultra-fastidious, follow-all-the-rules-or-perish types till I saw him at an after-hours all by his lonesome gulping Cognacs.

KJ sluices hyperspeed through a press (even he handles it the way I never could), tries to split a three-man trap, and dribble-kicks the ball out of bounds. He boots the ball and watches rapt (a regular midcourt Madame Tussaud statue) while it scrawls its way to a stop, while the white-socked sideline crew soundtracks his gaffe with a loud-ass, Ooooooh!

Shake it off, shake it off, I yell from up top, and people below twist around to look.

Mom shows near the end of the first quarter. She's got her coat, not a winter coat, zipped to her throat and her cheeks are flushed. She searches the stands for so long I'm compelled to get up and wave. You can see it on her way up: either Mom's getting old or she's laying serious hot sauce on the trouble it takes to climb.

So, new wheels, but on the same old CP clock, I say.

It wasn't me this time, it was them, she says. Caseworker popped up right when I was about to leave. Oh my gosh, these folks and their rules, she says. I'll be overjoyed, you hear me? Overjoyed when this is done. Mom's new 'do still looks proper, but her nails could use new paint. This is how I'd describe her to strangers: Perfect minus a touch or two. She unzips herself, snakes out her coat (it's thinner than I thought, with rips in the lining), and asks what she's missed.

Not much, I say. Coupla points, an assist, a bonehead play.

Good or bad? she says.

Try average, I say.

Next thing I know, Mom's screaming KJ's name when I swear the boy ain't done shit but toss the ball inbounds. KJ gazes up at us with game-time eyes as fierce, no, fiercer, than mine ever were.

That's my boy, she says. My baby.

When I was my brother's age, with not a care I'd admit to beyond my box score, I lived for playing games in front of my family, ached for the times when a cousin or an aunt or unc would attend, but especially Mom, who missed many more than she made.

How's the electric-blue chariot? I say. You still in love?

Yes, in love, she says.

All to the good, I say. So everything's working? No troubles.

None that I know of, she says.

Great, I say. So you good on funds for gas? Your pockets straight otherwise?

Son, you've done enough, she says. More than enough, she says. Let's enjoy the game.

Next time downcourt KJ dribbles hard left and banks a layup over a boy that's hit his growth spurt hella-early. It's a nice play, but you'd think my bro rescued a newborn from bullets, with the racket Mom makes: thunderclaps and stomping and high-pitched rah-rahing.

Mom, I say. It's two points. One. Two. That's all. Which means it's our two points.

No. It's your brother's two points, she says. You could show more support.

Support, I say. Me? Wow, Mom. Like really, wow, forreal.

KJ's game is one of those back-and-forth contests where each mistake is mega, the extended remix of an original blunder—BKA nerves for the players, fever for us. You know what I'm saying, an atmosphere to birth a hoop hero—or lay a hyped prospect's name to early rest.

Midquarter of next quarter, KJ shakes by his man, spins out of control, and slings a pass that smacks his teammate dead in the face: *BLAM!* His teammate drops to a knee and then falls on his back. He covers his mug and moans. The coach flurries off the bench with a towel in hand. Bench-warmers fly on the court and make a half-moon around the boy. Can't tell you how long the youngster mewls, how long the coach presses a towel against a gang of blood and tears.

Oh my gosh, Mom says.

He'll be cool, I say. Bloody nose or a headache. No worse.

Well, I hope so, she says. But I meant your brother.

KJ is gaping at the harm from steps back, his face my face from years ago, high school, maybe further: a boy with something precious knocked clean the fuck right out of him.

Second half, no fist-pumping pom-pom plays for Team KJ—not a one till minutes in, when he reaches for a steal, lets his man slip past, and, trying to recover, hazards a hero-block that damn near decapitates a boy. The refs' whistles trill in sync. The opposite bench screams flagrant foul. The boy lays out for counts, gets up woozy, heads to the line. KJ's coach calls time-out and hastens to meet his players, but KJ drops his head and drags tacit past the huddle. He grabs the farthest seat, a chair a motherfuckin city block from anyone else, and makes himself an avalanche. With attitude like this, he seems headed down the same road I was, seems a trial or two from blowing the faith of the ones who believe and don't have to. This is what I'll tell him later, when we're away from the lick of this flame.

Better for him is what I want for him if better for him exist.

The coach sends the team out minus KJ. He stomps to my brother's distant seat and screams. KJ drops his eyes. Do you hear? Coach says. I know you hear. He grabs a clutch of KJ's jersey and yanks him to his feet. He pulls him so close it's lash to lash. Get out of here! he says. Get out of here now, he says. Go!

KJ snatches away. He turns and kicks an empty seat legs-up. He marches into game play and stands at center court. He tears off his jersey, slings it across the floor towards his bench, balls his fists, and seethes—at his coach, his teammates, the boys sprawled by the baseline, the adults who've peeked in from concessions; he seethes with his muscled gut swelling and the veins standing out in his neck.

Mom springs to her feet, but I catch her wrist and hold her still, feel her pulse as a song in my palm.

Don't, I say.

She stills a beat, a beat and shakes free. She scrambles down the bleachers, leaving her coat back, as if she isn't as old and harmed as she is.

Me chasing her.

She chasing him.

KJ a hurricane now whirling outside.

We keep it alive.

It was Big Ken and his brothers (my pimpish uncs), it was Uncle Sip, who made me dream and kept that hope buoyed as best they could. It was them who bought me mini-balls and mini-hoops for birthdays, who drove me to Biddy Ball camps, who would take me to the park for one-on-ones and practice. It was them who talked of the neighborhood legends, the city's rare semi-pros, the small few who got a chance to see the lights. It was those men who preached to me, Make them all know your name. But it ain't them and me no more. Or it is me. But me and my bros. Me prodding KJ, prodding Canaan. Doping them with this dream. But tell me this, will you, is it so wrong? Is it? What kind of solipsistic black-hearted robot would I be to wish against my brothers succeeding in ways that I failed?

FIRST ZION BAPTIST CHURCH
Est. 1863
4304 N. Vancouver Ave.
Portland, OR. 97212

NEW MEMBER REGISTRATION

Would you like to become a member of our church? Have you been praying about joining one of Oregon's oldest ministries? Are you new to the area and want to transfer your membership? If you answered "yes" to any of these questions, then please take a moment to fill out the information below and drop it off to our church offices. Open membership is held once monthly. For more information, please stop by the church office or call us 503.281.9220.

Name_____

Address_____

City _____ State _____ Zip_____

Home phone _____ Cell_____

Email address _____

Age ____ Marital Status: Married __ Single __ Divorced __ Widowed ___ Separated ___

Have you ever been a member of our church? Yes _____ No _____

Have you ever been baptized? Yes ___ No ___ Would you like to become a candidate? Yes__ No__

Are you saved? Yes __ No __

Would you like to transfer your membership to this church? Yes ___ No ___

If yes, what church are you transferring from?

Name of church _____

Address _____

City _____ State _____ Zip _____

Phone _____

What areas of church are you interested in?

- o Choir
- o Education
- o Family life
- o Men's ministry
- o Women's ministry

- o Ministries of hope and healing
- o Prayer
- o Young adult
- o Youth ministry
- o Missionary work

One of those places you think can save you
if need be, from yourself.
—Grace

IT'S MORE A DRONE than singing that fills the room when I walk in. It's a warble and then not one. The deacon approaches the podium and I make my way past a white-gloved usher woman to a pew near the back. The deacon's suit coat hangs knee-length. He reads announcements and when he's done he calls up Pastor Hammond. The pastor, a freckle-faced man with black back-combed hair, rises from his seat and strolls up to the pulpit, where a massive Bible rest under a bent microphone. Amen, he says, offering a glimpse of a gold-capped front tooth. He nods at the choir and they stand and the choir director moves out in front with his hands at his sides and his head down. The director lifts his head and the choir hums the first notes of "Amazing Grace."

Pastor Hammond—he was a guest speaker at my last church—asks the church to be seated. He clears his throat and sips from a goblet. Today, saints, he says, I want to speak to you about temptation. He unbuttons his jacket and grips the lectern and gazes out. The devil tempted Jesus to make stones into bread, he says. But Jesus refused. I said, the devil tempted Jesus to make stones into bread but Jesus refused. And when Jesus said no, the devil took him to the highest mountain and said he'd give him all the kingdoms and the glory if Jesus would get down on his knees. But Jesus, the pastor shouts, told that devil, I only worship *one* God. Jesus, amen, told that devil, I serve one God and one God only. And surely, the pastor says, and slaps the lectern, if Jesus could pass up all the world's glory, then we can forsake the tiny temptations of our lives. He goes on and while he does the pews fill up and the members clap and here and there shout amen. The pastor stops and wipes sweat from his neck and face and waves his handkerchief and calls up his wife, the first lady. He fades to a seat pushed against the wall. The first lady takes the podium, looks out at the church, lays her Bible on the lectern. Today, saints, I'd like to speak to you about marriage, she says. The Bible tells us not to count another's blessings. It warns us not to live beyond our means.

Not often, but sometimes talk of marriage makes me think of my ex, a man I met in NA—this should have been my first clue!—of the time I fell in starry-eyed love and married his non-working self at the courthouse months later. His name was Larry and he smoked and drank. The day after we exchanged vows, Larry earned a key chain that might as well have been the master key for every liquor store in the land. He jumped right back on the bottle, and before long, before I'd relapsed myself, he fell right back into puffing too. The man was an expert if ever there was one. He left on a hunt for his potion one October night and we didn't see him until after New Years, the cold day he strolled in whistling as if the world had wound to a halt while he was gone.

The first lady preaches and the pastor, legs and arms crossed, beams from his seat. She finishes and the church applauds, big booming claps. The choir stands and sings "Soon and Very Soon." The members sway in their dark blue robes with yellow stoles, the faces of praise. The women wear dark coats of makeup, the men sport beards edged just so. The pastor strolls up after the song and he thanks the choir and his beautiful wife for her kind and wise words.

Now, saints, he says, and saunters to the edge of the pulpit. I'd like to hear of the Lord's good work.

The first to testify is a couple—the wife wears a diamond spec for a ring, the husband a crushed tie—who sit in my row. The husband thanks God for clothes, for a roof, for a decent car to get back and forth. God is good, he says. Praise Him.

A woman testifies next, tells the church how after her husband left, she stayed home a month straight trying to starve herself blind, says she would've whittled to dust if the pastor hadn't came by and prayed her back to faith.

The next to witness is a man at the front of the church. He says that the Lord brought his daughter back after she'd been gone so long it gave him a stroke. He tears up, and there's a certain part, a better part of me, that sympathizes.

The first time I was grown and joined a new church was after what happened to my cousin. She was younger by not many years and more of a sister. I introduced her to one of Kenny's brothers and they dated against our family's wishes. She went missing months later, and we all assumed she'd ran off with him, that Kenny's brother had convinced her to prostitute. We didn't believe otherwise until we found out the brother had been in jail. My cousin was gone from summer through fall. Then one night the news ran the story of a woman found in Overlook Park. The anchor said the woman had been stabbed dozens of times and left for so long her body had begun to decompose. The next morning the boys and I drove to Mama Liza's. We hadn't been there long when the police knocked, asking questions and I could feel right off why they had come.

The next Sunday I joined First AME Zion and gave my life to Christ, for my cousin, my sister, for what I'd done to my family, for what I must've known I'd do all too soon to myself.

The choir sings "Bridge Over Troubled Water." The pastor dabs his face once more and waits for calm and glides again to the edge of the pulpit. Is there anyone here who needs prayer, he says, who wants to give their life to our Lord and Savior Jesus Christ?

An elder woman in a gray wig, a boy in slacks that stop too high, a man in an oversize double-breasted suit, they amble to the front of the church and kneel before the pastor and the cross. Those who stayed back hum and sway. My neighbor nudges me and asks if I'd like to go and I shake my head. If I was a girl, Mama Liza would lead me to the front and stay by my side. But she's gone. The organist fingers chords and it's a language all its own. More of the brave drift down and submit.

John 3:16, *For God so loved the world, that He gave His only begotten Son, that whosoever should believe in Him should not perish, but have everlasting life*, the pastor says. Father, we ask that You come into our house today. We ask that whatever is troubling the hearts of these men, these women, these children, your creations, Father, we ask that You come into their lives and heal it. Let us put our faith in You, Lord. Everything works together for the good of them that love You. The pastor strides from one side of the stage to the other and stops under a giant painting of Jesus. He drifts down the steps and lays a hand on those that have come forward to be born. He looks up and roves his eyes around. Then with his face shining and shining he starts up an aisle. It's my aisle.

God, some of us have been before You once, but it wasn't our time, he says. God, some of us have been before You twice and it wasn't our time, he says. But dear God, this is our time. The pastor stops next to my pew. The organist fingers chords and the drummer taps his cymbals. Satan, the pastor says. You are no match for my God. You are a coward. I said, Satan, you are no match for my God. You are a coward. We rebuke you in the name of the Lord. The pastor stomps and shakes his fist and snaps his head back. We rebuke you, Satan, in the name of the Lord.

The pastor gazes along my pew. He reaches out. Reaches out to whom?

This time I want to turn away. This time I can't.

He wades into my row and they part. Come, come, my saint, he says.

Good sense says I've hurt her too much to keep her.
—Champ

HERE'S THE STORY that changed my mind about this love shit. Not by itself, but still. This happened back in high school, so it goes: me and the homies went to see the new black flick (you know how they do us. We had to roll to the outskirts to catch it; not that that matters, but it matters), and while I was in the lobby buying a Slushie and some ransom-priced popcorn, this super lame guy I'd seen in traffic bopped up. He asked me if my girl was my girl and grinned. I told him yeah and asked him, what about it? Bro, I ain't no snitch, he said, but she's in there with another dude.

This wouldn't have been so bad if my girl wasn't distinguished, if she hadn't been the only girl in the history of my postpubescent fuck spree—which began in earnest in eighth grade and was full tilt by that point, who had ever inspired me to pass on a shot of ancillary pussy. We (the we being me and my homeboys, whose fatmouthing made a worse situation worser) found her in the theater sitting with this supernaturally pale half-a-nigger who hooped (I told y'all we all hooped) for a private high school in the burbs. So how did a fledgling Don Giovanni handle such trials? I tapped old girl on the shoulder and beamed high-watt and sat behind her and the half-a-nigger the whole flick, making a

symphony of sucking down my Slushie and smacking my popcorn with true ambition. The credits rolled and I let them empty
into the aisle and followed, trading big-ass guffaws with my boys.
For the rest of the day and thereafter, I played like wasn't shit
wrong, that I was cool as the temperature (it was like they double-
dutied the joint for storing cadavers) in that theater that day,
though the truth was I was an emblem for grief.

Wouldn't you know, when I got home, Grace was nowhere to
be found. MIA until days later, when she slumped in too looped
to lend advice of any kind of efficacy. When she finally got right,
I told her what happened, expecting the kind of coddling my
young self was too old for even then. That's what I wanted, but
this is what I got instead: Son, if you're going to risk your love,
save all the space you can for hurt.

Beth answers barefoot in a silk robe with music playing in the
background, a surprise since I called her crib not an hour ago and
she didn't pick up. She lets me in, heads for the fridge, pours a glass
of wine. She sways into her room and through her robe, through
the silk-something under it, you can see her ass cheeks jump
(picture two koala bears wrestling) just like I lust.

Damn, I say.

Damn, what? she says.

The kitchen's light is lush. I weigh the dope, mix it with soda,
and set a pot to boil. Then it's back and forth from the kitchen to
the peephole, my hands no good for anything steady, the sound
of my pulse not the sound of a pulse. This happens every time I
chef. It happens and I mind it or else. Beth ask me to top off her
glass and I pass again by the peephole. This is intervention, no

less, which is a priority when you've had dreams like mines, sleep wrecked for weeks with visions I can't even speak on.

I take the pot off the stove and let the work lock.

I dump the water and let the work sit on a paper towel to air-dry.

But this is as far as it goes with the play-by-play. This ain't no how-to guide.

I lie across Beth's bed. She asks me about school, and I tell her about an essay on happiness that I had to read for class. What would you rather have, a trick knee or a broken leg? I say.

I beg your pardon? she says

Of the two, I say. Which would you rather?

The leg, she says. It'll heal.

Beth, her big brown nipples pressing through the silk, sits against the headboard with her knees bent and parted, no panties. An invite. And how could I pass on an invite like this? With Kim's face a foosball knocking around my skull, I strip down to my boxer briefs and tell her she ain't cool for seducing me.

So this is what you call seduction? she says.

Peoples, pause please before you blister me too tough. Me and Beth, we ain't all the way reckless. We've got rules: no open-mouth kissing, no proclamations of love, a limit on postcoital pillow talk. Before that, though, I make a rhythm that lasts a few songs and part of another. She rests her thigh, warm and twitchy, across my stomach when we finish, while we lay looking at the TV without watching it, a paranormal quiet between us. This goes on till I get up to clean off. Our postsession cool-off is pretty much standard but what happens in the bathroom borders on the semifantastic. What happens in the bathroom is this: it hits me that I couldn't, for a jackpot, recall Beth's last name. Oh boy, talk about all bad intimacies. I grab the sink with both hands and look into the mirror. See a face that's the face of a sucker who could do this on a whim to a good chick. I rub my nuts and smell a finger. To smell another woman on your nuts when you love your girl (I know, I know, I know) is foul. To be stumped on the last name of the girl that's all over your nuts when you love your girl is no less than lowdown dirty despicable. I mumble the alphabet, hoping a letter will help the name catch hold.

You want to know some funny shit? I say, back in the room, stepping into my boxer briefs. I can't remember your last name for shit.

Are you serious? she says. Do you think admitting that fact's a little foolish? she says.

Admitting that fact might be the least of my fool, I say.

It's Ford, she says. And for the record, you're the worst.

Beth's an army girl, a corporal, which in a strange way makes our setup extra-special. I bend to lace my shoes, see a fitted cap under the bed. I should shrug it off, but what can I say, I'm an opportunist. I toss it on the bed and ask if it's competition for the crown.

Beth smirks. She asks if I can give her the storage fee. It's early I know but things a little tight this month, she says.

You need it? I say.

Wouldn't ask if I didn't, she says.

So check it, I hope you don't be letting your less special houseguests snoop, I say. Can't have nobody stumbling on my stash.

If I have a guest you can believe he's occupied, she says. The last thing he's worried about is playing a sleuth.

What's the size of the thing it takes to kill it, whatever it is?

Beth says this and I can hear Half Man in my head (the old jabbering voice of dissent) warning me against hitting Beth raw, reminding my silly ass that she's in the field in a major way.

If your dad's a plumber, you learn pipe work, how to dredge a pipe; if he's a writer, he gives you books, show you how to write a decent sentence; if Pops is a preacher, maybe he teaches you Sunday sermons. My dad (by *dad* I mean Big Ken, who isn't my real dad, but stepped up when my biological pops was into sleight of hand) was, Ibullshityounot, on everything I love, right hand to God, a pimp. Some days he'd take me along while he checked his hos: white girls who lived in dank apartments, who wore robes well into the afternoons and who smelled of cigarette smoke. Sometimes he'd have other errands to run, and would leave me with them. They'd occupy me the best they could, and when he swooped in an hour or so later, he'd stuff fives and tens in my pockets and let me lap-drive to the next spot. He never talked about what he was, and when I got older he never held his hustle up as a model, but for the last long while I've wondered how much of what he was is what I am.

Beth gets up to take a shower. She leaves her door cracked, tells me that the sergeant pulled her aside and said she might get stationed in another state, that I might have to find another spot to stash my work. She says I've got a few months, maybe more, but she wants to give me a heads-up. I lay her cash on her blanket and stroll in the kitchen, where I prep a few oz's and scrub the pot and utensils clean. Forget the cliché: in this life cleanliness is next to freedom!

I leave with a swollen plastic sack stuffed in my sleeve and my eyes stabbing every which way.

Here's the mantra of me and my homeboys: Don't let daylight catch you! When you live with your girl you can explain away loads of suspect business, but strolling in at the crack of dawn ain't one of them. The homies, some of them would rather catch a misdemeanor (a couple of them actually have) and spend a night in a holding tank than face their girl after she's spent a whole night seething. Now it ain't a hard fast rule break when I creep through my front door, but it's that hour when the sun ain't far off from being an orange badge behind the clouds. I hope Kim's asleep, but hope, what's that? She's on the couch with the blinds open and the lights off. What you doing up? I say. Kim keeps her back to me. Long strands fall over her shoulders. Long legs sprawled in shadows sectioned by blinds. She don't say a word; matterfact, she don't shrug or jerk or nothing. She's got it bad, that not-answering shit, but all I can do at this hour is sigh. What you doing up?

The news, she says. Guess you didn't see it.

Who watches the news? Why would I be watching the news? I say.

Why wouldn't you? she says. If you did, you would've heard about the big bust.

What that got to do with me? I say. I know you ain't worrying over the next nigger's troubles.

Kim throws a small and hard thing across the room, knocks a picture of us at the Rose Festival carnival off the wall. I tip over and rehang it.

Keep thinking it's gonna be the next person, she says.

She looks fierce. She never looked this fierce. Not when we met. My freshman year at P State. She was walking up to the bar on campus, a sway of hips and a strut to annihilate a young punk. Where we met should have been the harbinger of harbingers, but I didn't have it in me to dismiss a girl with a walk like that. She's couple years older but I lied about how old I was (claimed the age I am now) and we were shacked up quick enough that the shit might've been bad judgment. And the truth is, though I talk tough, and these last couple years ain't been no romance novel (show me a love that is), I wouldn't trade her for no one— period. What'd your boy Nietzsche say: *There is always some madness in love. There is always some reason in madness.*

Maybe the old German saw into the maw of my tomorrows.

The stories I could tell. How once she found my car outside a chick's condo and sliced my tires; how she once wrote, *Fuck You Champ*, in red lipstick all over my windshield; how, after a random fuck rang our home line, she ripped my laptop screen off its hinges; how the night of the day her girl *allegedly* spied me on a lunch date she doused me out of a dead sleep with a pot of cold water and warned next time it'd be hot!

Good sense says I've hurt her too much to keep her, says too that I'll never find another who loves this hard, who knows what it means to have a home, knows too what it means to have a home and lose one. I sit down beside her and pull her close, wishing I could snatch out my heart and show her, but knowing, with all the room I've saved for hurt, this slab ain't much to see.

She breaks loose and flurries into the room, me chasing. She flops at the edge of the bed and takes off her top. It's hard to see where she starts and the dark ends. If this were another night, I'd lay her down, work her panties low, and slide inside—the only alibi she'd believe. But I don't have the mettle for it. Or tonight I'm made of too much steel for it.

Kim gets up and walks to the dresser. She takes out a paper and pamphlets and tosses them on the bed. The pamphlets show pregnant women. What's this? I say.

A decision, she says.

Decisions. Our last was not long ago and we said never again.

But the punk in me knows I'll press soon enough for another, a last (you would hope) clinic visit.

What the pimps in my life, what all the two-bit players and the model apathetic lovers never told me, was this: For those of us who can feel, the guilt never leaves, it only ever gets displaced.

Do you know how many times I've tried?

—Grace

BIG STRENGTH WAS MY MOTHER'S BLESSING.
The strength to birth Pat and me in less than a year. To wake
every day before dawn to cook and ready us for school and spend
the rest of her day mopping and folding and washing and scrub-
bing, to do that and look past what her husband's family, Andrew's
parents, Mama Liza and Bubba, who were well off from bootlegging, said about her and hers. Since I wanted to be strong too, I
was Mom's shadow, scouring the tub with ammonia, and hand-
mopping the tiles till they were clean as our silverware. For this
my mother treated me as a friend, told me secrets she never told
Pat, roused me from sleep some nights to sit with her well after
she'd sent him to bed.

The morning it happened, Mom kissed my eyes wide and told
me to wake Pat and I hustled down the hall and up the steps to
the attic, where my brother slept in a room that, no matter how
bad Mom stayed on him to clean it, forever smelled like feet. To
wake Pat you had to snatch the covers off him, which he knew
but never liked. We headed downstairs to a breakfast of bacon,
grits, eggs, and homemade biscuits. Mom was standing over the
stove and Andrew was reading a paper, wearing a shirt Mom had
stiffened crisp with homemade starch. My mother was wearing

the same thing she wore each day: a nightgown, a black head scarf, and fall-apart house slippers. Mom fixed Andrew's plate and hovered close while he took his first bite. She asked him if he was going to fix the blinds and he said that he would and that he didn't need any more reminders. When he finished, Mom stalked him out of the kitchen and into the living room. We heard her ask again about the blinds, heard the door slam shut.

Pat and me were finishing our plates when she came back in and ran a tub of water and piled pots and pans and skillets in the sink. All you could hear was those dishes and Pat scraping the last bits of food off his plate. Pat swallowed his last mouthful and pushed away from the table and stood gazing at our mother.

Mom, he said. Is Daddy a good man?

Of course, she said.

Mom, he said. Do you love him?

What kind of question is that?

She snatched his plate off the table and grunted it back to the sink. Pat looked at me and I looked away.

Well, if you love Dad, Pat said, then why do you get mad and try to hurt him?

This sucked the color out Mom's face. She dropped a plate and stared into the sink. You could count the words she spoke to us for the rest of the morning and that afternoon after school. She was more of herself later that night, letting me piece puzzles in the living room while she hummed along to her favorite 45s and waited for Andrew to come home.

He slugged in late and slumped on the couch. He kicked off his shoes, undid the throat of his shirt, propped his feet on the table, and lay his head back. My mother watched all this, waited till he was settled, and asked again about the blinds, asked if he planned to fix them that night as he had said he would. He said no, he'd do it the next night.

Mom stood and sighed. She sighed from a deep place and you knew it. She walked over and dragged a needle across her 45. She tied her scarf and smoothed her gown and sent me to my room, where I lay in my bed counting, counting, counting, how long it would take for her to erupt. It didn't take long at all before the screaming began, before Andrew whisked past my door and up the steps to Pat's room. Then I heard Mom in the kitchen. Then I heard Mom stomping up the steps. The boom of their voices coaxed me into the hall. That's where I saw Mom and Andrew tangled at the top of the steps, saw light catch the blade of a long knife, saw Andrew push and my mother tumble down the steps. It hurt to look, so I didn't look, not until she was at my feet, a blade in her chest, blood soaking through her gown. She died before I let her go.

I'm parked near the hydrant outside Andrew's place, the house he bought with his wife. He's got his front porch primed and his handrails sanded and his siding power-washed. You can see his wife—his sun, moon, stars—inside with a TV dancing grays across her face. She peeks up at me at the sound of the doorbell, then strolls into another room. She lolls out with Andrew behind her. He's the one that answers. He jitters the handle to open the storm door. Grace, he says. To what do we owe this surprise?

Afternoon, I say

He steps aside to let me in. I say hello to his wife and she plays like she doesn't hear it. Humph, I say, and follow Andrew into the kitchen. Out in the world this man is meticulous—shirts with creases in the sleeves, slacks with all the wrinkles knocked out, wing tips polished. But today he's dressed in a T-shirt and un-pressed khakis with his belt unfastened.

Drink? he says.

No, thank you, I say.

He pours himself a vodka straight, no ice. He asks me what I've been up to. Says he hasn't seen me in days.

Days, weeks, months, I say

So let me guess, you're back in church, he says.

How would you know? I say.

It's about the only time I see you, he says.

It's the only time I can come, I say. The only time I can stand that woman, what you've done.

Which church? he says.

First Zion, I say.

That Baptist? he says.

Andrew's a Catholic, attends St. Andrew's hour-long Sunday masses, Wednesday night choir practices, takes minutes at meet-ings of the local archdiocese.

He's right too. This isn't the first. First Zion, First Baptist. St. Mark's. Maranatha, Parkside Missionary, New Hope. I join and go a Sunday, go Sundays, steady until a weekend binge keeps me away for a week, for weeks at a time, for too many Sundays to brave the faces, to face the pastor, the first lady, a deacon; I join and attend until a choir member or an organist or an usher sees me wild and stumbling outside myself. The times that's hap-pened it's been much easier to find a new place to pray.

How long, how long? When will you let it go? he says.

Lose a mother, and lose a father, get replaced, and all is well, I say. It's just that easy, is it?

Grace, he says. Give me chance.

Chance? You have no clue, do you? You could never know how it feels to be left behind and cast back?

The wife sweeps in and stands over the stove. She asks Andrew when I'm leaving, if I might stay through dinner, says she didn't fix enough for company. Andrew grabs prescription bottles off a carousel and shakes out pills and downs them with his vodka.

Is that safe? I say.

These old things? he says. He re-racks his meds. We're Thomases. We're built to last. The wife clears her throat and makes noise in a cabinet over the stove. She tramps out.

What do you call that? I say.

Oh, what can we do? he says. What can we do?

The time for doing *been* passed, I say.

He says my name again and throws up a hand. This man is an expert too, has lied to himself about what he's done to me. Their old Chihuahua barks in a back room. The refrigerator groans. It wouldn't kill you to call me Dad, he says. That is, after all, who I am.

That is, after all, who who is? I say.

Is this why you came? he says. I know this can't be why you came.

Correct, I say.

Then why? he says.

To invite you to church, I say. Come with me one Sunday, I say. Just one.

I'm not so sure about that, he says.

Why not? I say.

He gets up and pours himself another drink and pours me a

glass of water and carries them both over. What is it you want from me? he says

You don't get it, do you? It's not what I want *from* you. It's what I want *for* you.

He's glum under the light, this man who's been a man for all but me. I shove away from the table and stomp into the living room, stopping to gawk at the shrine of Pat and my adopted sister, a girl who was more of the girl he and his wife wanted than me—the first true hurt. I turn a family portrait of them face-down and whisk into the living room, where the wife is sitting on the couch smoking. I stop a few feet from her. She crosses and uncrosses her legs and blows outs smoke. God bless you, I say. May God have mercy on your soul. She looks over my shoulder and I look over my shoulder at Andrew, her husband, who's standing in the kitchen's entrance.

He has the face of a martyr, this man, he who hasn't been crucified enough for his sins.

What I could tell him about my Sixth Street crew.

—Champ

UNDER A SKY the color of dried tears I push past a politician's campaign sign. The sign is plunged into the front yard, into dry grass, cause it ain't been a drip of rain (which you should know by now is a small-scale miracle) in the P for days on end. I knock and stand back, peeking through a split in the curtain of the front door's oval window, hoping for a few smart words, maybe a sentence, weighing one last time if bothering these people that don't know me from the next nigger is worth what it might cost in expectations.

Life has what?

Breaking out now is still one of them. Abandoning this shit altogether, before the door swings open and my options (what options?) taper to none. Got that coward's-retreat weight on my heels when a woman answers, standing barefoot and blowing on a black mug with her long gray hair parted and her eyes creased with lines. She greets me with a smile that's straight and blanched.

Hello? she says. Her voice means peace.

Hello, I say, and pause.

Blame these sprint-twitch shivers. There's still time to turn tail, to claim I'm a Jehovah's Witness, a salesman hocking magazine subscriptions, a distant neighbor hounding after a lost puppy—still time to claim any one of these excuses and she'd probably close the door and spare me the risk of making a fool of myself.

But what do I do? Apologize for the bother and ask if I can speak to her about the house.

Our place? she says. She cups her mug and moves to where I can see her better. She gives me the once-over. I give her a twice-over on the sly. She's got green eyes, a regal neck. Do you mind? she says. She eases the door shut, leaves me on the porch, and through the glass I see her evanesce.

I swing around to face Sixth, see the wind blow the peak off a pile of old leaves in the yard, shiver a naked tree branch. This is a last chance, and because it is, I plant a foot so as not to be foiled by my wayward courage.

The woman opens the door and there's a man standing behind her. He steps out in front and introduces himself and offers me a palm knobby with calluses.

What can I do for you? he says.

Sorry to bother you, sir. This may seem strange. Well, it is a bit strange. Okay, let me back up. I used to live in this house. My family and I. This is weird, I know, sir, miss, but I was wondering if I could have a look inside, I say. If it would be too much of a bother to maybe have a look around at our old place.

And your names is?

Sorry, sorry. My names is Shawn, sir. Shawn Thomas.

Shawn, a look, you say? You mean a tour? he says. He turns to his wife and she looks at me. He steps aside and points me to the living room couch. His wife asks if I'd like a drink and shuffles into what was the kitchen and probably still is. There's glassy magazines fanned across a nicked wood table, framed pictures hung on the walls—a black-and-white wedding photo, a flick of what looks like the husband holding a fish long as a shark. He lowers himself into an easy chair and leans forward and clasps his hands. One of his thumbnails is obsidian.

Worked construction most of my life, and let me tell you, they just don't build them like this anymore, he says. These days they pour a weak base, slap a few beams together, and tack up thin Sheetrock. Do it all in a matter of weeks. Used to be we'd take our time. Lay a thick slab of concrete, plaster the walls, drive a nail with the intent the beams would last. He falls back. But hey, it's hard to find anything of character these days, he says. And that goes for house or human being.

Sir, I say, extra emphasis on the *sir*. I don't know much about building a house, but I know how a home can make you feel.

Right, right, he says, and stands. You're probably itchin to see what we've done.

We start in the basement, in the same back room where Bubba, my great-grandfather, used to collect his junk. Bubba was a heavy-weight hoarder, believed that everything he touched deserved a second life. We (the *we* being my bros, my cousins, the neighborhood kids) spent hours rooting through what Bubba had saved to resurrect. The old junk room's a hardware store now stocked with shelves of hand tools, and power tools with cords looped and tied. Nubuck belts hang against a wall, a massive metal cabinet is pushed in a corner. This is my sanctum, he says, sweeping his arm. A man has got to have a place that gives him peace.

He snaps his suspenders, snaps them joints the same way Bubba did. My great-grandpops wore the same thing every day save Sunday: a flannel shirt and gray slacks up near his navel. It was Bubba that did most of the disciplining back then. He had this way of standing, when he was about to soften a tough ass, with his head cocked and his thumbs hooked in the waist of his suspenders, that let you know he meant business. He'd seize you in one of his Nordic glares, make you kneel, lock your head between his legs, and ask if you knew why you were being punished. Then he'd tan your ass, open-hand, no belt, or with a thick black whip (a real whip!) so tough you wondered if he was working for honor.

But one thing about Bubba, he never exacerbated a mauling like Mama Liza, never said shit like, This is going to hurt me more than it hurts you, never proselytized: If I spare the rod I'll spoil the child. Not him. He'd whoop you with heroic silence, then offer you the hankie forever folded in a pocket.

We wander into the basement's main room. He shows me his wife's potter's wheel. This here is where she spends her time, he says, plucks a paintbrush from a handmade cup, and runs that dark thumb over the bristles.

We stroll past an ancient fridge and stove into the room where Mama Liza kept a contraption that dried fruit (you've never seen a family more stocked with raisins, prunes, and dates!), a room that's empty now. When I was young, they kept the room decked with tweed couches that we'd stand on to watch the foot traffic: a man collecting shopping carts, a chick tottering home from a night on the stroll, grandmothers carrying jumbo Bibles into the storefront church next door.

He asks me if I'm ready to head upstairs.

We start in the kitchen. And this ain't what it was. Gone the teacup wallpaper, the painting of *The Last Supper*, the decorative copper spoons, the sloppy white paint that sealed our cabinet drawers froze. They've refinished the cabinets, fastened them with bronze handles, laid tiles over our old Formica counters.

Our fridge used to make the sound of a band warming up, but theirs could lullaby a nigger to sleep.

We hit the second floor. Stop in the room where Mama Liza and Bubba slept, a room they kept locked during the day and while they were gone. We meander into Uncle Sip's old room next. Uncle Sip's room stayed fragrant with cologne tester bottles he stole from the mall, was stacked with men's fashion mags, stacks that, no matter how tall I got, were taller than me.

The husband asks what it was like growing up in the neighborhood.

What I could tell him about my Sixth Street crew. My homeboy from next door who was the king of all tumblers, who could backflip on command or challenge for a whole block. My other boy who lived in the cluttered house across the street, the one we all envied for his lax curfew. There was my boy, who was less of my boy, with the palsied arm, the last pick no matter what game we played. And there was the big homie Scoop, the most resourceful of us. Scoop was the one who knocked the bottom out a milk basket for a makeshift hoop, who built a go-cart we crashed wheeling down a steep hill.

I could tell him about the old homies, but what I say is, it was great. Lots of friends. Lots of good times.

Upstairs, they've pulled up the carpet in the hall and laid down hardwood. Upstairs, he takes me into the bathroom. The clawfoot tub (it's refinished) that I'd bathe in for school still takes up most of the space, but otherwise the bathroom's revamped: a recessed fan where the old bulb hung, new sink and porcelain toilet. We head into Mom's old room, which is now a shrine of trophies, helmets, mitts, balls, a pair of grubby baseball cleats encased in glass. We roam the rest of the floor and the attic, which ain't an attic no more, him pointing out this and that, calling out types of woods and metals, the names of manufacturers. Did most of the work myself, he says, and please believe you never seen a man more proud.

There's piano music playing when we get downstairs. It lures both of us into the same nook where Mama Liza would lie on a couch and demand I tweeze stubborn hairs out her chin, where us kids were forced into torturous hours of song, prayer, and Bible verse recitation. The wife fingers a piano that looks like our old one. She asks if we had one when we lived in the house, tells me it was left inside when they bought it.

We did, I say.

Then we owe you thanks, she says. Thank you.

They walk me out together. We hope this was all you hoped it would be, he says. They stand on the porch and watch me leave.

For Mom and my bros, for my girl, for Uncle Sip, for my aunt if ever she needs, even a room or two for my cousins who never reside too far from grief, if I can buy this, *when* I reclaim what by ethic is ours, there will be rooms for the whole battered bunch of us. The owners, yes, they were cool, but they must be told—it takes more than hardwood floors and paint, more than tile and granite, more than a new keyed key; they must know it takes more than a deed and mortgage for a house to become your home.

What you got, some big old plan?
                    —Grace

THERE AIN'T A MERCIFUL BONE in his body, the way
he struts in my job full of himself and some. The way he tarries
inside the door looking around, the way he finds a free space for
his bigger, swollen self, and, till the front counter clears, plays as
if fixing his shirt is what matters most in the world.

Afternoon, Grace, he says, strolling up.

Most of the years we were together, Kenny wore Jheri curls,
wore velour tracksuits and tenny shoes, but this newfangled
Kenny wears a low fade, tailored suit, and glasses never sold as
two-for-one.

Good afternoon, I say. What's up?

How you been? he says.

Blessed, I say.

So this, he says, it what they call blessed.

That a joke? I say.

Came to rap to you a second, he says. Can we? Won't be but a
hot second. I promise.

I ask my coworker to watch my till, find an empty booth. You
can see that he's losing his hair. So when you start wearing glasses?
I say.

It's been a minute, he says. But only to work. When I need whitey to take me serious. He takes off his frames and blows on the lenses. So here's the deal, he says. Christmas, me and Helen taking the boys to Hawaii.

He sweeps straw scraps and shredded cheese off the table.

Taking them for Christmas? I say. You asking or telling?

Which? he says. Would you prefer?

What, you got some big old plan? You taking them to see your brother?

Both, he says.

Taking my boys to see a man who still call himself a pimp? I say.

He's a preacher now, Kenny says. Ordained and all. Matter-fact, he's doing the ceremony.

Ceremony? I say.

Yes, wedding, Kenny says. His smile is steel. A brotha held out as long as he could, he says. Anyhow, thought I'd give you a heads-up in case you want to do something with the boys before we leave.

Once during a trip to Vegas Kenny and me meandered near the end of the strip. We were steps from a chapel with a bright fluorescent-light sign outside. We saw a groom carrying his bride out across the threshold, and I mentioned to him about how beautiful it was. Kenny screwed his face and crossed his arms. That depend on who's doing the seeing, he said, and neither he nor I broached the subject again.

Oh, I say.

You know it ain't like me to show up at person's place of

employment, he says. But I tried your crib a few times and I couldn't reach you. He taps the table a finger at a time, his nails clipped to slivers of clean white.

Been working, I say.

Say, if you don't mind me asking, how much you making here? he says.

Is that important? I say.

Is it important that I know, or is it important how much you make? he asks.

My take-home is less than my old state checks, but I'd never give him the pleasure.

You might've run out ahead of me, I say. But I'll catch up.

Bet you will, he says.

Yes, I will, I say. God provides.

He puts on his glasses and gets up. Figured you say something of the sort, he says. The boys told me you mentioned to them about going to church, which is a good thing for sure, Grace, a real good thing. And you probably right about the Lord providing, he says. He fixes his tie and sweeps his hand over his slacks and shoulders. But I'll tell you this: Fordamnsure I can't speak for no one else, but for me, he says, for me, I ain't cashed check the first from the Father, the Son, nor the Holy Ghost.

There's new construction at the bowling lanes. Long tarps make temporary walls. The whole place fumes wet paint and paint thinner. The boys break up stairs splattered with dried putty and wait on the floor above the lanes, the arcade floor. They sprint for the games while I exchange bills for quarters from a girl with purple hair and piercings in her lip and nose. When I get down to where the boys are, I count them out equal sums. When it's gone, it's gone, I say.

Champ is nowhere to be found.

I find a seat and watch them play. This goes on for games and still no sight of my eldest. I tell the boys to keep an eye out while I head for the restroom to fix—I'm always fixing my face. All I have is my face—my eyes and lips. There's a woman in a stall who isn't smelling womanish, so I take less time than I would. When I walk out Champ calls me from the steps.

Did you forget what time we said? I say.

He taps the face of his watch. You know me, he says. I might be late, but I never miss the show.

We mosey to the games and catch the boys standing toe to toe and woofing at one another, a gauzy light glowing from a screen behind them. Cut it, Champ says, and the boys break apart. Damn, can't take ya'll nowhere.

Champ rents shoes and picks a lane and types our names in the machine: CHAMPion, BROLOSS 1, BROLOSS 2, THE MOMS. He points to the board, asks us if we see it, tell us it's prophetic.

Champ must've watched one too many pro bowling tourneys or else my brother Pat in his day at the lanes. He picks a cobalt-blue ball and you should see his ritual. Before every turn he glances back at us, does a shuffle, twists his cap backwards, strolls to the dots, waits a movie pause, and rolls, leaving his wrist cocked till the ball strikes a pin. He don't bowl many strikes, but he rarely misses a spare, but on the occasion he does he falls to his knees. The boy competes at everything, has done it since he was young.

I asked him why once and he said he'd taken enough losses for his life. Who was I to argue?

He leaves pins on his next frame and I ask if it's the best he can do.

If that's the best you can do, I say, you best pray.

We play out the games Champ bought, Canaan pitching gutter after gutter and KJ leaving half his pins. We play out the games and my strikes and spares won't stop. One strike I do a victory dance and ask Champ for a critique.

Funny, Champ says. Real funny. But a little sunshine don't make a summer.

What the boys don't know is there was a time when summers ran forever, when I bowled every week, a time when weekends Dawn and me would meet and pair off and play. Would roll until they called last game. What the boys don't know is there was a time when I carried my own pink ball, years I bowled not a point below 180.

Champ begs a rematch, but I'm too tired, so he bowls alone, tells me he's aiming at my high game. The boys and I eat chili dogs and chips and drink frigid Cokes. They tease Champ with a chant: Mom's the champ, Champ's not the champ.

This is a charm, but these wins will cost. These wins have cost, and I feel the price in my back and feet. Canaan helps me slip out of my rented shoes and I prop my socked feet in an empty chair and wait for Champ to tire of falling short.

We leave out together, Canaan and KJ—my babies—flitting up ahead and Champ slugging behind me with an honest frown. The garage is bright and empty, a car here, a truck there, the Honda. We stop outside of my car.

That was luck, Champ says. You know that was luck. Next time.

You still salty? I say. Look, if I win, you win, I say. If one wins, we all win. Besides, that was a blast.

Kaboom, he says.

He waits while I find my key, while the boys and I climb in, while I start the engine. I give it gas and it growls.

My son says he's suffered a life's worth of losses, but how many losses have I?

Here's my wish—let the world see me now, a conqueror, high above my sorrows, a flagpole pushed through the pile.

Around these parts, it ain't but three types of men.
 —Champ

DO YOU WANT TO KNOW what kind of guy I am? Do you really want to know what kind of guy I am? I'm the type of dude who takes hellafied relational risks in hopes the fallout (often a result that features acute physical pain) coerces me to some decisive act. Take my girl: She's a good woman, one of the best I've been with (and we know we're not talking no short list neither), but sometimes, no lie, I wish instead of always accusing me, always threatening me, instead of doing that, I wish sometimes that she'd just leave. I mean, how many times does she have to discover a random number or an empty condom wrapper in my pocket, how many times does she have to suffer an acidic message from some scallywag (she breaks my codes like a federal agent!), how many 9/10 true rumors of me banging some chick with an ass that's a small planet does she have to endure before she splits? Not threatens to bounce, but sashays right out of my life for good, those lustrous tresses waving good-bye, so long; have a cursed life. But since it don't, as I said, seem like she's making no definitive plans to break, I revert to my assbackwards tactic of inviting atomic consequence. Only here's the thing, it hasn't worked; matterfact, the most it's done is flame already tense situations—e.g., she won't leave and I can't leave a woman who loves this hard and hurts this true, so I figured I'd go raw a few times in hopes I'd knock her up and she'd stay for good or, postconception, she'd realize I was not the one, visit the clinic, and flee for all time, though all the while, in the deep recesses where my purest sense exists, hoping my little spermatozoa would swim right past the target, cause truth be told, I'm about as ready for fatherhood as any old young punk you see on these streets with his pants hung low and a permanent sneer. In fact, in most of the ways that matter, I might be the paragon, the one who's aborted (admitted wrong word choice here) by logic at the most inopportune times, then left to feel ambivalent about decisions that affect not only my well-being, but somebody else's baseline joy. Real talk, if making tough decisions is part of being a man, then I might wind up a Geritol-popping juvenile, which is fait accompli for guys like me who screw up our lives one lousy judgment at a time.

But wait, the retrograde choices, they just might be in my genes. Case in point, my biological pops. Dude had three babies in less than a year by women who lived on the same block. One year, same block! Who could or would concoct such a tale? My mom was the last of the threesome, claims she didn't know about the others until right after her grand old valedictorian speech (besides birth, the proudest moment of her life), the one she made the night after she found out about tiny fetus me. And talk about timing, this was a few years after the first Supreme Court abortion ruling, a couple years after *Roe v. Wade*, and, and, and, if you add to that my pop's apparent predilection for barebacking, to the assured detriment of Mom's nursing school dream, you can see how I could have easily ended up a coat hanger victim or the refuse of some clinic. To her credit, though, Moms wasn't having it. She traded in plan A for plan B and set about becoming the best single mother she could.

At moments, the best single mother there is.

If we all could be so selfless.

It's cold as an Eskimo's nuts outside, colder, but the weather hasn't thinned the crowd. We (the *we* being me and Kim) check in and luck out on seats beside an über-pregnant woman that's putting a whole lot of pressure on the seams of her long dress. The lady has two tykes with her, neither of them old enough to tie their shoes. Old enough to tear up some shit, though, and they're working at it with toddler flair: tugging things off the tables, pushing the cold button on the water cooler, ripping jagged pages out of pamphlets. On a break from a reign of infant terror, one of them wobbles over by me and yanks at my pants. Are you okay? he says, craning up and flashing a jagged-spaced grin. Yes, I'm okay, I say. Mommy say we get grocery, he says. You take us get grocery? Before I can answer, his mother approaches shouting his name (something multisyllabic a linguist would have a tough time pronouncing) and draws the little man backwards. These boys, she says, and shakes her head. Oh my gosh, my boys.

The infant attraction ain't new. That's always been me, the one who turns colicky babies into cooing machines, who attracts the little ones like the North Pole magnetic pull. My mom said it's cause I got a good soul, that babies can see though your blunders and masks right into the maw of you, but little multisyllable, he must not sense my intentions, the visions I've had of discarding one last life.

A duo manages the front desk, a twosome I'd bet not more than a few years removed from bittersweet sixteen, one of them wearing earrings big as bracelets, the other with a set of flushed cheeks. Kim says she's thirsty and sends me to the cooler. She swigs what I fetch as if dying of thirst. Meantime, my nerves are straight anarchy! How, I say to myself, how, self, did we ever end up here? I ask this knowing full well the answer: Last week she asked what I had planned on this day at this time, knowing good and motherfuckin well I don't plan much of nothing outside of school, then said, Well, since you're not busy, why don't you come to the appointment? She granted me all of a nanosecond to grab a wispy excuse (I didn't) before ambushing me with one of those two-part gold medal questions only a half-wit botches: Don't you care about me? Are you concerned with our baby?

And let it be known for the lifetime ledgers, I may be a whole bunch of things, but believemewhenItellyou, a superfool ain't one of them!

Well, not always. Well, not then, at least.

Still, a baby don't calibrate with me, not now, and maybe not ever, which is why these last few weeks I've been wrecked, one of those freeway accidents it makes you shiver just to see, which is why I've spent whole days consumed with finding just the right thing to say, just the right time to say it.

Let's talk

Speak.

Are you sure?

No, I'm not.

Then we should wait, babe.

You think so?

No, I know so. Timing.

As I said, Mom's a Mother Teresa type, magnanimous as they come, but me benevolent? In a world remade to my selfish specs, just that easy, Kim would concede, lay her aquiline cheek against my chest, and have a different kind of appointment by day's end. But who am I supposed to be fooling? This is the first time *ever* she asked me to attend a visit, the first time *ever* that appointment wasn't at a clinic besieged by around-the-clock picketing, the first time *ever* we've treaded anywhere near a second trimester.

Translation: These are desperate days.

Urgent days indeed.

I don't know how it is where you're from, but around here, the words *planned pregnancy* might as well be some kind of next millennium Martian language. Around these parts, it ain't but three types of men:

Dudes who didn't want to be fathers and made convincing cases otherwise.

Dudes who didn't want to be fathers and got bulldogged into becoming them anyhow.

Dudes who didn't want to be fathers and pulled Copperfield-ish escapes before or right after their baby's birth.

A nurse steps half in, half out of the lobby and calls a name. The pregnant woman labors out of her seat and totters with her charges trailing her. I watch the new foursome disappear.

Look at that. That can't be me, Kim says. I would never do this alone.

How do you know she's alone? I say. Could be the dad couldn't make it. Stayed in the car. This place ain't exactly male-friendly.

You see a ring? she says. Where was the ring?

One has to know when is when and when is now, so not another word from me. Instead, I grab a magazine. The cover girl is a pregnant girl wearing a bikini. She's posed with an arm above her belly and another near her navel and her smile's a normal smile on narcotics. This is the kind of picture that misleads, that makes pregnancy seem like one glorious journey for all parties involved. I peek up from the cover and see another couple enter, the man carrying a detached car seat, AKA a walking, toting sign.

As if I need one.

Every week she announces what's new: He's got a brain and spinal cord; by now he's got hands and webbed feet; he's not an embryo anymore, he's a fetus. Updates I'm guessing are meant to beguile, but instead keep me awake late nights, staring at the swell of her belly, the broadening of her dark areolas, that, many-a-night, have shot me out of bed in sweats, my heart sailing like a souped-up metronome.

Right, my silly ass should've seen this coming.

Right, my silly ass didn't see this coming. After she'd broke it off with her ex, after she and I began claiming one another (I shouldn't have to tell you what a big step that was!), she duped me with that line of questioning that has sent many a believes-he's-keen young skirt-chaser hightailing for an exit. We were at the open-air hot tub spot where I'd taken a few prime prospects, drinking white wine from smuggled plastic cups.

Are you the type of man to leave after the chase? Is this all about a challenge? she said.

No, not at all, I said. I really like you.

You do? she said. How long does that last?

Saecula saeculorum, I said.

What's that? she said.

Forever and ever, I said. To the ages of ages.

And peoples, let's admit that line sounded real slick, ultra-suave

if I do say so myself, which I do. And where I'm from, the suavest shit you ever said to a chick is a superhero's superpower.

Kim rummages in her purse and I scan the office playing the
game where I imagine lives for absolute strangers. The guy in
the mesh hat was a high school football star stiff-arming his way
to the NFL till word leaked of test scores even a D-1 coach
wouldn't fix. Now homie hangs drywall to pay the rent and
scrimps all year for fishing trips. The chick in the corner answers
phones at a downtown dentist office, drives a minivan, cooks her
husband two unappreciated meals a day, and sends him to work
with a slapdash sack lunch and, every season or so, a shot of
half-ass head! The female by the cooler is a former coed who
volunteers at shelters and spends her weekends rock climbing,
kayaking, hiking the Cascades.

I'm just about to dive on someone else when another nurse
pushes through the door and calls Kim. We follow the nurse to a
scale in the hall and afterwards to an empty waiting room, where
Kim climbs on the table and kicks the shoes off her swollen feet.

Have you started prenatals? she says.

Yes, Kim says.

Great, she says. Concerned today about anything especially?

No, not that I can think of, Kim says.

The nurse checks the rest of her vitals, marks them in her
chart, and sets the chart on the counter. She fishes a gown from
a top drawer and tells us the doctor will be right in. Kim strips,
folds her pants and top, and gives the neat stack to me. She turns
in the mirror in her bra and panties and it reminds me of the cover
girl. Before this, seeing my girl in any degree of naked would

excite me to off-the-Mohs-chart stiffness, but today she inspires not even a tingle. She puts on her gown, unhooks her bra, slips out of her panties, and I'llbedamned still nothing.

Why are you so quiet? she says.

There a law against quiet? I say.

You aren't any other time, she says. Why now?

Let's not do this here, I say. Not now.

You almost don't hear the doctor come in. The doc's got silver hair above floppy ears but most noticeable is that he's huge. I'm talking retired-hooper-big, alien hands and feet.

How's my favorite patient? he says.

Hey, Doc, she says. I'm great.

And you must be Shawn, he says. I've heard good things. Good, good things. Doc seems intent on turning my fingers to mush, waits waaaaaay too long to let me loose. He stoops to tie a faded off-brand running shoe, and a thatch of surly chest hair sprouts from the V of his V-neck. He picks up the chart and reads. Okay, okay, okay. All is well, he says. You're a few pounds off weightwise, but no worry.

So, Shawn, he says. How're the studies?

Good, I say. Pretty good, I guess.

Looking forward to the Christmas break? he says. You two have any plans for the holidays?

Just dinner, I say.

Nice, he says. I love holiday meals. So, Kim tells me you finish this year. Have you decided on a grad school yet?

Not yet, I say. Not sure about grad school.

He gazes at me through what must be the clearest Aryan blue eyes in the hemisphere. You should make that a surety, he says.

You know a bachelor's is just the start these days. Besides, this new life will need an example. Gorgeous girlfriend, new baby, you are one lucky young man, my friend. He stuffs his hands (it's miraculous they fit) into a pair of rubber gloves. Enough about school, he says. Let's have a look at that uterus. He turns his head and slips under her gown. Ahh, this feels like ten weeks, he says. Feels like eleven weeks, he says. Maybe twelve.

Sixteen weeks, state law, twenty-four if there's a grave risk to the mother. This kind of info is everywhere in those cheerless clinics. We last visited one not enough months ago. I dropped off Kim, gave her a knot of fifties, and, with a tornado whipping my guts into a FEMA site, waited some safe blocks away. They called for pickup, and I drove to the clinic's back lot, where a frowning woman wheeled Kim down a ramp and helped me load her into the car. Kim grabbed my arm before we left. That's it, she said. That's it and I mean it. No more.

Doc snaps off his gloves, trashes them, marks notes. Well, we're far enough along, he says. How'd you two like to hear the heart-beat? Kim, of course, says we'd love to, and while the doctor is gone, she puts on her pants and inspects herself in the mirror. She catches me gazing. In truth it is half at her and half at what could be the rest of our days.

Please tell me why you don't seem excited, she says.

You're excited enough for us both, I say. But I don't know.

Don't know what? she says.

About this, I say.

You are *not* sayin what I think you're sayin, she says.

Life has options is what they preached in my old youth program, but to keep it all the way funky, options are forevermore my trick knee.

But like I said in so many words, maybe my affliction's a product of genes, biology.

Dude was a magician, my biological pops, showed up when Moms was in labor but when it came time to sign the birth certificate: POOF! For the better half of my life the nigger was a hocus-pocus Harry Houdini. But check it, don't throw me no pity parade, nor chasten Pops too tough. There's no doubt at all a third baby in less than a year was not, if dude had any, part of his plans; plus, with the efficacies of Big Ken, there's a chance things worked out fine, finer, the finest.

The silence is an overripe piece of fruit between us yearning to be split wide. Let's talk, I should say, gash the gushy quiet right down the center and seize this fleet-footed moment before it puts on track shoes and sprints off.

They've told me for most of my life that my life is optionful, but what they should've said was this: You've got a choice, youngin, till you don't.

Doc tugs in the Doppler (it's a machine resembling an oversized CB), and tells Kim to lie down. He spreads gel over her taut belly and circles it with a wand. He turns a knob and the room fills with a *swoosh-swoosh, swoosh-swoosh.*

Now, there's a healthy heart, he says.

We listen. The light in her face says it's an all-around charm for her. It's a charm for me as well (how could it not be, this living being that we made?) but also a dread.

Doc kills the Doppler, scrawls more notes, tucks Kim's file under his arm. You be sure and take good care of her, he says. You be sure and take great care of her.

No hype, there might be a curse in how hard he slaps my back.

My girl sits up, yearns her head at me. Her eyes could spark flames.

Say it, she says. Go ahead and say it.

There are options. There are choices. There are chances. There are last chances. There is the last chance of the last chances—the end.

Outside, a hall scale clanks, a baby wails, someone calls a name.

Look, I'd like to believe that about mines, about the one who'd burst squalling and splashing into the world, that we (me and you, you and I) could bet breath, that I'd be no spine-chilling or mind-bending nothing, no part voila or poof, not one scintilla of abracadabra alakazam.

Or would I be?

Or would we all?

Can I ask a question?
—Grace

SOME PEOPLE ARE LATECOMERS to themselves, but who we are will soon enough surround us.

Kim stands back. She's wearing pajamas and an apron over them that reads CHEF. STAND BACK. She wishes me a merry Christmas and helps me with my bags—the gifts and desserts. Soon as my hands are free, I hike for the bathroom, where I run the sink till the water steams and run my hands in the hot stream and rub my hands on my face to unthaw. When I come out, she's laid my desserts on the counter. She stands by the stove with a rolled bundle under her arm. She snaps it open, shows off an apron that says NUMBER ONE CHEF.

How about that? I say.

I've been making holiday dinners since Mom was alive, and I wonder when was Kim's first dinner, how much she knows about these kinds of meals.

I should get to it, I say. Or we'll be eating at midnight.

Don't you need help? she says. I was hoping I could help, she says.

Later, I say. I do my best work alone.

Don't mean to exclude but what could she know about the frying or baking or broiling, what it means to season with heart? Go ahead and rest while I get things going, I say. She skulks into the front room and sprawls on the couch and powers the TV—the screen's so big the actors are life-sized!—and raises the volume to a level that might peeve the neighbors. Champ lazes in a commercial or so later wearing long johns with his hands dug in his crotch. He stoops by Kim and whispers in her ear and she sits up and shakes her head. He calls me into the room and I take seasonings out of the cupboard and follow him. He mutes the TV and throws his eyes, those big innocent eyes, from me to Kim, from Kim to me. Kim has something she wants to tell you, he says. We have something we'd like to tell you, he says. He pushes Kim closer and takes my hand and lays it on her stomach. Feel, he says. Can you feel it?

Her stomach is firm and swollen.

I drop on the couch and shake my head.

This is a blessing, I say. Such a blessing. How far are you along?

Sixteen weeks, Champ says.

Amazing, I say. Your first child. My first grandchild.

One look at them together and you can see into their trials. How tough it will be to hold a baby above all else. But they will have me. This is another shot for me.

I get up and go into the kitchen and Champ follows. He stands behind me, his chin on my shoulder, while I prep. Mmmm, can't wait, he says. He turns me around and pecks me under an eye. He grabs milk from the fridge and gulps and puts it right back on the shelf—a sin in my home. He smirks, a little rim of white over his lip. Yeah, I know, I know, he says, wiping the white with his shirt. But I'm grown, he says. Overgrown.

So grown you lost your manners, I say. I sure hope that isn't what you teach your own child. That's not what I taught you.

Geesh, so serious, he says. He does a shuffle. It's the dance he'd do when he was young and wanted something I couldn't afford. Before there was little I could afford. Before he stopped asking me for anything at all.

Boy, stop, I say. It won't work.

It's Christmas, Mom, cut me some slack. And a little time too, he says. I need to let some water run on this overnight funk. Let me shower and dress and it's Chef Champ at your beckon.

This is a joke. He has to know he's no help whatsoever in the kitchen. It's a miracle that he and she don't eat out evermore or starve. His brothers have been cooking full meals for years, but Champ might burn down a house, though you can't blame anybody but me. Frying a burger or boiling wieners is about all I ever tried to teach him, which almost doesn't count since I never let him practice. He'd amble into my room at all hours— mashing a fist in his eye and complaining he was starved. Whenever he did, I'd stir and fix him a snack or meal or whatever he thought he wanted—a response, God knows, that never once felt wrong.

A firstborn could be the most we'll ever see of bliss.

The food cooks, and I stroll into the living room. The tree's decked in gold and silver, and presents that match the color scheme. This sure is a beautiful tree, I say. You think you guys bought enough gifts? I lift a box tagged for KJ and feel its bulk— pounds of it.

You know your son, Kim says. Too much isn't enough.

There was a time when Thanksgivings Champ would produce a Christmas list with his gifts ranked. He'd give me the list and ply me with the sweetest gapped smile and I'd appease him with the promise that I'd do what I could. Every year for years too, that's what I did. Why wouldn't I? He kept A's in school, never got time-outs or notes home or suspensions, not to mention in those days Kenny was paying most of the bills. If ever there was a time, that was the era when the world felt abundant. When I felt big in the world.

Champ lazes out and we open gifts. You should have seen me last night wrapping and rewrapping what I bought, fussing over the tape and folds. Kim opens hers first, detaching the bow with care, pulling the tape gentle. Not the fancy you're used to, I say. But it's the best I could do on a budget. She pulls out the pants and rubs the cotton against her cheek and tells me they're so soft and kisses me on the cheek. Thank you, thank you. I love them, she says.

Champ don't go at his gifts like he used to; he used to shake the box and guess and guess what it was, but now he peels the tape back slow and lifts his gift into view—a Bible. He touches the gold-painted finger tabs and fans the pages. Oooooh, good-lookin, he says. The Good Book. Been looking high and low for a new one, but my fair luck, they been sold out since Black Friday.

Funny, I say. But I was hoping you'd think it was thoughtful.

Sheesh, Mom, he says. Where's our sense of humor? Thank you. Thank you so much for the gift.

You're welcome, I say, and ask him if he remembers our Christmas Eve plays, how he used to whine and pout the years he wasn't cast as Jesus.

Sure do, he says. Jesus of Nazareth, that was me. But now I know for sure that paying for the next man's sins ain't the shot.

There's snow left from last week's storm and winter's glow is a presence among us. Champ hands me a long box topped with a yellow bow and I strip the wrapping as if I might reuse it—waste not, want not—and uncover a three-quarter-length lamb's-wool coat, dead-on the one I've been eyeing for months.

Only the best for me and mines, he says. He leans back, full of himself, a munificent smile. You shouldn't have, I say, and trace the arms and the shoulders and around the collar. He helps me try it on, tells me to go into the room and check it out in the full-length mirror. I flit in his room and check myself in the mirrored closet doors, turning one way and then the other and flipping the collar and fingering the buttons, having my moment.

He or she has left one side of the closet half closed and you can see an open safe on the floor among boxes. Easy, I slide the door to get a better look inside, see stacks and stacks of bills—not sure how much, but I'd guess more than I ever made in a year of work—see gold jewelry, see what could be hard dope wrapped in plastic. Of all what I see the drugs are what shoot the air right out of me, and all the light.

I am new.
I am good.
I am strong.
I am powerless over people.
I am powerless over my children.

I drag out working to fix my face.

So what's the full-length verdict? Champ says.

Can I ask a question? I say. How much did you pay for this?

Mom, it's a Christmas gift. A gift. Asking about price is bad etiquette.

Champ, how much?

It's a gift, he says. He makes a face he made as a boy. And I'd give the world for him to be that boy again, without ever worrying when I might come home, whether or not I'm safe, where I've been, without ever the wonder of why I'm not myself.

Okay, I say. You're right. It's Christmas. I'll let it go for now. Let's enjoy.

Later, Champ sets the table and Kim serves the drinks and I bring out the food, the turkey and dressing, the candied yams, the macaroni and cheese, the collard greens, the roast, the deviled eggs—a feast to last for days. He carves the turkey and says grace as well. We eat with the TV showing sports. They don't have much to say and I have less to say than that. It takes much too much strength to fight what I see. My son on a corner, his pockets swollen with a sack of shards, or him holed in a dank house. You wonder if he treats them as the worst of them do. How could he let me see it when I told him not to let me see it; now how can I ever see past it? Canaan and KJ call after dinner and wish us all aloha. I leave with unopened gifts under the tree.

New Years, the morning of my first day off in forever, and this return is a resolution. I lug a Hefty bag laden with all Champ has bought me these last months into the building: the coat, the clothes, the clock, everything. He answers wearing a wrinkled V-neck T-shirt and tuxedo pants, a gold chain lying over his shirt, bright diamonds in his ear. I drop the bag by his feet and by his eyes he can't believe it.

What's this? he says.

It's yours, I say. I can't.

Can't do what? he says.

I told you not to let me see, I say. You should've kept it from me.

See what? he says.

Too much, I say. It was all there. I saw it all.

What time is it? he says. It's too early for this. Come inside.

No, I say. I take the car keys out of my pocket and drop them on the bag.

Oh boy, he says. Ooooh boy. That Bible got you tripping like this? What the Bible teach us but how to suffer? he says. That's what you want for us? Suffering?

Son, we can get away from *Him*, I say. But no one gets so far they can't get back. I leave, track the line of lambent bulbs to the stairs. There's a cold that belongs outside, belongs out of this world, in the lobby and through the lobby glass there's the Honda, parked by the curb, its wheels flecked with dirt. I totter outside and into the street and face the building and search the windows, and there's my son gazing at me with his arms crossed and a face I can't make out. I turn away from him and close my coat, this nothing coat, and march off against a treacherous wind.

You hate to think it, hate to say it.
                —Champ

LAST SCHOOL YEAR me and Big Ken were the emergency
contacts. What that meant was, the times they couldn't reach
Big Ken or when they could but he couldn't get away from work,
they called me. They called me more than once too. Baby bro
stayed in some elementary school strife: backtalking the teacher,
scuffling in the lunch line, forging notes home, was in the office
so much the little nigger damn near had a reserved seat in detention. The last time they called they were vague about the transgression, but were clear it was grave, that he had to be picked
up ASAP. I got the call while I was on campus between classes. I
blew my next class and drove the fast lane most of the way to his
school. When I got in the office, the school's hawk-beaked secretary thrust a stack of carbon copies in my face. Meanwhile, I
glimpsed the principal (he and I had had words) in his office
nursing a vainglorious-ass smirk. The secretary had security take
me down (as if I needed directions) to the detention room,
where my bro was stooped over a lefty desk with his faced
smashed in his arms. I caught him by his collar and, with the
security (a fossilized waif who couldn't make an infant follow
rules) stalking us, I drug him out of the school. It felt like there
was a set of eyes pressed against every single window, watching

me shove Canaan into the car and slam the door, watching me storm around and seethe at him through my windshield. Me huffing and groping for slick calm. Don't ask me why I was so hot without the details. Could've been the way the principal looked at me or the latent grudge over it being me once again attending the issue instead of Big Ken, instead of Mom, who was still in her program; don't ask me why, but that day I had a mind to fire on baby bro right there in the bright broad light of the lot. Lucky for him the watchful gaze of a building of witnesses made me think twice. I took out Canaan's paper and read the script:

Canaan Thomas, a student with a history of behavioral problems, was involved in an altercation with Mr. Glisan. Mr. Glisan ordered Thomas to run lines for dressing down late for class and Thomas refused. Mr. Glisan then asked Thomas to leave the gym, at which point Thomas cursed Mr. Glisan in front of the class. Mr. Glisan requested once more that Thomas leave the gym and report to the principal's office at once. Thomas responded by tossing a ball in the stands and threatening to bring a firearm to school to shoot Mr. Glisan. School security was alerted and Thomas was escorted to the main office. Thomas is hereby suspended from school pending a hearing for expulsion.

What to do??? Read it once. Read it twice, then asked him, with fist and heart open, for his side of the story. He said he showed up a couple minutes late for class, and in front of the whole team the coach fired a ball at him and said to run suicides. He (my granitehead bro) tracked the ball and kicked it to the other end of the gym (this was a bad move, of course, but as it turns out the lil homie was locomotive) and told the teacher what he could do with his suicides. He claimed that day that the teacher called him a loser and a waste and only then did he curse (another dandy move but youngster was caught, bad breaks to boot, on that steep, steep slope of flawed judgment) and say he'd get his older brother (me) to come the next day and whoop the teacher's ass. This was what made the teacher call security, not, as baby bro alleged that day (his eyes leaking Oregon raindrops) because he threatened to bring a pistol to school.

Man, they got you in the system now, I said. Satisfied?

For the record, my peoples, yes I know it could have been a snafu picking a side. But who gives a rat's ass whose story I believed? The end game was this: my baby brother won't be back in "regular" school (oh, the shit we forsake) for at least a year if ever at all.

At Canaan's new school (an alternative school housed among a bunch of warehouses) the office, or what I'm guessing is the office, is empty, desolate, so I stride down the hall and peek inside the first open door and introduce myself to a lady sitting behind a messy desk. She greets me all cherry-like, and I tell her why I came. She knows Canaan, his grade, his class, and offers to walk me over.

Canaan's class is in another building, and from the office to his class you can see the shabby warehouses, forklifts, bereft wooden pallets. Up ahead a semi pulls onto the lot, its engine making the sound of tools knocking, and muscles towards a garage where men in grimy jeans and hooded jackets wait in the cold. My escort stops and rubs her shoulders and points to the building. It's really awesome you came, she says, her nose and ears chilled soft red. She strides off hugging herself.

Dinged lockers, a lone lefty desk tagged with *Fizzuck Mizz. H*, a dented trash can, that's what I see inside. The classroom door is closed, but you can see the teacher (I'm guessing she's Ms. H) through a window cut in the door. She's standing by a portable chalkboard dressed in slacks and a blouse. She points to the word DREAM written in giant letters on the board. I crack the door and wave and she smiles and waves, and I stroll in searching for baby bro in the seats. He's posted in a row nearest the back and sinks in his desk when I look at him. This classroom is all these classrooms. There's a hand-drawn box on the board with a name in it, a wall of maps showing countries these youngsters, like it was for me and my patnas, got a 0.01 percent chance of seeing as nonsoldiers, a laminated poster of the classroom rules. Ms. H announces me to the class, all boys, and warns them on their best behavior.

What, he posed to be babysittin or somethin? says a youngster with level-five acne. Ms. H tells him to show me respect and the little peon balls a sheet and shoots it well short of the closest trash can.

She asks me if there's anything I'd like to say.

What pops in my head is the story of old classmates, a pair of fine young gentlemen who had a dope spot near my high school. Every day they'd slouch in a desk by the window and eagle-eye the shit out of their spot, and each day whenever either of them saw a potential lick, they'd blast out their seats and scramble out the class and out of school in competition. They both (go figure) ended up in alternative school and I lost track, but no sooner than I'd waltzed offstage in my grad cap and gown, I heard they got rocked with state racketeering charges. Their fates beyond that? Gent A got bludgeoned to death with a bat in a state prison, and Gent B, well, let's just say that by the time he sees the free world again, we'll be booking weekend trips to the moon.

That's the story that pops in my head, but what comes out my mouth is this: Hey, guys. I'm happy to be here. But we can pretend I'm not. That I'm a ghost.

This, of course, goes for everybody but my baby bro. I pick the desk right behind him and he twists around. I give him the you-best-not-embarrass-me-or-I'll-fuck-your-young-ass-up look and he slumps lower than even I thought he could. Ms. H waits until I'm settled, then writes REM on the board. When we dream, our brain all but paralyzes us, she says. That's what happens to us physiologically.

Physio-what?

Physiologically, John, she says. That means what happens inside our bodies.

Ms. H asks them to take out a sheet of paper and write down their last dream. Most of the class cracks open a notebook, all but the acne-struck youngster who says he don't do no dreaming. Not only does he participate zilch, he balls up another sheet and tosses it haphazard. John, do you need a break, do you need to take a trip to the office? she says.

Nah, he says. Do you?

You hate to think it, hate to say it, but there's a kid like him in most every class (well, the ones I was in), a rogue-in-training who's at worst beyond rescue. Ms. H tours the desks and lets them write till they slap their pens on top of their sheets. She walks to the board and ask for volunteers.

One of the boys in the front shoots up his hand.

Go ahead, Juan, she says.

Okay. I had dream something chase me, he says. But I no see

who chase. The chaser get loud and faster. And I kept run and run right off edge. Then I run in air and fall same time. I no hit ground, but I no stop fall either.

The tiny black interlude (you know I know about those) where don't nobody right off say a word.

Thank you, Juan, for sharing, she says.

You won't catch me calling myself a scholar, but I've cracked a book or two, one of which was the text for my Intro to Psychology class. (Don't those psych electives look lovely when you're working with your counselor on degree plans?) The psych professor was heavy into your boy Carl Jung. Jung, who was Freud's patna, believed dreams are the way we acquaint with our unconscious, the way we try and solve the problems of our waking hours, and you can bet the theory would've been even more accepted if Jung wasn't a German, if he was not, per the historians, a Jew-hating, self-aggrandizing, cock-chasing German. But, (alleged) Reich research, top-flight narcissism, and Aryan ass pursuits aside, home-boy's theories are nottobefuckedwith! For proof I submit exhibit A: Jung's seven dream archetypes: *persona, shadow, anima/animus, divine child, wise old man, great mother,* and of course the *trickster.*

Why oh why, Ms. H calls on young Scarface and he reminds her he don't dream.

But everyone dreams, she says.

He scratches on a sheet, slams his pencil down, and swivels to glare at the class. Well, I ain't everybody, he says.

Ms. H takes off her glasses and rubs the bridge of her nose and puts them back on and simpers. She marks a check by his name on the board.

She picks more boys to share, calls on Canaan last. My brother works a stash of transparent stall tactics. He ends up telling us about this dream he's been having where he's hooping in the coliseum. He says at the end of the dream they pass him the ball with seconds left on the clock, pass him the ball while KJ, Mom, and me cheer from courtside seats. The worst part, my brother explains, is not that he misses the last shot, but that he dribbles out the clock and never takes the shot to miss. Everybody boos, he says. Mom. My brothers. The crowd.

At lunchtime, Ms. H. escorts us to the teachers' lounge. There's a male teacher sprawled on a couch napping, another washing a Tupperwared meal back with a massive bottled juice, another plucking drenched red onions from a salad. Ms. H says for us to sit where we like and takes her sack lunch down to a seat beside the picky herbivore. Canaan rustles through his brown bag for a sandwich, takes it apart, and checks the joint as if he's never seen roast beef. For me lunch is a vending machine special: chips and a cold pop.

So talk, I say. Spill it.

About what? he says.

How you like it here? I say. How you're getting along.

I don't, he says.

Good, I say. This ain't no place to like.

Then why'd you come? he says.

Why you think? I say.

Noone else do, he says.

Now look, I say. At how smart you've become.

Ms. H finishes her lunch and leaves. The napping teacher wakes and hunts the faculty fridge for a plastic-wrapped plate. Others wander in and out with supplies, spoons, paper plates, plastic cups, water from the cooler, coffee. Baby bro and me watch the weak action and eat, no words.

Ms. H gives a lesson on prefixes, suffixes, and root words. She asks if I'd like to help and I stroll between the desks checking sheets. Every third boy is struggling, makes you wonder what made them "alternative" picks, if all their hellified delinquency is no more and maybe less than a thin cloak for some innominate at-risk-low-income-single-parent syndrome.

Ms. H grants free computer time for the boys who've made it thus far without their names on the board in the box of shame/pride. Towards the end of class, for everybody else, that everybody being miraculously or predictably Canaan and the quietest boy in the room, Ms. H offers two options: silent reading or cleanup duty. Pow! Just like that, you never seen a group of hard-heads more eager to tidy and sweep. She assigns them to keep a dream journal for a week, then asks if I have any parting words. What pops in my head this time is the premise of one of my favorite books, a nonfiction joint from my I've-taken-too-many-black-studies-classes-and-ended-up-a-green-militant era. The book's called *Brothers and Keepers*, and tells the story of two bio-logical brothers raised in the same house who end up with fates stark miles apart: one a famous writer with a grand professorship and the other a former dope addict doing life in prison. I tell the boys about the book and end with the question for all the ox-blood marbles: The question isn't which brother's life would you rather live. That's easy, right, fellas? The question is how do you avoid becoming the other?

Ms. H forces a smatter of mumble-mouth thank-you's. The

boys grab their bags and coats and bolt, all but Canaan, who I tell to wait outside.

Then it's just she and I in the room alone.

That book sounds interesting, she says.

Oh, it is, I say.

Shawn, I really appreciate you coming, she says, and orders a stack of papers. These boys need more of this. Need someone who takes an interest. Who can model what it means to be a student.

They do, I say. But I don't know if I'm the guy.

She puts on her coat.

That brother of yours, he's just the sweetest, she says. He doesn't belong here.

You think not? I say.

Oh, I know so, she says. I've seen the ones that do, and he's not them. What he needs is an outlet. A person he trusts that he can talk with, who'll listen when he speaks.

I'm with you on that, I say. But he keeps so much to himself.

She scoops an armload of files and books and papers. He thinks the world of you, Shawn. All of it.

I'm fine, I say. Let me go.
                —Grace

IT'S FRIDAY NIGHT, a payday. I'm waiting at Check Mart, my uniform reeking of ground beef, worrying over how I'll pay my fees and fines, my bus pass, my woman products, and groceries with yet another anemic check. All day, I've been back and forth, back and forth, about whether to call Champ. Whether to tell him giving it all back was mistake, that I need him after all.

Up ahead a stumpy Mexican is giving a cashier the Spanglish blues.

ID, sir, I need to see your ID, she says.

Que? he says.

ID, sir, she says. I-den-ti-fi-ca-tion.

Yo no tengo. Pero, necesito mi money, he says.

No ID, no check cashed, sir, she says.

The fine print of the Western Union poster that's pinned to the back wall, that's what I'm reading when Michael, yes, Michael pushes inside with a girl my first mind tells me has a suicide soul. She and he and what comes to mind is not tonight. I turn my back and spy them in the mirror, see him fix his shirt and tie his shoe and whisper to her. See her cover her mouth and titter. I scrounge my bag for coins and rub them together. Emergency change.

The Mexican gestures and grouses while the cashier looks on through bulletproof glass all tagged with rates and policies and wanted posters. Next, next, she says, and the Mexican grabs his check and stomps out the door cursing in English.

I slug up to the glass feeling every second of this week's shifts in my legs and feet. The least they could do if they gone keep sneaking across the border is learn the damn language, she says. Up close the cashier has a soft chin and the cheeks of a baby. She slides my check through a scanner and asks for ID. The scanner lights green and spits out the check. She asks me how I'd like my money and I tell her, Big bills, please. She drops the coins on top and shoves all I have in the world—it wouldn't pay rent— through the slot under the glass. Thank you, I say, stuffing the cash in my bra. He and I catch eyes. He motions for me to stop. Be blessed, I say, and flit by as fast as I can.

The last time I saw him was at a meeting. He moseyed in scruffy, in an overstarched shirt, jaws working triple-chew on a wad of gum, and plopped in a seat a row ahead of mine. Should've seen him for the first half of the meeting—reciting the prayers and traditions, clapping for testimonies; he even dropped in dollars when the basket came around.

The break came, and I ventured into the lobby, found a seat out of the way, took out my pocket Bible, and turned to Revelations: the verse where John describes the throne of God. I peeked up from my book, and saw Michael swanking over with his arms raised into a white flag.

Good day, he said. I come in peace.

Not to worry, I said, marked my place, and asked him why he was at the meeting.

Damn good question, he said. Heard this was the group of groups. Thought I'd stop through, see for myself.

Well, welcome, I said.

He pointed to my Bible and asked if I was back in church.

Why? I said. That a problem?

Oh, not a problem at all, he said. The problems is what hit us between groups, Bible study, and church.

Just then my sponsor—she'd been clean for an age and counseled in a group home—came out the meeting room. I called her over to us.

Hi, Grace, she said.

Hey, Judy, I said.

How's the journey? she said

Just fine, I said. Called you over so you can meet my old friend. This is Michael. He used to be a trigger. Seems he'd like to be a trigger. But he isn't anything anymore. Isn't that right? I said.

Michael jerked his head and smashed his eyes to slits. Wow, MCA like that? he said.

Like that! I said.

Then I should leave you be, he said, and slunk off while Judy stood by.

Outside the Check Mart there're ominous clouds and the promise of rain. I can smell it, feel the mist against my face, hear it whispering, What we gone do now? Do it and do it quick. I strike off, turning on a side street, the first of shortcuts to my apartment. I cut though an alley and hear a car pull in behind me, its engine rumbling. MCA, MCA, thought that was you. Damn, I see we just gone keep bumpin into each other, he says. Where you headed?

Home, I say.

Where that at? he says. His partner—the girl—cranes in her seat to see me. She's not much more than a set of eyes in the cabin.

Close enough, I say.

I got you, he says.

No, thanks, I say, and feel the first light drops on my head, feel it touch other places where my skin is bare.

C'mon, now. I can't let you get caught out in this, he says. It's fixta pour. He sticks his arm out the window. Can't you tell?

I'm fine, I say. Let me go.

Go where? he says. Go how, walkin? Come on and get in before it comes down.

I say his name weak, a protest he couldn't believe.

Michael stops the car and hops out. He sprints ahead and stands in my path. The drizzle frosts his afro. Oh, you must be waterproof, he says. A Z of lightning gashes the sky; thunder reaches inside me. The rain falls slanted and snarling, turns my clothes into soggy mass. See! What I tell you? he says. He stalks me to where the alley lets out, his feet slapping in fresh puddles, the both of us getting farther and farther from his lights. Streaks of grease fall into my eyes. And here comes the feeling that my whole life has come to this.

Help is a call away.
I help others by asking for help.
I am not alone.
Faith without works is dead.

Michael touches me as though he cares. It's his touch from once a life ago. We were at the end of a binge, in an empty attic smoking resin. He unzipped my pants and I let him. Said not a word while he thrashed inside me either. He finished and wiped himself on his shirt. You and I could be something, he said. The two of us is linked.

That night is all reason I need to say no. Every reason to say yes. Reasons to hope against what I know: That it isn't in him to be someone else. That the best for him is becoming more of who he is. All right, I say. But take me straight there. I really just need to get home.

We rush to his car while the rain thumps trash cans and metal awnings and parked cars. The girl hands me and Michael napkins. He dabs his face and asks where I'm headed.

Piedmonts, I say.

Well I'll be gotdamned, he says, eyeing me in the rearview. Got you right there in the hurricane, huh?

He shifts the car and we stall and pitch forward. Check this out, he says. We got to make one stop. Just one stop is all, but it's on the way.

What happens?
—Champ

PEOPLES, PEOPLES, have you been wondering how I got in this shit in earnest?

How it starts is this: I'm a freshman in a polytech high school and homecoming is coming soon, too soon cause Mom's been out for days doing what I know she does plus a whole bunch of shit I don't even want to imagine with a welfare check that won't be a welfare check when she comes home. How it starts is Mom's on a mission, which means the chances of her, as promised, copping me a homecoming suit, homecoming shirt, homecoming tie, of her having the ends to give me to cop my homecoming date (a pretty young thing it took a whole quarter of school for me to step to) a box of chocolate and corsage, the chances of her footing one penny of my homecoming expense when she slogs in, is looking about the same as the odds for us (me, mom, and my bros) making a year in any one place without a shutoff notice: lights, phone, heat. So what do I do? What I do is approach my friend who's only a year older than me but already a young star in the curb-serving cosmos. My friend agrees to front me a "sack," which ain't a sack, but a few blonde shards wrapped and tied off in plastic. He offers me the dope on consignment and tells me that if I do it right I'll double-up. Both petrified and excited, I carry the

178

dope home, carry the package in my fist and keep my fist in my pocket the whole way, terrified it might slip through an unbeknownst hole into the abyss or, worse, into plain view. That same night (no need to sneak, cause Mom is still MIA) I wait till my bros fall asleep, lock the windows and both the doors, and strike out wearing a hoodie and jeans with my tiny package held so tight this time it leaves an imprint. That same night, I head out dreaming of easy double-up, of a sale, a sale, a sale. I dream of returning triumphant to school the next day to pay off my debt and cop another package, dream of hustling the cash I'll need for fresh new homecoming gear, a flower for my pretty young thing, and enough left over to line my impecunious-ass pockets with loose bills. I trek to a part of Northeast everybody with an active brain cell knows is crack central, a mise-en-scène chockablock with aspirants like me, with not-so-young dealers, with dopeheads darting in and out of shadows or grumbling up in cars with their windows dropped low. Only I go out that first night without clue the first of the protocol, not to mention with a heart much too meek for the comp, serious motherfucking competition. I'm talking a wannabe or in-the-midst-being D Boy on every corner. Talking one man shows, two man shows. Motherfucking triumvarates. And all accosting, without a second's fear it seemed, each and every would-be buyer. Me out in the thick of it, bones a-rattle, too punkish to open my mouth, and after a while cursing myself for being out at all. Me posted on one corner and then the other with hope rocket-blasting out my chest towards the stratosphere. Plus the brand-new dread that my mother, that Grace, might be wandering this dim universe.

What happens? I don't make a dime that first night. Don't

make a nickel, nor penny either. Don't make a cent that next
night or the one thereafter. It takes about a week (I have to sneak
out after Mom comes home) of dry runs to realize I ain't built for
this business, that if this is how it has to happen, my too-soon
homecoming will come and go without a working budget. Yeah,
I catch a tiny epiphany, but what about my what I owe my friend?
I'm new in the game, but smart enough to know the rules, the
tacit laws on returns and refunds. It takes a week of ducking and
dodging my friend (known for his quick temper and quicker
fists) in the halls before I work up the nerve to approach him in
the lunchroom, to explain that I tried and tried but couldn't get it
off, to admit I ain't cut out for the game, to say sorry, sorry, but
can he please take it back and squash my tab.

My luck, sometimes it's luck. And lucky for me he does.

So I quit. That's it. Quit and don't see another one of those
plaque-colored pills (Mom's always managed to keep them from
us) in person till right after high school. But the week after gradu-
ation, with my corner shortcomings worn down just enough, I buy
a sack with part of the scholarship I won, buy the sack dead set on
being discouraged, buy it with the intent of softening (I didn't win
a D-1 hoop scholarship) the fact my D-1 hoop dreams are all but
deceased, that for the next two years of life it's community college
and a twin bed at my mom's. But of course I take the scholarship
loot and cop a big double-up sack from my quick-fisted high school
homie and trek one night to a brand-new crucible. But this time I
make a sale. This time I make a second sale. Translation: this time
it's on! I go from double-up to a quarter ounce, from a quarter to a
half, from that half to the full oz. Go from one oz to two oz's, two
to three oz's, three to four and half oz's, and some nights I feel as if
I can't be stopped. In a half year, as if by some stroke of the blackest

magic, I'm buying quarter kilos (along the way graduated from copping from my high school patna) from a dude with a mint-condition old-school Benz and a bevy of gold chains.

You want to know how this starts in earnest? You listening?

It gets better. Or bigger, I should say. A year or so later, it's drought status, and my gold-flossin connect has been out-of-pocket for so long I'm thinking the nigger may never be in-pocket again. So I make a few calls to see if I can get a pack to last until the golden connect re-ups. This friend of a friend gives me the number to Mister, who I hit up and ask to speak about business. Mister (his voice is hella-whisperish over the phone) tells me to swing through. I count the ass-end of my re-up funds (got dough enough for a couple and I mean a couple, of oz's) and drive to meet him. It's an early Sunday, so the streets have that empty apocalyptic feel they do before the city stirs. Mister's store is closed, and I knock an eon before he answers. He locks a behemoth bolt behind us and leads me to the back of his store, but instead of discussing what I came for, he goes on about this mentor he had as a boy growing up in South Central. He explains the mentor was a white man from London who ministered to him and his boys on British culture, about places like Buckingham Palace and the houses of Parliament, on shit like bespoke tailoring and the King's English. Mister tells me that years after he started clocking the kind of bread he needed machines to count, he'd spend a few weeks a year in England, every time copping a closet of Savile Row suits, spread-collar shirts, and silk ties fat as a forearm. He gives me the monologue, and only when he's done does he lead me downstairs. He stands at a bistro table stacked with bills (he's crazy insouciant about the shit too, as if it's no more than a table scattered with old copper pennies) and asks what he can do for me. I show him the cash and ask if he can sell me a little something till my connect gets right. Mister flashes the kind of teeth Hollywood types pay a grip for and tells me its too bad about my boy being out-of-pocket, but that he's a man of abundance. He waves off the money I brought and digs into a duffel bag at his feet, and takes out a duct-taped package the size of a book—the first whole one I've ever seen with my eyes. He quotes me the price (complete with a new customer discount) and tells me to bring him what I owe him off the top. He leads me upstairs, unlocks his many-bolted door, pushes it open, says, Be safe, hella-dispassionate. With the first brick I've *ever* lay eyes on tucked in my sleeve, a trillion doubts knocking around my hard skull, and a ruthless rapid-ass heart, I totter out into the maw.

How this began in earnest, there it is, peoples, there it is.

How goes it? Mister says, standing beneath a light that makes his bald head glow. He's wearing a white shirt that's almost iridescent, a double Windsor tie knot (Mister's your GQ uncle or spicy grandfather, depending) as big as a baby's fist. Ain't but a few customers inside, a wino clutching a jug of Rossi, a clique of youngsters wearing creased jeans, and an old lady pushing a walker past canned goods. The wino staggers up to the counter smelling as if he'd soaked overnight in his potion. Mister, I'm a little short on my medicine, he says, searching for a Lagrangian point in his shifty balance.

How short? Mister says

All of it! the wino says, and flashes a jagged, yolk-colored grille.

Mister touches his gray-speckled goatee, tells his brother Red to grab a broom so the wino can sweep out front, and Red (he's laconic as they come) slogs into the back.

You know we quit drinking once, the wino says, at last unswaying.

That right? Mister says.

Yes, sir. It was four days back in '82. As it happens, I blew out my knee and couldn't make it to the store, he says, with a laugh that hacks up a mouthful of phlegm.

Mister gives up a grin. Red reappears with the broom.

Make sure you sweep out front and out back, Mister says. Get it good and clean around those cans. And don't crack my wine till your done.

Sir, yes, sir, the wino says, and bends his arm in a broken salute. Not a sip until I'm finished.

The youngsters stroll up to the counter. Mister eyes his gold watch, the only piece of jewelry I've ever seen him wear, and asks the boys about a missing member of their crew. The boys snitch that their patna is home faking sick.

Oh, you don't say, Mister says. Well, I tell you what, you all hold on to that chump change and pick what you want. Take it and tell your boy I let you do it. Tell him I said when he don't go to school, he misses out.

You'd think these youngsters just finished a booster's prep school, the way they stuff their pockets to balloons and airwalk for the door screaming, Mister, you tight.

Mister calls Red to cover the till and waves at me to follow. We stroll past a partially opened safe and a card table scattered with dominoes (he's no joke on the bones, knows your next move before you do, and on the dice, forget it, he'll lick you for everything in your pocket, plus whatever's in your stash), down the steps and into his dusty basement. Barred widows. Pinstripes of wispy-ass light. He shuffles over by a table decked with a cash-counting machine and an unopened bag of rubber bands. And below sits his famous duffel bag. I give him what I owe on my tab. The money is stuffed in a paper sack.

Now, not then. There's no time. With the baby, with what it might cost for the house, our home, this is the time to ask. You think we could bump it from one to two? I say.

One to two whole ones? he says.

Yes, I say.

He takes the bills out of my sack and stacks them in the counter. We could, he says. But you'd need to be sure you can move it. Your ambition and your business match up.

Oh, they do, I say. They do, trust me, I got it, I say, though why should he trust, with so much of me that doesn't believe?

Mister's phone rings. He answers, tells the caller, Everything is everything, his code for being in-pocket. At his age, middle age, Mister's the best you can hope for in this life or else the worst of dooms. He lifts two bricks out of his duffel and passes them to me. One or two or twenty—get all you can while you can but not a gram or dollar more than that, he says. You want to last, that's how you last. He moves closer. He clicks on the money counter and the bills whir. Listen, don't forget this. Don't let this slip your mind. Most of us, if we're lucky, we see a few seconds of the high life. And the rest are the residue years.

Red is helping a customer when we get upstairs. Mister tells me, Be safe, on my way out.

Half Man, my transport guy, twists his face when I climb inside.

Took you long enough, he says.

I hand him the packages and on everything the nigger's eyes look bedazzled.

Damn, two, homie! You doing it like that? he says.

This fool, it's nothing to see him at the gambling shack, high as a neutron star, spluttering my business in earshot of a hear-fast hustler with hopes of snagging a get-out-of-jail-free card. You think you can move em? he says.

Who's sure about what? I say. They mines now. What choice do I have?

This fool, right hand to God, he leans out the car and empties a blunt. He's my boy of all my boys, no doubt, but sometimes he's straight imbecilic.

C'mon, dog, you can't be serious. We got all this work and you rolling a blunt! I say, my voice close to breaking. Is this some kind of spoof?

This is for later. Not now, he says. Quit being chickenshit. They ain't arresting niggers for no blunt.

Man, put that shit away, I say. Now! I strap my seat belt and eyesweep the lot.

Damn, dog, he says.

You keep on, I say. You just keep on and you'll see. Guess who the fuck won't be with you when you do.

If you believe the streets, Mister's store is under surveillance, under the attentive eye of a task force team. Agents crouched on rooftops with long-range mics and long-lens cameras. No lie, every time I step out this joint, I get the feeling I'm the blind subject of a secret photo spread, one destined for a precinct or judge. The only way to keep sane, to keep a pulse that ticks on pace, is to say not me. It's not me they want. Why would they, when they could have him? My self-talk is self-deceit at its finest, AKA a reckless heart. And what they *should* say about that kind of heart is this: It breeds state charges, bow-legged bids in the feds.

Half Man lifts his tall tee, loosens his belt, and stuffs the bricks in his waist. We pull onto MLK, with me working my mirrors with monk-like vigil. I make a turn and another a turn, doing a mile or two over the limit since a mile or two below looks hella-suspicious. I cruise the block twice to be cautious, which ain't in no handbook, but should be. While I'm stopped at a light I see a ghost, alive, but three-quarters dead or more. Dawn, Mom's ex–best friend, is sloped against a pole, a PSA for a crack life specialist. She wobble-head totters into the crosswalk. She stops and peers into the car and squints and stutters around to my side. She shakes her finger, does a happy dance. Nephew. Is that my nephew? she says.

There's no doubt whatsoever that I should mash off the next green, but what instead do I do?

Oh my God! Oh my God! It's been so long, she says. Look at you!

Years ago, when her son, my best friend in those days was alive, Dawn was the undisputed beauty of Mom's friends, but look at her now: a pound away from levitating, with a butch haircut and a bad blond dye job and lips the shade of an oil spill.

She perches in my window and don't move when the light goes green. Don't so much as flinch when cars zag and blow their horns. Nephew, you think you could ride your auntie up the street? she says.

I look across at Half Man and the homie don't say shit. It been years since I visited her son's grave, and I can see his face in her face right now, her face in his. Let me pull around, I say, and wheel into the nearest lot. Dawn jams behind us. Can't give you no ride but take this, I say, and I give her cash. Thank you, thank you, thank you, she says. She stuffs it in her bra and keeps her eyes fixed on what's left in my fist. You think you could spare a few more dollars for Auntie? she says. Got some things that came up. Some things that won't go away. Behind Dawn I see police pull up to a light; they are too far away to see if they see us. This is the millisecond when you tell yourself this could be nothing. When you say this could be a motherfucking problem. When you say to yourself, self, let's not find out which.

You know what, Auntie, it's cool, I say. Where'd you say you were headed?

We (the three of us) ease off. Me and Half Man are locked in a white-boy rigidness (the anti–Invisible Man), heads straight, contrived tranquillity. No, there ain't no handbooks for this, but if there ever was or is, what pose to strike when you're dirty should make the final script.

You see them? he says.

What you think? I say.

See who? Dawn says. See what?

No worries, I say.

The police bust a U and, *bam*, it's like someone tripped a stopwatch in my chest. Here's the nanosecond you say, self, keep your head straight, your hands at ten and two, make no, copy that, not a one sudden move.

If they flash us I'm breakin, Half Man says.

Breaking for what? Dawn says. What's going on?

It's all good, Auntie, I say. Not your worry, I say. But as soon as I say it, my guts jump out my chest and break, leave the punk in me all by my lonesome. We're cool. We're cool. Just sit back. We got a good L, insurance, good tags. This is me talking to me.

We straight, I say. This is me talking aloud.

Who straight? Half Man says. His face is bled. How I'm straight when I might got a warrant?

Oregon state law: Attempting to elude police could be charged as a misdemeanor. State law: A warrant is all the probable cause they'd need for a search. With what's stuffed in Half Man's waist (soft grams in the thousands), by the time they set us free, we'd be decades into the new motherfucking millennium.

They drilled it into us: Life has options.

But what they didn't say was how those options dash with the hurry-up.

Elude or not.

Half Man sits or bolts.

Take the risk or risk the loss.

Wait too long and you've waited too gotdamn long.

They trail us for blocks before they hit the lights. I pull to the curb. Uniformed blockheads take their punk-ass time climbing out. They stomp up on both sides, all shoulders and grudge. We got this handled. We got this handled, I say to myself, and my self disbelieves. I touch my foot to the gas thinking, Which risk is the riskiest? Which risk is the riskiest? Which risk is the most risk? Hello, sir, I say, cheesing beyond all reason and nursing the prayer the *sir* sounds incontrovertible true. Did I do something wrong?

For starters, he says, how about soliciting a prostitute? He taps the back window. Well, well, well, if it ain't old Dawn, he says. You're still at it, are you? Didn't we tell you that last time that the next time we were taking you down?

He asks for my license, insurance, and registration. I glance over at Half Man, who's flushed.

Dawn calls the officer by name, assures him she isn't turning a trick. Tells him that I'm her nephew.

Nephew, he spits. He scopes my L. Then you should have no problem confirming his first and last name and year of birth.

Dawn shifts in her seat.

This is my life.

That was my life.

It can happen that fast.

Boy, you don't have a worry that ain't my worry.
　　　　　　　—Grace

EVERYONE, WHEN YOU THINK OF IT, is trying to
buy time, and what's more expensive than that? The buzzer
sounds, and before I can get my bearings there's banging at my
door. It's Champ. How'd you get through the gates? I say, standing outside the light.

It's late, I say.

Or early, he says. He wipes mist from his face. He looks past
me into a living room too dank to see much of nothing. Well, do
I get to come in or am I banned? he says. I stall. I step aside, hoping he won't speak on the shake in my hands, what the rain has
done to my hair. If he'd come an hour ago, I would've been in
the midst, doffing my wet clothes, checking myself, saying affir-
mations by the mirror.

He smells like an ashtray and I tell him as much.

Been out, he says. Damn smokers. Be glad you quit.

Would it have been too much to wait till tomorrow? I say.

It is tomorrow, he says.

The ride with Michael could've cost me more than I had to
give, but this isn't the time to mention it. I ask if he's thirsty and
offer him room-temperature tap or tap on ice. Ice, he says. I tell

him to sit, but he stomps into the kitchen behind me and throws open the fridge. He checks best-by dates, tugs open the empty drawers. Where's the food? he says. What're you trying to do here, starve?

Not even, I say. Just haven't been able to get to the store. Been working and working and when I get home it's too late, the walk too far.

You ain't got to walk and you know it, he says. This is crazy. He takes a clutch of bills from his pocket and waves them at me. Why're you being so stubborn? he says. Why are you killin your-self when we got this?

That's yours and nothing's changed, I say. He looks at the bills and stuffs them in his pocket and slams himself into the chair. My refrigerator rattles and growls. The faucet drips in hi-fi.

I saw Dawn, he says. She's some of the reason I come to see you.

Did you? Haven't seen her myself, I say. How is she?

The same, he says. Or worse.

That's sad, I say. I'll have to put her in my prayers.

She could use it, he says. And while you're at it, pray for a date to pick up your car. To pick up your bag, he says. They'll be there when you come.

Give the bag away, I say. Someone could use it.

Right, he says. You!

Champ, I say.

Grace, he says. Besides food, what else do you need? Are you straight?

Lord willing, I say.

How about we give the Lord a break? he says. Leave Him out of it for a sec.

What I need are my babies, I say.

What we need is the house, he says. That's what I'm going to buy.

What house? I say.

The house, he says.

Have you lost your mind? You must have lost your mind. Buy the house when? With what?

That's my worry, he says.

Boy, you don't have a worry that's not my worry, I say. None. Do you think you're the first one to bet on a dollar? Don't you know what you're into won't save us, that it cannot save us? she say. You need to see it, son. You must. You either see it now or see it when the seeing is priceless.

He springs out of his chair and clicks on the light. I lose sight, find it again.

Look at you, he says. How about I ask questions. Where you been? For how long? With who?

It's not what you think, I say.

I'm supposed to believe that? he says.

It was a ride. That's it, just a ride.

Just got a ride to where? he says.

From Michael, I say. But believe me, nothing happened,

He tells me to show him my hands—it was always in my hands. He fumbles across the table for them, and I cede. Do you see? I say. What don't you see? I say. You have to know I made him bring me home. He had to. I won't give him that power. I can't give anyone that power. Champ releases me and sits back in his seat, rocking, his face softened. I ask him to wait and pad into the room to find my spare key, to fetch the cash from my check, and the receipt. I tell him to check the receipt against what's there, but he won't.

I'm sorry, Mom, he says. Straight up.

I lay my spare on the table. Come and go, come and go, I say. There's nothing for me to hide. He takes up the key and turns it and touches the ridges and grips it in a fist and taps his fist against his head.

You think you could stop by the county office? I say. They got me working a double, and I'd rather not risk being late paying my fees.

Done, he says. He leaves the bills on the table and tells me to use them to buy food.

Take the money, I say.

Keep it, he says. You need it.

Oh God, Champ. Never mind, I say. I'll go myself.

He gulps water and slams his cup, and cubes leap and skip to the floor. He pushes from the table and snaps to his feet and clomps for the front room and I follow—me chasing my eldest, so many of my days pursuing us. He rages outside and I strive after him until he stops along the path and turns to me, huffing, his arms hanging limp at his sides. Someone snaps a light on in a second-story unit. Something fat and small darts across the lawn.

Champ, please, don't do this, I say.

Please Champ don't do what? he says. His eyes drift over me, all of me. In a flash, he whips away and hikes for the gates.

But can my boy be blamed? Can he? So help me, what in God's name on God's earth can he do with all I have done to us?

Man, she been trippin.

—Champ

NO MIGHTS OR MAYBES to it, in the public my home-
body is a helluva right-hand man, but minus a crowd, he's a jabbering voice of dissent. Prove it! he loves saying, which is second
only to his favorite: Man, what kind of fool-ass shit is that!

Was making my case on the ride over, schooling the homie
that a generation was all it takes. For evidence I used the Kennedys and Joe Sr. (John, Bobby, and Teddy's pops), he, who clocked
beaucoup bread doing stock business that, these days, would get a
motherfucker locked up under a jail; he, who made a king's ran-
som off his side hustle as a grand, maybe the grand puba of prohi-
bition bootlegging.

Tell me the Kennedys ain't American royals, I said.

And your point is? he said.

This is when I mentioned Big Ken's oldest brother, Uncle
Cluck, who well before his passionate crusade for crackhead of the
century graduated cum laude from the U of O and ran a profitable
legal businesses while becoming (per the newspaper headlines of
his bust) the biggest dope dealer in the land.

My point is you've got to be more than ambitious. You got to
have that capital-*V* vision. Just think where Big Ken's fam would've
been if Uncle Cluck was farsighted.

Half Man made the sound of a fat stabbed balloon. Bro, your uncle Cluck was a dope dealer, he said. Not no politician. You got a bunch of book smarts, homie. But I do believe sometimes you lack in common sense.

Maybe he wasn't, I say. But what if it ain't who you end up, but who you were or could've been?

It's the Shamrock, but we call it the Sham. And the Sham wouldn't be shit without Sweets. Sweets, Ms. Do-It-All here, is chatting up a guy with a grizzly beard. The TV bolted to the wall plays a football game on mute. A pair of chicks hunker near the poker machines, one with a head of frozen ripples, the other trawling a purse you could use for baptismals. Ain't but a few working bulbs above the pool table, which makes for terrible light, but once your eyes adjust, you can make out rips in the felt and sight a clean shot. I hunt a pair of straight sticks and check the table for warps and Half Man slinks over to buy the brews.

Oh, you trying to get me buzzed, I say. It won't work.

No, I'm trying to cut trips to the bar, he says. Besides, your luck has run out.

Since when, I say, is luck a synonym for skill?

The sun shines on a dog's ass every now and then, he says.

My favorite unc, Uncle Sip, was the one who schooled me on how to hold a brew, how to lap it before you swallow, a skill at which (I've seen him down 40's on the hour every hour all the day long) he must've been an expert. But Unc didn't bestow me his tolerance. Me, who's almost always buzzed from the first swig on. Liquored or not, though, Half Man ain't half no comp on this felt. The homie don't know nothing about my Shaolin secret. The key to a straight shot is balance. The trick to balance is accepting the fall.

I break. Balls scatter but nothing drops.

Losing your touch, Half Man says.

Or touched, I say, by another loose rack.

Half Man scouts a shot, eyes a solid, and sinks it. That's your ass, he says. You luck done run out.

Bet money, I say.

What, now I'm supposed to be spooked? he says.

We both know I'm not to be bluffed by quasi-cool. I slap a couple bucks on the rail and, true to form, he short-sticks his next shot.

So much for being fearless, I say. Let's hope we never get into another event with the police. You was damn near an albino.

Sheeit, he says, and catches his brew by the neck. What you know, when you ain't been locked up?

You ever check on that? I say.

Bro, who checks on warrants? he says.

Boom! This dude burst though the saloon doors hauling a bloated garbage bag. He struggles over and drops his bag by us and scans the room from Sweets and the bearded man, to the chick gamblers to me and Half Man. He digs a black box from an inside coat pocket and asks us if we like gold and diamonds. Check this out: Knocked All That Glitters for proper shine, he says. He pulls out a thick copper-colored chain and a men's diamond ring. Chain worth a few hundred. Ring worth a few grand, he says. But I'll take half a stack for both. That's a bargain right there.

You call that gold? We must look like marks, I say.

Nah, nah, not at all, boss. Check it out. Got the fourteen-K stamp and all that. The shit's authentic plus ten percent, he says. Ask anybody. I do my business on the up-and-up day- and night, seven days out the week.

Half Man asks what's in the bag.

Oh, this right here? he says. This what I happened upon this morning. A few personal items. Household necessities and such. Got a twin sheet set with a thread count high as a house note. Got a nice comforter too. Calvin Klein drawls, got T-shirts, the premium kind with that thick-ass cotton, got flashlights and batteries, a couple pairs of leather gloves. And you know them gloves gone come in handy. Be cold as an Eskimo's balls out here fore you know it. Altogether the shit come up to bout rent on a one-bedroom. But I ain't gone stick you up like I do them white folks. The shit's all yours for the fair bid.

Half Man slaps his bottle down and digs in his pocket. He spreads his offer into a fan.

You serious, dude says. For almost five times that worth of merchandise. All brand-new with the tags attached. Damn, boss, I know I'm fucked up, but you ain't got to do a brother like that!

Man, you want this money or what? Half Man says.

But that's bad business, he says. Can't do it for that.

Half Man stuffs his cash out of sight and dude tucks his black boxes and reties his bag. He fathoms the room and idles, begins to schlep off with his wares.

Hold up, I say. How much for the bedding?

He stops and turns and brightens and asks me what I think is fair. We haggle a second or two and settle. He throws in a pack of batteries, which is, as he calls it, a new business perk.

Me and Half Man split games and finish the rest of our brews. I'm good and buzzing by the last one but miles from slurring or swaying. Or so it feels. Meantime, one of the gambler girls wins big and brags about it to her friend. Sweets asks if we'd like another round, but I order water instead—another tenet of Uncle Sip's drink-for-life manifesto.

The side door swings open and in rushes a clique of dudes wearing black parkas and blue Chuck Taylors. There's a funny-ass joke running between them right up until the time they see us. Seeing us is the same as someone muting the laugh track on a sitcom. These clowns (in a city this small we all do) look hella familiar, but I couldn't tell you from where or name a single name. They pull up seats, place an order for a round of Rémys, and keep right on snickering. They glare at us and bet money they're measuring their reps against ours. I walk over and ask Half Man if he thinks there might be a problem and he says, Shit, if it is, it's for them, maybe.

Got to dig the homie for that. True, there ain't no superheroes here (all of the tough dudes end up dead or defeated), but some guys, guys like Half Man that live by pistols and pathos, there's just ain't no persuading them they're capeless, that, no matter, white tees over flesh never amounts to Kevlar.

The wannabes spread out. One of them (dude smells like a lit blunt) spreads quarters on the rail and hovers without a word. We take our time finishing, and play another game just because we can, and when we're done, Half Man snatches our bets off the rail, while I grab the stuff I bought for my mom. We blasé to the other side. It crosses my mind to hum.

On the other side we order our usual: burgers big as Frisbees, crispy fries, biggie pops. We grub by the big picture window. Outside, the wind throws trash across the lot. A trucker climbs into his semi. A woman flits towards the hospital with a thick parka up top, scrubs down below, and gleaming white nurse shoes.

Half Man asks about Mom.

She's cool, I say. But she needs to get out of that spot. I need to get her out of there.

Where she stay again? he says.

Piedmonts, I say.

The Piedmonts, he says. Damn, dog, I see your point.

She gave me a key, I say. I'ma shoot this bedding there ASAP. If she don't see me leave it, she might keep it.

Why wouldn't she keep it? he says.

Man, she been trippin, I say. Asking about where I get the money to help. On her holy shit again.

You still scheming on ya'lls old house? he says.

Yeah, that's the plan.

Oh, so they selling it now? How much?

Ain't got that far, I say.

You can bet that shit gone be a jug, he says.

Why you think I'm into it like this now? I say.

Half Man scopes the restaurant and cranes across the table. Dog, what you think about fuckin with meth? he says. It's crazy-low startup cost and stupid net. My homeboy knows some white boys in Southeast that be making bank.

Bad idea, I say.

No, serious, he says.

Me too, I say. How about we stick to what we know fore we get knocked?

My pager goes off and it's a lick. I chomp another bite of burger and scribble a fry in ketchup. You ready to roll? I say. Let's be out.

Peoples, peoples, keep it one hundred with me. You've been wondering about us improvidents—my uncs, the booster, Half Man, the antiheroes on the other side of the Sham, me. You've been wondering, what is it that sets us apart, haven't you, wondering how are we all, all, all, all, one in the same?

So simple—but for her not much of a care.

—Grace

YOU STEAL ONE DAY OFF from no days off.

And laze.

Unplug the phone and carry in a radio. Tune it to a station that dulls the noise—a tantruming baby, neighbors barking back and forth, the thumpety-thump-thump of a neighbor that keeps his beat box blasting—that seems to never cease. You run the hottest tub you can, a temperature that steams, and, if you're short on essentials, dump capfuls—shampoo, dishwashing soap, liquid detergent—of something to bubble and foam. No one's home, but you close the door and seal off the world. Light a candle and place it close, and by candle flame pin your hair off your neck and take your time stripping out your clothes. Climb in one foot first to test if it scalds, then full in. Roll a bath towel and prop your neck. Fold a facecloth and lay it across your eyes.

Be who you want, where you want, for as long as you want.

Forever.

Soak, and when you're done, dry and rub down—cocoa butter and cream that's sweet—and get dressed, make a mug of hot tea or hot cocoa or warm milk, and saunter into the front room to be still with yourself.

The door.

The door and a voice I can't make out behind it calling my name.

I walk to the curtains and crack a slit and peek to see who it is. It's my caseworker here unannounced, which, pursuant, as they've told me, is well within her rights. I don't so much let her in as she rambles past as if she owns the place and leans her tall umbrella against the wall. She's dressed in a wool coat, checkered wool scarf, and the kind of low-heeled heels that— forgive me, God—they sell at stores for old hags. She tells me to help her out of her coat, that she prefers it hung on wood, and I scuttle off to the closet with it over my arm. She tells me to have a seat when I come back, that this will take as long as it takes. Then she's off down the hall and into the bedroom and I can hear her slamming drawers, hear her dragging open the sliding closet that never stays tracked; if she wanted, she could turn the pockets of my old coat inside out, shake my pants wrong side up, snatch the lid off my precious few shoe boxes. She'd be justified tearing off my sheets, shaking the pillow from its sham, flipping the mattress, and with the time she spends, this could be what she does. She stomps into the bathroom next, creaks open the cabinet, and rattles bottles and bottles of pills and makes a fracas of restacking them on the metal shelves. She uses the toilet and runs the faucet twice as long as anyone should. Then you can see her in the hall, rustling through the hall closet, a cubbyhole understocked with secondhand towels. She passes through the front room and into the kitchen, where she slams the cupboards, clangs the silverware, clashes the pots and pans; where she hounds through a drawer I keep stuffed with pens, papers, broken knickknacks, condiments from work. She opens the fridge and it grunts on

cue. If the fruit and vegetable bins weren't empty, she'd probably hunt them too.

It hasn't dawned on me until now what a former tenant might've
left. That this woman could happen upon that last person's loose
pill, empty gram packet, that she might find an ancient antenna
pipe, a scorched spoon, a burnt pop can with a pencil hole punched
through it. And if she does, it's trouble—a bench warrant, in-
creased fines, a mandate for day-reporting, jail time that lasts for
months, a possible request for revocation, a brand-new charge. She
makes her way back into the front room. She takes my picture off
the wall, snoops the seams of the curtains, kneels to check the
innards of the baseboard heater. She ask-tells me to stand and pulls
the couch cushions one by one. Not until all of this is done does
she settle, take a steno pad—you can see the handcuffs attached at
her waist—out her purse and start to scrawl. Looks like everything
checks out, she says. Impressive.

Thanks, I say, and cinch the tie on my robe. So I've been
wondering, is there a chance of me being cut loose sooner than
my contract date? I say.

To be honest, I'm not a big fan of that, she says. But I'd listen.
Where are you on fines and fees?

Caught up, I say. And I'd work to pay them early if need be.
There's plenty hours down at my job.

She tells me I'd have to be finished, that we can discuss the
prospect at my next scheduled check-in. She says it, too, as if
it's so minute. The strings on my life low on her list of concerns. Makes you wonder if she's ever needed permission to
come and go, if she's ever been afraid of what comes next.

The door. The door—again!

This time a bam, bam, bam that cracks it from half cracked to half open. It's who else? Seeing his face I could lie down and die.

MCA, don't act all like that, he says. I came to make amends.

Now's not the time, I say. Not now.

C'mon, now, thought it was Christian to forgive. It been bothering me ever since, he says. He huffs a facsimile cloud and shivers and rubs the sleeves of his stretched knit sweater. He jokes he's far from weatherproofed and asks to come in. The man smells as you'd expect he would.

My caseworker appears at my back, exhaling what must be stones.

Oh, you got company, Michael says. He pats his misted afro. There's a cake cutter stabbed in it.

The way she says my name. Oh God, the way she says my name.

Michael beams that jagged yellow puzzle. He swaggers in and introduces himself. But pretty as you is, he says, call me what you damn well please.

May I ask how you and Grace are acquainted? she says.

He scratches his beard. Sheeit, me and baby girl go way back. Ain't that right, MCA? He stoops to tie his shoe. He gets upright and brushes the knees of his corduroys.

Interesting, she says. She tells him her name, her first name.

Beautiful name, he says. And biblical too. Now, if you don't mind me askin, how you know old MCA?

This is my caseworker, Michael, I say, and feel sparks in my chest.

Oooooh, Michael says. Oh, I see. You mean as in an outstanding member of our county's fine, fine Department of Community Justice.

Yes, that's correct, she says. And can you clarify when you and Ms. Thomas last convened?

Michael jabs his cake cutter into another spot. He turns to me—slow; he turns to her—slower. Now, that's a damn good question, he says. Hmmmm, let's see. Well, if I'm not mistaken . . . No, no, no, as a matter of fact, your forgiveness, please. The date seems to have escaped me. These days a brother's mind ain't worth a quarter, he says, nor nickels, he says. But I can vouch it's been a good minute. A good little minute, indeed.

She asks for his full name.

He gives her a false surname and bows and backs away.

Look like you two tendin official business, he says. Think that's my cue to get the hell outta Dodge.

I close the door with strength, and twist the locks back and forth, back and forth, and turn by increments to face her and all of what she is. She moseys over to where she left her purse and roots through it. She culls a pad and scribbles in the pad and packs it away. She touches the cuffs at her waist. Ms. Thomas, I take it you know the rules of your contract, she says. And the penalties for breaking them.

Wait, I say. Please let me tell you the truth.

She crosses her arms and cocks her neck. The truth, is it? she says. Let's hear this.

But now?

—Champ

THIS WAS AFTER MOM and Big Ken had split, a night KJ
was off with Big Ken, so it was just me and Mom at the crib. It
was one of those nights when my gut was doing Béla Károlyi
backflips. One of those nights when I slunk into Mom's room
with the hope of coaxing her into fixing a snack, fixing a meal,
fixing a grain of anything. That night, though, I found her lying
across her bed with her face smothered in a pillow. I asked what
was wrong and she rose and told me not to worry, that what was
bothering her was grown folk's business, and since it was, I should
go on back to my room and lie down. And go on back to my
room was what I did. But no sooner had my stomach settled and
let me close my eyes than Mom shook me awake, rushed me to
get dressed, and tugged me out the front door. She hustled me
into our compact car and told me we were going to see Dawn
(her best friend, my play aunt), that we wouldn't be but a minute,
and drove us across town with me complaining the whole way till
she promised me a Burger Barn burger, my favorite. We drove to
a mangy motel at the end of Interstate Ave., climbed flights of
stairs, and knocked on a room with its numbers scribbled in thick
felt-tip. This man straight out a nightmare answered, raked us a
good one with his eyes, and let us in. Mom's friend, my play-aunt

Dawn, was sitting on a bed cluttered with clothes, looking as though she'd been mauled by pit bulls. I may have been a month or so shy of finishing fifth grade but it didn't take no adult foresight to see what was happening was all to the bad. Mr. Nightmare cleared the clothes (beeper tags still attached) off the bed, turned on a show, and tossed me a tepid can of pop. I watched a black-and-white TV with bad V-hold till the credits scrolled on a kung fu show or a cowboy show or a hero show—whatever they played before the networks went off-air. By that time my bladder was good and full, but the problem was, Mom, Aunt Dawn, and Mr. Nightmare were locked in the bathroom. What could I do? What I could do is what I did: squirm with my eyes stinging and the pop about to burst an organ. Near the time that I was about to erupt I scrambled over, stuck my ear to the bathroom, and heard whispers that made me hella-hesitant. Picture me doing a rain dance for courage. Picture, just when I worked up the nerve, Dawn cracked the door on a bandbox of gray haze. Picture clouds rushing out and my mother wild-eyed and sucking a pipe.

That first time is on my mind—here now cause she's at work and it ain't much happening in the courtyard, here and there a roving eye peeking through a sheet-tacked window or a split in diaphanous-ass drapes, eyes trailing me to Mom's apartment, where it takes me forever (so long, I'm thinking maybe she got it changed) to get her janky lock to click. I haul the bag into her bedroom and strip a ratted blanket and mismatched sheets off her bed. I remake it with the new sheets (the thread count is mean; for once a booster wasn't false-advertising) and tuck the sheets with tight-ass hospital corners. I fluff her flat pillows and slide them in the new shams.

On the way out, I see Mom's left her tenny shoes kicked off by the front, with the laces yanked tight and knotted. I stop and pick them up. I untie the knots, loosen the strings just so, and set them flush against the wall. This was the most I could for her then.

But now?

Later, the storm has stopped (the worst of the storm anyhow) by the time I swoop Half Man and head for the spot everybody's been bragging on the last couple weeks, and if the cars in the lot are any clue, the word wasn't no hype. Half Man hops out and strolls ahead, unzipping his parka. Look like it's off the chain, he says, his voice pulsed. The wind sighs damp leaves and cigarettes butts, scatters a few loose flyers. There's a line stretching around the side of the club, but we swank to the front, shake a dub in the door guy's hand, mosey in, and on our way to the bar shoulder-bang a few wassups. I order a vodka and tonic and Half Man opts for a (he loves that dark potion) Hennessy double. Soon as I get his drink, he says, Let see what they bitin like, and strolls off.

The club's hazy with smoke, smoldering under strobes. I find a close-to-empty corner and watch the set. *Dance Fever* types doing what they do on the parquet dance floor: a chick rubbing her ass against some dude's crotch, a buffed dude convulsing as if by electric shock, a couple of cool-ass two-steppers. This kind of stuff goes on uneventful for songs, but when the DJ spins an East Coast set, a scuffle (wouldn't be a weekend without a fisticuffs) breaks out. The DJ mutes the music and shouts over the mic. The floor clears, leaves these two dudes tussling center stage without a single punch thrown till bouncers with their polo shirtsleeves rolled to their rotator cuffs (there must be an unwritten bouncer rule: the bigger you are, the smaller you buy your shirts) rip them apart and drag them off in choke holds.

With the brawl cleared, the DJ spins a slow set and that's when I see a girl across the room mouthing a chorus. We smile at each other (an invite), and I stroll over. We rap a taste, and guess who you won't catch saying too much of nothing, not cause I'm at a loss, but more so cause I trust old head advice: If a chick is feeling you, she'll wait for you to say the right thing. But if you say too much, you raise the risk of saying the wrong thing.

Half Man, on the other hand, plays percentages, philosophizes that if he spits at the right number one will bite.

But myself, I ain't built for such sufferings. Trust and believe, my friends, it's suffering.

This chick isn't a Half Man gamble, but she also ain't looking like a one-night hype. You can see the obsequious ones from miles off, the ones eager to offer up a piece of themselves for a few drinks and a rote flattery—the hurt and the hurt communing. With this chick, though, it'd have to be another night or week, which might work for a dude with more time on his hands, but here's the thing: A month from now will be too close to June, when the baby is due. Each month it becomes harder and harder to risk our good thing.

I offer a drink and she accepts, but on the way to the bar, Kim's a straight masochist—her sweet face, sweet voice, her sweet-ass presence dogging me to no end. It's torture to the point that, by the time I make it back, no B.S., I can't even look the chick in her eye, much less lay down a mack. The best I can manage is, Nice to meet you. Then I bounce. No numbers exchanged, no promise to meet again.

I tramp across the club. Strobes pulse light off earrings and watches, off rhinestones and sequined tops, a tinseled tooth or two, off a fellow hustler's hella-big medallion. The DJ plays a West Coast rap set and the floor fills up again, with a bouncer roaming the border, his ponytail noosed in a rubber band, his triple-X shirt stretched to a test of physics. I down a drink and search for a place to make a call (I move mindful of my space; you never know when a mean-mugging misanthrope is itchin to spark a beef over an accidental nudge or a scuff on his new white kicks) from indoors, since the club don't allow reentry. I end up in the restroom. It's empty, but for caution's sake (yeah, I love my girl but I can't have one of these fly-by-nights thinking I'm whooped) I close a stall and cup my cell.

Kim picks up short-time.

Guess you were up? I say.

Something like that, she says. Got a call not too long ago. Whoever it was called and listened and hung up. Probably one of your broads.

Stop it, I say.

She exhales in a way that lets you know she's alive.

Anyways, why're you calling so late? she says.

Do I need a reason to call my woman? I say. Can't it be me thinking of you? Me calling to see what you need?

This, of course, is truth (this time), and it hurts that she can't trust it.

What did you do? she says.

Damn, here we go with the indictments, I say. A nigger can't be concerned?

'Bye, Champ, she says. I'm fine. We're fine. See you when you get here.

Half Man's posted in a corner blathering to a chick wearing glitter on her arms and a cheap necklace. I tell him I'm ready to leave and he pops up and pulls me to the side. Damn, dog, all this work and you wanna bounce? Why?

Man, look, I say. Stay if you want, but you're on your own.

Think I'ma hold tight, homie, he says. You see that? A few more stiff ones and she's a go!

Outside, there's a gust of feral wind and the moon's so low you could jump and touch it.

It's true, all true, it makes me sad that my girl's instinct is to doubt my word, but I've told so many lowdown dirty pitiful lies, how could she ever, ever, ever with her whole heart believe?

IN THE CIRCUIT COURT OF THE STATE OF OREGON
FOR THE COUNTY OF _____

In the Matter of:)
)   Case No. _____
_____,   )
                   Petitioner,   )   PETITION FOR CUSTODY AND PARENTING
)   TIME under ORS 109.103
        and   )   ☐ and CHILD SUPPORT
)
_____,   )   DOMESTIC RELATIONS CASE SUBJECT TO
                   Respondent.   )   FEE UNDER ORS 21.111
)
        and   )
)
☐_____,)
Child who is at least 18 and under 21 years)
of age, unmarried and unemancipated.   )
(ORS 107.108)   )

1.   Petitioner is the ☐mother ☐father and Respondent is the ☐mother ☐father of (names of children):
_____, born on the
following date/s: _____

2.   Paternity has been established:
        ☐ by filing with the State Registrar of Vital Statistics a voluntary acknowledgment of paternity,
concerning the following child/ren (*e.g., birth certificate*): _____
_____
                              (*list name/s of child/ren involved*)
        ☐ by administrative order docketed with the following court: _____, as
case number _____, located in _____ county, concerning the following child/ren:
_____
                              (*list name/s of child/ren involved*)
        ☐ by judicial order entered in the following court:_____, as
case number _____, located in _____ county, concerning the following child/ren:
_____
                              (*list name/s of child/ren involved*)
        ☐ by another method: _____
concerning the following child/ren:_____
_____
                              (*list name/s of child/ren involved*)
///

They're all I got and you know it.

      —Grace

THEY FIND YOU WITHOUT FAIL, Godspeed, the creditor letters and bills for unpaid lights and heat. They find you without fail, reach your next forwarding address—dollars and dollars of bank overdrafts, parking fines with interest and penalty, Sallie Mae stalking you on a default loan. Bills that turn a simple trip for the mail into sad, sad business, a reason to check it once a week, if you check it at all.

This morning, stuffed between secured credit offers and unmarked collection notices, is a letter from the Child Services Division. The letter says Kenny is suing for full custody, that I have to show in court in May. I rush inside and pick up the phone and punch his number. Kenny answers as if he's been waiting for the call as long as he's been living. This is a joke, right? Early April fool's? I say.

No, Grace, he says. It's no mistake.

So this is you now? I say. You itching to steal my boys?

Nobody's stealing your boys, he says. They're our boys. Ours, and they're settled. It makes good sense to keep it that way.

Good sense to who? To you. Or you talking for her now?

No more back-and-forth, he says. This is best.

Won't be any back-and-forth, I say. My boys will live with me and that's that. Oh God, you're dead set on causing me grief.

This isn't about you, he says.

You black bastard. It won't happen. God as my witness, nobody's taking my boys. They're all I got and you know it.

I slam the phone and sit with my eyes dropped against the world.

Faith without works is dead.
Faith is spelled a-c-t-i-o-n.
The task ahead is never as great as the power behind.

Times like this, who to seek? Who shall I seek when I can't do this alone? When I will not try to.

If you can catch my brother sober and on a break from bickering with one of his kids' mothers, which when is that really, he's about as reasonable a voice as to be found. His is the voice I need. Without a bus that runs the route I need—why oh why did I give him back the car?—I hike across town to the tavern. It's blocks, but I don't feel them. I am in it before I know how I got here, in the midst of this dimness, of a room that reeks of ammonia and whiskey. There's a man at the bar and sparse bodies plunked around tables and what I know right off is this: This room's too quiet for Pat to be anywhere in it. I ask after him anyway and the bartender tells me he hasn't seen him in days. He don't say how many, but I gather it's been enough, that there's a chance—if I can track him—of my brother being sober and keen. The man at the bar catches my sleeve, asks why I'm leaving so soon, and offers to buy me a drink, but I shake free and seethe. Didn't mean no harm, he says.

There are times when I can do it alone. There are times when doing it alone is the surest way to fall. And what now would happen if I so much as stumble? Pat, where is Pat? There isn't another way or anyone else.

You count on this if you can't nothing else: The bus never runs on time when you're rushing.

I stand and sit and troll my bag for who-knows-what and wade into the street and back to the curb, the whole time listening for the sound of the bus against the sound of my body moaning its dread. Cars slog past. Time ticks off and still there's no sign of the bus—further chaos in me. I shoulder my bag and march off for Pat's place, saying my boys' names to myself block to block just because. This time I can feel it, every step. When I get to Pat's woman's place, his boys' are out front roughhousing. I see his youngest take a gut blow and drop to a knee, see his oldest begin to laugh. Don't I know, don't I know, I say and help the youngest to his feet. Pat's youngest, like my youngest, attracts trouble, is who you most hope to rescue before it's too much of a charge. I stamp both boys with a kiss and climb the porch and find the front door cracked and knock to be polite. Pat's woman tells me to hold on. She answers wearing a gown and slippers with a scarf tied to the front. I ask for my brother and she twists her lips. Ain't seen his triflin ass for the better part of a week, she says. You check the tavern?

That's where I coming from now, I say.

Well, shoot, she says. Then I don't know. Maybe he's locked up or been staying by one of those nasty heifers. You know how he do? she says. He'll breeze on by when he gets good and ready—or flat broke, one of the two.

She makes a comment about my face and asks if I'm thirsty or hungry and roves through a maze of clutter into the kitchen. While she's gone, I swipe a finger of dust from the table and lift my foot from a sticky patch on the floor. She's got a pure heart, as my brother has said himself, but she can't keep a clean house— period.

She carries out pops and snack bags of chips. So what's the trouble? she says. You don't seem yourself.

You know, I say, if it ain't this it's that.

Who you telling? she says. Your brother's this and that combined.

I wish I could laugh but I can't.

Is it money? she says. I don't got much, but if you need it you can sure borrow. You family to me—brother or no brother.

Oh, girl, you know I couldn't, I say, but can I use the phone? She hunts a cordless from under a pile of clothes and hands it to me and leaves the room. This first place I call—I used to call for Kenny, and you never forget the number—is the Justice Center and lo and behold my brother's in the system, held on one count trespassing and one count menacing. Pat's woman strolls back in chomping a mouthful of chips. She asks if I found him and forgive me God this once but I lie. I tell her, Thanks and sorry to rush, and hotfoot out, hoping to catch the county's last visiting session. My nephews are in the front yard, and I say good-byes and kiss them on the cheeks.

It's one bus and a second bus and a transfer, the everlasting story of my life.

It's scarce at the county check-in—a woman stuffing clothes into a locker, an old man searching his wallet, another female checking the placard of contraband items. I stow my bag and stuff the state letter in a pocket and breeze through the detector about as fast as they let me and flit down the hall to the room. There's a deputy outside the room and he waves me in and I find a booth beside a girl who, by the face, is at the end of a bad run. The girl and me trade a glance and she goes right back conversing with a baby-faced twenty-something with a head of messy braids and script across his neck.

Pat struts out as though all is right with the world. He plops in his seat and eyes me through the Plexiglas and leans back and leans forward and yanks the phone off the holster. Hey, sis, he says. Fancy seeing you here.

Look who's in good spirits, I say.

Ain't I always? he says.

What you do this time? I say.

Sis, you know how it is with us ladies' men, he says. Either they can't get enough or they've had too much, and it's hard to know any given day which is which. They gave me a court date the day after tomorrow but she ain't gone show, so this ain't no big old whoop-de-do. Be back shooting cupid arrows by the end of the week.

Boy, you still a magnet for lightweight trouble, I say. You gone get enough of that.

Nah, I'm a heavyweight, he says. That's why this don't count. But I know you didn't come to lecture me on spending a petty few days in the county.

What I came for is this, I say, and take out the letter and press it against the glass and leave it for him to read.

Well, I'll be damned, sis. That's serious, he says. How you plan on playing it?

That's why I came, I say.

Right, right. Hmm, well, I'd say you need a lawyer, he says. You got some dollars set aside? They ain't cheap.

Pat, I say. Let's be real.

Best call Nephew, then. Have him shell out some bucks. The boy buying cars and whatnot, he should have it.

No, not Champ, I say. He's not an option.

Not an option? Now look, who ain't being realistic? he says. Allbullshitaside, you gone need references too. Law-abiding, tax-paying, God-fearing citizens to speak on your behalf. And if you still fooling around in the church, you should see about the pastor, if not him a deacon. Plus, call Pops. I know you lifetime pissy with him, but you know like I know that Pops still got clout with them white folks. He pushes his face closer to the glass and asks to see the letter again.

Okay, got it, got it. That date gone be here fore we know it. Barring any unforeseen female troubles, I'll be free and present and ready if need be to speak on your behalf.

The tears come on, little reservoirs in the cup of my lids that I dab at with my fist. I hate for him or anyone else to see me falter.

Say, sis, keep your head up, he says. You got this. He presses his palm to the window and smiles. It's Andrew's smile, the smile of his sons, the smile from when he was a boy, those years the world tore us apart.

I can only hope, beyond this, baby bro feels the same.
                                    —Champ

A COURTHOUSE IS AN OMEN for a nigger like me, but
I'm four-flats down for baby bro, so here I am, here we are (the
we being Ms. H, the rest of his knucklehead class). Our tour
guide is a jolly twenty-something short-cropped blond that, by
the face, ain't got a criminogenic bone in his body. He meets us
at the building's entrance and welcomes our group to the Multnomah County Courthouse. We're at the midway of a line that
winds out the door. What must be the usual sorts filing in, filling
in swift-like too, though soon as I think that, our good fortune
dies a fast death at the hands of the slow-moving or slow-witted
or both, stalling progress with over-metaled belts, pounds of jewelry, pocketfuls of change, and way too much electronic shit for
an earthling. But today's our day. Our guide escorts us to the head
of the clog and holds it while we amble through the detectors,
while, on the other side of the machines, we fall into an oblong
circle under the semi-circumspect gaze of stout sheriffs. And let
me say this right here, right now: Whoever designed the sheriffs'
puke-green uniforms gave a rat's ass about the stain they'd leave
on your eyes, my eyes, or anybody else's.

Our chipper blond lodestar leads us to a conference room on
the second floor and we pick seats at a massive oak desk that must

be old as all of us added together. It takes a spate of shushing from Ms. H to coerce the boys out of fidgeting and talking and general unconcern, and in that tease of hush, our guide points at the enormous portraits of stern white men lining the walls and asks if anybody can name the name of a Supreme Court justice. Wouldn't you know, the boys turn absolute mutes, search here and there for an innocuous spot to fix their eyes. I taunt baby bro into response. He guesses wrong, but give him credit. Not a single one of these nascent knuckleheads risks a next try.

Our guide stands at the head of the table and asks another question. He waits. He waits in vain. Okay, well, let's get started, he says. Our court system has three basic functions. To interpret laws, settle disputes, and strike down laws that conflict with the Constitution. He stops and rakes his hair—you know, that patented spread-finger white-boy rake. There are four types of courts: trial courts of limited jurisdiction, trial courts of general jurisdiction, intermediate appellate courts, and courts of last resort. This courthouse is a court of general jurisdiction. He explains how criminal courts are the body of law that preserves a person's basic rights, that anyone that violates those rights has committed a crime against the people.

And who the people posed to be? says one of the boys.

You are, I am, we all are, the guide says, and flashes one of those halcyon smiles that could only be a birthright. Felonies, he says, are the more serious crimes and punishable by a year or more, while sentences for misdemeanors seldom run more than a year. Later today, he says, you'll see criminal proceedings. He goes on and, no lie, to say the least, old green eyes is loquacious as they come.

Canaan folds his arms on the desk, droops a few times into my fam's famous somnolent nod, and lays his head in his crooked arms. Almost everyone else around the table has wandered off into never-never land. This I take (it's why I'm here, right?) as my cue. I march around to baby bro's seat, tell him he best not embarrass us, and joust a finger in his back. He straightens, jerks his arms off the table, a beacon for his boys, you'd hope, but hell nah, they carry on in the clouds. Towards the end of his spiel, our guide cites a long list of phenomenal stats, the last of which is how every day the courthouse produces a stack of papers tall as a full-grown man, what he calls the paper trail.

Morning court. We're some of the first inside the courtroom and take up an entire bench back in the back and part of the next row up. We're the first, but a finger snap and the room is chock-ablock with all sorts: with attorney types carrying leather briefs, with dudes who look as though they ain't bathed since the new year flipped, with chicks who've graffitti'd their faces in colors (stark mascara, layers of blush), with ladies who've pinned broaches to their lapels. On the other side of a waist-high wall sits two tables, bare minus a pair of angled microphones and yellow note-pads. The jury box, the court reporter, the witness stand, it's all there just like you see on TV. The bailiff asks the room to stand while His Honor strolls out to his bench, a throne of polished wood bedecked with a gavel and a life-sized bronze sculpture of our glorious state bird. He takes his seat beneath a huge replica of old Harvey Gordon's (disclosure: our guide told us this in the intro) state seal.

I clamp Canaan's shoulder and give it a squeeze. I am here, it says. We are here, it says. And it counts.

Once, when I was working for a summer program, we took a vanload of problem campers to the Justice Center for one of those scared-straight shock visits. The first stop of the visit was the booking room, where severe deputies fingerprinted the boys (never dawned on me till now they were entering them in the system forreal forreal), snapped their mug shots, printed the mug shots, and gifted the prints as souvenirs. Next, they dumped us in a holding cell supercharged in world-class funk, I'm talking a stench to make your respiratory system shut right the fuck down! But the holding-cell funk wasn't the pinnacle. They escorted us past pods of inmates banging against thick glass and booming (See you when you get here! Top bunk's all yours, baby boy. Look at the cutie pies!) to the cafeteria, where, after they fed us a jailhouse special: tuna fish on stale white bread, acerbic potato goop, and fruit cups with dubious expiration dates, they marched out a trio of lifetime felons to rant from a kissing distance on the pitfalls of crime. Can't say for sure the effect the trip had on the boys, but what I can say is this: When we left, all I could think was, Not me, no way I could stand even a second locked up. And here's the truth of the truth of the truth: I can only hope, beyond this, baby bro feels the same.

We are not this, I whisper to Canaan. This is not for us.

Watch enough TV and you'll get to thinking, like me, that judges spend most of their days sentencing headline cases, but His Honor (dude looks a little too affable for the job) presides over a lineup of anonymous business: a discovery status hearing, a preliminary hearing, a suppression hearing, a probate hearing, a show-cause hearing for an unpaid fine, a motion, an arraignment, an appeal, a criminal trespass charge, a charge of felon in possession of a firearm, and, of course, of course . . .

The deputy escorts a dude dressed in county blues that I used

to see out working the curb. He strolls in uncuffed, his arms behind his back anyhow. He glimpses me over his shoulder and
gives me a dispirited what's-up nod.

Canaan peeps this and asks if I know him.

Not really, I say.

Dude's lawyer (by his suit, he must've cost a few bucks) asks
to approach the bench. You'd need bionic ears to hear the exchange between him and the judge, but whatever it is, they seem
to agree. The judge trumpets dude's charges, Distribution of a
Controlled Substance and Possession of a Control Substance (the
infamous DCS/PCS one-two punch), lists the conditions of
homeboy's plea (he won't be home no time soon), launches into
a soliloquy about how disappointed he is, how it bothers him to
convict so many men who look like him, young black men for
drugs, and so on. He asks dude's lawyer if his client would like
to speak.

The lawyer announces his client wrote a statement.

Ms. H glances down the row at us. I catch Canaan whispering
across me to one of his boys, and give him a merciful elbow-jab.

Dude stands and glances from side to side and back at us. He
pulls his shoulders tight and sighs. Your Honor, I'd like apologize,
he says. I'd like to apologize to you, my family, my community, to
God. My actions were wrong and harmful and cannot be justified.
He blathers another couple lines of canned contrition, then stops
abrupt and balls his sheet to zilch. The move plunges the room into
a Catholic hush. Fuck this! he says. You think this gone stop? It
won't. And whoever think so, need think again. Cause we out here
neck-deep, he says. If one go down, one come up. If one go down,
one come up. That's the rule, he says. One down, one up is the
only law that counts.

Dude swings to face us and sorts the crowd and stops on me. Ain't that right, bro? he says. Tell em I'm right, bro, he says. We look each other dead in the face, in the eye. He spares me the homicide of saying my name.

The judge drops his gavel and calls the bailiff and the bailiff stomps over and catches dude by the shirt and lugs him into the aisle and towards the exit. The whole time he chants, One down, one up, one down, one up, one down, one up, his head cocked in such a way you'd think he was a saint.

And shit, maybe he is. Church and court, it's all the same—pews, a throne, a God, the accused.

I need you.

—Grace

THEIR VOICES FALL TO ME on the street. Call me to
gaze up at the stained glass until I hear a break in the song. I skirt
inside and mount the steps and, when I get upstairs, stand back as
far as you can from the stage. Up front near the choir loft, a
circle of members laugh and chat. Okay, okay, the director says,
and the members file into the rows of the loft. The organist
plays a chord. The director waves fingers bedecked with silver.
La, la, la, la la, they sing, and somebody's off-key.

I stroll down and find the pastor sitting in a front pew with a
Bible balanced between his legs.

Well, well, well, he says, and sits the Bible aside. If it isn't one
of God's glories. Let me guess, you came to lend us a voice.

No, Pastor. I say. I came to see you.

Then here I am, he says.

Do you think we could talk in private? I say.

He leads me behind the stage and pulpit, past a closet packed
with the choir's new robes, leads me into a dank room with walls
lined by rusted pipes. He clears a fold-up chair and places it before a desk scattered with MLK fans and a portrait of him and
his wife. He stacks the fans into a pile and turns the portrait to
face me.

I need you, I say.

He loosens his tie and undoes his top button, exposing an inside collar rung with black. He asks what's the trouble but I can't tell him. He glides around the desk and lays a palm on my head, a touch full of a man's strength and the fear of God. He prays, and while he does, I think, Yes, yes, there *are* such things as happy endings; they are wrong, those who say the happy ones haven't lived long enough. He lifts his hand and opens his eyes and holds me in them an instant. The choir's next hymn floats in faint from outside the walls. He asks if I'm in danger.

No danger. But trouble, I say, and compose. I am dignified, and this I want him to see. Pastor lifts a Bible from his drawer, thumbs pages, asks if he could read me a verse. Corinthians 3:17, he says: *If anyone defiles the temple of God, God will destroy him. For the temple of God is holy, which temple you are.*

I take out the state papers and show him and watch his eyes track along as he reads. He finishes and he smooths the paper and lays it across his desk. How can I help? he says.

Pastor, I know I haven't been here long, but if you could come, I say. I would love it if you could come and speak. If you can. If it's not too much trouble.

Pastor folds the letter into fourths and slides it across to me. When you're one of us, you are one of us, he says. And we take care of our own how we can.

When we leave we float past the choir and down the aisle and down steps and out of the church and onto the street, where this early spring warmth drops from the clouds. Hope to see you Sunday, he says. He catches my hands and presses them into a form of prayer. Keep faith, keep faith. We push on. We testify, he says, and glides back into the church.

Me alone hoping the choir sends another song falling. Where to next arrives as a taste in my mouth. I troop around to Big Charles's store to buy a pop and chips and my first pack of cigarettes in months.

Thought you quit, he says.

I did, I say.

He shakes his head.

It's one of those days, I say. But just this one time, that's it.

He snatches a pack off the shelf and thumps it and lays it on the counter. Boy, if I had a dollar, he says. But fuck it, you good for business.

Best to pay and leave before I have the chance to reconsider. A foot out the door it's as if I've wandered into a new county. The first drag stokes my chest and feels better than it has, the best it might feel ever again.

Answer A is this:

—Champ

WHEN WE WERE KNEE-HIGH to an ant, wet behind the ears (you know all the little sobriquets the old heads love to tag you with), and everything else they called us in those days, every time we were doing something we (the *we* being me, my bros, and any one of my intractable-ass first, second, or third cousins) had no business doing, Mama Liza would say it's all fun and games . . . It's all fun and games till somebody gets their eye gouged out . . . It's all fun and games till somebody busts their head wide open . . . It's all fun and games till somebody scrapes all the skin off their knees. When we were older, she didn't even have to finish the sentence. She'd catch us committing some stark crime, shake her wig askew, make her eyes go all ecclesiastical, and say, It's all fun and games . . .

Professor Haskins is hunched over a stack of papers with his door cracked. He hacks a loud cough into the crook of his arm and swivels slow at the sound of me entering.

Got a sec? I say.

For you, he says, sure.

He pats the couch, tells me to have a seat.

The cushions suck me low.

What can I do for you? he says.

About the program, I say. Can you tell me more?

He grins, taps a ditty on his desk. So you changed your mind? he says. Ready for politics?

No so much politics but school, I say. Do you know the dead-line, what I'd need?

He frowns and shakes his head, his frosty natural going back and forth. There's meat under his eyes and a bulge above his belt. Well, Shawn, he says. I'm afraid the deadline has come and gone.

Oh, I say, and fight the suck of the couch cushions onto my feet. Guess my next question is moot.

Not so fast, he says.

But I thought you said I missed it, I say.

You did, he says. He shuts the door, sits at his desk. He pushes his specs up the bridge of his nose, wheels his seat close. Now, this stays between us, he says, and puts a finger to his lip. The word is there's one spot left and pressure from the dean to fill it. He ex-plains how to apply—the recc letters, the essay, a speech.

What I tell him is all I need is a shot, as if I've considered the whole process all before. But that's always been my gift: Say it first and believe it second. I tell him, no sweat, that the info goes no further than me. He tells me start quick, recites the drop-dead deadline. You should see me when I bop out all buoy-ant—a theme song playing in my head. The recc letters: cool. The speech: cool. But the essay—not so much. Though you all know me; by the time I stroll out of Smith Hall, I got the inkling of a half-ass plan.

The campus ain't but yay big. But that ain't stopped me from exploring, from getting my Jacques Cousteau on in buildings where they seldom hold classes, where the rooms are so cold that even this time of year, sitting alone in them like I do some days, my blood runs cooler. No bullshit, every now and again, on days when my meter's full and there's time to burn, or days when you can bet there's a ticket waiting on my windshield, I search the campus for a quiet space. This is how I found the elevator where I used to steal off with this chick from my black studies class. What can I say about her? She was a superbad, smart, with fierce short hair and heart-attack hips and thighs, the kind of chick who makes me feel inferior. Add to that she had an ass that could turn staunch assologists into teary-eyed swains. Fortunate me and she were assigned to work on a project. We stopped by the campus bar the night we finished the project, tested our threshold for microbrews, and somehow ended up on Marine Drive watching planes take off. I'm not sure when, but sometime that night I said some slick shit (or maybe it wasn't so slick and she was hella-credulous) I've been dying to rehash: We got to make the most of this, I said. This moment right here is history right after right now.

Now, maybe that sounds corny to you, some world-class drag, but say that sitting on Marine Drive, say it with the right song playing and the rain making music on your hood, and beyond-your-limit of alcohol swooshing your brain, say it right then, and it just might sound like the suavest shit you ever said in your life. And I don't know how it is where you from, but I told you all a while ago what that equals around here.

Here's the extended remix of the story: She let me hit in the car that night and, after our next class, was game for a second go-round in the elevator I'd found in the emptiest, coldest building on campus. Even more unbelievable was this: For the rest of the quarter, she'd let me coax her to that same building for another shot.

Why'd I tell you? Answer A is this: I don't fuck for the sake of fucking or fuck for sport like other fools; I fuck for stories, tales I can trade with my boys after. Shit, if they cared more about chess than chasing skirts, I'd set my sights on becoming a black Bobby Fischer, but since they don't, and since, how I see it, lying on your dick is a transgression worse than treason, what else can I do?

I stop by the phone booth and return a couple pages before I bounce, the last of which is to Todd, who says he wants to up his usual buy. The timing don't surprise me. For as long as we've been doing business, he's been a godsend. He never flakes on a meet time or dickers with short bank; what he does is once a week or so call to meet and pay with big bills arranged faceup and folded over. I swear, clients like him make this life feel infinite.

Hold up, *godsend*? What the fuck? One of you should've checked me for that.

Todd's a great, great customer, but, real speak, he's also a sucker-for-love type too. There was this one time when I stopped by his old crib to handle business and he answered the door in a wife-beater and boxers, with his braids undone, looking like he'd just got his ass whooped, when in truth he was damn near disembowel-ed over a broad. Most guys, in front a crowd, they'll claim they're tough boss-mack-player types, but away from the public, in those recesses where the lie of us won't live, they're Romeo-drink-the-poison-for-a-pretty-young-Juliet kind of punks, and choice cli-ent aside, count Todd in that group. That day I stopped by, he whined and whined about the broad and likely would have kept right on whining if I didn't cut him short: Listen, man, it's all fun and games till they got you where you like them more than they like you, I said. You need a new plan. You can't keep treating these chicks like crystal statues.

I don't know, man, he said.

Damn, thought you was a player, I said. Thought a player like you would know some of them is dying to be dogged. C'mon man, a gang of broads is mystic flagellants.

Homeboy lit up a blunt and sucked. Like many a cliché dope boy, his whole crib was redolent of some of Oregon's finest, reason why a contact high was wagging its middle finger in my brain.

And I ain't talking physical either, I said. You'd be surprised how many chase heartache, need it to feel whole.

He took another pull and gazed at me, sclera the color of blood, a half-moon of white in the crease of his scorched bottom lip.

I'm tellin you some real shit, bro, I said. Put the cease-and-desist on the search-and-rescues.

You will never guess what homeboy's response was after all that free G. (G as in game, peoples, stick with me!) It was this: Champ, what the fuck's a flagellant?

Why did I mention the story? Right here, right now? Reason why is what happened at Todd's was on my mind last week when I went to this super-hood hole-in-the-wall in Southeast, a spot where the chicks looked hella-weary, and every other dude wore a just-paroled-long-pinkie-nail, a spot where I ended up rapping to this chick I knew from jump I had no intent on pursuing. Macked her digits out of no more than habit, stuffed them in my pocket, and took my black ass home. But my luck, if it's luck, you've got to love and hate it. Kim sleuthed the shred of paper out of my jeans (since a real player checks his pockets before stepping foot in his crib, what am I?) while I was in the bathroom and wouldn't hear word one of my sorry-ass excuse. She cursed me into a salt pillar and cried and cried. You would've thought she'd cry till dawn, cry for a day, sob all the way till the new year. She's got a bulging heart, my girl, one that stumbles outside her like a sixth sense, feeling. But the cold part, the part I know deep deep at the source, is that she'll hurt for now and forgive. Can she hurt for now and forget? Tough guess, but against myself most times, I keep giving her chances to try.

Peoples, peoples, ladies especially, you few sentient gents. Tell the truth, you *got* to be tired of my vagina monologues. You've got to be tired of all this wannabe boss-mack-player talk of pussy and conquests and general female malice. Let me apologize in earnest to those who've had it up to here. For you, you, and you who've passed that point. Trust and believe, trust and motherfucking believe, I'm tired, so tired, of *living* this talk. It's hard, maybe impossible to believe, but I'm not a bad guy. Maybe chickenshit beyond recourse but not mendacious. All my skirt-chasing and tough talk is no better and mostly worse than a flimsy shield. From more than you all will ever know. From more than I may ever know. From more for sure than I could ever call up the courage to speak on.

But what I will say is this: Who's your first love? What happens when that first love warns you to save room for hurt and spends half your life applying the most harm? How do you protect what bleeds?

Forget that shit they preach on risk and reward. When it comes to a heart, my heart, being butt-naked and swollen in the world, it's the greater the risk, the deeper the scar.

But weep for me not, though. I don't want no parts of it.

That's not why I said what I said. I said all I said to ask this: Can you do me a huge, huge solid and translate? Cause the times I'm talking pussy and conquest and general female abuse, what I'm really talking is wounds.

Wounds and salves.

Wounds and bows.

Wounds and deeper wounds.

Then here I am.

—Grace

I WATCH THE NEWS till the news goes off. I lie down and
sit up. Lay down and sit up. I edge to the edge of the bed and half
watch a late-night show. I lie back, force my eyes shut, and pray
for a dream. Nothing, so I get up and throw on my robe and
slink into the kitchen and fix a hot tea. I leave the mug to cool
and take out my pack—it's lasted all week—and light a cig on
the stove. It flares orange and shivers in the slice between my
fingers. The smoke shakes in me as I sit crossing and uncrossing
my legs.

What about my boys? What about all I've missed? The one or
two birthdays. The umpteen missed games—T-ball, football, basketball. The nights I blew school plays, recitals, parent-teacher
conferences.

Thoughts like this can bring it on, and when you feel it building, you make a list of who to call. Of who will offer a haven. Of
who will remind you how far you've come.

My God. I could call Champ, Pat if he's out, my sponsor, but
there's a strength to be gained from fighting this urge alone. Get
through this and I can escape them all. I smoke another cigarette
too close to the brown, stub it out in a bowl, slink into the room,
and lie across the bed wishing this time sleep finds me, but instead

end up splashing in and out of sleep with these nerves, with my neighbors keeping up noise above my head. I take out the state letter and read it once more, remind myself to keep faith, that this will all work out in the end. It will all work out for us in the end. I drag out of bed and dress and tramp to Big Charles's corner store. Big Charles is hunkered behind the counter and don't look happy to see me. Don't look surprised either. Let me guess, he says, and slants his mouth. So much for the last time being the last time. Look like you well on your way to puffin again like an old broke stove. He pulls my brand without me asking and tosses me a book of matches that he says are on the house. I pay and skitter out with my eyes cut to the floor. I stop and trash the packaging and light up and feel the first sweet pull knock the shake from my hands. I give the second pull time to do its work and flit down Williams for home. The block is wet and clear but for two bodies up ahead hard to make out. This late I should cross the street, I think, but I don't. Closer, I drop my head and blow a wreath and judge the distance between us by the sound of their voices, the footfalls of a heavy boot. When I'm a step past them, she calls my name and frights me into a dead stop. I turn slow and Dawn and I are face-to-face. Knew I'd see you, she says. Knew it soon as I seen Champ. She steps closer and presses a cold bony cheek against mine and asks why I'm out and what I've been up to.

Working, I say. Just working and going to church. There ain't much time for too much else.

I know that's right, she says. I seen Michael the other night and he said ya'll was out together not too long ago. She steps back and swings an arm over the man's shoulder. This is Jerry, she says. Jerry drives trucks, but he's off two days and wants to party.

She and I so many times out. The nights she coaxed me from bed while the boys were asleep with a promise, never kept, that I'd be home before they woke. The nights we crouched in a black corner and went rock for rock through every red cent of a state check. This woman was in the room when Champ was born, is the godmother of my baby boy.

What do you do with all of this?

We either are or we aren't.
Where we go, there we are.
I am new.
I am strong.
Faith without works is dead.

No, thanks, I say. Not for me.

Oh, girl. Did I say? she says. It's all-expense paid.

Makes me no difference, I say.

Come on, girl, she says. Just like old times, you'll be back fore you know you was gone.

There's strength to be earned in facing it alone. But how often can we beat the risk? Here I am—once more. Here we are. It—a tightness in your stomach and taste lying on your tongue—comes on in a flood and you can't fight the tide.

Next thing, we flit almost single-file, Dawn at the head, Jerry bopping behind us—the brim of his trucker cap bent to a V, his long hair flopping underneath—and me fighting my steps, pills of sweat scrawling my side, something inside me a thunder in my ears. Our makeshift envoy stomping from block to block till we reach a street that's not a street but a tunnel under arched trees.

Dawn stops at a house with a spastic porch light and a hard fast dopehead standing inside a waist-high fence. He calls her name and tips up to the fence.

Dawn loops her arm through mine. These my friends, she says. We trying to see who got it.

Not a problem. Not a problem, he says. Long as you straighten me out on the back end.

Jerry shows the man what, in the wrong place, in a place like this, could get us robbed. He brags we came to party.

Well, say no more, the man says. He tours us a few doors down to a narrow house with every other window boarded and an old car raised on bricks in the yard. We wind a concrete path to a side door, where our guy tells us to let him do the talking and knocks a knock that must be a code. Dawn clasps my hand, but there's no comfort in it. The boy that answers wears a folded blue bandanna around his head, a dress-long T-shirt, and pants that could fit him and someone else.

Bear in-pocket? our guy says. Brought him some business.

The boy glares and points us down a hall and we scoot past a clique of other boys still in age range for a good whooping, to a half-opened door with a hole punched though it. Our guy pushes inside. There's a beasty hunk of a man hunkered at a table with a tiny TV playing shadows across his face. Speak, he says, without bothering to look up.

What it is, our guy says. Got some folks lookin to spend. Told em you was the one to spend with.

Dawn gives my hand another crush. It should be a sign to flee but it's a sign to be still.

Jerry steps forward and tips his trucker cap. Howdy, he says. If you don't mind, we'd like to start small, and if it's prime, we'll spend a whole heap witcha. He yanks a crisp twenty from a fat chain wallet.

What the fuck's that? Bear says. He stabs his yellow eyes at us one by one. What, you ain't told them we don't fuck with no minor licks? he says. He waves a paw. Miss me with this nickel-and-dime shit. Sixteenth and up or no go.

It would be a blessing if Jerry takes offense and we leave. The perfect chance for me to admit I've made a mistake, that I've got no business here, that I should run home as fast as I can. The problem is, in this life, when you expect it most, no one takes offense enough. Jerry jerks a hundred from his wallet. Not a problem, he says.

We follow our guy downstairs. He tells us not to worry, that as long as we're spending, it's all good with Bear. He asks about his pay no sooner than we clear the last step and Jerry unsheathes a pocketknife and slices a generous chunk. Our guy bounds the stairs with his fee stashed in his cheek. This place is like so many others, gloom and dust. A chair with its fourth leg snapped off, a leather love seat ripped to flaps, hole-punched pop cans strewn on a low table. Jerry loads our first bowl, and we spark the blast we'll chase the rest of the night. Then the circuit: we smoke one pill and another and burn time and who knows what else, and Jerry tramps to see Bear while Dawn and I sit far apart and silent. He buys more dope and returns with a face that, on a night like tonight, you might mistake for love. Jerry wipes his face and shakes his hair and refits his cap. He stands and belts a blues tune, belts two. A boy shuffles to midway on the steps. Ya'll gone have to bounce with all the bullshit, he says.

Jerry apologizes and the boy disappears upstairs. For a time after, we talk in taps and touches. Jerry goes up and comes down with a face you might mistake—on a night like tonight—for faith. Then more of the same. We pop and sizzle for hours, a day, for what could last a life. We keep on till birds chirp outside and light pipes through the boards covering a busted-out window.

Dawn, poor Dawn, claws the pipe to her chest like the Lamb of God, but we coax it away and pass and pass until the dope is gone and Jerry's wallet has thinned almost flat. I'm afraid it's true, he says. What they say about all good things. He turns what's left in his wallet into a flag and fans it. He plods upstairs a last time.

The end is always so sad, Dawn says. She hacks a cough and worries the cuff of her shirt.

What time is it? I say. What time you think it is?

Why? she says. Who got someplace to be?

I do, I say. Work.

Work will be there, she says. That's how jobs is, just waiting around for somebody to do them. She stands and throws her arms up: Work, work, work, she says. Jerry floats down with a good-sized sixteenth. He lays it whole on the screen and we burn it down to a shard. We smoke the shard, and when it's gone Jerry scrapes the resin with the tip of his knife—collects a tiny farewell bump.

That's it, I say. No more.

Dawn's face falls down. She turns to me. Maybe not, she says. We could barter.

Barter with what? I say.

With this, she says, and points. I'd do it myself, but I'm on my menstrual and you know how heavy it is. Messy ain't worth as much.

What? I say. Who? Not me.

... And we all by now should know what that is.
                              —Champ

IT'S NOT HOW IT STARTED (Mom carried newborn
me from the hospital back to Sixth Street—back home), but by
the time I was waddling around on my own two, it seemed like
we were on a quest to live everywhere there was for us (the *us*
being anyone within a grade of our hue) to live in the city. There
was the rental house off Powell where we lived when KJ was born,
a place infamous for its pothole minefield. There was the duplex in
Southeast that, whenever we tramped inside from the rain (when
wasn't it raining?), our shag carpet stunk of a wet dog. There was
Big Ken's mother's house on Seventh and Shaver, the place we
lived when, one Fourth of July, an atomic-ass firecracker blew in
my fist. There was the shabby apartment on Lombard where me
and my homeboys would meet under the carports, lay cardboard
over oil-slicked concrete, and break dance till the batteries drained
on a boom box. How could I forget the two-bedroom townhouse
with stucco walls on Thirtieth and Stark? This was where we lay
our heads the time Mom and Big Ken took their longest hiatus,
where we lived when my guess Canaan was conceived during a
bout of make up sex, where we stayed when Big Ken bought me
a cherry red moped that, against Mom's rants, he'd let me wheel
on backstreets alone. We moved here. We moved there. We moved

for a time back to Sixth. There were those years when we lived across the water in a giant apartment complex called the Wingate Estates. Tennis courts, swimming pool, a rec room, the complex had the works. This was the place we lived the summer I learned how to swim, the summers I rode bike trails and skateboards past Mom's lax sunset curfew. Twentieth and Belmont. Twelve and Klickitat. There was the month or two for some reason or other I lived with Uncle Sip and a white broad in Tigard. There was the half year we suffered in a raggedy studio on the corner of Williams and Killingsworth, the place we moved to when Mom checked out of her inaugural in-patient program. There and there and back to Sixth—back home. We'd spend months in a spot. A year. Sometimes weeks.

. . . Then Bubba died and, months later, Mama Liza (how's that for a lifetime love?) and my avaricious great Uncs strong-armed my granddad into the idea that selling the house on Sixth trumped keeping it in the family. This was around the time white men in khakis and polo shirts were skipping around the neighborhood, smiling sly, knocking on doors, and coercing hella-gullible residents with what must've seemed like unrefusable sums. Next thing we had an estate sale in the house on Sixth. Then a for-sale sign popped up. Then I drove by one day in my high school bucket and saw a minivan parked in the back driveway and movers ferrying taped boxes up the front porch steps.

You'd be surprised at what you can find in the classifieds. Case in point, I search the real estate section and luck upon an ad (bet it cost a nice piece of change) that takes up the most space on a page. Big bold letters too.

THE REAL ESTATE GUY

BUYING OR SELLING

BANKS OR PRIVATE

NO MATTER YOUR REAL ESTATE NEEDS

WE'RE HERE TO HELP!

503-555-9000!

What do I have to lose? I call, and a couple rings later a wispy-voiced dude picks up. He calls himself Jude the Real Estate Guy, and says he's at my service. Off-top (maybe it's the feathery-ass falsetto), the dude sounds super-sprightly, too chipper, really, but I give him my name and the barest details of why I called. He tells me, from what I said (how he can know this now is beyond me, but I'm desperate enough to buy it), there's less reason to be worried than I think. No joke, not only is homie's voice cherry to the utmost, it's also epicene, which in a strange way gives me peace and hope.

He asks me when and where I'd like to meet and I say as soon as we can at the coffee shop near the mall. How's today? he says.

It's easy (it ain't but two customers inside, and one of them is an Asian) to spot Jude a couple hours later in the coffee shop. He's the one crammed in a corner booth. I call his name and he looks up and ekes out. Right off you can't help but notice he's as bulky as I am thin (wonder if he feels about his girth how I feel about my slight), with dark hair silvered above his ears, saggy jowls, and a snout that's a normal nose squared; scratch that, with a nose that's two human noses cubed! What I mean to say is the tiny voice I heard over the phone must be stuck inside the wrong dude.

Nice to meet you, he says. He asks if I want coffee or water and unbuttons a loose sport coat. Judging by his smile (too toothy for a grown-ass man) homie's cool tank is running on fumes—if you ask me another positive sign. He excuses himself and bops to the counter, hella-tons on his tippy-toes, and returns with bottled waters. I twist off the top and swig. He rifles through a folder embossed with his name and slogan. Bud, I always like to start with two things I believe about business, he says. You've got to be able to give people what they need, sometimes even before they know they need it. The second is forget what they say about mixing business and personal. That's a load of crapola. I do my business with people, and to me that's always personal.

Jude's voice is, at best, an infinitesimal bit off the sissified, an octave or so below what mines was in high school, those years my teammates used to bust my balls about my pitch, the years I would tense something treacherous at the prospect of answering a phone and being mistook for a chick.

You ever met a stranger who confides their life story (lowlights, highlights, dashed dreams, five-year plan) a second past an intro? Have you ever? Jude tells me he was born in Lubbock but lived a little bit of everywhere, says his old man was a die-hard lush who could never hold a job and every year disappeared for a season. Jude confides that he's childless, with an ex-wife who wants to fleece him to pennies, and at present is doing a helluva helluva job. He claims he was a D-1 philosophy-minoring middle linebacker headed for the pros till he tore an ACL and took up binge-eating and pill-popping. The confessions go on. The man admits that ever since he wrecked his knee, even though he kicked the pills, he hasn't been able to shed the weight. So I ended up here, Jude says. Cause every smart real estate man knows this city is the new frontier.

But enough about me, he says. What about you, bud? What's your story?

Show me a nigger with that much trust and courage, who's that open from jump. Forsure, forsure, I can show you a nigger who ain't. What I don't tell Jude is what I shouldn't tell Jude. And we all by now should know what that is.

Jude says his old man preached that a man's business is a man's business, so he can understand keeping some things to myself, but when I'm ready, if I'm ever ready, that I could breach the code.

I tell him about the house, the backstory of my sacrosanct great-grands, and how long it was ours; about the new owners and my tour and the fact it isn't for sale; about what I think I can hustle if, no, make that *when* we convince them to sell. Meantime, Jude jots notes in the pad he pulled from a folder, turning animate tufts of dark knuckle hair.

He sets his pen aside and gulps his drink. Bud, I've never been one to mislead. This sounds tough, but I promise to do the best I can. He slides out of the booth and flashes those seismic teeth. What am I saying? he says. If it can be done, we'll do it. Rest assured you've found the right guy.

Outside, Jude throws on his thin standard-issue (two ovals stretched out to points, the same style for every white male on earth!) white-boy shades. He asks how far we are from the house, and when I tell him, he says that we should go have a look-see, and offers to drive. His ride is a white rental with shampooed cloth seats and logo-stamped rubber mats. He keeps his hands at ten and two the whole way there and hazards not a single mile per hour over any posted speed. Better safe, he says.

When we get to Sixth, he cruises by the house and keeps going around the block, to get, he says, a feel for the neighborhood. The next time around he parks a distance back and gets out and tippy-toes up to the house. He gallivants (if he's worried about the owners thinking he's a snoop specialist I sure can't tell; got to love that white man's audacity!) around the front, the back, the side facing Mason. Meantime, I'm leaned in my seat invisible-man style on straight tenterhooks that the husband or the wife will spy Jude or me or us both, believe me shady, and ground this whole expectant business before it ever grows wings. I peek over the dash and see upgrades from the last time I drove by, new paint on the porch and what looks like a good power-washing for the rest of the place—signs I can't or won't decode. Jude makes another trip around the house and tippy-toes back to the car.

Wow! Now, that's what you call a home, he says. You know, there's nothing like owning your own piece of terra firma, Jude says. If this was the Middle Ages, when land was your one and only piece of wealth, you might have to fight for it. In those days, possession ruled, he says. If you had it, you owned it; if you found it, you kept it; if you wanted it, you had to fight. And that's pretty much how it stayed till William the Conqueror came along, defeated King Harold, and declared ownership of every square inch of England. It was the new king that gave land rights to his officers and made them tenants-in-chief of huge plots of land. Wasn't long before those chiefs were getting rich subletting their land, then passing their riches and rights to their kids. They called it the feudal system, Jude says. But some people call it the birth of the aristocrats. He takes off his standard-issue shades and wipes his nose. And Shawn, let me tell you, after all this time, a home's still the best way to leap from one class to the next, to get a foothold in the world.

He leaves the car off and we sit. I watch an old man hobble up the steps of what's maybe still Miss Mary's house. Watch a boy skip his scooter along the sidewalk. Mist gathers and Jude lowers his window and sticks his head into it. He reels himself in, straps on his seat belt, grabs the wheel on the numbers, and turns to me. Bud, whether they will or won't, we hope for the best. And I'll do all I can. All I can and more. But I can tell you one thing sure, he says. This won't be cheap.

Got it, got it.
　　—Grace

I'M TIRED, TIRED, but early for the shift after the shift I missed. In the ladies' room I soap stains—when was I supposed to have made it to a washhouse?—and splash my face alive. I step out of the restroom a tiny bit staggered and see Pam leaning against the wall with a clipboard tucked. She cuts her eyes at me and inspects nails this week she's painted in triple fluorescents.

Missed you, she says. That's how you do? No call, no nothin?

Oh, I say. Was I on the schedule?

Nice try, but don't try it, she says.

Try what? I say.

Enough! she says. I told you from day one, I need workers I can trust.

It won't happen again, I say. You have my word. Next time I'll double-check.

If there's a next time, it's your last time, she says.

Got it, got it, I say.

Great, glad you do, cause I meant it, she says. Now tell me what's wrong. Why you don't seem yourself.

Just tired is all, I say, though as soon as I say it, I hate her for the fact she won't seek the truth. Hate myself for needing to be pushed to it.

Pam shakes her braids—thick ropes plaited wide and pulling at the edges of her scalp—off her shoulders. Come, she says, and drags me into the office. She lays her clipboard down, collects time cards spread across her desk. I snatch off my visor and smooth my hair; what I wouldn't give for another visit to the stylist. She searches her drawer for a stack of checks and hands me mines.

I know you say you're tired, but I might need you for OT, she says.

That's fine, I say, and stuff the check in my pants and walk out to the front counter.

There's a baseball team—snap-back hats and raglans—in the lobby, boys about the same age as KJ, and it brings me low to see them laugh and joke. I open a till and wave over a scrawny boy with braces. Welcome to Taco World. How may I help you? I say, and wonder if he too can see this blight.

Fucking refuse, do you hear?

—Champ

THE WIND SENDS a broken branch into the same bed of sawdust where, one night, my girl stabbed my toothbrush so deep in the soil, you could only see the tip. Why? It's a long, long story, both the original version and the extended remix. I'm trying as best I can to keep you from getting distracted. That's a lie, but I'd rather not speak on it. I couldn't stand any of you thinking less of me.

From the room where I keep my computer and books, I watch my neighbor, the one from across the hall, pull up in his dented compact. Dude's a teacher, which I know because he corners me everywhere he can (in the laundry room, in the elevator, by mailboxes, near the trash) and dupes me into saga-length Q&A's. I'm so serious, if he catches your ear, it's the Indefatigable Express, with nonstops till you break, either that or smack (never did it, but believe me it's crossed my mind more than once) him right in his trap! Guys like him, if I was less prone to fits of guilt and shame, I'd curse them to hell, but since I'm not, I cut him slack cause we know how it is with those college-educated middle-to-ruling-class whiteys: Everybody's business (how else to keep the rest of us on lock?) is their business.

Tonight, Mr. Chat-You-to-Sleep lollygags in his ride longer

than the norm. He climbs out, finally, holding a clutch of papers and a lunch pail. He loses a few sheets and chases them down. He presses the damp papers and his metal box to his chest and scurries inside. End of show.

The encore ain't the chatterer, but a clique in letterman coats slapboxing their way along the block. Every few steps, they drop their bags, square off, start a new round. Nothing special really, but *bam*, just like that, I got an idea for my personal statement. An anecdote about the time one night I was coming home from a game and a carload of gang members cruised beside me, screamed, What up, blood? and dumped a few shots my way.

Now, having an idea is one thing, but the real work is turning a blank screen into words, into sentences, into a few fucking paragraphs. My laptop's fan is whirring, that's how long it's been since I last tapped the keys. A slew of starts and stops, starts and stops and deletions then back to ogling the cursor, the glowing white screen. Wasn't checking in the least for grad school before now and look? I want in on my accord, though. On merit or not at all. No handouts, no punk-ass affirmative actions for me. I get the few first lines tapped out, but after that—nathan. Just me fumbling for a next sentence and losing track of time. Maybe I was wrong: What's tougher than a blank screen is a sentence or two and nowhere to go from there. I get up and walk again to the window, thinking it worked once, why not? I look far, far down the street and then up at the clouds, always the clouds, where a star or two twink. I slug into the kitchen, grab a two-liter (real pop too, none of that diet crap) out the fridge, and meander back to my laptop, where I take a swill that crawls down my throat. Then it's me back gazing at the screen and praying for afflatus. A prayer answered when, I'll be gotdamned, words arrive, begrudged, one word and then the next, and after a while I got a whole page and I'm dancing around the table. What is it? What is it? Kim says, from the front room. I carry my laptop to where she is and peep her doing what she does best besides harangue your boy: laze on the couch and channel-surf. She's got her feet (bare toes cause the doc said polish could poison the baby) on the table and her shirt hiked above her tumescent belly. She pats the couch for me to sit. It's the statement, I say. I think I got a start. Let me read it to you two. By the way, this reading to the baby is brand-new.

Not baby. It's a girl. It's a girl. We're having a baby girl!

Tell me, what was the sense anymore in fighting it?

Yes, I was hella-resistant at first, but hearing the heartbeat did a retrograde number on my resolve. These days I'm a baby-book bibliophile: *The New Dad's Survival Guide, Man to Man on Child, Daddy Prep, A Father's Firstborn* . . . these days, I'm a neophyte baby-supply specialist, packing our closets with all things infant: the stroller, the car seat, the booster seat, the high chair, the potty chair, a swing, a bouncer, a bottle warmer, a breast pump; catch me stocking an oversized toy chest with rattles, dolls, building blocks, touch-and-feel flash cards. I've bought cases of diapers, wipes, bottles, washcloths, bought doubles and triples of baby soap and lotion and shampoo and oil, stockpiled bibs, burp clothes, blankets.

Got to the point where some mornings I stand at the mirror and sing lullabies. Cause between you and me the near birth of my future Princess has my vulnerability levels dropped way down, any lower and I'd be on par with dudes like Jude, the proud owners of lifetime weep-for-free passes. But all in all in all it's for best, right? Who among you would claim different?

You hear that, Princess? I say, to Kim's navel. Dad's going to grad school.

Say it first and believe it second; that's my psalm.

Okay, and what happens after? Kim says. What happens all the while?

We went over this, I say.

We did, she says. But what if it doesn't work out the way you think?

Don't let her hear you, I say. You best not ever let her hear you doubt me.

Champ, she needs to survive, she says. We do.

I'm supporting us now, ain't I? I say

You need a job, Champ, she says. A job. Why don't you just finish and work?

You act like you don't know me by now. You act like you don't know better than judge me by these local-ass standards. My dreams are bigger than this place, and you nor no one else is going to kill them.

What's that supposed to mean? she says.

You know what the fuck it means, I say, and whip her around by her chin rougher than I should. I refuse to be one of these fools anonymous everywhere but inside their head. Fucking refuse, do you hear?

Kim falls quiet. She tugs her shirt over her stomach.

My pager goes off. It's one of my regulars calling too late for a lick, but I need the dough—and that's that.

Who's that this late? she says.

It's business, I say. My business, I'll be right back.

Funny you should ask.

—Grace

THIS HEIFER—FORGIVE ME, LORD—is wasting too much of my precious time, treating me as though I begged for the world, when all I asked for was change to make a call. At my back, rowdy kids knock over piles of folded clothes and kick overstuffed shivering washers. Metal clinks in multiload dryers. A giant steamer hisses somewhere unseen. I snatch the quarters and head outside to the phone booth.

I call expecting the line to ring and ring with no answer, for their machine to pick up.

Oh, so it's you, Kenny says. Didn't recognize the number.

It's a whole lot that you don't, I say. Where are my boys?

Grace, I don't think I'm feeling your tone of voice, he says.

Cut the games, I say.

They're at the park, he says. Call back.

I'll do you one better, I say.

He lets the phone go quiet.

A barefoot toddler darts past me into the parking lot with no one giving chase.

Guess you didn't hear me? he says.

Why should I be listening? I say.

See, that's it, he says. We got court coming up. We'll let the judge decide when you will and won't.

Judge who? I say. I'm coming to see my boys.

Grace! he says. In all honesty, you can't dictate shit, he says. What you need to do is get yourself situated, so when all this is settled, you'll have a decent place for the boys to visit.

We shall see, I say.

Yes, he says. We shall.

The way I slam the phone knocks a quarter out the coin return. I turn my back to the booth, but don't know where to go, don't know what to do, but what I need is someone close who'll listen, who could help. The nearest one I can think of is Kenny's older brother Chris, who used to live not too far from here. Chris, who was an ear for me when his brother and I had troubles, whose advice Kenny would mind when no one else could get through. I hike Fremont, too tired to know how tired I am. A car toots at me, but I don't bother looking up. I make a turn and amble by young girls twirling double-Dutch ropes. A block or so beyond, there's a young couple carrying groceries into the same house where years and years ago I almost got caught in a drug raid.

That night the police kicked in the front door, guns drawn and shouting, and I burst out the back barefoot because I couldn't run in heels. There was a dog chasing me till I hit the first fence, and I could feel the air from its bark at my feet. I sprang one fence and another, cut through black yards, my feet not feeling a thing. All I could think of was being caught, of having to explain what I was doing in the house in the first place. This fear kept me tearing through backstreets until there was nothing behind me but wind, until I reached Dawson Park, where I crouched behind a bush and waited till the sun rose.

You can hear the girls twirl their ropes and sing a tune. The woman grins at the man from the porch. He climbs the steps with armloads of bags and stops on a landing and a dog bounds out on the front to meet him and nuzzles against his leg. A last turn puts me on what used to be Chris's block and what in a fair world still is. You can see a man that looks like Chris in a driveway, hovering over a two-seater with a hand sheathed in a fluffy glove. I huff to within a shout.

That sure is a nice ride, I say.

Hey, hey, hey. Well, ain't this somethin. What's happenin, sis? he says, snatches off his mitt. Ain't seen you since can't even call it. He rubs his pants, the hands he shares with his brother, thick and hairless, though his pinky nail is filed to a spike.

Happened to be in the neighborhood, I say. Thought I'd drop by and make sure you was still alive.

Now you know us pimps don't die, he says, and moves closer. His cologne could knock you down.

Well, I see you ain't lost your sense of humor, I say.

Ha! Never that. But on the serious tip, sis, what's been up? When you last seen my thickhead brother? Me and Blood ain't got up in a few.

Funny you should ask, I say. Cause I just got off the phone with him. Can I tell you I'm so finished.

Chris's eyes linger on places I'd rather they wouldn't. Makes me think what's left to see in me of my last time out, what signs might give it away.

Yeah, Blood done flip-flopped, but that's how it be when

them white folks put you on payroll. Enough about him, though. How's my nephews?

Getting grown too fast, I say. Actually, they been living with your brother this past year.

Oh, he says. Oh. That's news to me. That a long- or a short-term deal?

Supposed to have been short, but your brother trying to see it turn permanent, I say. We go to court coming up here soon.

Court! As in before a judge? You *got* to be bullshittin! he says. That yellow nigga really is out his head. Chris throws his mitts on the hood. He swings open the driver's-side door and plops inside. He thumbs the replica emblem anchoring his gold chain.

But on a happier note, I say. What's the latest with you? You still ripping and running the streets?

Oh, you know how it go with me, he says. Get rich or go to jail trying. He laughs. He checks himself in his car's tiny side mirror, pats the graying sides of his Jheri curl, pinches his hoop earrings. On the serious tip, though, sis, I got a little business I'm bout to start. Soul food restaurant by them old motels on Interstate.

That sounds nice, I say.

Hope so, he says. Got to find a way. But how about you? he says. You back working them corporate gigs?

Not so much anymore, I say.

He cocks his head and looks up at me. Well, I tell you what, I ain't got but a couple weeks till my doors is open, and when they do, you got a job, he says. That's my word.

Now, I just might have to take you up on that, I say.

Cool, cool, he says.

Chris asks where I'm headed and I tell him Kenny's place. He asks if I'm driving and I admit that I'm on foot, catching buses, the train. So is Blood still out there in the boonies? he says. I nod and he offers me a ride. He collects his supplies in a bucket and sits the bucket by the garage. He tells me to wait in the car while he runs in to change. He struts out hot seconds later wearing a Hawaiian print shirt open to flash his chain and terry-cloth sweats. His Jheri curl is not of want for sheen.

We get on the road. The way he drives, you blink and you're on the freeway, whipping lanes, his engine revving in low gears and whistling at a high speed. Off the bridge, we almost miss our exit for the highway heading east. He keeps the music off, and we end up trading stories. The road trip where Champ locked him out the car while we stopped to get gas. The night I punched his prostitute for cursing in front of the boys, the year we all flew to Canada for the Fourth of July. He and I have always had such an easy time. It reminds me how often between men—between brothers even—that a girl chooses wrong, and how, after a time, the wrong choices become us. Chris whisks the east highway in high gears and nothing else. The wind twirls my hair into a swarm. We get off the exit and catch the light and I tell him how an ex anything brings me down. He lets the car coast down the slope. Sis, you know it wouldn't hurt for you to try and see the world sunny side up sometimes, he says. We ride the next lights in pinched quiet. He pulls over just inside the subdivision. I'd drop you right out front, he says, but it might be best for you if I don't.

This hair, I make to smooth it and thank him for the ride and sling out the car. Hold up, he says, and reaches in his glove box for a napkin, and scribbles his number. He tells me to remind him of the court date: And I'm so serious about the job, he says. He backs out rather than risk a drive by his brother's.

Kenny's neighborhood is a world of its own, a world away from the Piedmonts. Boys shoot baskets at a curbside hoop; a man trims his front hedges; a couple power-walks toward a distant cul-de-sac. I stutter up to Kenny's house, a sight in this season, a spread of lush grass cut sharp at its edges, bark dust smoothed over blooming weedless flower beds, paint that almost gleams. You can see how tired I am—the wrung eyes, the pillows in my cheeks—in the glass of Kenny's front door. I take out a tube of gloss and paint my lips and practice a mock smile. Right now I could leave. There's a feeling in me to leave, to whisk past the boys, beyond these perfect lawns and cheery strolling pairs, to sprint till I reach the other side of the brick walls that cleave this place from what could never equal up. Kenny throws his front door wide and frights me. I didn't hear him walk up.

Figured you'd show anyhow, he says. You never was one for listening.

Where are my sons? I say.

They gone, he says.

That's a lie, I say. Where are they?

Lie to you for what? he says. Who are you to lie to?

He looks over my shoulder and I turn to see what he sees. It's a car coming towards us. Kenny struts down the pathway and waits on the slope while I'm held stillest. Helen pulls up and he helps her out of the car and makes a show of whispering to her. She frowns and tucks a bag that cost my life, all of my life, to her side and waves a ring awesome even in this failing light. KJ climbs out and squints at me as if I'm a thing made of steel and wood, and stands in place with his arms at his sides. It takes him forever to lope over and begrudge me a limp squeeze.

Aren't you happy to see me? I say.

He answers too low for me to make out.

My youngest climbs out and stands, looking doleful, his eyes on this man, this woman, on his brother, settling on me. We step to meet each other and he presses his head in my chest and pulls me close. His heart knocks against mine and when we break, he takes his time slugging for the house. He gives me a farewell glance before crossing the threshold. Then it's me and this man and this woman face-to-haughty face. Kenny kisses Helen on the head and cossets her ring. They beam at each other in a way that makes me want—the lucky ones get more of a life than they've earned—to do them harm. She huffs and flounces off, and Kenny stands back, arms folded. You've never seen a man this smug.

Yous about a dirty, I say. Plain dirty, I say. What you been telling my boys?

Grace, you don't get it, do you? You still don't get it, do you? he says. The boys got eyes. They can see.

That's why we do business.

—Champ

THE COME UP.

Try one without them.

My first regular was this cluck who called himself Showtime who used to rush for me during my second go 'round on the curb. He was as old as one of my unc's and had a hairline caught in a permanent zeek—a push back to the fulfillity. For a pinch off one of my fatter pills (if you ain't peeped it yet among othings we call them pills) he'd roam a shout distance off and wouldn't show his face until he had a buy. He was good for hustling up twenty licks, forty licks, the odd fifty, miniscule ends in retrospect but business that popped my profit cherry.

Then there was this white man across the water in Vancouver who wore black biker leathers and a long-ass ponytail. He ran with a band of methheads turned crackheads or methcrackheads, most of them longshoremen or truckers by trade. Clockwork, he'd hit my line for a few hundred dollars worth of dope (pill for pill too so choice profit!) for him and his seafaring, long-haul buddies. We used to meet in this department store on Mill Plain and do the swap in a vacant aisle. You should have seen him after that, a hirsute blur out the store. But me, more cautious then, made habit of lagging, would drift into a longer line, buy a load of knickknacks, and stroll out proxy-blithe.

You want to come up? Trust, you ain't coming up without them.

Without clientele like this full-time hustler/part-time basehead. Picture this husky dude with skin three times onyx, eyes that shine hepatitic gold, and a flat-backed head swathed yearlong in a linty skull cap. But don't let aesthetics or the fact that he partakes of the occasional beam-up throw you. Homie is oh so serious about his (our) bread. Orders an ounce every other day and by the day near the first of the month and has never once dickered for a bulk deal, complained the dope's discolored, nor said a foul word about an aftertaste.

No bullshit. Where would I be without them?

Without dude I've been dealing with off and on, more steady than not, since I first started getting fronted whole ones. He's this OG Crip with fat cornrows and a cold-ass effluvium and who, on the low, might be part bigfoot—a size to, with no windup at all, slap a bantamweight non-pugilistic nigger such as me into forever sleep. But rancidness aside, homie orders a minimum of four-and-a-half and most times more with the drawback being a drawback I can bear: he rathers I deliver to one of his spots (boarded shacks where hordes of destitute clucks burn through settlement checks, SSI and state checks, through what's left of their crippled pride), pop-up dopehouses he runs with crews of young blue-rag deuces.

Nah, wouldn't be shit without them, minus the one I'm here to meet tonight. Best customer of the bunch. Past or present.

I'm parked by the corner store, shadowed, solicitous, half a whole thing (the shit was too bulky for my boxer briefs) stuffed in a Ziploc in a paper sack that's crammed inside my sleeve. Half a whole one is a big fucking lick, could put a nice dent in whatever down payment (no, not if but when and how much) Jude works out. This happy shit is what's on my mind when a car pulls up in the rear and flashes its lights. Budging for headlight blinks while hitting a solo lick for a half kilo? You would think not, but . . . I stick my head out the window and see an arm waving me back, hear a voice, Todd's voice, calling my name. The part of my brain that makes sound, the most sound, decisions says let him come to me and do the deal in my ride, but you know how I do.

This a new ride? I say.

Rental, Todd says.

Oh, okay. What kind? I say.

You got that on you? he says.

Fasho, I say.

Cool, he says. Let's roll.

We pull off slow, with Todd finger-steering and the music on whisper and the wipers lulling and the dashboard lit in neons. We make a few turns to the drum of languorous rain.

This lick has got me breaking my embargo on business after sundown, but we know why, correct? Plus, as I said, me and dude go back. Way before his sucker-for-love scene, we both pledged Brothers Gaining Equality, a fledgling high school fraternity (you wouldn't catch me pledging a college frat now, plodding campus with an ego gassed on Greek myths) made up of upperclassmen and a freshman or two. BGE held can drives, coat drives, community cleanups, spoke to kids, danced at step shows, threw parties, volunteered weekends at old folks' homes. As it happened, Todd pledged a couple months after me and rocked with the group till years later we lost steam.

He pulls to the curb on a gloomy side street, and I give him the sack. You can feel how heavy it was when it leaves me and the shit ain't in any way negligent.

This everything? he says. Homeboy's redolent of high-powered chronic, got lower lids the shade of sliced peaches. Of course, I say. You know how I do. He hands me a brown paper sack with its edges rolled closed. All there, he says, a scarlet sclera dialed to me, the other scoping the road. Yeah, I know it is, bro. That's why we do business, I say.

I open the sack expecting a bundle of big faces arranged faceup and folded but scoop a handful of fucking board-game bills!

Ha, I say. Good one.

Todd hits the locks. He hits the locks and, on God, dynamite would make less boom! The click is a brisance that shoots through my ears and into my head and stomps down my spine. What's worse, someone springs from the backseat and chokes me around the throat. That someone smashes a gun against the side of my eye and, on my life, this can't be true; how could it? That fast my face goes cold; that fast the rest of me does too. Don't say one motherfuckin word! he says, and grinds the gun till the gun breaks skin. There ain't no life flashing past. No white lights. No image of Jesus floating above my head. There's a trickle of blood scribbling into my eye and this nigger easing off with lethal calm.

I need to find him.

—Grace

ANDREW'S TRUCK ISN'T OUT FRONT, so I sneak around back to check if it's garaged. I'm peeking into the garage when I hear the patio door slide open. It's his wife.

What? I say.

Why you look? she says. She can make her eyes into swords when she wants. Or lances.

Where is he? I say.

So rude, she says.

Where? I say.

She looks into the alley and asks if I'm alone.

I need to find him, I say.

He downtown, she says. Rally at the square.

I stomp for the gate. She calls after me and I decide to stop. She comes down the steps and whisks across the patio with her arms in a gesture of peace.

This way with us, she says. It is no good.

This could be a ploy. Why here? Why now? This woman who long ago plied at Andrew to send me away. Who all these years has dug a moat between us. The hard heartbreaks don't soften this fast.

★ ★ ★

My brother Pat used to tell me stories about Andrew, how he'd made the local paper for his role in a school board meeting, about him marching in police beating protests, how he'd sit front row at a city forum to rename a street. Times he was present for others when that presence too was at my expense. When it meant missing a recital, or school play, or a track meet. Andrew oft absent, though in this way we've been more alike than we have not.

There's a Measure Eleven protest at the courthouse square. A slew of folks shouting and stomping and waving and pounding cardboard signs tacked to sticks. There are so many of them, all that shows through the mass of feet and bodies are bits of red brick. I stand on the fringes with what seems little chance of finding Andrew inside the crush.

My eyes dart from this to that one and Andrew is nowhere to be found. I wade closer and see a man on the steps dressed in khakis and a windbreaker, a bullhorn in hand. He jumps and barks through the horn. The veins in his neck flex to tight ropes and his face blushes to the red of a fresh scratch. Police with helmets and clubs and shields show up and stand shoulder to blue-uniformed shoulder—stewing, but where don't they?—around the sides of the square. I skirt around to Broadway to look from higher up. But there's no sign of Andrew, so I ease down the steps and into the horde. The speaker points to the sky and the crowd roars. They spike signs and pump their fists and chant, and I sift for Andrew, feeling as if each step places me more and more in harm's way, as if finding his dark face would be the same as seeing Christ. It isn't long until I'm in the center, suffering bumps and nudges, with my arms stiff and my shoulders pushed tight, me on the verge of a full cardiac stop or else an organ about to burst through my ribs. It's too much. It isn't anything left for me to do but brace and wait for the crowd to grant me a safe distance.

The touch on my arm you couldn't mistake. It's a father's touch, a kind touch. Grace, he says. What are you doing? Why are you here?

So this, this, is why these niggers feel super.

—Champ

SECURITY AT THE SHACK SHAKES me down at the
front and turns an aphasic tower till I ask where I can find Mister. He nods towards the steps at the end of an unlit hall, steps
that announce my weight all the way down. From down here
you can see Mister through an archway among an ambit of gamblers, hustlers fatmouthing with fat stacks in their fists and piles
of bills underfoot, an august vision when you've lost what I lost:
thousands, in one whop! I stand by while they bicker over who's
next on the dice, who hit what point, who made what side bet,
stall with no clue of what the fuck I'll say. Mister gets his turn on
the dice, and that's when, trepid as shit, I slug inside. Mister
nods. He's got a knot of bills in his grip, money flapping out his
pockets too. One of the old heads asks if I'm shooting and I shake
my head no. The old head who asked about me playing ain't the
only one of them I've seen before, and I'm wondering which
one, if any, knows what happened last night? What happened to
me last night is the kind of news that travels at Mach speed, light
speed, motherfucking god speed. It's called the wire. And it's the
same kind of wire that turned these dice games into legends.

You hear of fools losing new car money in a night, losing that
much and returning the next day, hear of games going all night

and through the morning, shoot-outs that start with bet the dub and end with two men standing and heaps of cash. And if the games are legends, Mister's (it's almost impossible to beat the in-exhaustible bank) the hero, mythic for winning big, for never getting duped by a scheme nor jerked on a debt.

Mister smooths his tie, brushes dust off his knee, gives Red, who's holding his sport coat, a clutch of wrinkled hundreds. He blows on the dice and shakes them near his head. Taking all bets, gentlemen, he says. Tonight's a good night. Tonight could be your night. His first roll shows four and five, and he scoops the dice and rubs them together. Who else wants a shot at the bank? he says, and taunts the reluctant into wary side bets. Mister kisses the dice and shoots. He shoots and shoots and shoots. You could fall out and die waiting for him to hit his point or crap out, and, shit, I almost do. But he does—he hits it and sends Red around to collect the loot.

The hope, a foolish hope, fleets that his mood is such he might forgive what I owe. We (the *we* being anyone with even a toe in the streets) all know if you owe this man a cent, you pay this man that cent, or else.

Don't leave, gentlemen. Please, he says. He gives the dice to an old head and signals me and I follow him into a room cor-doned by a dingy curtain and stacked with dusty crushed boxes. The room is either twice as hot as anyplace or else the day's long dread is a flame in my gut.

It's about last night, I say.

Mister throws up his hand. So I hear, he says.

You heard? I say.

A long shadow flits past the curtain. The dice game kicks into a next round.

He moves closer and rolls his shoulders.

Did I ever tell you how well Red could swim? he says. Did I ever tell you how strong he was, how fast? Back home, we never lived more than a bike ride from the beach. We lived that close and my brother was always there, always in the water. Don't know why, but this one day I decided to go with him. Not too long after we got to the beach, we started woofing about who could do what, and who was the best and biggest and strongest. The woofing ended with a bet to see who could swim out the farthest. On the face the bet was a no-win for me. Anyone who'd ever seen us near water knew Red was twice the swimmer I was. Red knew he was twice the swimmer I was, but I knew what he didn't. We both dove in and right off Red was Red, out front going fast and strong, while I lagged stroking slow and steady. I kept the same pace until I passed the buoys, until I couldn't see my brother swimming beside or ahead of me. I swam till I was out so far that the current was tugging me where it wanted. Got out that far and swam farther, swam as a matter of fact until I thought I might die. That's when I turned and headed back. It took every ounce of me to make it to shore, Mister says. And collapsed as soon as I touched the sand. The next thing I knew, Red was standing over me shaking his head, calling me crazy, asking me how I did what I did, claiming it must've been a trick. He hovered until I caught my breath. He asked again and I told him yes, it was a trick. And the trick was, he swam worried the whole way whether he'd make it back to shore, but making it back was never the bet.

Mister walks over, parts a crack in the dirty curtain, and shows me his brother ghosting over the game, mute and thoughtless, a sport coat (Mister's coat) draped over an arm. Look, Mister says. I love him, but he and I are not the same. Mister eclipses the space between us and turns to me. But the question is, which one of us are you?

Mister unbuttons his cuffs and rolls his sleeves and gapes at me and my one safe resort is to look away.

Hold tight, he says, and saunters into the gambling room. I can feel myself shrink while he's gone, hear broken parts in the unfit machinery of me. If I were braver, I'd mention my plans to buy the house and ask/beg for tolerance. That's what I would do if my nuts weren't, right this very second, the size of mustard seeds.

Mister returns carrying a strap in plain view, its barrel facing the floor. He hands it to me by the grip. It's black and sleek, with its serial number scratched off, and feels lighter than you'd imagined it would.

So this, this, is why these niggers feel super. Held this shit for all of a nanotick and now, this very instant, I'm as gallant as a nigger with nothing whatsoever under the sun of value to him to lose.

They take from you. They take from me. And we can't have that problem, mister says. You don't want that problem, he says. With them or with me.

I'm going to get you what I owe, I say. All of it.

Mister slaps me on a trapezium and smirks a smirk to melt my face. Sure you will, he says. Sure you will, and soon. That's the way this works.

And you don't know what that means.

—Grace

SHOULD'VE SEEN ME.

In the lobby fighting myself. We can't do this. We can. We can't do it without him. We can. What's different about where it will come from? Should've seen me a foot in and a foot out the door, riding the elevator for trips. But in the end, what else can I do?

My eldest answers dressed in a tank top and basketball shorts and this is the first time I've noticed his arms, a man's arms, protective. I need you, I say, and fall into him. He catches me, holds me up, presses his chin to the top of my head. I step back and gather and we step inside. He pulls out a chair for me at the table.

Is this about Big Ken? he says. The custody?

How do you know? I say.

He mentioned it, Champ says. But I didn't think he meant to see it through.

Well, he has, I say. Or he intends to. I'm scheduled to go to court.

Court? he says. When?

In a month, I say. Champ, I thought I could do it on my own but I can't. I can't keep fighting this fight by myself.

You're right, he says. So what now?

We need a lawyer, I say. Can you pay for one?

He sighs from someplace other than himself. He drops his head and rubs above his eyebrows. He lifts his eyes and looks away and looks at me.

What's wrong? I say.

Timing, he says. You wouldn't believe this timing.

So do you have it? I say.

No, I don't, he says. But how much do you need?

Forget it, I say. I'll find a way.

No, you won't. I will, he says. How much?

He leans into a shaft of light and you can see a tiny scab on the high side of his face, see flecks of red in the white of an eye. I don't know. I don't know. I don't know. I don't know, I say. Whatever you can spare and I'll make do.

He ventures into his room. There's the sound of the closet door sliding open, of Kim murmuring. This while I jitter in my seat and wonder whether I should stay or leave, whether this is yet another test of what I sacrifice *every* time the time comes. Champ slugs out and plops in his seat. Let's start with this, he says, and slaps down the key to the Honda. It's attached to a silver key chain. That and now this, he says. He takes out a knot, counts out a stack, and lays it in front of me. I don't pick it up to count. Whatever it is, it's what I need. What I should know not to accept.

My God, I say.

Mom, let's leave Him out of this, this time, he says. You came for help and here it is. My help.

Son, thank you for this. For all you've done.

We listen to what wafts in from the street, a motorcycle revving by, the shrill voices of kids. Kim, in leggings and a tentish shirt, totters over to us and she lifts the bills off the table showy and sets them down. Wow! Looks like you won the lotto, she says.

I scoop the money off the table and dump it in my bag. How's my grandbaby? I say. How are you?

Me, still instasick every morning, Kim says. But she's just fine.

Did you say she? I say.

Yes, she says. He didn't tell you? Your son will soon have a baby girl to care for. He might want to start practicing now.

I throw Champ a look and he shrugs and says that he's sorry, that he meant to mention it sooner.

Kim wanders over and checks herself in the hall mirror—pinches her thigh, turns this way and that way—and groans. She takes out a jacket and wrestles on the sleeves. Oh, I sooo can't do this, she says.

You sooooo can't do what? Champ says.

Look! she says.

Why don't you quit complainin and get some that fit? he says. It's simple if you ask me.

She toddles over and poses. All right, Mr. Simple, she says. You must be feeling generous today.

What about what I gave you last week? he says.

That was last week, she says.

He looks to the ceiling. This isn't a good time, he says.

Oh, so you don't care if I feel like this another week? she says.

He thumbs what looks like less than he gave me and holds it up for her to grab. Take care of me, you take care of her, she says. She pecks him above his eye and dodders out, the sweetest scent in her wake.

He apologizes for Kim, but I shrug it off. He asks if I'm

hungry and tells me to stay put and goes into the kitchen. He fixes us breakfast—sausage, eggs, toast—which is more than I thought he could do. He makes me a place setting and serves me with that gap-toothed grin of his and sits across the table with his back against the chair and his elbows off the table just like I taught him when he was a boy.

Since when did you start cookin? I say, forking a mouthful.

Since I live with a girl who scorches meals on the reg, he says. A man can only stand but so much suffering.

She'll get better when the baby comes, I say. And the baby will be here before you know it. How are you two doing otherwise?

You just seen it, he says. And that's been for weeks.

Hormones, I say. The first time's the toughest. Be kind. Be patient.

Yeah, the estrogen attitudes I get, he says. But she's been talking marriage.

Has she? What's wrong with that? I say. That is how it's supposed to be done.

Says who? he says. Not for me. A father now, yes. But a husband, hell no.

Champ, that's foolish, I say. And selfish. Don't be so selfish. You've got to learn to give, son. More than what's in your pocket.

We finish and he digs the bag—it's as swelled as it was when New Years I brought it back—from a closet stocked with boxes for my grandbaby. He carries it out behind me to the Honda. It's filthy; its hood and roof are painted with bird drops. He drops the bag and kicks a hubcap. As you can see, it's been sittin since you left it, he says. It wouldn't be a bad idea to spend a few bucks on new juice. He loads the bag in the trunk while I circle the car checking for dents or a low tire. I climb inside and he closes the door and stands at the window while I settle, while I grip the wheel and let it go, while I adjust the seat and shift, while I flip the visor and case myself in the mirror.

He motions me to lower the window. He ducks inside and keeps balance on his arms.

If it ain't enough let me know and we'll see what else we got, he says.

Thank you, thank you, thank you, I say, and ask if he can get his brothers together before we go to court.

Done, he says. I got you.

Yes, you do, Champ, I say. And you don't know what that means.

He taps the car and backs a step away.

Do you really think it's selfish? he says.

Do it for you. For you and for her and the baby. Champ, you have to believe me. Living against the risk of love is no way to live.

Look, he says, and points to the sky. Birds sail high and silent, a prayer in flight, their flock formed in the shape of a V.

How are we supposed to do that?

—Champ

THIS STAYS BETWEEN US PEOPLES.

The us being you and me. The us being you and me and no one, meaning—No. One.

That cool?

Okay cool, if it's cool with you then put that on something.

As a matter of fact, swear on what you need.

Mom says I'm selfish, but that ain't it and though I can't, no, I won't say it to her, she should know. All this time I didn't bare it because I couldn't and I couldn't because there was only so many times she could leave before the next time was it, before the next time turned me into another me. Wasn't but so many times before that happened and I knew, even back then when I knew next to less than nothing, to be scared of who I'd become. So I put this abject slab where neither she nor no female could reach it forreal. And that's where it's been for so long you can't know, where it's been stashed until just this blink. But between us (what's your word worth?), I'm going to risk it out again for my mother. It's time to chance it out a last time for Grace and for me.

For the address that Jude gave, there ain't no sign at all, just some copper-colored numbers (damn near nondescript) painted on a metal door smack between a tax prep business and Lock and Key Security. How I know, the windows of the others are scripted with company names, with phone numbers and slogans, the whole nine. The blinds are drawn to the window of Jude's business, got me questioning whether I wrote the address down right or not. Even more uneasy, cause where Jude's office is (or should I say where I hope it is) is out here where I don't much roll, where most of the people I know don't go either. Am I surprised when he answers? Let's just say I wouldn't have been shocked if he didn't. Hey, he says with the zealousness of someone who's lived evidence that the world plays fair. He slaps a sweaty palm in mine and invites me in. He tells me to have a seat and smashes into the leather office chair beneath a gargantuan plaque.

The Real Estate Guy

BUY. SELL. INVEST.
SINCE 1990

The office is sparse. An oak desk, metal crates stuffed with manila files, tweed-seat chairs pushed flushed against a wall, FOR SALE signs stacked in a corner. Jude tells me to pull up a seat and pushes a slab of bound sheets at me with the words BIG BUST written on the cover. I scan the top pages, peek to see Jude reclined in his chair, his super-sized dome pressed against the wall below his plaque. When the market is strong, people think the goodness will last forever, Jude says. That they've stumbled upon the gleaming gold gates of the kingdom of fortunes. And history says that's all the people need to toss the old rules right out a high-rise window. Jude blathers (imagine a hella-effeminate Don LaFontaine) minutes more of voice-over, and might keep on if I don't speak up.

What is this for? Research? I say.

You could say that, he says. But more pleasure. This is the best thing ever wrote on the twenties bubble bust.

Okay. Got it, I say. History's cool, but I'd love to hear about the house? Don't mean to be so direct with dude, but who has time for the sidebars? Shit, we all know my bind, slap a blood-pressure cuff on me right now and witness a nigger that measures close to a stroke.

The house. Oh, that old thing, he says, and laughs. Even his laugh is mellifluous.

The other day I told Half Man about Jude's dainty timbre and its comfort to me, but the homie wasn't hearing none of it: Fuck how he sound, dog. That shit could be cahoots. Here's the thing—he could be right. But here's the thing, too—the homie could be wrong. And peoples, this ain't in the least about what I stand to lose if this whiteman is playing me for a mark; it's about all *we* stand to gain, what we will achieve cause I spoke it so (and what else must we need to make the universe acquiesce?) when this deal, that ain't yet a deal goes through. Oh, you don't know by now what that is? What, you ain't been tracking? What's in this for my beloved, for us few dear Thomases is this: a chance to resurrect and live. And for all the extraordinary bookie-types please, please, tell me how much for that is too much to risk?

Jude tippy-toes to the window and twists open the blinds and brightens the office. The security company's van pulls up (I know this because even the van has signage) and a duo of stiff rent-a-cop types hop out and strut into the office next door. Jude takes his seat and checks a file. He shakes his mouse and stares into his computer. Bud, he says. I've always believed in educating my clients. So here we go. The first rule of real estate is, it's never about buying or selling. It's always about wants and dreams. About who wants what and when.

The night the owner dreams of a condo in Phoenix or a ranch in Durham, that house is as good as yours.

Huh? I say. Is that the plan? That don't sound promising.

No, he says. That's not it. But I want you to see how this works from the inside out. We've got good news. The husband has been eyeing early retirement. Says he and his wife may sell the house and move out of state.

Thinking or doing? I say.

Buying and selling is one big narrative and you have to realize if you're at the start, rising in the action, have reached the climax, or are falling towards a denouement. That's what I told them, and the good thing is, they're listening. The trick will be convincing them that this is the perfect time in their story to sell.

How are we supposed to do that? I say.

Here's another helpful bit of intrigue, Jude says. As it turns out he has family from the town over from my hometown. You'd think that stuff wouldn't make a difference, but, bud, it all makes a difference.

My pager goes off. It's a number I don't know. A number I won't answer. A number I won't be calling back.

I'd love it if you could spell it out in plain English, I say.

There's a true opportunity, Jude says. But I have to tell you. It's hard as heck to be convincing without talking concrete figures. My question to you is, are you ready to talk numbers?

He quotes me what he thinks I'll need to make as an offer they'll accept, and shit, if my pressure was stroke-high a second ago, it's got to have shot up near cardiac arrest. The number would be beyond my means if the hustle gods blessed me with a string of solid gold licks, but figure in what I lost and what I owe and believemewhenitellyou it may as well be the payoff for the fucking national debt. I tell Jude what I think I can raise, though in truth it's about double what I believe within reach. I ask if we can make the down payment in cash.

Cash! he says. So you're a cash guy? I love cash. Cash rules. But, bud, I'm afraid we can't very well hand the owners a bundle of hundreds and fifties. We'd have to find another way to transact, money orders or a cashier's check or some such. Let me think on it a bit. Jude don't bother to ask where the money might come from—and let's all call this benevolence.

Do we have a shot? I say. A real shot?

Of course. Of course. Don't worry, with what you quoted we should be good, and if they ask for more, it shouldn't be by much..

What about how much you want to do the deal? I say.

We can figure my fee later, he says. We'll get a deal with them in place first.

Jude says sometime soon we should check out at least a few other properties, that he'd love to show me his neighborhood, his new place. He lives in Beaverton, and why oh why am I not surprised? There can't be a swath of my fair city even a scintilla more befitting of a homogenous middle-aged white man.

You got it, I say.

We shake and he shows me out. I totter across the street with a math problem for a brain. Right, so oddsmakers there's a forever source of ways this deal could fail, but as I said for my family, for all of us, I can't let this dream defer, won't let it fall apart. I glance back at Jude, and his chubby mug is lit with mirth.

Do you understand?
    —Grace

WE MEET OUTSIDE OF ANDREW'S.

Champ shows with his brothers, my babies, who I haven't seen since I went out to Kenny's place, and I don't know what they've been told. They sit and I sit and for a moment it's a schism that can't be breached. I get out of the Honda first—this is what mothers do—and gaze at my babies through the back window of Champ's car, see them from the neck up, dark caps cocked sideways and bright tops. Canaan climbs out first and then KJ. They haste over and crush me in a double hug. Meanwhile, Andrew strolls out of the house onto his porch. His pot-belly presses against his shirt; gray stubble speckles his bald head. He looks like a father, that he should've been my father, that he will be if he isn't now. He slinks off the porch and over to us. Well what a surprise, he says. So I guess you were all itchin to visit old granddad, he says. Or is something else?

Something else, I say. A family outing. We're going out to Multnomah Falls. Where we haven't been since God knows.

Now, there's a great day in the works, he says. He straightens the boys' hats and asks what's new, if they've been misbehaving, and the boys answer in voices too low to be believed, the pitch of my speech when the truth isn't holding it up. Champ pops out and says hello to Andrew over the roof. Andrew mentions something to me about court, says we need to talk later.

Guess I should let you all get going, he says. If memory serves me correct, it's crowded up there this time of year. You guys have a blast and be safe up there near the water, he says, and backs onto the lawn.

We load up. I give KJ the front seat so I can sit in the back with my baby. Andrew stands in the grass and waves good-bye.

Champ takes the busy streets to the eastbound on-ramp. We pass 33rd, 42nd, 82nd, 102nd, 122nd . . . farther, he lowers the music to white noise and tells the boys that when we get where we're going, they best act like they got some sense. For a time after that, there either isn't enough to say or is too much to say, as we ride with the wind no more than a hum through the sunroof's angled slit.

This feels as if we could ride to the next morning, ride right on until we reach the next coming. We cruise easy along 84 East. We get out to where for stretches and stretches they raise the posted speed limit. Out where semis think they own the road, where a camper hogs two lanes. We wheel by a four-by-four tugging a winched boat, blow past a long trailer hauling a manufactured home, past roadkill and a fat tire blown to shreds, past a car stranded on the side of the road with a man kneeling near a fender. We go farther, through the Gorge, highway flanked by the river on one side, woods on the other. I reach over the seat and touch KJ to see if he's asleep. I snug next to my youngest, see a car float past with a bumper sticker that says BLESSED TO BE ALIVE. There's a tiny stretch on this trip that's a place between places. Canaan, mouth hung, nods on my shoulder and catches himself and rights. You gonna be there, right? he says.

Be where, baby? I say.

There, he says. In court.

KJ twists around. Yeah, dummy, he says.

No one in this car is a dummy, I say.

Mom, do you know what will happen? Canaan says. What they gone have us do?

Nothing you don't want to, I say. I promise you that.

The car goes quiet and I close my eyes and drift. When I open them, there's a sign ahead that says the falls is next exit.

Out front there's a welcome sign and a paved lot and today must be the day. Trucks and buses and cars and vans and SUVs—all colors. License plates from Oregon and across the bridge, California tags, states farther east. We hunt lanes and luck upon a van pulling out to leave. My boys, awakening, slink behind me through the maze of cars to where you can first see the lodge. There's a crowd gathered, and we huddle a good distance away while a guide trumpets instructions. The space clears, and I make the boys read the sign that list facts about the falls. That it's the second tallest year-round falls in the country, that it's fed by underground springs, that this time of year it flows its highest, that millions visit each year, that it's such and such feet to the falls' peak.

Before we start, I announce the rules: No horseplay, no hiking off alone. If one makes it up, we all do. And your mama's making it, I say. So we all will. Champ takes the lead when we get on the trail, complains within steps of scuffing his new tan boots. My youngest boys fight the incline in matching black tenny shoes, while I caboose it in the flattest flats I own. In flats I hope are flat enough. Farther up my knees and back are signing pay back, and this mist is turning my hair to shriveled knots. My boys and me among a trickle climbing as singles and couples, the smart ones trekking wary of the slick spots hard to see until it's too late.

A man carries his son on his shoulders. A woman totes a baby in a sling. A pack of boys stomp with fanny packs strapped on their waists. There's a sparse trail floating down from the top, flashing faces of pity—or pride. Meanwhile, I keep my arms and legs pumping and my chin held high.

Champ, in the lead, stops and turns to us. Ya'll cool? he says. If one make it, we all make it, right? That's the deal.

His timing is spot on. We are past the point of turning back being easier than pushing ahead. We reach the feeble swaying bridge. People lined up for pictures with a wood statue. From here the falls gush from above and below. From here the river, blue, a deep blue, funnels between steep slopes. Come, I say, and bring my boys into a circle. We take up hands, and I look each one of them in the eye. I want you to hear me, I say, straining against the spill of the falls. There's nothing for you to be afraid of. All you have to do is tell the truth, I say. Today's truth. The next seconds stretch; my God do they stretch. Remember this, I say. You, me, us—we can't ever get trapped by who we were. Who we were is not who we are. Who we are is right here, I say. And right now. The truth of us is on this bridge. Do you know what I mean? This, I say, is us.

That's all well and good, Mom, Champ says. But here's a truth: We're beat. How about we hike back down? The boys snicker and our circle breaks apart.

Oh no, I say. This is a good hurt. An earned hurt. We can't come this far and stop short.

Don't matter?

—Champ

FROM MY BIDDY BALL DAYS all the way through my
senior year, this place was a home, which is how (they skimp on
the light bill and keep the heat so low winters a nigger could
catch frostbite) the people who run the joint treat it. To top it off,
it's funky—or worse, we're talking reektastic.

But ask anybody and they'll tell you this gym attracts the A-1
ballers, hosts the top runs in the city. You ain't got a name if you
didn't earn that name breaking ankles and sinking game points
when it's game point apiece both teams.

The dudes balling now, though, ain't exactly the best index of
the lore. A crew of old heads and has-beens running a game the
short way, sideline to sideline, shooting bricks, hobbling into the
key, and talking old school smack: In your face! Swish! Money! I
watch till, by what must be magic, one of them sinks a bank shot
for game point. A guy with the next game asks if I'm down to
run and I tell him not today, that I'm helping my bros practice,
which is today's truth, but not the whole truth, which at present
I'll keep to myself for fear it might sound malicious.

The other side of the gym is empty. KJ pokes the ball from
me, dribbles over, and jacks a janky lefty jumper that falls short
of the rim. Canaan jogs off alone, scoops another ball from a

corner, and pounds it. He goes between his legs and around his back and crosses over, moves he mastered that year and change we lived across from a half-court, those days when he'd burn hours (in particular when Mom was out on missions) practicing, heaving his rubber indoor/outdoor rock at a rim with no net (sometimes kicking it on a missed chip shot), those months he'd spend a whole day seeing how close he could come to touching the rim. Practice that paid off. Already baby bro is the owner of a mean floor game (cut him slack on last season's fiasco) and a crossover that could send one of these has-beens to the ICU.

Let me see it, I say, and clap at Canaan for the rock. He tosses it at me, and with no bounces I sink a jumper from out-of-bounds. It's one-quarter luck but I say, See? What good is all that fancy dribbling if you can't put the ball in the hole?

I can, Canaan says, and takes a shot that smacks the side of the rim.

That don't look like you can, I say, shaking my head. I hope that ain't what you're calling a jimmy.

At the other end, the old heads yawp until one of them snatches their ball, tucks it under his arm, and stomps towards the door.

We (me and my bros) decide on a game of crunch and I toss the ball to Canaan for him to check it up top. He rubs the ball and he sizes us both as if he really believes he can win. If I was more magnanimous, right now I'd go lace these dudes with keen secondhand coach encouragements: Ain't nobody giving you shit. Always outwork the next man. The only thing to fear is not having practiced enough. But that's if I was more magnanimous, key word: if!

If you played ball like I played ball, you'd know it's every man for himself, so don't go to blaming me for pushing, for hand-checking on D, for tagging them with semi-benign elbows. KJ goes up and I whack the ball *and* him out of the air, as if we ain't got (so says the hoop gods: Spare the hard foul, spoil the sibling) the same DNA. It's first game: Me. Next game: Me. Third game: Who you think? We ball till there's a reef of sweat in the front of my tee, till my boxers are stuck to my legs. A win is a win is a win is a win, I tell myself as I'm bent over gasping. We watch the old heads at the other end while I catch my breath for rematch a million. They've got another game going and all you can hear is the squeak of old high tops and the backboard reports of a bricked-jumper jubilee. Watching this sad show of basketball skills inspires me (maybe I'm more generous than even I thought) into a jump-shot tutor session.

I send Canaan to the free throw line. All right, I say. Elbow straight and fingertips. Snap your wrist and follow through. See the rim and nothing else. I school Canaan first and then KJ. We shoot an hour so, me shagging most of the balls. Canaan nets a shot and I carry it over and ask him if he's talked to Mom since we rode out to the falls.

What's there to talk about? he says.

You need a reason? I say. About what's going on.

It don't matter, he says.

Don't matter? I say. What the fuck you mean? I rush him and slap the ball out of his hands. It dribbles away but Canaan shags it and carries it over and the three of us meet in the free throw circle. That's our mama, I say. Our mama. She needs us and we need her.

But Champ, if we live with Mom, where we gone stay? Canaan says.

In the house, I say.

Which house? he says

Our house, I say, assured overmuch, though not forreal.

KJ bends and stretches his shirt over his knees. Canaan hugs the ball to his chest.

How's that? Canaan says.

Grown folks' shit, bro, I say. Leave it to me and stick to being a kid.

They vote for pizza when we leave, so I drive to the parlor near the mall. Been here a gazillion times and always the same thought bubble hanging above my head: Who was the genius who okayed parking a big-ass fire truck (complete with a varnished wooden ladder and a barefoot mannequin frozen for good on a fireman's pole) dead center in the floor?

This is the thought, but I don't know why, cause we've never come for the sights. We're here for the thin-crust, the paragon of thin-crust pizzas. We order a thin-crust with extra everything we like, find seats, fix our table with plates and a fizzing pitcher of pop. KJ pours us each a full mug, and I set my pager on the tabletop just in case. If you're wondering, we're still wearing our hoop gear; yep, we brothers fine-dining with sweaty balls and all.

What's this I hear about more trouble at school? I say to Canaan. He turns a worried face to KJ and back to me, his diffidence amped up.

Miss H always on me, he says. He reaches for his drink, but I catch the handle of his mug and hold it.

So what? I say. That's her job.

The boy nods a weak-ass nod; he's always resorting to weak-ass nods; if he keeps on he'll be the pubescent prince of weak-assness. Look, man, you can't be tripping in class. You want to get back to regular school, don't you?

But she only be sweatin me and no one else, he says.

That's a favor, I say. The fact that she gives a shit is a gift. You best check yourself for me and you got problems, patna. Serious problems.

Okay, Champ, okay, he says.

Okay, my ass, I say. Don't fucking okay me.

A clique of juveniles troop in vociferous as shit and my bros and I can't help but look over, can't help but eyeball them till they find their seats.

So ya'll tryin to hit that game room or what? I say. I fleece my sweats for cash. Spend some and put the rest in your sock, I say, but already baby bro is trucking off for heaven.

What about you? I say, and peel off KJ's loot.

I'm good, he says, waving his hand.

Oh, like that? I say.

Yeah, I don't feel like playing, he says. He wipes dried sweat from his forehead. He looks more than ever like Big Ken, who, as I've said, is his and Canaan's biological pops, but was my pops in every other way that counts.

Suit yourself, I say. But tell me this: What we gone do about our rockhead baby bro?

You're the big brother, he says.

Before Canaan was born, Mom and Big Ken brought me and KJ here on Saturdays. Big Ken would cop extra-large pizzas with extra pepperoni and iceless pitchers of off-brand pop. Mom, for her part, would bless us with handfuls of quarters and tell me to keep an eye on KJ in the game room; KJ, who, the minute he got his issue, would fall over himself trying to land first game on his favorite game, an intergalactic joint he couldn't play for shit. He'd plow through his stock of quarters, burn through whatever was left of mine, which mattered less to me since, whenever we got to our last, Mom, the patron saint of extra coins, would appear with cuploads of replenishments. Sometimes she'd hit us with a refill and vanish, others she'd watch until we'd spent our last and/or a kid stretched his face from being sidelined diutius.

What I wouldn't give for a rebirth of those blithe days.

What's the deal with spring league? I say. You ballin?

Nothing, he says. He pours salt on the table and finger-swirls a design.

Tryouts is soon, right? I say. You got action at JV if you play tough D.

The high schoolers climb into the fire truck and howl as if it's the funniest thing on earth.

Don't know if I'm playin, he says.

Why? I say. Thought you was a hooper. Is it grades? Please tell me you not fuckin up in school too, I say. You fuck up now and you've fucked up. You ain't no little kid.

I know I ain't, he says. You the one who thinks I am.

Yo, don't get clocked, patna, I say. You wanna get slugged?

He turns away. I touch my face and rub circles under my cheeks.

Is it grades?

No, he says.

Well, how are they? I say.

All right, he says.

Just all right, I say.

Yeah, he says.

Here we go with this one-word-answer melancholy shit, I say. I'm trying to have a dialogue.

My pager buzzes but I don't bother to check who it is. Yeah, I need what I need, but there must be a time that's off-limits.

What about the broads? I say. You got a girl?

Yes, Champ. I got a girl, he says.

Those years when me and my mom were still an inseparable tag team tandem, the years before my brother was even born, Big Ken pimped for our bread and meat, and though by the time KJ came along Big Ken was ebbing into retirement (maybe the smartest move he ever made), that nurture might of turned my bro into a super-bathetic anti-pimp.

Only one girl? I say.

Yes, one, he says.

Damn, well, have she gave you some womb? I say.

I don't have to tell you, he says.

You don't, I say. But check it, you're already a year older than I was when I hit my first, so if you ain't knocked one down, you best get crackin.

He squeezes his lips and glares. We've got the same dark brown eyes, the same long wild lashes. Champ, he says. Who says I want to be you? I don't want to be like you.

They call our number over the speakers—a motherfucking boon—and I grab the marker and push away.

Right, I say. Right. If only you knew.

My bros when we leave slug out in tandem slow and rebel-like. Steps through the lot, KJ falls back and when I look to see where, I don't know what to make of his face. I stand beside the car and track him over the roof. He stops to look at what I can't see, stalls until I walk out to meet him. What's the holdup? I say and catch him by the arm. He yanks away, jerks so tough he sends a small package tumbling. He breaks to pick it up.

What they'd told me for most my life is life has options.

But whose life, and when?

What's that? I say.

Nothing, he says. It's nothing. He looks shook and keeps the bit balled in his fist. Meantime, Canaan climbs out and gawks.

Let me see, I say. As if I need to see.

No! he says. He backs away, but trips in a pothole, and lands on his ass. I pounce on him, pry open his fist, and find the bit wrapped and clipped just like mine.

What in the fuck is this! I say. What in the fuck are you doing?

Mr brother stands on his own and brushes gravel from his ass and elbows. He tugs his shoulders, and as if by some sort of supernatural gift, he's heads taller—has never looked this big, nor this sure, nor this doomed.

Answer me! I say.

He twists to look at Canaan and swings to look at me. His eyes and my eyes dueling.

What *I'm* doing what *you* do, he says.

Right now, now, it takes nothing to see me beating him half to death. Though when I wind up to swing, I can't swing. My kith as my witness, I drop the bit, and stomp and stomp and stomp until I've crushed it all to dust.

PORTLAND POLICE BUREAU

INVESTIGATION REPORT

CRIME ANALYSIS INFORMATION 3 CODE LIMIT

CASE NO.	REFER CASE NO.	CLASSIFICATION		CLR

DATE/TIME REPORTED	DATE/TIME OCCURRED	TYPE ACTIVITY ☐ PHONE-IN (P) ☐ S/4 (S) ☐ RADIO (R)

LOCATION OF OCCURRENCE

ONE SENTENCE SUMMARY OF INCIDENT

PERSONS CO—COMPLAINANT OW—OWNER WI—WITNESS BU—BUSINESS PF—PROPERTY FINDER

ADDITIONAL PERSONS IN NARRATIVE Y N

CODE	NAME	CRN	SEX	RACE	DOB

CASE NO.

COPIES

☐ DET
☐ CENT
☐ EAST
☐ NORTH
☐ NE
☐ SE
☐ DVD
☐ ID
☐ Crim Prev
☐ Intel
☐ JUV
☐ JDH
☐ SOSCF
☐ CAT
☐ C/S
☐ DVCS
☐
☐
☐

COMPUTER ENTRY

☐ Person

OPR
☐ Vehicle

OPR
☐ Crime/ Prop

OPR
☐ Book

OPR

HOME ADDRESS	ZIP	HOME PHONE
BUSINESS/SCHOOL ADDRESS	WORK HOURS	WORK PHONE

CODE	NAME	CRN	SEX	RACE	DOB
HOME ADDRESS		ZIP	HOME PHONE		
BUSINESS/SCHOOL ADDRESS		WORK HOURS	WORK PHONE		

CODE	NAME	CRN	SEX	RACE	DOB
HOME ADDRESS		ZIP	HOME PHONE		
BUSINESS/SCHOOL ADDRESS		WORK HOURS	WORK PHONE		

A1,B2—SUSPECTS MI—Missing RW—Runaway DK—Drunk DE—Deceased OD—Overdose AS—Attempt Suicide ME—Mental

ADDITIONAL SUSPECTS OR ANOTHER INCIDENT? Y N

CODE	NAME	CRN	SEX	RACE	DOB
AKA/MONIKER		HT	WT	HAIR	EYES	IN CUSTODY Y N
ADDRESS	PHONE	OTHER DESCRIPTION			

CODE	NAME	CRN	SEX	RACE	DOB
AKA/MONIKER		HT	WT	HAIR	EYES	IN CUSTODY Y N
ADDRESS	PHONE	OTHER DESCRIPTION			

VEHICLE S—Stolen R—Recovered L—Locate A—Abandoned T—Towed V—Victim's Vehicle X—Suspect Vehicle

ADDITIONAL VEHICLE IN NARRATIVE Y N

CODE	LICENSE NO.	STATE	LIC YR	TYPE	VIN	STLN/RCVD VALUE
VEH YR	MAKE	MODEL			STYLE	COLOR

DELIQ PAYMENTS Y N	KEYS IN VEHICLE Y N	THEFT INSUR. Y N	PERMISSION GIVEN Y N	TRANSMISSION ☐ STANDARD ☐ AUTO	BODY DAMAGE Y N EXPLAIN:

CHARGE/CITE NO.	HOLD Y N REASON:

TOWED BY/TOWED TO	☐ DEPT REQUEST ☐ PRIVATE REQUEST	UNIT & PERSON NOTIFIED

O.R.S. 162.375 SECTION 212 INITIATING A FALSE REPORT. (1) A PERSON COMMITS THE CRIME OF INITIATING A FALSE REPORT IF HE KNOWINGLY INITIATES A FALSE ALARM OR REPORT WHICH IS TRANSMITTED TO A FIRE DEPARTMENT, LAW ENFORCEMENT AGENCY OR OTHER ORGANIZATION THAT DEALS WITH EMERGENCIES INVOLVING DANGER TO LIFE OR PROPERTY (2) INITIATING A FALSE REPORT IS A CLASS C MISDEMEANOR.

☐ I UNDERSTAND THAT I AM LIABLE FOR ALL TOWING AND STORAGE COSTS INCURRED DURING THE RECOVERY OF THIS VEHICLE.   ☐ I WILL TESTIFY AS A WITNESS AGAINST THE DEFENDANT WHEN HE/SHE IS CHARGED WITH A CRIME.

☐ RELEASED PROPERTY/VEHICLE TO

☐ THE NAMED CHILD (ADULT) IS PRESENTLY A RUNAWAY (MISSING) AND I REQUEST THAT HE/SHE BE TAKEN INTO CUSTODY FOR THEIR OWN PROTECTION.

SIGNATURE OF PERSON REPORTING THE INCIDENT

CRIME PREVENTION INFO DESIRED? Y N	IDENTIFICATION DIVISION NOTIFIED? Y N	OUTSIDE AGENCY NOTIFIED/REFERRED TO? Y N	WHICH ONE:

REPORTING OFFICER(S)	DPSST	PREC/DIV	RLF/SHIFT	ASSN/DIST	SUPERVISOR'S SIGNATURE

PPB-IR-10/84

767 (05/01)

Sometimes you have the strength to face them;
sometimes you don't.
—Grace

A KINKY-HEAD BOY RUNS UP beside me while I'm in
the store searching for snacks. He asks if I can buy him a pack of
Capri Suns. His dimple is in the same cheek as Champ's. There's
only one other person in the aisle, a pitiful-looking something,
somebody's baby herself, her arms tattooed to murals, who I
suppose is the boy's mama, but hope she isn't, since she hasn't
noticed how far the boy has roamed. I take a knee and explain
I'd love to, but we'd have to ask his mother. He leads me to her,
and as soon as he's within reach, she slaps him as though he's
grown. What I tell your mannish ass bout runnin off?

This is the time to turn and scoot off before I say something I
shouldn't. Rather, something I should.

The checkout line could trick you. Ahead of me kids fidget
with handfuls of bagged candy and ahead of them a frosty-haired
woman a few weeks by the looks—God knows I don't say it to
be facetious—from needing a wheelchair or walker. The woman
slumps over the counter and so slow, so so slow, trawls her purse
for change with a stack of coupons slabbed on the counter for
signing checks. There's a thin girl right beside her—an aide or
something, I guess, since they don't resemble—bagging the

lady's trickle of buys. The woman finds a second, thicker stack of coupons and starts to sort. Patience, patience, I say to myself. Though I can say for true: It won't be me worrying a cashier or a manager over the small print of the weekend special. Will never be me but how could I ever know?

The woman moves snoozy against the life of the store. Carts squeak, tills open, a glass jar breaks in an aisle close by; a man calls a special that's off special by the end of the day. I sift through my snacks, picking a choice for my one night off this week. The boy, my friend, wanders up, with his pitiful mama groping after him.

You buy Capri Sun? he says.

It hurts too much anymore—which is I why I can't, won't let Kenny win—to be a boy's disappointment, overmuch. I ask his mama if she minds and she curses him and twists his arm and tells him to say sorry for asking. He apologizes. His face a face that makes me wish he was mine. I tell her it's no trouble. That I'd love to do it, that I've got boys, and know how it is. Then, shit, I guess, she says, which is all the consent I need.

It's misty when I leave the store, but we can't let that stop us. I toss my bag in the backseat and climb in. The car clicks cold the first turn of the key—I've got to get this checked—but catches the next try. I drive blocks down to a roadside flower stand owned by a man who used to work at one of my old jobs. He crushed on me for years, used to offer lunches and buy flowers for no reason at all. Then one late night he saw me at the end of a binge. Since then, the few times we've seen one another, he talks to me soft and makes it a point to ask how I've been. Sometimes you have the strength to face them; sometimes you don't. I get out and pick a bouquet. He gives it to me for discount and says he hopes I'm doing well, that it looks to him as if I am.

The ride to the cemetery takes you by the zoo. The zoo should be the next outing for the boys and I.

It's been too long, much too long, since my last time here. There's a new sign at the entrance, or else an old sign I'm first seeing. The first time I came, I came alone and got lost, and all these years since it's easy to get turned around, to lose the route that leads easiest to his marker. The surest, fastest way is to find it on foot. I hike past the mausoleum—muddied patches suck at my heels—push over slopes, wend through cypress trees and mini-gardens of blooming yellow tulips. I tread the maze of markers, stepping around and between but never over a stone. The grounds crew has set up a tent, dug a new plot, laid straps across it. The man stacking chairs under the tent calls a twangish Howdy, and waves for me to stop. He wipes his hands on overalls stamped with islands of dirt, tips a checkerboard conductor's cap, and dabs his face with a stained cloth. He asks if I need help finding a stone and I tell him I'm fine, that who I came to see should be just over the next hill.

All righty, he says, and goes back to his business. I feel his eyes at my back as I leave.

By the time I reach my godson's marker the bouquet has leaked a rose-sized stain on my blouse. I take a knee—feeling the wet grass soak through my pants—and clear loose grass and dirt from his birth and death dates. I take out the flowers one by one and lay them around the border and when I'm done I bow and pray. Not sure how long this lasts but when I look up the over-alled man is standing nearby.

Oh, I say. Didn't hear you walk up.

It's an ancient Shaolin secret, he says. Or is it Alabama? He simpers. It's the smile of an honest man. Not a church man, but an honest man—the toughest to find. He asks if Dawn's boy is my boy.

He's my godson, I say.

He snaps the straps of his overalls. Excuse the manners, he says. My name's Henry. I'm the head groundskeeper here.

Grace, I say. Good to meet you.

Grace, he says. I got a cousin named Grace. And she's a beauty just like you.

Thank you, I say.

No thanks due, he says. I'm just a bystander is all. Miss Grace, let me guess, you're from someplace else original?

What makes you say that? I say.

Where I come from we honor the dead. But not much here, from what I can tell. Got me to thinking that it's the place, that it's the way folks are reared up north. But here you are visiting alone, paying respect, restoring my faith.

He helps me to my feet. He refits his hat on snug, checks his watch. Welp, I better get a move on, he says. My shift's about done. He asks if I can find my way out, says it's hecka easy to get turned around.

Thanks for the offer, I say. But I can find the way myself.

Hurrah for independence. Have a good day, he says, and moseys off. For as far as I can see, the man rambles between and around markers, but never over a single stone.

Mom and I are alike that way.

—Champ

THE DETAILS, the details would about bore you to a three on the old Glasgow Scale.

But read on if you don't mind taking the risk.

The basics: Each week we'll meet at the bank and I'll give Jude the cash (a buck less than what they're required to report to the Feds) and he'll deposit the funds. This will go on until we reach the figure (a month or so, by my count) we need for the down payment. Jude will cut the owners a check, buy the house in his name, then after the close of escrow (who says the average white man means us new Negroes no good?) will transfer me the deed by quitclaim. Then, *bam*, I'm making the mortgage, and me and mines are legal and rightful owners of our very own piece of terra firma, our slice of the American Dream.

Peoples, are you with me? Still awake? Cool.

You may be wondering how I'm going to raise the bread to pay Mister, raise what I'll need for a down payment on the house—and futhermore how I'll support my sweet, newborn baby girl when she arrives. Well guess what, I've been wondering too. Nah, I'm bullshitting. I got a plan. What's the plan? My plan is no plan for now. Winging it. But how about I promise (you never know when there's a vitriolic superhater afoot) to share a plan when and if there is a plan after we (the *we* being you and I) have spent more time together? Won't knock you specific, but we all know a nigger can't be sure about human beings in general. Add to that what's been happening to me in recent times, and forgive me for not being the most trusting brother around.

The bank is on a busy street, close by my old school, and right across (of all the branches) from the Northeast Precinct. To top it off, I got my pistol stashed (I've suffered the first and last of five-digit mishaps) in the armrest. I'm strapped and don't you know every other white sedan spooks me to the brink of mashing out the lot. Not that I'd have the nuts to lead police on a high-speed. Me, who's never pushed to triple digits a ride with 180 on the speed dial, me the same trepid dude who yields on yellows. But please don't bust me down about it too much. Admitted, most days I'm percents of a stone-cold fraud, but which one of us is authentic 24/7?

Stayed up late last night counting and recounting this first payment. All of which, to be safe, I should be using to pay Mister. The whole time I counted, Kim sat by looking pugnacious. Whole time too, I pretended not to notice and kept right on counting. Fell asleep on my nth recount, woke up this morning on paranoid, and called Half Man. Called the homie hoping his natural born hatetrocity would push me to scrap the plan. Surprise! He didn't pick up. I wasn't lying what I said about dude being the CEO of the year of Never-There-When-Needed, Inc.

Our meet time comes. Our meet time goes. Still no sign of Jude. Bank customers come and go. An old man waltzes out all smiles. A redhead woman winds out of the revolving door with the I'm-a-bounced-check-away-from-having-my-account-closed mug. A short line builds for the ATM.

The cash, the pistol, and no Jude. If this goes another nanotick somebody best call an EMT. Disclosure: When I'm doing even the slightest of wrongs (not that this ranks that low on the scale) I feel the intractable horror that every lawman or lawwoman in the world is scheming for my arrest, and that once in custody, no matter my crime, no less than a death penalty will do.

Where the fuck is this man?

Couldn't reach Half Man, Inc., this morning, but I did catch Mom before a shift. She and I talked about the lawyer and court, expected, but when we were done, she asked about the house. She's been asking about it as of late: if I think I can get it done, who'll live in it when I do. Asking how long, how much. Been asking, but I get the sense she's still afterall ambivalent, though what sane person could hold it against her? Hope for the best and brace for the worst, Mom and I are alike that way.

At last, Jude shows. Arrives in a car (a Taurus with a primered quarter panel and a temporary tag taped to the rear windshield) that, driven by anybody other than a nonthreatening descendant of the Caucasus, is called a bucket, a stuffer, a hootride—a worthy suspect for police attention. He waves at me. He parks spaces away, spills out, tippy-toes over, and lets himself into my ride. He don't so much sit as plop the fuck in the seat. His cologne could blast a plugged nose clear. All my windows were up but after whiffs of him, all my windows go down.

Bud, do you feel as good as I feel? he says. He has a fresh haircut, the sides trimmed, over his ears.

That depends, I say.

Well, you should. This is it, he says. The president's first pitch, the Final Four tip, Indy's green flag.

He takes the money and stuffs it inside his jacket and tells me to sit tight while he carries my scrilla into the bank. There's a bantamweight bout between me and me on whether to stalk Jude into the lobby, on whether to stalk his ass while he deposits what amounts to the lion's share of a nigger's depleted net worth. But the numbers hold me still—i.e., the distance in feet we are from the precinct. Jude pushes inside and I'm left praying against a grand mal seizure. Left feeling time as a trickle in my throat, and a boom, boom, boom behind my eyes.

Jude bursts out of the entrance beaming as wide as a bridge is long. He steps out and gazes around the lot and bops over and climbs in. All according to plan, he says. He shows me the deposit slip and asks if I'd like to grab a celebratory lunch. It's on me, he says.

He explains there's a place he's been meaning to try and offers to drive, and since I'm always looking for a reason to shirk touching a wheel, I hop out with no further prodding. Jude's spot is downtown, Northwest (did anyone expect otherwise?); you know, White Folks R Us. The man wheeled slow mo for real in his rental, but in this hootride, homeboy's a PSA for the Department of Motor Vehicles. He (even when he's in yap mode, which when is he not?) keeps his eyes on the road, inch, creep, crawls us along with, true to form, mitts glued at ten and two.

If there is such a thing as a low-speed bandit, he's it.

If you didn't know no better, you'd think *he* was the one worried about whether he's dirty or clean.

He pats the dash at a stop. Finally got the old workhorse worked on, he says. Now all we need is the green light from DEQ. He points at the odometer, asks if I've ever seen mileage this high on anything still running. We take the Fremont Bridge into downtown, and head into Northwest. Northwest, most everywhere else our city's paved smooth. But down here make a turn and catch a cobblestone throughway. The new cafés, new boutiques, new galleries, new condos. The old warehouses, apartments, decrepit restaurants.

Look and see what the city was, see maybe what it will be, even if it resist.

Jude's restaurant pick is chocked with a bunch of working stiffs: clean-shaven faces, nonexistent sideburns, bleached teeth, a third of them with suit coats thrown over their seats. Working stiffs, AKA All-American anglos of the sort with stay-at-home wives that, soon as they're of age to suck a nipple, tote their pride and joys to Kumon and Mandarin lessons, to ballet, piano, violin, fencing, who torture their poor innocent kids (this before they hit pre-K!) with weird white-people shit like anxiety-release acupuncture and vision therapy. Peep game, I'm all for pushing posterity to strive (no way I let my Princess be a slacker) but I pray to God, Jesus, Muhammad, Yahweh, Allah, and the rest, that I got the good sense to mind limits.

And feel free to apply my theory anyplace.

Where there's All-American white men, trust and believe there are All-American white women. These apples of the universe wear either skirt suits or designer workout gear, sports 'do's with highlights, and makeup so subtle you can't be sure if they're wearing any at all. The maître d' leads us to seats in a ill-lit section. Jude don't waste a second splaying open his menu, but I, on the flip side, begin with my test, lifting the cutlery (the heavier the fork, spoon, knife, the better the chef) to judge my chances of catching tasty grub. A woman (her jet-black bob cut don't fit) strides over to our table.

Juuuuuude, Jude, how are you? she says.

Oh, hey, Jude says. I'm well. Doing quite well. How are you?

Excellent, she says. Didn't know you came here, she says.

My first time, Jude says. But I've heard such good things.

Jude introduces me, tells her that I'm his new favorite client. Her handshake is hella-firm. She flaunts a smile made of moonglow—that white.

Don't mean to keep you two, she says. But can I say how much we love our new place? How much we absolutely love it.

Awesome, Jude says.

She looks at me and says Jude's an angel. She turns to Jude. You really are, for what you did for us, and we can't thank you enough. Well I should be getting along, she says. She suggests an entrée to die for, and saunters off into brighter light.

Our waiter must be on protest. Or maybe our wait time is racial. (We're post what? Only a silly nigger's insensate to racial slights.) The room. You can see inside the kitchen. A chef (white jacket and toque blanche hat) tossing chopped bits out of a pan, a dude in a black suit glaring at a mannequin-stiff busboy, a bartender slapping shot glasses on the counter. Jude reminds me it's open season on the menu, says his motto is to spend what he can before his evil ex claims it. Our past due server slugs over. He quotes the special of the day, segues into a cheerless spiel on menu favorites, asks if we'd like drinks. We pick starters and main courses. Jude, too, orders champagne by the glass, and while our waiter flits off (right now, all of a sudden he's in a hurry) for them, Jude smears hunks of butter on the gourmet bread and gets to work. No wonder! No wonder! No BS, homeboy's chomped through almost the whole basket by the time the waiter comes back with our drinks on a silver tray. Jude lifts his flute for a toast and waits for me to join.

Here's to us, he says. May the best day of our lives be worse than our worst to come.

That was a proper, I say. Did you make that up? I might hafta steal it.

Bud, feel free, he says.

He slops another glob of butter on his bread and swallows the shit whole. Next week, no carbs, he says, his mouth full. But this week . . . He taps his pocket, takes out a low-ringing cell, puzzles his eyebrows at the number, answers. Hello, he says. Yes, this is he. Jude frowns. He covers his phone, says excuse me, and bustles out. You can see him pacing, see him snatch his cell away from his face and ogle it in disbelief. He's out there woofing long enough for his main course to arrive and cool, for his drink to arrive and go warm. He slugs back inside. His face is flushed, and his eyes have gone a darker blue.

Bad news? I say.

The ex's vulture lawyer specializes in bad news, Jude says. That woman's the blight of my life. Wants more, more, more. Whether there's more or not. Bud, when it comes to getting married, be sure or for God sakes be against it.

The part of my brain that makes sounds decisions says it's best not to prod him further, and this time, I heed the wiser me.

God knows what I should say.

—Grace

FIRST YOU MAKE YOURSELF a believer and then if need
be you can say it to someone else and mean it. This is the last
pack, I say. This one and no more! I can't subject (when they
come home, and they will come home!) my boys, my babies, to
this poison. This one last time, I say, and slip on the clothes I
wore earlier and my heels and tear out of the apartment. You
could walk, but I drive down to Big Charles's market. He's
stranded behind the counter, dumping a grab bag of chips in his
mouth. Let me guess. Let me guess, he says, and crushes bites.

No guessing, I say. But this is the last pack. I'm done.

Then it look like you shoulda made the last pack the last one,
he says. I'm all out, Less you puffing nonfiltered.

Oh no, I say. Who's open and close by that might have my
brand?

Hate to break it to you, smokella, he says. But they robbed the
truck that delivers this zone. Your best bet's out by the airport.

That far? I say.

That far, he says.

He hands me a book of matches and says it's the best he can
do, and I whisk out to the car, which cranks easy enough.

Where to next? I pull off with mist beading the windshield: a forecast. I leave my radio off. This isn't a night for music; it's a night for what I'm out for, with a taste in my mouth, and the rest of me longing for that deep first pull. Bodies roaming. You wonder who's running from something. Who's running to something. How few this hour could be up to any good. You'd be surprised what and who you would need, to keep from feeling alone. The Honda hits a pothole and the rear wheel squeaks. This car don't sound like itself. You hope it isn't falling to pieces: the car—your life. There's time to stop now, go home, and rest. The weekend. There's work tomorrow. Sunday's an off day. Then, the big day: Monday, which is court for my boys, my babies. God knows it will come sooner than it should, knows there's a strange old urge to fight before then. I check my tank, it's quarter full. It hits me to ride until the tank runs out. The mist turns to rain, the rain to something else. I set my wipers to full speed. I stop at a light and watch a man stutter into the crosswalk with a coat tented over his head. He stumbles and finds balance. My light turns green and I lose him from there. Blocks farther, I see the sign for the tavern flicker the red and blue of warnings. I pull over and rush in as though I was headed here all along. The tavern is dim. The jukebox plays R & B. Nothing but men inside, scattered, and I can feel them hawk my path to the machine and it's stocked with my brand. I lay my bag on the machine and scrounge for dollars and coins. An old man wobbles over. The man's eyes are wet as anything outside, and he can't quite find his poise. He asks my name and offers to pay.

It's Grace, I say. And thank you but no thank you.

Well Grace, he says. May I at least interest you in a drink? Word is they go well with a smoke.

I'm rushing, I say.

This late? he says.

Yes, I say.

Must have a big day ahead. How about just one drink, he says. Don't crush an old man's hope. He drags me to the bar and pulls out a seat and tells the bartender to fix a special, and the bartender pours a vodka and cranberry—much more vodka than juice—and tops it with a wrinkled cherry. He presents it as though it's a gift. Do you mind? I say, and take the wrapper off my pack and shake out a cig. The old man finds a lighter and thumbs a flame and holds—he couldn't keep his hands still for a hero's treasure—it quivering between us. The first pull under-whelms. I sip at my drink, once, to be polite, but won't be tak-ing many more. No way I let the numbers undo me. Not now, and not—if it's up to me, and it is—ever. The old man lets me smoke in peace. Someone staggers for the exit. Someone feeds the jukebox, picks a song filled with static and a deep voice moaning. Others go on with the rest of their night. The man orders himself another drink and the bartender warns it should be his last.

Don't I know it should be, he says, and downs it in one swal-low. He pushes an ashtray closer to me, and I tap my cig and blow a ring towards the lights. The next sips are against my will.

Where you headed? he says.

Home, I say.

Home's the big rush? he says.

No it's not, I say.

He's prying. I don't like men who pry. I swear off men who pry, but I am not myself, and this much I know. I confess to him about Big Ken and the boys and court and he listens as if I'm the last living soul among the dead. He pinches a napkin from the counter stack and gives it to me. Now, now, not those, he says. We don't want those. I dab at my face and say sorry. He says it's nothing to be sorry over. He orders another drink and swears it's his last of the night. Where's the count on what I'm losing, on how much, how fast?

I'm so embarrassed, I say.

Listen, he says. I been everywhere, done everything, seen all the shit you ain't supposed to, and trust an old man the judge that rules against you got two glass eyes and a heart more dense than stone. And what my fair lady would you say are the chances of that? He rolls his neck, excuses me from my drink, walks me to the door, and kisses my hand good-bye. Till then, he says.

Right outside it's take-cover weather, stay-home weather, melt-away weather. I hunt for my keys and make a dash for the Honda and, wouldn't you know, it won't start first turn. It won't start second turn either. I tap the gas and try again—and nothing. Not a grumble, stutter, or click. I take out another cigarette and let my seat back and fog the car with smoke. This goes on until the rain bears down, until I pop the latch, climb out, and, with no clue of where to look or what I'd do if I found the trouble, I gape at a strange maze of metal and rubber and plastic and tubes and cords and bolts and screws and blocks and caps. I peek up from under the hood and see headlights flickering in the distance, the shaky light of a car that, by the way it knocks, couldn't be in much better shape than the

Honda. The car stops beside me and a bolt of fright almost breaks me in two. I keep my head ducked under the hood; maybe the driver will move on.

Well, well, well. If it ain't Ms. Corporate America. What you doin out this time of night?

It's him. You can't believe it. You can.

Michael swings his car around so it's hood-to-hood with mine and vaults out, taunting the rain. He tells me to get inside my car and ducks under my hood and fusses parts and tells me try the start—dead. He walks back to his car and searches his trunk for cables and tethers us and revs his engine and tells me to try it once more—dead. He walks around and plops in my passenger seat. He smells of rain and smoke and grief.

It takes another cig to keep my eyes dry.

Battery. Starter. Solenoid. Hate to be the bearer of bad news, he says. But this here ain't movin nowhere tonight.

My life, I say. And mean it.

Not worry, MCA. You know I got you. Where you headed? he says. His eyes shine and spark.

F.E.A.R. Frustration. Ego. Anxiety. Resentment.
F.E.A.R. False. Expectations. Appear. Real.
F.E.A.R. False. Evidence. Appears. Real.
F.E.A.R. F—. Everything. And. Run.

God knows what I *should* say. But what I do say is, Anywhere, please, but home.

Funny you should say that, he says, cause it just so happens I got a coupla dollars burning a hole in my pocket.

Before we pull off, I mention my work shifts tomorrow and

next day, about court on Monday. Cool, cool, he says, and assures me I'll be back before I know it, that what could go wrong
won't.

Michael's spot is out, the next one too. The next place tells us to
hold on, so we hold until we can't. Must be drought, he says.
He's not quite dry and sounds discouraged. This till I say I might
know someone else. His eyes say he can't believe it, and what's
true is, I can't either. We either lose a first life riding or make it so
fast that I can't keep track. The block's dark as ever and cemetery-
dead, and even the boys always out and never up to any good had
sense enough to escape this storm. We park as close as we can and
jaunt around back, Michael covering our heads with a mildewed
shirt from his trunk. The bandanna-wearing boy that answers
could be someone's baby I know, and probably is. I ask for Bear
and he lets us inside.

This place is like it was, like the others, like them all.

No one belongs, but everyone buying is welcome.

The boy points to a distant room, and Michael frontiers a step
ahead. He swaggers inside and up close to the table where Bear
roosts before a tiny TV. What it is, boss, Michael says. We came
to spend a few bucks. Bear sizes Michael, sizes me, small, smaller
behind him. He declares his nonnegotiable minimum buy. Cool,
cool, not a problem, Michael says. Matterfact, let's kick off with
double the fun. Bear masses upright and claws a sack from his
crotch. Half his dreads are undone. His white T-shirt isn't white.
His nails glow burnt beige. They make the exchange and Michael asks if we can smoke in one of the rooms. Bear sends us to
the basement, and you wonder how far it is from hell. It's the
same filth and dust below. Michael loads a new glass pipe and

gives it to me for our first blast. He asks how it tastes, says there's been bad batches, rocks overcut with acetone making rounds. He tells me that the money he's spending, big money, comes from a check scheme, that there's no need for us to pace.

He says there isn't a more fitting smoke buddy in all the land, says it as though it's praise, and my God, it feels not far from it.

Michael goes alone to buy the next blast. And the next. And the next. And the next. The man back and forth, so fast. We start where we left off and the question is never if you want to, but instead how long it will take to burn through it all.

There's a shattered bulb in the overhead fixture, the bulb's foot still in the socket. CRIP LIFE FOR LIFE is scrawled on unfinished drywall.

Michael gets up and pumps the fist that isn't holding the pipe. See, people get it fucked up, MCA, he says. They say it's where you been and with who. They say it's where you're at and when. But what don't they say? He bucks his eyes around the room and settles a naked gaze on me. Be happy? he says. Be happy how? Where? When? Happy—don't fall for it, he says. You can't trust it, he says. He holds the pipe to where the light should glow. This here between us is happy, he says. All that other shit is fairy tales.

One. Two. A thousand. You lose track of the trips he takes upstairs. I float, fly to a street-level window, see dark between the boards, and I can't know for sure when I last saw light, if we've been at it hours or a day or days.

What time is it? I say. What day?

Noon, midnight, next week. What difference do it make? he says.

The difference is I work, I say. I told you I have to work.

Michael shakes his head and yanks his pockets inside out. We musta been here a few minutes, he says. Ain't no more encores.

No more? I say. That's it?

Well, they say all's well that ends . . . or whatever the fuck. Michael's eyes are spangled. His lips the color of wet bark.

Work or no work, God knows you hope this lasts forever, knows too you hope it ends right now, and in time it does, though it always does before its time.

No, too soon, I say. It's too soon.

The. End, he says.

Or next act, I say. My head is fogged, I shove on my shoes. Come, I say. Let's go.

That's me talking to me.
　　—Champ

IT SHOULD BE JUDE PICKING up or his voice saying
leave a message, but it's neither. It's a dial tone and the lady that
says a number has been disconnected. First thing I tell myself is
not to panic, that I must have misdialed, that I should try again.
So I do. I do again and again and again. Every time suffering the
same grim result. You should see me snatch the phone from my
face and stare at the dial pad, expecting I don't know what. Dis-
heartened? Damn skippy, but I keep at it more times than I'd
admit, keep right the fuck on dialing until I'm convinced the
recording ain't a fluke, that it ain't a joke being played by a
clown with loads of free time and a sadistic streak. I'm a photon
out my crib. Zip! I jump in my ride and catch rubber out the lot.
Some things happen and in an instant it's so easy to think the
worst, so tough to stay composed. But I tell myself this ain't one
of those times, that we (me and me) should stay positive—deceits
that keep me sane for blocks upon blocks, keep me from blowing
yellows and reds, which is genius, with this strap in my ride. The
first time I drove to Jude's office I needed directions, and directions for my directions, but right now homeboy's cross streets are
a compass point on a map stamped in my brain. A right here, a
left there, all I got to do is listen and steer. The freeway gods

show me favor till the last few exits, then, *bam*, either there's a major pileup up ahead or I'm caught in an ill-timed experiment of time-lapse photography, slowed to a crawl, then a standstill, with gloomtastic math knocking around my skull: This + that + this = the sum that might be lost! Then there's a sliver of daylight in view, and boy, that's all I needed. Here I go weaving through cars, blasting the slow lane, tailgating niggers Sunday driving on a Friday. It's a wonder that I don't get stopped. I get to Jude's office, park across the street, hop out blind, and feel the gust of a truck this close to killing me forever. I squeeze my eyes tight, pause while my heart falls back in its cage. Jude has a sign on the door which makes me hopeful. That lasts, what, a second, till the moment I peer into his office window and despair: no desk, no plaque, no chairs. It's barren but for scattered papers and an empty cardboard box. I yell his name and rap the door. Pound so hard I might've broken a knuckle. Bang with one hand, then the other, then, *blam*, try to kick that bitch off the hinges. No go, so I go around back and repeat. This time, I press my ear to the door and listen for a sign of life. An also-ran top-flight security type in uniform moseys out and tells me Jude's moved, that he packed up earlier this week (what was supposed to be my last down payment). I ask dude if he's sure and he tells me he's positive, that he helped Jude load a truck hisself. Did he mention his next address? I say.

The rent-a-cop pokes out his chest and asks can he ask how I know Jude. I tell him I'm an old friend, a new client.

He gropes his baton, juts one leg out in front of the other, says No offense, guy, but you don't look much like either one. The top-flight rent-a-punk strolls back into his office, tapping his baton and whistling. The part of my brain that makes bonehead choices says to bash a window, tear up the place: smash lights, graffiti the walls, piss-soak the floor, all of which I'd do if I suspected it would help even an inkling. Come on, man, let's not get out of character here.

That's me talking to me.

In a masochistic fit, I pull my cell and once, twice, ceaseless call Jude. We're sorry . . . We're sorry, but the number . . . We're sorry, but the number you have reached . . . The one person I can fathom to call besides the culprit is Half Man. So I call my homeboy and he, hella-astonishing, answers. You ain't gonna believe this shit, I say, and explain the drama.

Quit bullshittin, he says. Put that on something.

On my mama and baby, I say.

Static cackles across our line and we wait for it to clear.

Damn, so the whitey tryin to pull the okey on us, huh? Hell nah, hell nah. Come swoop, he says, and we'll find this motherfucker.

Next thing I know, I got Half Man barking in the passenger seat, swearing what he'll do when we catch Jude. Serious threats I'm hoping ain't a bunch of fatmouthing on his part, cause about now I'd be happy to see Jude waylaid, flogged, water-tortured, Chinese-style. Sounds extra, but I'm so so serious: When we catch him it's whatever, zero interference on my part. Better yet, why stand aside when I can partake?

Me nursing visions of grave physical harm. Half Man's a mute-mouth, don't utter a motherfucking peep till we wheel into a suburb, and even then, all he asks is how much farther, how do I know that we're headed the right way.

Cause I been here once, I say.

So we're relying on your faulty memory? he says.

Who's the one who's fucked? I say. Who wants to find him more, me or you?

We're in Southwest, which means we're suspects. (Try not feeling suspicious when you're treated suspect.) We journey long suburban blocks, stretches and stretches minus nary a familiar sight. We do this for what feels like an eon of hearthurt, and just about the time I'm about to wail a dirge I see, if my memory can be trusted, Jude's house up ahead. There, it's up there, I say, feeling pleased for a snap.

He asks me if I'm sure, this dude and his assurances, and I park right in the front, lift the armrest, hand him my strap. He tucks it in his belt, and about now it's looking like an amulet, though how long can good fortune last in this zip? We bandit out the car, policelike, hunterlike, bounty hunters who've fallen under the gaze of wish-they-were-circumspect citizen detectives: a woman tending plants in her front yard, a guy reading a paper on his porch, the person spying us from a Red Sea part in a curtain— all waiting for an excuse, legitimate or not, to call Officer Arrest-a-Nigger-for-Nothing's direct line. Maybe they're too preoccupied to notice we don't (or do) fit the neighborhood profile, but maybe, just maybe, they ain't.

Scratch what I said about the pistol offering comfort. It's an onus.

The back and forth, the back and forth, Ibullshityounot, if you snatched off the top of my head, you'd hear me pop and fizzle. Half Man follows me onto the porch, and if he's attentive at all, he mocks my best nonthreatening Negro gait, the one full of leisure and anti-bounce. I rap the door and stand back and it's déjàfuckingvu. I hit it again, inch closer. I twist and catch a detective (the green thumb lady) peeking up from tending her plants. She sees me see her and don't bother to look away, the white woman's audacity in the flesh. Half Man hits the door this time, and bet a life, you could hear it for blocks. That loud, and still no answer, not a sound. Stand close to me this second and hear hope's slow leak. *Sssssssssssssssssssssss* . . . Half Man says we should go around back, bust in, see what's what.

You call that a plan? I say.

You got a better plan? he says.

Yes, I say.

Oh, he says. How could I forget you're the king of gold plans?

Who the fuck are you, I say.

He crosses his arms and smacks his lips, and we could be anything to each other. We could be not nothing at all.

It's empty, says a voice. It's the green thumb detective. She wipes a tool on her apron and climbs the steps.

You mean not home or empty? I say.

I mean empty, she says.

But my friend lives here, I say.

My friend lived there, she says.

Do you know where I can find him?

Heaven, she says. Let's hope.

Me and Half Man swivel mouth to wide mouth.

Dead, I say. But I just seen him last week.

Saw who? she says.

Jude, I say.

There's no Jude at this address, she says. That was Ted's place. Mr. Rose.

You sure? I say.

He was my neighbor before my boys were born, she says. And they're all grown men.

This is how it feels to have all the thew knocked right out of you, to be one of those fat monster truck tires stabbed flat. Let's go, I say, and slog off the porch. Half Man complains in the car that this don't make sense, that the lady might be lying, that we should circle back, break in, ransack the place.

It's a fool's idea, and I tell him so.

Just trying to look out, he says. But fuck it. You're the one taking the L. Half Man's braids are skinny limp ropes on his neck. I could twist them into a noose and hang him, twist them into a noose and lynch myself.

Because Jude's not there and hasn't been and I know it.

Watch, he says. Next we gone find out we don't know his real name.

Leave it to my homeboy (is he my aceboon?), or else glimpse my bleak-ass future before me.

Here's a foolproof plan for an express pass to prison: Run up in a bank acting a fool. Now, I know this as any mentally fit human being does, but since most days, today being one of them, it's disputable whether Half Man's one of us, I have to remind him to leave the strap in the car. We get inside and Half Man (thank God) finds a seat and chills while I scan the lobby checking to see if by some great change of fortune (my luck?) Jude can be found lollygagging in a line. Is he here? What you think? I stretch my face into a suburban-block-long ersatz smile and bop over, nonthreatening Negro gait every step to a young banker's cube.

Good afternoon. I was wondering if you might be able to

assist me? I say, so pusillanimous somebody should punch me dead in my face.

Sure, sure, he says. That's what I'm here for.

Dude ain't much older than me, which another time, another day, would count for something, but I'm sure it don't count for nothing. Since I can't at present, for my life, concoct an acceptable lie, I settle on the truth, most of it anyhow, which spills out in a fusillade. The banker waits for me to finish. He taps his keyboard and squints at his screen. He says he wishes he could help and blames his punk ineptitude on bank rules and privacy laws; he prattles a hyperbolic list of bureaucratic bullshit that boils down to this: Hell no, leave! It's not that I don't believe you, he says, capping his bulletin, but we've got rules, strict rules, and stiff penalties.

I ply longer, fall, fall to the other side of desperate, and when I reach the end of my wits with him, I ask to see the branch manager and the banker calls over this middle-aged dude in a cheap suit and scuffed brogues. Here I go pleading again, asinine, but at least the manager fronts as though he's listening: giving me hammy head nods with a grip on his concave chin. He lets me vent, indulges a second of mock musing, then quotes, with zero compassion, from the same trite script as his banker.

You can't do nothing? I say. Nothing?

The man's *no* is implacable and I know it. He tells banker to take it from here. He excuses himself and moseys off the way anyone would whose life was still intact.

Half Man's across the room, thumbing a brochure. Long white tee, those killer braids, they might think he's casing the joint. We don't need that heat.

Common sense says it's time to break, but I ring the bell on another round with the banker. This time I describe Jude, his tippy-toe gait, his silvered sides, his hulk nose, his indelible-ass voice, but the banker says he can't recall him, tells me he wishes he could be of more help, asks if he could assist me with anything else, a new checking account, a savings account, a CD, a reply that got me considering a bribe, a threat, of snatching his computer and breaking out the front door, going back for my strap and taking hostages till they unass every copper cent in Jude's accounts—got me thinking all that plus a host of other numbskull moves. Who's fooled? We all know by now or should that I ain't got it in me to be that bold. I ask him (it's a hairsbreadth from a teary plea) to please give me a call if he sees or hears anything, anything at all, and limp out, Half Man behind me, defeated, demolished, fucking disemboweled. Outside, the sky is a battered blue, and I'm convinced the color's a sign for me and me alone. We sit in the car, me with a tick, tick, tick, in my ear and a bully twitch. I bash the wheel and a part shakes loose and clatters. I smack the back of my head against the seat rest and scream a scream that Miller-knots my gut. I look over at Half Man, my terror gauge, who at times is unshakable, and he looks worried beyond belief.

Mister's in the back of his store slapping bones with old heads. A quartet roosted around the table with piles of cash at hand. All told, it's ends that could probably pay off what I owe him and replace most of what I might've lost to Jude. A come-up, I'm thinking, which means it's true, it's true, that bad luck can hatch a wrong idea, yank all the scruples out of even the purest of motherfuckers. There's Mister. Does he see himself as the man with an IOU on my life? A hoary old head calls domino, smashes the table, and the bones leap and fall rearranged. The players swap bills, and Mister gets up and motions me out of the room.

He tells me he's been calling, asks why I've been hard to find to which I explain about the house and Jude. Mister rubs his slick head and rubs the face of his watch with his shirt. Hate to hear that, he says. But what that have to do with what you owe me? That don't have nothing to do with my money.

I quote him all I have to my name, which is thousands less than I owe, and ask him for few more days to pay in full. He pushes up close and pats my cheek, tender. Time, he says. And patience. In time all patience wears out. He tells me to go and bring what I have, all I have, to go and bring it back tonight. Bill's due, he says. Past due. I nod and drop my eyes to the floor. Counting the most that's inside my safe, what's left of my last package. He stops by his safe and twists it open, takes out a wrapped stack of bills, turns them into a fan, waves the fan. You see this? he says. You don't get this by giving it out. He stuffs the stack in his pocket and marches me to the front and unbolts the door, sounding that fucking bell. A van stutters down MLK, its taillight bandaged with duct tape. Mister claps me on the back. Trust me, he says. Trust me, you don't want this problem.

Tonight's as wet and warm a Saturday as any this month, but MLK is cold and empty, and I stumble to the car with a rock the size of Augustus lodged in my gut—or maybe, just maybe, it's my heart. Half Man snaps up in his seat when I climb in. Damn, homie, that was quick, he says. What's the word?

The word is you go home, I say.

You can guess what time it is when I get home. It's late. Alibi-late. No-excuse-late. I hit the lock praying Kim's asleep, but my girl is wide awake, vivid, with all the lights up in the room. I shuttle in, slide the closet, crank open the safe, empty it but for a few bills, and tramp into the front room. I lay it on the counter and count (it's less than I thought—anemic) and she stalks in behind me and hovers, her belly pressed against my back. She don't say nothing at first. Lets me count and recount in what, on another night, could be peace.

What's this?

This, I say. Is business.

At this hour? she says.

My business, I say.

I grab a paper sack and load the cash in it: the rent, light bill, re-up, the rest.

What business?! she says. Champ, you need to explain.

Look, leave me the fuck alone, I say. Not tonight. Of all the nights, not tonight.

Mister's brother Red lets me back into the store. You can hear the bones sliding across the table in the back and the same old heads barking at one another. I slug into the back room and stand against the wall while someone washes the bones, while they pull their hands, while they eye the black dots as if them shits are talismans. Mister lays big six, lays the rest of his hand facedown, tells Red to stand watch. Give me a sec, fellas, he says, and gets to his feet.

He takes me into the basement and wades between delivery boxes to the bistro where his money counter sits. I pull out the bag (it may as well be a sack of blood) and give it to him and he drops it on the table. He asks how much is there, how much I'm short. I tell him and he warns me to have the rest next week.

Oh, for sure, I say, though I'm not and he knows it. He clicks the overhead bulb, turns the basement blackish, leaves me groping behind him through a maze of dark. He stops in the stairwell and turns to me, the light sourcing behind him. Everybody ain't built for this, he says, and glides the rest of the way up.

Outside the store I get a page. It's a lick, my regular, the one with a spot. One of the ones who buys his work already rocked, and shit, shit, all I have left is soft. All I have left is stashed at Beth's crib. She don't pick up (a theme) when I call, but that don't no matter, I ain't about to miss his bread. Damn right, I can't afford to miss this bread. Under a dying quarter moon, I fly out 26 west, a lone traveler part of the way, to her place. She answers, thank God, (Why is a nigger thanking God?) in a loosened robe and nothing else. She makes a face, asks what time it is. Late, I say. No, early. Time to handle business. She shakes her head and tells me to come back later—this afternoon or this evening, says she's got company. But I need it now, I say. Just give me a few and I'll be out your hair. Just keep him in the room and let me grab my things. She concedes, strolls into her room, pulls her door shut. Swift I gather the work, the scales, the Pyrex, the baggies, an unopened box of baking soda, and I whisk outside in the claws of paranoia. Tough to know whether it's day or night.

It's Sunday. Early Sunday, when I get in, and the apartment's teeming with the orange of dawn. I hustle into the kitchen and empty the backpack. I find a pot, fill it, set it to boil. I knock a chunk off the work (the smell, a nigger never can get used to the stench), weigh it, and dump it to boil. This feels like day one. It feels like the end. I stand by the stove, stirring, adjusting the heat, praying Kim don't wake, wondering what I could say if she does. There's a knock at the door that, on my life, shoots my heart up into my throat. I freeze and wait to see if whoever it is has the wrong place. The next knock is a statement. She calls my name, and I creep to the door.

Who is it? I say.

The voice is garbled. I crack the door and here she is, my mother, rancid, her eyes glassy, charred lips slopped with gloss.

Son, I don't know what I wanna be when I grow up, she says. And I'm all grown up.

What? I say.

What do you want me to say? she says. Can't you see? She has as much chance as earth does of keeping still.

You bringing this here? Where I lay my head? I say, like I can. I look to see who else in the hall.

No lectures, please. Just give it to me. I need it. Let me have it.

Have what? I say.

Champ, don't make me go through changes, she says. Okay, I can't right now.

You come to my door at the crack of dawn.

She fixes her shirt. Please, Champ. Give it to me and let me go.

Give you what? To do what?

The water splashes out of the pot in hi-fi. Much longer, and I'll lose grams, longer than that it might cook down to paste and come back at almost naught.

Do you know what tomorrow is? I say. I know you know what tomorrow is.

Yes, yes, yes, I do. I'll get it together. I swear. Just give it to me, Champ. Don't make me beg.

Leave! I say, and shut the door. Shut it so it doesn't slam. I stomp into the kitchen, see my work cooked down to a loss. I take it off the eye and drain it. I look up and see Kim, tumescent, standing in the kitchen entrance. Who, she says, was that? And what, she says, is this?

Go back to sleep, I say.

This is what you do and where you do it now? she says. This is what you feel for us.

Grace shouts again from the hall, and I creep over and watch her through the peephole. She bangs the door with her fist and winces. She takes off her shoe and blams the door with her heel.

Honor thy father and thy mother. That thy days may be long upon the land which the Lord thy God giveth thee. She bangs her shoe once more. *Cursed be he that setteth light by his father or mother.*

Are you fucking serious, I say. Leave, I say. Go now, before one of them calls the police.

Grace holds her heel. Her hand is bleeding. Let them call and let them come, she says. Let them call and let them come. And when they do, let's tell them how you won't give your mama a few dollars to keep her from dying.

My neighbor, the nosy-ass schoolteacher, cranes his head out of his apartment and ask if everything's okay?

It's fine, I say.

No sir, Grace says. It's *not* fine. My son, here, do you know him? Do you happen to know how he makes his living?

This snoopy mother fucker's face is a fireworks show. He gaps his mouth as if to speak, but I snatch Grace inside, slam the door, press my chin into the top of her head. I fleece my pockets, give her what's in them, not much, and tell her to go and don't come back. She stuffs the cash in her bra and drops her heel on the floor and slips it on her foot. She hobbles off, the click of her heel echoing.

I walk to the window to see if I can see her leave and when I come back Kim is standing near the stove. She asks again what I'm doing. I grab the pot and utensils and dump them in the sink and run a sink of water. She gapes while I set up: the scale, baggies, paper towels. Her eyes, those eyes, brimming with tears. You said you wouldn't, she says. What good is your word? I stab cracks in the work and lay it on the paper towel to air-dry. Why, Champ? Why? I have a right to know, she says.

You have a right to know? A right. People's rights are violated every day, I say. What the fuck's so special about yours?

She shakes her head and touches her belly and slumps off for the room.

My lick pages me again, adds 911, and I chop the work, weigh out oz's, tie them off in plastic. Kim wobbles out about the time I finish weighing. She's dressed and tugging a messily packed suitcase.

Oh, here we go with this, I say.

She yanks open the closet packed with things for the baby, snatches a jacket off a hanger, struggles into the sleeves.

Miss me with this bullshit, I say. Where're you supposed to be going?

I dump the work in a sack and fold the sack down to a grip.

You promised, she says. But you won't stop unless they stop you. You won't, and we won't be here when they do.

You wanna go? Then go! I say.

That's all you got left?

—Grace

MICHAEL HAS THE CAR RUNNING when I limp out, a
deep throb in my fist. He tinkers with knobs and opens and
searches and shuts the glovebox. He gazes at me. He's never seen
the heart of what's wrong, or else maybe he's checking for the
wrong hurts. I rest my busted hand on the dash, see blood on my
knuckles, new bruises. He asks if I'm ready, and I lift what
Champ gave me into view.

Say no more, Michael says.

The mission. Back at the spot. This time I tell Michael to let me
take the lead. You'd swear Bear's bigger than he was when we
left. I order and he paws a dwindled plastic sack from his crotch.
There's a cascade of sweat on his nose, disks of yellow in his pits.

That's all you got left? I say.

Not your worry, Bear says. Supplies is my business. Demand is
yours.

We could whine about the size of what he gives us but who
has the strength? Bear says there's a crowd downstairs, so sends
us this round to the attic. There's a black tunnel leading upstairs.
You wouldn't be surprised if you fell through a step. We make it
up alive. Up here there's old wallpaper peeling in strips, dusty

330

plastic bins shoved in the corners, a stained-to-death fabric couch, a chipped wood table built too low for an adult.

Tiny windows filter morning, light, and in that light Michael is maimed. Or maybe it's how I look to him. Or maybe I'm seeing myself in him.

He proclaims we have to make this stretch.

We puff. Spell as long as we can between blasts. Sit and stand. Float to corners where the light doesn't reach. I press my face against a window, and see far, far up, something metallic twinking by.

Between my last blast and the one to come I may well lose a year of life.

But why stop now, though? How can you stop when you can keep on? When the strongest urge is to reach the end.

Here comes big trouble: a deep pull and no new feeling. Here's Michael silent, beyond words now, a distance into his next dream.

They say what you do is who you are, and is the only voice to heed, but sometimes, some days, who am I? The Grace I don't know stands and screams, WHO THE HELL GIVES THEM THE RIGHT? She climbs on the couch, loads a bowl, and strikes a flame. She squeezes her eyes into magic and sucks down her *and* his share. WHAT DO THEY KNOW? JUST WAIT, I'LL SHOW THEM ALL!

That's cool, MCA, but get down fore you fall down, Michael says.

He gropes for the pipe, hugs it against his chest, gazes into its black foot. I see, we being selfish, he says. He scrapes the resin and burns it and drops the hot pipe on the table. That's it, he says. The end of good things. The last dance. Show's over.

No, no, no; the show must go on, I say, and flash the money I meant to keep for myself.

This time I go down alone.

Bear's eyes are red smears. They make you wonder how he sees, what he sees, if he sees at all. Back, he says. Where dude? Upstairs, I say. Bear this time serves me from a tiny sack in his sock. The pills are anemic. You think you could throw in extra.

We don't do no extras, he says.

After all we spent? I say.

After who spent what? he says.

That's how you treat people, I say. Why not be more kind? It wouldn't hurt to be more kind. You know God has a plan for your life.

What the fuck? he says. God ain't nowhere near this muthafucka. Take that dope and get the fuck out my face.

Bear shoos me and I backtrack with these scant pills cupped.

Michael frowns at my purchase and sighs. He tells me to have at it, hands me the lighter and pipe. The boys make a racket below. Bear's voice booms through the floor.

The lighter lashes a bright flame and I suck as slow as I can. What I have won't last anywhere near as long as I need.

What could go wrong? is what you ask yourself, and you could just imagine, or maybe you can't. The courthouse tomorrow, the Multnomah County Courthouse on Salmon, the same one where, on the first floor, you come to pay a traffic ticket or parking fine or start the process to reinstate your license, where in a second or third or fourth floor room you might find someone crying innocent of theft or pleading guilty on assault, where you might see a boy not much younger than my eldest begging a judge for probation, where in that building so many just like Michael or me, or so near us the difference can't be ranked, will have their distribution charges dropped to possession. A judge will sit in his chambers studying dockets and sipping plain black coffee while the building fills, while the checkpoint clogs with visitors wearing belt buckles and bracelets and rings and necklaces, stalls from screws in a foot or a pacemaker, while guards snatch others out of line for wand searches, and trash a small thing they huff is within the rules. Visitors will slide or eke by security and reach for papers and slips and copies they brought folded in their pockets or buried in a wallet or purse, stuffed in a legal envelope, notices and subpoenas and warrants and summonses and paternity test results and reccs from a teacher or a pastor or a boss; imagine them slogging into the building with, tucked under arm, probation files and police briefs and psych briefs and transcripts and community service contacts, carrying orders of protection and tax returns and pay stubs and bank slips and W2's and deeds and judgments and drug program intake and outtake papers and receipts and passports and licenses and SS cards and adoption papers and notarized letters of insurance; imagine them bearing deposition transcripts and affidavits and every other form or letter or printout or triplicate carbon copy you could think of, plus a whole slew you couldn't—any card or file or scrap they think will swing the law in their favor.

Tomorrow AM who will be among them?

Andrew will arrive first, with his tie Windsor-knotted and shirt tucked perfect in his slacks he's owned for an age. Picture Champ not far behind, swanking inside in polished black shoes and a dress shirt buttoned at his throat. Picture the pastor floating in. Picture Chris who said he'd show, keeping his word, and, just far enough behind to miss conflict, Kenny and his tramp traipsing in arm in arm with my boys, my babies, in tow. Picture their grinning lawyer toting a briefcase full of lies. Picture all of them filing into the courtroom and the judge taking his bench, and calling Kenny's name and my name. Picture them all—my babies, Champ, Andrew, the pastor, Chris, that man, that woman, their smirking counselor, searching the room for who's missing: me!

Missions. You know you should stop, but . . . You end up downstairs, empty-handed, face-to-mask with Bear, and asking for a favor—or is it a blessing, or is it a curse? You end up downstairs and on your knees in every way that counts.

We don't do no extras and we don't do no favors, he says.

But I swear I'll pay you tomorrow, I say. I'll give it to you with interest.

He bends the antenna on his tiny TV and turns a knob.

Don't make me go home, I say. I can't go home.

Well, you sho in the fuck can't stay here, he says. We accommodate paying clients.

Just one, I say. Please.

Hell, nah, he says. I let you slide, I may as well spot every muthafucka who come in here with a sob story. This ain't no nonprofit, he says. This a business. And if you ain't got no bread, we ain't got no further business.

The voice in the TV says good day to Oregon. Bear dumps a bottle cap of ashes on the floor and rakes me with his rheumy red smears—false spells. I can't feel my busted-up hand, can't feel my face. I turn to leave, but his bark stops me cold. He grunts out of his seat and undoes his belt and snorts. Check this out, he says.

We don't do no extras nor no credit. But we do got one helluva motherfuckin payment plan.

He plucks a plump pill from a sack in his sock and gifts it into a sacrament.

This thing can't jack his TV to loud enough.

That's my mama, I say. My mama.
　　　—Champ

THIS YOUNGSTER THAT'S OUT front don't know me and looks spooked when I ask for dude. He tells me to go around back, where a dude with a blue fitted cap dipped low points me past a group of young Crips camped by a TV. I got my pistol tucked (trust who?) in my waist and the sack of oz's stuffed in my drawls: reasons A and B, respective, of me stepping hesitant as shit down the hall towards a room at the end of the hall with a TV blasting inside.

When I get in the room, this sasquatch nigger is on the floor, pants dropped, his nasty hairy ass pounding a female body. It's one of those times I want to look away but can't. The female's got her head thrown to the side and is a corpse but for a twitch in her feet. And it's the feet that give her away. It's seeing those feet that cracks a fault line in me. He stabs her again with a deep grunt, and growls what I can't hear over the noise: over the TV, over the chatter inside my skull. I take out my pistol, trip the safety, and materialize at his side. I drop to my knees and jab the pistol with all my might into the meat that covers his ribs.

Get off of her, I say. Get off of her now.

Bear freezes, holds himself prone, keeps his eyes low.

My mother's eyes snap open and plead me in the face with a face that's three-fifths of a suicide.

Bear hefts to his feet, yanks at his pants, fumbles with his belt buckle. His white T-shirt's soaked with yellow sweat. I keep my pistol (I can feel it shaking, and hope he can't see) aimed where his heart should be.

That's my mama, I say. My mama, I say. Say it as a man, a boy, a child.

The woman who gave me life stands butt-naked, all bones, her pubic bush glistening wet. Well, here it is, no more secrets, she says. The truth, all truth. Now are you satisfied? She martyrs her arms out. Her eyes are wrung dark. One of her penciled eyebrows is swiped clean. Her hair's a spiked swarm.

The room reeks of blunts and sweat and raw sex—a kick in the soul.

Get dressed, I say. Put your fucking clothes on, now.

Bear don't speak nor move. You've never seen a nigger this size be this still. He and I looking into each other, judging worth. It's tough to keep strength on the trigger. My mother dresses too slow, takes too long to slip on her panties and pants, her bra and shirt, her shoes. I snatch her by the shirt and it tears at the neck. I grab her by the arm and, with my back to Bear, jerk this wispish woman into the hall and down the hall and past the young Crips (none who rouse for a nigger dragging a basehead to destination unknown) and outside, drag her to the car, where I shove her in it less all of my might. I safety the pistol and stash it under my seat. It hurts to breathe. It hurts to be alive. We ease off.

Where are you taking me? she says.

Shut. The fuck. UP, I say.

It's Sunday and the world sounds like Sunday. Mom rocks in her seat, turned from me, praying hands pushed between her legs, a tear lolling on her sharp cheek. Whatever she is, I am far less than I was when I needed her more. What now can we do for each other? I drive all backstreets, Rodney, Roselawn, Holman, Failing. The city steady turning its back on us.

We stop at a four-way stop and Portland's finest idle across from us. You can see them spy into our car and look down at something out of sight. We pull off and they pull off and I see them see me in the eye. They crawl past and bust a U and you don't know a nigger, never seen a nigger, it couldn't be a nigger with this much base panic. They follow a pulse and hit us with flashers, trouble that should spark a high-speed, but I pull to the curb.

We're straight, we're straight, I say to myself. Be cool and we'll be on our way.

It's a duo and they strut up on both sides. I let the window down, say hello (with honor), and ask if he could please tell me why I was stopped.

For starters, a seat belt, he says. He's got a weak chin of salt-and-pepper stubble and a nexus of paunch.

Oh, I say, glance at my unstrapped chest and touch where the strap should be.

He asks for my license and stomps back to his motoring cruiser. Its lights flash red and blue in my mirror. This is my life. These are my options. Choices flushed to two: Run or stay. Run or stay put. Run or stay the fuck put. Take the risk or risk what's stuffed in my boxer briefs paroling me into my afterlife. I whisper to my mother for her to, no matter, keep her mouth shut. Be cool, be cool, I say again to myself. The partner plods back to the car and hands me my license. Clean, he says, and just that fast I feel my heart slow to the speed of a human being. This time we'll let you slide, but next time it's a ticket, so buckle up, he says. Never know when it will save your life. He pats the hood and asks his partner if he's ready to roll, but his partner (you know him: he'd misstep on a beating heart and wouldn't think twice to check his boot) is rapt by Mom. He knocks on her window for me to let it down and I do. You don't look so hot, he says. You look not-so-hot hot *and* nervous. Now, if I didn't know any better, I'd say you've been doing drugs. Illegal drugs.

Mom sits mute, and I pray to God, Jesus, and all the saints she stays just so.

Yep, he says. I'd say you're showing telltale signs of illicit drug use. That or a rough night turning tricks.

I reach over and touch Mom's thigh and there's no greater wish for my life than for her to feel its warning.

Mom shuts her eyes tight, opens them slowest. She turns to the cop, her neck first, then those stormy browns. Turning tricks! she says. Who the hell you calling a prostitute!

Well, now that you ask, that's a good question, he says. How about we find out who? He reaches through the window and asks for her ID.

Mom gropes around. She slams her back against the seat and pats her pockets. She dips her hand through the throat of her torn shirt into her bra. I left it, she says. I don't have it.

Then I'm afraid you and I have a problem, he says. He orders her to step out of the car, says it almost as if it's a choice. He posts her for search, asks if she's carrying any drugs or paraphernalia, if he should worry over needles or glass. Mom releases a deep breath and looks to the sky. He frisks her from her feet up. He digs his hand in a pocket and pulls out a matchbook and scraps. He leaves the pocket inside out and lays his finds on the hood. He fishes another pocket and sifts small trash.

BINGO! he says, and cups a puny find.

I don't have to see it to know what it is.

The cop at my window frowns and tells me to step out of the car. My options now *an* option: RUN!

But run and leave who?

My legs are all flesh, no bones, as I fall out, wouldn't carry me a foot. The cop jerks my arms behind my head and kicks my legs apart.

My option: no option.

Are you clean? he says. Tell me now if you're dirty and we can save ourselves trouble. He frisks me from the top down, tapping my arms, chest, gut. He gets down to my crotch and pats the sack—once, pats the sack—twice. He tilts his head and grins, a big, wide, grin. Uh-oh, what's that? he says. What do we have here?

No lie, about now, a bullet would be mercy.

He digs into my jeans and lifts the sack (my work rocked up and packaged in plastic) to the sky.

Partner, he says. Will you take a look at this.

They toss us cuffed into their hard backseat and boom the doors shut. Leave me and Mom, mother and son—always.

There are. There are.

—Grace

I AM GOD'S CHILD. I place my life in the care of God. I am one with God and the universe. God, I can't, but You can, so please do. If He's too far removed, who moved? If you're trying to pray, it's praying. Let go and let God. I am powerless over people. I am powerless over my children. I am powerless over drugs. I believe in a power greater than me. Faith without works is dead. Faith is spelled a-c-t-i-o-n. When we do all the talking, we learn what we know. We are only as sick as our secrets. We either are or we aren't. Where we go, there we are. Sponsors: Use one. Help is a call away. I help others by asking for help. Drugs: an equal choice destroyer. Do it sober. Easy does it, but do it. Don't quit before the magic. Be grateful. Be sick and tired of being sick and tired. Before you say I can't, say I try. Life starts when you stop. Listen like only the dying can. Lead me not into temptation, I can find it myself. I forgive myself for hurting myself and others. I forgive myself for letting others hurt me. I deserve to be loved by myself and others. I like myself. I love myself without condition. I accept love. I am not alone. I am able to change. I am the change I want to see. I am the one who makes me whole. Using is death. One hit is too many, a thousand is not enough. F.E.A.R. Frustration. Ego. Anxiety. Resentment. F.E.A.R. False. Expectations. Appear. Real. F.E.A.R. False. Evidence. Appears. Real. F.E.A.R. F——. Everything. And. Run. F.E.A.R. Face. Everything. And. Recover. Give time time. Give it away

341

to keep it. Forgive to gain forgiveness. We didn't get here on a winning streak. The choice is yours: Choose wise. There will be pain in your progress. The pain I might feel by remembering can't be any worse than the pain I feel by knowing and not remembering. Have a good day, unless you planned to have a bad one. I am liked. I am loved. I am free. I am worthy. I am humble. I am happy. I am patient. I am valued. Just for today, I will be vulnerable with someone I trust. Just for today, I will respect my own and others' boundaries. Just for today, I will act in a way that I would admire in someone else. Just for today, I will take one compliment and hold it in my heart for more than a fleeting second. Just for today, I will try and get a better view of my life. Just for today, I will be brave. Just for today, my recovery will be my world. I am human. I am full. I am new. I am good. I am strong.

If you've seen this place once, you've seen it forever: a windowless room with beige walls and gray tile and new residents serving meals. Today's menu is yesterday's, the day before—Cream of Wheat, poached eggs, and fruit juice in cups the same size they use to test our urine. I grab a tray and find an empty table near a girl who was new when I left. She chatters at a girl who, by her face, is too young for these scars. Maybe they gossip of an expert released one day who stumbled back in the next, of fast friends who won't be friends outside these walls. Or maybe her story is the story of what happened to me. I pick at my plate, dump most of it, and loaf back to my tiny box. I unpack my bag and square my tenny shoes against the wall and as might my eldest—what will happen to my eldest?—leave my laces loosened just so. I hang the picture of my boys, my beloveds, from Canaan's first birthday in the corner of the mirror, trace the picture's scalloped edges, press them flat against the glass. Then I lie on my bunk and listen for rain. Here, when doesn't it rain? Times it could have been the rain. They slip a note under my door for me to report to the office. There's no need to fix my face, but I fix my face, and lope down the hall.

The counselor is squaring portraits on the wall of champions. She turns to me and hikes her frames up the slope of her nose. Her hair is wound into a fall-red bun.

Good morning, she says.

Good morning, I say.

Well I called you down to welcome you back. So, welcome back and I mean it, she says. Grace, we come to know there are much worse fates than this.

We do, I say. I do.

She reaches out to me—both hands. You have to leave it, she says. Leave it be and push on. Because it's this time. Not ever the last time but this time that counts.

Yes, I say. Yes. This time this is it.

ACKNOWLEDGMENTS

A special note of gratitude to my readers: Marco F. Navarro, Robb Todd, A. Van. Jordan, Carla Edmon. Many thanks to the "straight shooter" Kathy Belden for not only agreeing to publish my novel but serving as a friend and mentor. Thank you to the team at Bloomsbury: George, Peter, Laura, Marie, Patti. Thank you to my agent, Liz Darhansoff, for taking the risk to represent me. Thank you to my wonderful publicist, Michelle Blankenship, for believing and pulling out her trumpet. Much appreciation to my fellow writers, teachers, and friends: Marcus Jackson, Cleyvis Natera, Tom Spanbauer, Gordon Lish, ZZ Packer, John Edgar Wideman, Marie Helene Bertino, Jesymn Ward, Amy Hempel, Michael Kimball, James Yeh, Freeway Rick Ross, Felicia Quaning, Denmark Reid, Ramon Blackburn, Ruth Danon, Barbara Adams, April Krassner, Kenny Warren Jr., and the rest of my 833 crew. Thank you to the Center for Fiction and in particular Noreen Tomassi and Kristin Henley. Thank you to my SEEK department family. Thank you to Self Enhancement Incorporated. Thank you to Bob Quillin and Vanessa for your grand support. Thank you to Sandy Vasceannie for years of opportunity. Thank you to John Ricard for all your assistance. Thank you to those who worked on the documentary: Todd Strickland, Nehemiah Booker, Chris and

ACKNOWLEDGMENTS

Erik Ewers, Dwight Myrick, P. Frank Williams, Josh Milowe. Thank you to my siblings: Adrian, Chris, Wesley, Romla, Monique, Jibri, Jesse, Latricia, De'Andre. Thank you to the family and friends who encouraged me to prosecute my dream: Rhonda, Myasha, Anthony, Jasmine A, Ladawn, Dr. Wallace, Almamia, Teresa, grand dad, Tanya. Thank you to my love, Juliette, for being everything. Thank you to my children: Justice Serene and Jaden Truth. And what would all of this be without my mother? Thank you, Mom. If I have left off anyone who played a role, I apologize, and thank you to you too.